BEYOND IMAGINING

Needing Hank's warmth, his love, the comfort of his body next to hers, Jennifer paced the living room. The minutes passed slowly, agonizingly. She strained to hear his truck, but the night was deadly quiet. She shrugged into her jacket and went to the table for her purse. She would drive down to the restaurant, maybe meet him on the road.

Walking to her car, Jennifer passed through one of those eerie chills in the night, a pocket of air where death had passed. In the car, she removed the revolver from her purse and placed it on the seat beside her. She drove down the hill, still searching the night for Hank's headlights. She passed no one on the road to town.

The restaurant was dark. *Where is he? Dear God, where is he?*

Jennifer pulled around to the back. Hank's truck was there. The door on the driver's side was open. She switched her lights to bright. Then she saw him . . .

She choked back the scream. *Please, God. No. No!*

PINNACLE BOOKS HAS
SOMETHING FOR EVERYONE—

MAGICIANS, EXPLORERS, WITCHES AND CATS

THE HANDYMAN (377-3, $3.95/$4.95)
He is a magician who likes hands. He likes their comfortable
shape and weight and size. He likes the portability of the hands
once they are severed from the rest of the ponderous body. Detective Lanark must discover who The Handyman is before more
handless bodies appear.

PASSAGE TO EDEN (538-5, $4.95/$5.95)
Set in a world of prehistoric beauty, here is the epic story of a
courageous seafarer whose wanderings lead him to the ends of
the old world—and to the discovery of a new world in the rugged,
untamed wilderness of northwestern America.

BLACK BODY (505-9, $5.95/$6.95)
An extraordinary chronicle, this is the diary of a witch, a journal
of the secrets of her race kept in return for not being burned for
her "sin." It is the story of Alba, that rarest of creatures, a white
witch: beautiful and able to walk in the human world undetected.

THE WHITE PUMA (532-6, $4.95/NCR)
The white puma has recognized the men who deprived him of his
family. Now, like other predators before him, he has become a
man-hater. This story is a fitting tribute to this magnificent animal that stands for all living creatures that have become, through
man's carelessness, close to disappearing forever from the face of
the earth.

CREEPING SHADOWS

GARY AMO

PINNACLE BOOKS
WINDSOR PUBLISHING CORP.

For Nancy

With Love

PINNACLE BOOKS

are published by

Windsor Publishing Corp.
475 Park Avenue South
New York, NY 10016

First printing: August, 1992

Printed in the United States of America

So we beat on, boats against the current, borne back
ceaselessly into the past.

F. Scott Fitzgerald

PROLOGUE

It was the day Bobby Kennedy would be shot.

The woman who called herself Sierra—she was still a girl really, scarcely nineteen—walked through San Francisco's financial district at noon. She was tall and wore a blue corduroy skirt with black boots. A cape draped over her shoulders shielded the baby she carried from the cool breeze blowing through the concrete canyons. Straight blonde hair hung to her waist. Her face had delicate features, but concern and worry marred her beauty. She was hungry and needed money desperately but as she walked, Sierra eliminated one choice after another. She couldn't work because there was no one to look after Clea. Going back to her sneering foster parents and asking for their help was unacceptable. They had never loved her. Her usefulness to them had ended with the government's monthly payments anyway. Applying for welfare took too long and there were too many questions she was afraid to answer. Who is the baby's father? Are you married? Why doesn't he contribute to your support? Sierra was afraid they might take Clea away. And her husband, Jack—dear, wonderful Jackson—would kill her if he found her. Nor could she bring herself to steal, not even the food she needed to keep healthy milk flowing from her breasts. All morning Sierra had planned the foray into the financial district, preparing herself to accost the comfortable and well-to-do, begging for spare change. Others among her acquaintances did it, laughing about how much money they were able to gather in a day of drifting through the city. But now, surrounded by groomed and neat young executives and well-dressed secretaries, Sierra's pride would not allow her to plead for the money she needed. Instead, she adjusted the blanket around Clea's tiny face—bless her, she hadn't made a sound—and turned toward Powell Street, fleeing humiliation, rushing to despair. Only one choice remained. At least, she would earn the money.

Sierra missed the first cable car in a rush of tourists. She had better luck with the second, climbing wearily aboard after checking the conductor's location on the car. He was at the back. She smiled gratefully at the tall and courtly gentleman who gave up his seat to her. The grip man clanged the bells and they screeched away up Powell Street past the St. Francis, climbing the hill toward the Mark Hopkins. The conductor worked his way slowly forward, collecting the fifteen cent fare from the passengers. Sierra divided her attention between the conductor and Clea who was awake now, smiling up at her, gurgling happily. It was a race between the conductor and her stop. She would ride as long as she dared and then leap off before she would have to pay the dime and nickel she didn't have. Please, God, she prayed silently, let me get to the top of the hill at least. I can walk the rest of the way. And then the cable car topped the hill, but the conductor was too close. Sierra left the car, lost among another group of tourists clambering aboard. She reached the sidewalk and started down the hill to North Beach as the cable car rushed past her with another furious burst of bells.

Clea stirred as Sierra hurried through North Beach, past the multitude of topless bars with their barkers already on the sidewalks in front, chattering loudly to

8

pedestrians. Residents ignored them. Tourists from the midwest giggled nervously, peeking at glossy photographs, both shocked and intrigued by the fantasy of bare breasted women behind the curtained doors.

"We're amost home, baby," Sierra whispered, lifting the child close to her face as she weaved through the people crowding the sidewalks. "We're almost there."

Clea smiled and reached for a strand of Sierra's hair with a small clenched fist. She quieted again, reassured by the warm breath on her face.

Sierra turned off Broadway and cut down a narrow side street, weaving through the interior of the real North Beach, where old-time residents gathered at small family restaurants to eat spaghetti and drink red wine. Sierra felt the weakness again as she climbed up the hill toward Coit Tower. She was growing faint by the time she plodded up the wood stairs to the tiny apartment, her refuge, her hiding place.

Inside, she rested for a moment, leaning against the door before she placed Clea carefully in her crib, adjusting the rattles hanging from a string so the baby could reach them. "I'll feed you in a minute, sweetie. Just let me get something first."

Sierra poured the rest of the milk on the cereal. The sugar bowl was empty. She had been living on cereal for three days. As she ate the cereal, Sierra looked at the telephone. At least, it wouldn't be cut off until Friday. "I have to do it, Clea," she said. "I don't know what else to do."

Sierra carefully rinsed the bowl before going to the telephone and dialing the number on the pad beside it. "Arthur, it's Sierra. I'll do it . . . I'm sorry, but it's the middle of the afternoon . . . All right, tonight's fine . . . Can you pick me up? I don't even have bus fare . . . And I need the money tonight. No credit . . . Okay, see you then."

PART I

ONE

Jennifer Warren's bad luck with men continued.

The annual holiday gathering of friends and family dispels loneliness for some, but not for all. There are those condemned to listen to the night track, that discordant sound track of our lives, a series of dissonant melodies played at the wrong speed in an endless cacophony, each strident tune a harsh reminder of frailties and mistakes. The music swells and builds to maddening heights in the mind, threatening to explode, until the weak seek oblivion. The strong endure.

Jennifer Warren endured, as always, listening to her own personal night track, punishing herself with the CD on random select, listening to the music of her youth—the Beatles, the Stones, Dylan, Jim Morrison and the Doors, Baez, Simon and Garfunkel. With each pause in the night track, the disks whirred and brought forth another memory. It was the year of love. It was dancing to Jefferson Airplane in a packed Fillmore Auditorium where the air was filled with the thick smell of grass, when you could get high by just breathing and listening to the blaring music. It was the nightly parade through the Haight-Ashbury and the runaways begging spare change from shocked and horrified tourists. Charles Manson and the Family had been there that year, along with the hordes of flower children and the dropouts; bikers and undercover cops, army deserters hiding out in the throngs, and draft evaders making a last sentimental stop before leaving for Canada; Weathermen and Black Panthers; SDS pickets at the Oakland Army Depot. It was that first chilling message from him. And it was the fear, the sickening, mind-numbing fear which, ever since that year, had been in uneasy remission. But it came back. It always did.

His holiday message, the first in nearly two years, had come this morning with the delivery of the newspaper. It was there on the coffee table waiting for her to look at for the tenth, fifteenth, twentieth time. But no matter how many times Jennifer Warren read the message in the Personals column of the classified section, it was like all the others that had come intermittently over the years . . . evil and threatening, his hatred only barely disguised. Sometimes the messages appeared on their anniversary. Sometimes it was a birthday message for her. Sometimes he just wanted her to know that he was out there, looking for her, waiting. And then another ad would appear in the Personals.

Jennifer was alone now in her Santa Monica condominium with the magnificent view. She sat in the darkness, still wearing the red evening gown, looking out at the array of lights that marked the long curving shoreline, stretching from beyond the Palos Verdes Peninsula in the south to Malibu in the north. The night air was crisp and clear. It was a view worth the pain Jennifer had used to pay for it, was still paying. Sensing that pain, the sleek black cat on her lap looked up at her with yellow piercing eyes and meowed softly.

The coastline was one long Christmas tree, festive with the glow of a million shimmering lights. Huge individual trees were gaily festooned with lights at civic centers in dozens of the cities that now make up Southern California. Homes in the beach communities,

14

large and small alike, were outlined with string after string of lights. Beneath the joyous atmosphere though, violence seethed, a restless throbbing drumbeat that accompanied hymns of peace and goodwill. Malls were crowded with shoppers, their parking lots filled to capacity. Angry curses shattered the peace and harmony of the season as fights broke out over a parking space. Inside, harried clerks struggled to keep up with the press of gift seekers, looking anxiously at their watches as the time crept slowly to closing time. Gang members—White, Hispanic, Black, Asian—cruised; predators seeking prey in a mugging, a household burglary, a drive-by shooting. But elsewhere, all along the coast, celebrants thronged pre-Christmas parties in a rising crescendo of homage to the holiday spirit.

In Newport Beach, Huntington Harbor, and Naples, Christmas boat parades brought revelers to hundreds of exclusive cocktail parties on chilly decks of multi-million dollar homes. Valets sweated despite the chill December night as they rushed back and forth, parking the expensive cars of their patrons. The privileged hugged and smiled, exchanging loud greetings with the false joy demanded by the season and then drank, ate, and watched as one crowded boat after another, huge yachts and tiny sloops alike, glided through the black waters of the bay in what appeared to be a never-ending line of lavishly illuminated displays of Christmas colors. Participants waved and shouted, lifting champagne glasses in repeated toasts to the season and each other.

Through it all, the demands of life continued. Hostesses worried when cocktail tidbits ran low. Married couples fought and argued over imagined slights, provoked by a careless admiring glance at another woman or that extra drink that induced slurred speech and reckless words. New matches began as men pursued women. Clandestine affairs were carried out in

15

public when liquor overcame caution. But all was not pleasure. Business was conducted, cards exchanged, deals struck. Lives were gutted and companies raped while their principals chatted unknowingly. Millions of dollars could exchange hands with a single word as a decision was made. Fortunes and passions ebbed and flowed like the tides. Life went on to the constant refrain . . . "Merry Christmas."

Jennifer had hoped and prayed that this year would be different, but Bennett Cameron had turned out to be another disaster. He had arrived in a sullen mood and the argument had begun over a drink before leaving for his agency Christmas party, progressing rapidly from a casual remark to shouting and screaming, bitter charges and countercharges, wounds that could not be healed now. Too much had been said, those painful accusations dredged from the darkness of the soul and yelled without thought or care. Bennett had slammed the door furiously, still shouting obscenities, leaving Jennifer slumped, pale and badly shaken, knowing that he had wanted to hurt her, coldly and with deliberate calculation. He couldn't just admit that he wanted her no longer, and was turning to a client, an actress half Jennifer's age.

Half-a-dozen times, she went to the telephone to call her daughter, wanting to make contact with someone. Each time she returned to her chair by the window without lifting the receiver. It would be the same as always, a few pleasantries exchanged and then the bitter recriminations—again. Neither of them could leave it alone for long.

Finally, Jennifer turned on a lamp and looked at the front page of the classifieds again. The personal message had not disappeared in the darkness. "Kathleen: The mountains will burn red and die." As always, it was signed simply with his initials. "J.H." Jennifer shuddered. Later, she would cut the page and put it with all the others. But not now. His touch was still on the paper, as though he had violated her living room with his presence.

Once more she looked at the telephone, but instead of calling Clea, she went to the bedroom and began packing, quickly shedding one persona when she slipped out of the evening gown, leaving it rumpled on the floor, becoming a new person identified by the freedom of jeans and boots, wool shirt, and leather jacket. The black cat perched at the edge of the bed and watched with interest, the yellow eyes following her movements from closet and dresser to the suitcase open on the bed. "Don't worry, Oscar," Jennifer said, scratching him behind the ears. "You're going too. We're going home."

Jennifer's neighbor from across the hall had found Oscar and two tiny sisters abandoned in an alley behind a local gay bar, three piteous balls of ragged black fur, crying desperately. Their eyes hadn't even opened yet, but still they hissed ferociously, baring toothless pink gums when Jerome picked them up, carrying them home where he fed them with an eye dropper, talking softly all the while, stroking their small bodies softly with one finger until they purred.

And then one evening Jerome had knocked on Jennifer's door.

"No," Jennifer insisted. "I don't want a cat."

"Just come and look at them," Jerome said. "They're so cute. You don't have to take one. I've already found homes for them."

"All right," Jennifer said. "But I'm just looking. That's it. Understood?"

"Of course, Sweetie."

And Oscar moved in that night.

But even now, months later, he followed her everywhere when she was home, as though fearing he would be abandoned again. Now Jennifer pulled his carrying case from the floor of the closet and put it on the bed. Oscar climbed in, kneading the thick bath towel that

17

was his bed, settled down, and waited for Jennifer to finish.

Jennifer took the other purse, the one that concealed the revolver between its two folds, and transferred wallet, keys, compact, lipstick, gum, tissues.

When she was packed and ready, Jennifer went across the hall and knocked on Jerome's door.

"That man's a real bitch," Jerome said opening the door.

"You heard him?"

"He shouldn't talk to you like that. You deserve better."

"I'm through with him."

"Good. I'll fix you a drink."

"No thanks. I'm leaving in a few minutes. I just wanted you to know I'd be gone. Keep an eye on the place for me? Save the newspapers?"

"Of course, Sweetie. Where are you going?"

"I just want to get away for a few days."

"You're being mysterious again."

"I'm a mysterious woman," Jennifer said.

"I like a woman with a past."

"You don't like women at all, Jerome."

"That's not true," he protested. "I like you. I just don't want to make love to you. And I think you're so brave when you go . . . there."

"It's not the end of the world, Jerome."

"Out there with the cowboys and the Indians. It's so . . . so . . . Wild West."

"Oh, Jerome, cut the flaming queen act. You know it doesn't work with me."

"Now you sound just like my ex-wife . . . so . . . forceful."

Jennifer laughed. "Have a good Christmas, Jerome. I'll bring your present back with me."

"A cowboy?"

"You're impossible, but you're a dear, Jerome."

18

"You are too, Jennifer. I'll miss you. Drive carefully."

Jennifer hesitated, looking up and down the hallway. They were alone. "Remember, Jerome, if anyone comes asking for me, you don't know where I am."

"I don't know a thing, but I wish you'd tell me what's going on. I could help."

"Someday, Jerome, but not now."

Carrying Oscar and the suitcase, Jennifer took the elevator to the garage and climbed into the nondescript foreign car. She fled, driving into the bright lights and heavy holiday traffic of West Los Angeles.

Jennifer followed her long-ingrained routine, driving aimlessly for awhile, checking the rear view mirror constantly, making abrupt turns without signaling, slowing for yellow caution lights at corners and then speeding through the intersection. Once, she nearly stopped for a red light and then raced through the intersection. No cars followed her.

When she was positive that no one cared about her movements, Jennifer retraced her path and then turned south, away from Santa Monica and the Westside, until she reached the storage area. She drove slowly through the parked RV's and boats on trailers, until she reached a row of garages at the back fence. Taking keys from a compartment in her purse, she said, "I'll be right back, Oscar."

She opened the lock and lifted the heavy garage door and climbed into the red pickup truck with Arizona license plates. It had an empty gun rack in the back window. Climbing into the cab, Jennifer pumped the gas pedal several times before turning the key in the ignition. It started reluctantly and only after several tries. I'm getting careless, Jennifer thought. I've got to get over here more often and run this thing. She let the big engine warm, before backing it out of the garage. She transferred her luggage and then Oscar to the

19

truck. He meowed plaintively, eager to be free of the case. "Just another minute, Oscar, show a little patience." She pulled the car into the garage, shut the door, snapped the lock shut.

"We're on our way now, Oscar," she said opening the carrying case. Once free to roam about, the cat was content to sit in the box, watching the passing lights with momentary interest as Jennifer headed for the Santa Monica Freeway and Interstate 10, ready to leave Los Angeles and her past behind for a time.

There was snow in the Cajon Pass above 3,000 feet, bright gleaming patches near the road and a solid white blanket that covered the mountain tops. The temperature was below freezing, but inside the cab of the pick-up truck, Jennifer was warm and happy, driving gratefully through the long night, leaving one life for another. Coming down from the mountain pass, the lights of Victorville and Barstow were isolated patches of civilization fighting against the black reaches of the high desert.

She stopped for gas in Barstow. A skinny high school boy left the warmth of the gas station office and walked slowly to the truck. He was wearing a high school letterman's jacket buttoned all the way to his chin. The big block letter on the jacket had the winged feet signifying a runner on the track team.

"Let me help you with that, ma'am," the boy said, taking the nozzle from her, inserting it in the tank, setting it on automatic. He started cleaning the windshield, sneaking admiring glances at Jennifer while he worked. Oscar stood, front paws stretched to the dashboard, and watched with interest as the boy wiped the water away with the squeegee.

"I could check your water and oil, ma'am."

"Thanks, but it's okay."

"Nice truck," he said.

"Yes," Jennifer said smiling at him. "You a track star."

He blushed. "Aw, no, I just like to run. Something to do after school. Before I come to work."

I'm a runner too, Jennifer thought, but I'm always running *away*.

The nozzle shut off. He topped the tank off slowly, as though reluctant to let Jennifer come in and out of his life so quickly.

"Is there someplace I can get a cup of coffee to go?" Jennifer asked.

"McDonald's closed by now. There's a cafe stays open all night though. Down the street a couple of blocks."

"Thanks," Jennifer said, rummaging in her purse for her wallet.

"I could let you have some," the boy said. "It's pretty fresh. Wouldn't charge you nothing for it."

"That'd be great," Jennifer said, "if it's not too much trouble."

"No trouble, ma'am. I got some big cups too. Tops and everything. Take anything in it?"

"Just black, please."

"Be right back, ma'am."

Jennifer watched as he loped back to the office. She could see his vague shape through a steamed and grimy window as he reached for a cup, poured coffee, carefully fitted a top to it and returned, holding the cup out shyly.

"Hope you like it, ma'am. Made it myself."

"I'm sure I will. Thanks very much."

Jennifer waved as she drove out of the gas station. He waved back and stared wistfully after her.

The Interstate split at Barstow, one path leading to Las Vegas and beyond into Utah, Salt Lake City, and then Wyoming. There were choices, always choices. She could have taken Interstate 10 out of Los Angeles all the way to Jacksonville, Florida. Instead she had

21

turned north into the high desert. Now, Jennifer took the southern fork to Needles on the Colorado River, sharing the desert night with the big trucks roaring through the darkness. Interstate 40 would take her into Arizona and beyond if she wanted, through New Mexico and the Texas Panhandle, Oklahoma, Arkansas, Tennessee, into North Carolina where it ended at Wilmington. Someday, it might come to that, but not yet.

She sipped the coffee, knowing it had been a love gift from a lonely boy. It was good, strong and dark. I'll stop there on the way back and tell him, Jennifer thought. Leave him a note if he's not there.

And so she drove through the desert to Needles, listening to the laments for lost loves on a country western station, realizing that Bennett Cameron didn't matter. Their relationship had seemed good for awhile, but it had been superficial, more the result of her longing for a commitment in a complete and satisfying relationship than love. "No more younger men, Oscar," she said ruefully, and put Bennett Cameron out of her mind and her life.

When they crossed the Colorado River, a sense of freedom grew within her, as it always did when she was going home. Oscar slept contentedly in his open carrying case. Occasionally, Jennifer reached out and touched his sleek black fur. Together, they left Kingman behind and climbed the winding road away from the desert, through the mountains to Flagstaff where she stopped for gas once more. And then they were turning south on the narrow country highway. Dawn found them, woman and cat, parked at the edge of the Mogollon Rim, watching as the first streaks of light pierced the eastern sky. Below them, the valley was shrouded in a thin misty fog that floated delicately down the slopes and through the majestic pine forests.

"We're home, Oscar," Jennifer whispered. She tried

22

to ignore the mountains that burned with the red glow of dawn.

Before time, there was the valley.

Created from the violent combat between gods of the nether world when ageless feuds erupted in monstrous volcanic explosions and anger flowed in rivers of fiery lava, the valley shuddered and was quiet, cowering in fear while ferocious battles raged all around. The earth shook and rolled. Poisonous smoke spewed into the heavens. Mountains rose and fell, bursting into the coarse dust of huge boulders that flew through the air. The warfare raged for millenniums and when it finally ended, a barren landscape stretched endlessly, a vast emptiness littered with the weapons of the gods, a battlefield that cooled through additional millenniums. But hidden away at the northern edge of the desert wasteland, the valley was serene. Creatures stirred cautiously, venturing into the cool forests of the mountain slopes and the grasslands that formed the valley's floor, where they lived in uneasy harmony with nature's cruel dictates. And so it was through the ages—until man.

Driving into the valley, Jennifer felt the power from a land that was an anomaly in stark contrast to the vast plateau of northern Arizona and the plains—the deserts and barren mountain ranges of southern Arizona. To the northwest, the San Francisco Plateau is marked by lava flows and dotted with volcanic cones. The San Francisco Mountains tower over the Plateau. Northeastern Arizona is cut through with canyons. Buttes and mesas mark the high country. The plains region to the south is largely vast stretches of desert, broken only by rugged and formidable mountains like the Superstitions. Between plateau and plains lies the mountain region of Arizona. Here, various mountain chains rise four- to six-thousand feet above their valley floors.

The valley was gentle and tranquil, seemingly imperturbable, but its history was harsh and bloody. Jennifer shuddered as she always did driving past the tall and stately pine tree where legend said Annie Potts and others had been hanged by vigilantes during the Feud. But that was another era, Jennifer told herself. And when it ended, the valley was ashamed and closed in on itself, stopping time, avoiding strangers and progress, isolating itself from the outside world. For Jennifer, each return to Hidden Valley was like traveling back through the decades of the twentieth century. But then she passed a highway improvement sign posted by the state government that proclaimed, PROGRESS AS PROMISED. Jennifer slowed for the survey crew in charge of planning progress. They waved as she passed.

Jennifer still found it hard to believe that when John F. Kennedy was setting the space program into motion with his inaugural comments for the New Frontier, the residents of Hidden Valley were debating the arrival of electricity. Even now, thirty-odd years later, there were old-time residents who marked the arrival of electricity as the demise of the Valley. Paved roads will do them in, Jennifer thought. And the hotel that's going to follow. They can't stop it.

Hank's Valley Cafe and Saloon still reflected Hidden Valley's reluctance to accept the twentieth century, with its parking lot still catering more to horses than automobiles. A hitching rail ran along the front length of the ramshackle wooden building. An old wooden trough was filled each morning with fresh water for the horses and Hank kept a basket of apples—winter and summer—by the front door. People who drove to Hank's parked their cars off to the side of the building or in back, where they would not disturb the horses.

24

There were several horses tied to the rail when Jennifer pulled into the gravel parking lot, stiff and cramped after the all night drive. Tucking Oscar under her arm, Jennifer pushed through the doors of Hank's.

"Hey, darling," Hank said in the deep rumbling voice that would have been the envy of Orson Welles. "Welcome home."

"It's good to be here, Hank," Jennifer said.

Hank left his customary place behind the bar and enveloped Jennifer in a massive hug, nearly crushing the breath from her body. Oscar squirmed free and leaped to the bar to watch. "God, it's good to see you, darling," he said, releasing her only to pick her up and twirl her around. "You're as beautiful as ever," he said, finally putting her down.

Oscar waited on the bar for his turn. Hank turned to him and gently scratched behind the cat's ears. "She still calling you by the pansy name?"

"He was not named for Oscar Wilde's sexual preference. I keep telling you that. He was a great writer."

"It's still not a fit name for a great big cat like this. Call him Clint. Something macho. Right, Clint?" Oscar purred contentedly beneath the gentle pressure of Hank's massive fingers. Hank had all of Clint Eastwood's movies on tape and when Hank tired of television fare, which was often, patrons were forced to endure another viewing of "Dirty Harry" or "High Plains Drifter" or "The Outlaw Josey Wales."

"But, Hank," one or another of his customers would complain, "I want to watch the Wildcats play UCLA."

"Ain't right to sit around and watch a bunch of dinks in short pants. Watch the movie. Learn something."

"Aw shit, Hank, give me another beer then." And that always ended any discussion of what would be seen on the bar's television that afternoon or night.

"Oh, Bear," Jennifer said, "what am I going to do with you?" Jennifer had given him the name. She was

25

the only person other than Clea who dared to call Hank by the nickname. But Clea didn't come to the Valley anymore. Clea hadn't been to the Valley for a long time now.

"Marry me, darling, and you can call me Bear forever."

"I could do worse, but all I want now is breakfast. Oscar wants breakfast."

"Chicken fried steak, hash browns, biscuits and gravy."

"I don't want all that," Jennifer said. "Every time I come here I gain ten pounds and spend weeks getting it off again."

"That's for Clint," Hank said, rubbing Oscar's ears. "What do you want? Some wimpy breakfast, I suppose? Dry toast. Black coffee."

"No, I want chicken fried steak. The works."

"All right then."

Nothing had changed since Jennifer's last visit over the long Thanksgiving Day weekend. Was it only a month ago? Not even a month, but it seemed much longer, an eternity to be endured in the facade of her other life. It was different here at Hank's, in Hidden Valley. There was none of the frenetic, swirling, restless fluctuation of Los Angeles, where change was constant. There, new buildings replaced old, seemingly overnight. Neighborhoods were always in flux as hordes of refugees from other states and other countries sought sanctuary. Ignore a section of the city for a month or two and it became unfamiliar. Not here. Change came slowly, grudgingly, to Hidden Valley. People who lived here for thirty years were still referred to as the new family up by Pleasant Creek. Jennifer had been coming here for five years and she was still viewed suspiciously, as an interloper. Her acceptance had been slow and remained incomplete. Hank had been the first. Slowly, grudgingly, others had come forward offering friendship.

Now, Jennifer found great solace each time she escaped the metropolitan area of Los Angeles and returned to Hidden Valley for a long weekend, sometimes a week, and on some all too infrequent occasions like now, a glorious ten days or two weeks, always stopping at Hank's first, finding comfort in the stability of the surroundings. Hank was invariably found standing behind the center of the bar, reading during slow hours, opening beers with dexterity when it was busy, engaged in wild rambling philosophical discussions with one or another of the regulars. Once, Jennifer had left in the midst of an argument over who was to blame for the split between Clint Eastwood and Sondra Locke. Sides were evenly divided between genders and the argument still raged six weeks later when Jennifer returned.

At the left of the bar, the dining room was brightly lit, clean and neat with checkered oilcloth coverings for the tables. To the right, another room housed two coin-operated pool tables. But the center of Hank's Valley Cafe and Saloon was the bar and all of the paraphernalia and knickknacks behind it. Tucked in among the bottles were tattered paperbacks—Hardy, Conrad, Dickens, Faulkner, Hemingway, Joyce, and Fitzgerald shared space with Louis L'Amour, Elmore Leonard, Noel Loomis, Tony Hillerman, Ross MacDonald, and John D. MacDonald. Next to the cash register, there was an old typewriter dating from the Feud. Hanging above the cash register was a .50 caliber Sharps 1874 sporting rifle. Next to it was a beautiful old violin, also from the Feud era, that Jennifer had tried to buy many times, but Hank refused to sell it. There were branding irons, also dating back to the Feud. And spurs. Bridles. Mounted heads of a deer and a bear. An old Coca Cola sign from the forties, perhaps even earlier. There were mounted covers of magazines—*Life, Saturday Evening Post, Collier's*. Behind Hank's post at the middle of the bar, there was an oil painting, a reclining portrait of a nude woman. Her long blonde hair billowed over but did not obscure full and round breasts. Her face was beautiful, her legs long and supple. Hank called her Amanda and had often said, "When a woman like that walks through my door, well, that's the woman I'm going to marry. No questions asked."

Hank served breakfast himself and than sat at the table with Jennifer, refilling their coffee mugs from a large insulated pot.

"Come for dinner tonight," Hank said. "Jesus has been cooking up his chili all week. It'll be ready." He hesitated. "We want to talk to you anyway."

"Who wants to talk?"

"Just some of the folks."

"What about?"

"That God damned hotel. What else? We need some advice."

"How can I help?"

"Better if you hear it all at once."

"I couldn't give you much advice right now anyway. I'm beat. Going home to sleep."

"See you tonight?"

"Sure, Bear. I wouldn't miss Jesus' chili for anything."

Exhaustion overcame Jennifer as she drove up the lonely and secluded dirt road to her home set on a slope high above the valley. Isolated in the pines, the large rambling house was in shadows for most of the day, but this early in the morning sunlight gleamed off a light covering of snow on the roof and the patches of snow scattered through the trees. Others thought the house was gloomy, dark. Jennifer didn't care, loving it from the first moment. And it was safe. No one could find her here, not even J.H.

She parked and climbed the wooden steps to the deck carrying her suitcase. Oscar pounced on a leaf, released it, watched it flutter away in the light breeze, pounced again. Yawning, Jennifer went through the cold house, flipping light switches, turning on the heat, opening blinds and windows to clear the mustiness out. Paper, kindling, and logs were laid out in the huge stone fireplace in the living room. The last thing Jennifer did each time before returning to Los Angeles was prepare the fire for her next visit. Still yawning, Jennifer lit the paper and watched with satisfaction as the flames caught and spread. Oscar sat beside her watching the fire with fascination. "Glad to be home?" Jennifer asked. "I am."

When the fire was burning brightly, she made a return journey through the house, closing the windows, letting the warmth spread through the living room and into the kitchen and other areas of the house. She pulled a large blanket from the closet and curled up on the couch in front of the fire to wait for sleep. But sleep would not come. As tired as she was, her flesh still vibrated from the long drive and her mind raced with disjointed thoughts—Bennett, Clea, the boy at the gas station, the hanging tree, Bear, sweet lovable Bear. When she finally dozed off, the thoughts followed her into dreams of the night track where she wandered aimlessly through a dreary landscape pursued by indistinct images from the past.

TWO

Washington, D.C. and the northern Virginia and Maryland suburbs were cold. As the late afternoon shadows lengthened, the temperature had already dipped below freezing, into the twenties, and weather forecasters predicted an overnight low in the teens. Along the parkways that led from Dulles International Airport to the capitol, the wooded hillsides that were so thick and green in spring and summer were now barren. Their trees, denuded of leaves, stood like skeletons escaped from the graves of a vast cemetery, reminders of nature's impermanence and a wintry, foreboding warning to man. The waters of the Potomac were icy gray below Key Bridge as the limousine crossed into Georgetown. Scores of headlights from early homeward bound commuters—the GS 11's, 13's, and 15's eager for a warm fire and the evening's pitcher of martinis—could not pierce the dusky gloom of the approaching winter's night.

Jackson Holloway stood on the sidewalk in front of the elegant old hotel, looking across Lafayette Park. Floodlights illuminated the White House. It looked small to him. There were larger estates in Newport Beach, Malibu, Beverly Hills. He wondered how many square feet there were in the White House. Pedestrians scurried through the park and down the sidewalk by the fence of the White House, overcoat collars turned up, heads bent against the biting cold. The national Christmas tree was in place, awaiting the presidential ceremony that would light it.

Holloway's driver waited uncomfortably. Finally, Holloway turned away from the White House.

"Seven o'clock, sir?" the driver questioned.

Holloway nodded and followed the bellhop into the hotel.

"Mr. Holloway," the desk clerk said, "how good to have you stay with us."

They met in the study of a beautifully restored home in Georgetown. Jackson Holloway was not awed by the gray-haired man who faced him across the coffee table in front of the fireplace. Jackson Holloway, rich and powerful in his own right, was never awed by anyone.

"If I bring you into my organization," the older man asked, "and make you a member of my team, is there anything in your background that will embarrass me publicly, or privately?"

"Of course not," Holloway replied, lying easily.

"No extra wives conveniently forgotten?"

Holloway only smiled.

"No drugs, alcohol, sexual deviations, mistresses, other women, men, boys, young girls?"

"Nothing."

"Sedition? Perhaps radical activities in your youth?"

"No."

"The possibility of tax liens by IRS?"

"I pay my taxes. On time. In full. My accountants are very good."

The gray-haired man smiled. "Like Job, you are perfect and upright, fear God, and eschew evil."

"Unlike Job, however," Holloway said, "I do not have seven sons and three daughters, nor do I have seven thousand sheep and three thousand camels."

"You know your Bible. I like that."

"I learned that you often cite the Book of Job in private conversations."

"I like that as well. Yes, you have done your homework."

"I am always prepared."

"There are formalities. I will order the security and background check. There will be no problems for a perfect and upright man who fears God."

"No," Holloway said.

"Yes, well, shall we go in to dinner?"

"Certainly."

"Oh, and I'm so sorry Mrs. Holloway was unable to join us. I hope she feels better soon. Please give her my best regards."

"I will," Holloway said. "Janice will appreciate that."

"Such a gracious woman. I look forward to seeing her again."

"Perhaps when you're in Palm Springs next week," Holloway said. Her bruises and the black eye should be gone by then, he thought.

Jackson Holloway sat in the first class compartment, sipping champagne, looking down as they crossed the Mississippi River on the transcontinental flight back to Los Angeles. The countryside below gradually slipped from beneath the cloud cover that had obscured the east and midwest. She was down there somewhere. The old hatred, long suppressed, welled up. She was the only one left who knew what he had been, what he had done, the bombings, the murders. The others were all dead. Twice before, she had escaped. But not this time.

This time he would do it himself, ensure that she could not harm him, destroy his ambitions, dreams, reputation. The bitch. The bitch and her daughter. They must die. He would make both of them pay this time. Holloway leaned back and closed his eyes. The steady throbbing hum of the aircraft engines fanned his hatred.

THREE

Sierra.
He was calling her name.
Sierra.
No.
She could see her breasts. They were huge, distended, and streaked with blue veins. The nipples were erect and swollen, aching.
The baby cried. Her baby.
Please give me my baby. I want my baby.
But she couldn't move. It was hot under the glare of the lights. Sweat glistened on her breasts and crawled over her belly. She struggled to break free, to get to her baby, comfort her, soothe her, stop her from crying. And she couldn't move. Her arms and legs would not obey frantic commands from the brain.
Please, she begged. Give me my baby.

Jennifer awakened, hot and sweaty, disoriented, tangled in the blanket, thrashing, striking out with her fists. Oscar leaped from her lap with a deep guttural growl. He stood across the room, his back to the fire, hair on end, arched, hissing.

"Oh, my God." Jennifer fell back, relieved at finding herself in familiar surroundings. She wiped the perspiration away from her brow. Her hair was damp and tangled. Jennifer looked down at Oscar. He relaxed and licked at one paw nonchalantly. "Did I scare you, babe? Scared me too." She sat up too quickly and had to wait for a wave of dizziness to pass. Still groggy, she went to the kitchen and drank down a glass of water thirstily, poured another and drank it slowly. Finally, feeling better, she went to her bedroom and undressed while letting the shower water run.

The long steaming shower washed fatigue away. Afterwards, Jennifer stood in front of the clouded mirror brushing and drying her hair, watching critically as her face and figure slowly emerged from beneath the condensation on the mirror. Although she didn't believe it, Jennifer Warren was, just past her fortieth birthday, a striking, even beautiful woman, tall, with long blonde hair that she had allowed to grow out again after years of keeping it shorn, severe. But instead of taking pride in the thick lustrous strands that fell naturally down her back, Jennifer saw only the first streaks of gray. Instead of seeing a face with eyes of an exquisite blue and red full lips, Jennifer saw the faint lines. She rubbed at the steam on the mirror, as though attempting to erase her face and figure, but succeeded only in clarifying the features of the woman, fresh and beautiful with heavy breasts that were still youthful and rose softly as Jennifer brushed her hair. Her belly swelled gently. Her legs were long and shapely. And the woman would not go away. She stood there with a faint mocking smile in her ice blue eyes, no matter how hard Jennifer rubbed at the reflection in the mirror.

Jennifer was just pulling an old red sweater over her head when the front door slammed loudly.

"Jenny?"

"I'm in here, Kathy."

A girl raced into the bedroom and skidded to a halt like a wobbly colt. "Hank said you were here," she said, suddenly shy, looking down at the floor. "Grandpa let me drive up."

"Come here," Jennifer said. "Give me a hug."

Kathy smiled and jumped into Jennifer's arms. "I'm so glad you're here. I didn't think you were coming until next week."

"Things change and here I am."

"It's so good to see you."

"It's good to see you too. And happy birthday. Did you get my card and the package?"

"The dictionary was great. Thank you. God, it's heavy though."

"An unabridged dictionary has to be heavy. Lots of words to cover."

"Sweet sixteen. Isn't it great? I got my license on the first try and everything."

"You've been driving since you were thirteen."

"Yeah, but now I'm legal."

Jennifer smiled and shook her head. "You're a real pill."

"I thought you were bringing your friend this time?"

Jennifer shrugged. "I thought so too. Things change." She smiled ruefully.

"Did you have a fight?"

Jennifer nodded. "A big one."

"He must be a jerk then," Kathy said. "To fight with you."

"Yeah, I'm so perfect."

"Well, you are. Beautiful. Intelligent. He must be a stupid jerk."

"That's an accurate description. Forget him. Is Dave here?"

"He's puttering around in the shed. Said he needed to chop some wood."

"Come on, let's go take a tour. I haven't looked around yet. Came right here and fell asleep. I just got up a little while ago."

"Want me to make some coffee?"

"Sure. That'd be great."

Kathy ran into the kitchen. "You go talk to Grandpa. I'll bring it out."

Jennifer stood on the deck for a moment, savoring the freshness of the cool air, the clarity of the view, the sweet smell of the pines and moldering leaves, the sharp sound of a squabble between a squirrel and a jay. It was a good place to live. She stuck her hands in the pockets of her red windbreaker and danced off the steps, the heels of her boots clattering on the heavy wood, and went around the house, following the sound of the axe.

"Why don't you use the damned saw, Dave?"

"Don't like the damned saw, Jenny. Makes too much noise. Stinks." The axe descended in a powerful arc and chips flew. Dave dug the axe from the log and raised it over his head. Again, the chips flew.

"How've you been?" he asked, prying the axe loose.

"Fine," Jennifer said. "Better, now that I'm back."

"Always good to come home," Dave said, spitting on the leather gloves worn black with hard work. "Better not to leave though." The axe whistled through the air.

Dave Mason was sixty-odd years old and had spent his entire life in the valley except for the time he had spent in the army during Korea. He had gone off to war saying little and returned saying even less. He was a hard worker and for decades had been employed by one or another of the ranchers while doing odd jobs for others in the valley, saving nickels and dimes, putting everything away for his granddaughter's education. The years spent in the open had burned and toughened his skin and he squinted perpetually, even when the sun was not bright and harsh against the eyes.

He was squinting as he left the axe blade sunk deep in the log and turned to Jennifer. "You heard yet?"

"Heard what, Dave?"

"Old man Lockhart's gonna sell his place to 'em. That gives 'em all they need now."

"Hank didn't say anything when I was there."

"He knew," Dave said. "Everybody does."

"That's what he wants," Jennifer said, kicking at the clean white chips scattered around their feet. "Said some of the folks wanted to talk to me tonight."

"I reckon so," Dave said, jerking at the axe handle. "Hope so, anyway. Somebody gotta tell us what to do."

"Dave, how are we going to stop one of the largest development companies in the west, maybe the entire country, from building on land they own?"

"There's my way and your way, I reckon."

"What's your way?"

"Take our guns and go have a little talk with them boys. Tell 'em we like our valley just fine the way it is."

"Just like the Feud," Jennifer said. "People around here are never going to forget that, are they? Cattlemen against sheepherders. Shoot until everyone's dead. We're not living in some western movie anymore. John Wayne's not coming. Clint Eastwood's not going to ride in on a horse and save the valley from a resort hotel."

"Well, there's your way."

"And what's that?"

"Get 'em into court and talk 'em to death. That's what lawyers supposed to do. Save us a bunch of bullets. I don't much care which way we do it, so long as they don't build no great damned hotel."

"Hey, you guys," Kathy called as she emerged from the doorway, "I got hot coffee coming right up." She carried two cups.

"Hey, sweetie," Dave said, "that's real nice. Thank you."

"You're welcome, Grandpa."

"Thanks, Kathy," Jennifer said. "Where's yours?"

"I'll run back and get it. I couldn't carry all three. Guess I'll never be a waitress."

"That's why you're going to college," Dave said. "You ain't gonna be no waitress."

"Oh Grandpa," Kathy said smiling affectionately at him. "I'll be right back and then we'll take the tour. Okay?"

"Sure, hon," Jennifer said.

"Thanks for sending her that dictionary, Jenny. Helps keep her mind on school instead of boys."

"And you stop talking about guns. That's not the way things are done."

"Hey, just because I live way to hell and gone out here, don't mean I'm stupid. I read the paper. Listen to the radio. Watch the TV news. Seems like guns is the only way things is done anymore. Back during the Feud, well, at least you knew which side you was on. Ain't so sure no more."

"Dave, you made a speech," Jennifer teased.

"Ready, Jennifer?" Kathy cried.

"You two go on, get outta here," Dave said. "Let me get my work done."

It was their own special rite. Kathy took Jennifer on a tour of the house, inside and out, pointing out everything that had been taken care of during her absence— the little repairs Dave had made, and, depending upon the season, the leaves that had been raked, a lawn mowed, snow swept from the rickety back overhang, everything that needed to be done to maintain a solid, but old home in a part of Arizona that combined forest and pastures above the northern edge of the Sonoran desert.

Jennifer loved the house.

It had been built after the Great War by one of the descendants of the Feud as a gift to his child bride. They had lived there happily for a decade until an influenza epidemic had carried away the still-youthful wife and their two sons and infant daughter. The embittered widower lived on in the house for awhile, drinking and blaming himself for carrying the killing disease home from Phoenix, finally ending his grief with a shotgun blast.

No one wanted to live there for a long time. Locally, the children believed the embittered ghost still haunted the bedroom where he had ended his life so abruptly. It was a test of boyhood to enter the death room at midnight. But finally an outsider bought the house, using it as a base for hunting forays into the nearby forests and mountains. Local legend had it that he even hunted with Zane Grey who had his own hunting lodge below the Mogollon Rim. After the hunter's death, the house stood empty for a year or two at a time, while undergoing its periodic changes in ownership, until a retired couple happened upon the valley. They lived in the house for years until they died within months of each other. Again, the house remained empty—until Jennifer Warren found it.

The Hidden Valley real estate agent had tried to dissuade Jennifer from purchasing the old house, steering her to other bigger, more modern, less isolated homes in other parts of the valley, but while Jennifer humored the agent for a time her decision had been made the moment she saw the old place for the first time.

Taking the now routine tour with Kathy always reminded Jennifer of how much she missed the place when she was in Los Angeles. Although Jennifer's time at the old house was limited, she felt it was her true residence. Her condominium in Santa Monica was little more than an apartment, a place to sleep and hide between trips to Hidden Valley. Almost simultaneously with the purchase, Jennifer had started preparing for the Arizona Bar examination, knowing that with luck Hidden Valley would eventually be her permanent residence.

"And that's about it," Kathy said. "You weren't gone so long this time."

"I'll be glad when I live here all the time," Jennifer said.

"Me too. I miss you when you're gone."

"By the time I can live here permanently though, you'll be away at college, falling in love. You won't

40

even think of me."

"I will," Kathy said. "You're practically like my mother. I wish you were my mother."

Jennifer looked at her namesake—she had been named Kathy once, long ago, in another life—and smiled. "I'd probably nag you then. That's what mothers do."

"You wouldn't."

"Don't be so sure," Jennifer said, thinking of Clea, wondering what had come between them. It was not a mother's loving nagging. Secrets had forced the chasm between them. One secret. Her secret.

A squirrel raced along the eave of the roof, pausing to chatter angrily at them, before leaping to a tree branch and climbing the trunk as if it were a circular staircase.

"What got into him, I wonder?" Jennifer asked. "Oscar's in the house."

"He's still mad because Granddad cut down the limb that was scraping against the house. He hollered the whole time we were cutting it down."

"I'll have to get him a squirrel treat. Soften him up again."

"So, that's everything now. Did we do an okay job?"

"You did a great job. As usual."

Later, Kathy waved as she proudly drove her grandfather's pickup down the hill. Dave sat stoically beside her, staring straight ahead through the windshield. Jennifer returned Kathy's wave, watching until the truck disappeared through a stand of trees into the growing shadows. Then, she went into the house to turn on lamps and place another log on top of the still-glowing coals in the fireplace. She sat for a moment on the couch, watching licks of flame dart out at the log. But Jennifer knew she could no longer avoid it. The two pleasant and happy hours spent with Kathy renewed too much of the old guilt. She had to call Clea. She had to try.

No answer.

Jennifer sighed with relief. It could wait until later. Tomorrow even.

It started at Hank's over hot chili and cold beer. "We'll go to the school after we eat supper," Hank said, "but we wanted to talk to you first, before everybody started shouting over there."

Jennifer looked at the others in the booth across from her. Harriet Spencer owned and ran one of the largest cattle ranches in the Valley and had ever since her husband had died ten years before. Paul Sutter's ranch was almost as large. Jennifer turned to Hank who had pulled a chair to the end of the booth. "What's going on here?" she asked.

"Go ahead, Hank," Harriet Spencer said. "Tell her."

"We want you to help us stop that hotel."

Jennifer toyed with her bowl of chili, started to take a bite of garlic bread, put it down again. The clack of pool balls and laughter drifted over from the bar section of Hank's.

"I can't get involved in this," Jennifer said.

"We don't know what to do," Paul Sutter said. "Me and Harriet, we know cattle. Hank's got a small spread, but he knows his bartending and his restaurant best. We thought it would be enough to go and tell the politicians we didn't want the hotel. Shit, they're our friends and neighbors. Supposed to listen to us. But they don't. They want the damn thing. All they see is money coming into the valley. They can smell the money and the payoffs."

"You know people," Hank said. "You're a lawyer. You know better than we do what can be done. We got to find a way to stop them if we're going to keep the valley the same as always. You're one of us now, Jenny,

42

and we need you."

"There's money to finance what needs to be done," Paul said. "A lot of folks are willing to help out."

"We need you, Jenny," Hank said.

Again, Jennifer looked from one face to another. What can it hurt? she thought. They're my friends. The only real friends I have. Finally, Jennifer said, "I don't know what good I'll be, but I'll do everything I can to help."

"Thank you," Harriet said.

"But there's a condition," Jennifer said. "I'll do what I can, but my name must not enter into it. I want my involvement kept secret, otherwise . . ."

"We never heard of you when it comes to this hotel," Hank said. "Now eat your chili, while I outline the plan for tonight."

The multi-purpose room at the school was still decorated for the Christmas pageant. A portable stage was covered with straw where elementary school children acted out the miracle of Christ's birth each year. Large red letters cut from poster paper spelled out holiday greetings above the stage.

The meeting was presided over by Thad Murphy, the township's mayor. Perhaps a hundred people sat in little groups scattered through the auditorium. Alternately loud and raucous and then quietly subdued by helpless anger, the residents of Hidden Valley raged at their fate. One speaker after another declared a personal fear.

"That hotel's gonna ruin the valley for sure."

"There'll be a bunch of outsiders bringing drugs and God knows what all in here. We just don't need it."

"Those damn politicians sold us out."

"Lockhart shouldn't have done it. Wasn't right to sell like that. Not to strangers. Developers."

"It won't be a safe place for our kids no more."

"Traffic'll be terrible."

"Eat up all the good land. Destroy the farms. The ranches. Might as well live in Phoenix then."

"Or Los Angeles."

"Is that what you want?"

Some few expressed support for the resort hotel, but they were quickly hooted down.

"We need the jobs and the economic growth . . ."

"You can't stop progress . . ."

"We have a right to do what we want with our property . . ."

"Traitors!"

"My God, get it through your heads. It's the twentieth century now and you're all fools if you think . . ."

Jennifer listened to the shocked dismay and vehement bitterness with misgivings and growing apprehension. The proposed Hidden Valley Resort was not a surprise. It had been talked about for years. But that's all it was. Talk. No one thought it would come to anything. Suddenly Hidden Valley Resort was a reality. And they want me to do something to stop it.

"Hank," Jennifer whispered, "I don't know about all this."

"It'll be okay, darling, we just gotta let all the fools talk first."

Crazy Maggie interrupted with a shriek. "Thad Murphy! I had my hand up for hours. You better recognize me." She was dressed all in black as usual.

"I was getting to you, Mrs. Henderson. Got to wait your turn like everybody else."

"I been waiting. But you let Jeff Peters talk and I had my hand up before he did."

"Let her talk, Thad."

Murphy sighed. "Go on, Mrs. Henderson. Speak your piece."

"I know what y'all call me. Just cause someone gets old and wears black to mourn her dead husband who

44

was a good man all his life don't mean that person's crazy. I see things but I ain't crazy." She laughed. It was an abrupt cackle and harsh. "I tell you what I see. Cause it's coming. Mean old octopus a coming. That's what you call it. Got a whole bunch of arms and gonna get all of us. Octopus coming and gonna drag us all down. That's what's a coming. Crazy Maggie sees it. You best be heeding my warning."

"You tell 'em, Maggie," someone shouted.

The old woman laughed again, but without humor, and shuffled out of the auditorium. The door slammed behind her, the clang echoed off the walls.

"She ain't so crazy, Thad. That's exactly what Kendall Enterprises is. Big old octopus and gonna drag us all down."

"Okay," Hank muttered. "That's just about enough of this foolishness." He stood up. "Thad," he said.

"Hank. Wondered why you been so quiet."

"Collecting my thoughts, Thad, collecting my thoughts." Hank left his place beside Jennifer and walked to the front of the auditorium to stand between Thad Murphy and the audience.

"You all know me," Hank said quietly. "I've lived here in Hidden Valley all my life, except for a spell in the Marine Corps. I like this place. I want to keep it the way it is. But we can't do nothing the way we're going tonight. Everyone shouting and yelling at each other. We've got to have a plan."

"You have a plan, I suppose," Murphy interrupted.

"I do, Mr. Mayor, I do."

"It's getting late. You going to tell us about this plan sometime before the sun comes up?"

"I'm going to tell you right now so we can get this meeting over and everyone back to my place drinking beer and spending money."

Hank waited for the laughter to die.

"We need a committee to organize our campaign against the Hidden Valley Resort Hotel. We got to get

45

smart and fight them rascals on their own ground, with money and votes and the courts."

My God, Jennifer thought, I can't do this. What am I getting into?

"I nominate Harriet Spencer to be chairlady of our committee."

"I second," someone cried.

"Nominations don't need a second," Hank said, "but we'll take them anyway. All in favor say aye."

"Aye." The chorus was loud.

"Opposed?"

"You're all a bunch of God damned fools," Tracy Hawkins said.

"I take that as a no vote," Hank said.

"Take it any way you want."

"Nominations are now open for the other members of the committee."

"I nominate Hank."

"Thad Murphy."

"Paul Sutter."

"That's enough."

"All in favor."

"Aye."

"Meeting adjourned."

"Hank, you manipulated this whole thing," Jennifer said when they were walking back to the bar. Her misgivings were back, stronger than before.

"Pretty slick, too, wasn't it?" Hank agreed.

"Damn it, Hank," Jennifer said, "I don't want to be involved in all this. I can't."

"Jenny, Jenny," Hank said softly. "We need help. We have to do something. There's no one else around here who can help."

"I don't even live here full time."

"But you want to."

"One of these days, yes, but . . ."

"When you're ready for the big move, do you want it looking like Los Angeles?"

"No, but . . ."

"All you have to do is come to a few meetings now and then. Give us the benefit of your experience. We'll do the rest. Nobody'll ever know you're one of us."

"I guess."

They walked in silence for a few minutes.

"There's something else, Jenny."

"Now what?"

"Aw, Jenny, darling, don't be like that," Hank said. "I just wanted to ask you to the Christmas party as my date."

"Oh, Hank, that's sweet of you, but . . ."

"But what? Anybody else asked you?"

"No."

"You still seeing that guy in L.A.?"

"No, but . . ."

"Why not, then? I'll even get dressed up."

Why not? Jennifer thought, smiling. "I'd love to be your date, Hank."

Jennifer sat brooding by the picture window, hating the past and dreading the future. She stared out over the deck at the few scattered lights that blemished the valley. The night was clear and cold. Distant stars glistened like diamonds displayed on a black velvet cloth. The moonlight reflected sharply off the snow. The slope of the mountains fell away into the darkness that frightened man. The lights were insignificant, faint illumination from other isolated homes, tiny pockets of life and festivity blending into a natural landscape yet unsullied by man's greed.

As she sat by the window, feeling the night chill seep through the cold glass panes, three deer—a small buck and two does—stepped gingerly, cautiously, into a snow covered clearing below the house. In the bright moonlight, Jennifer saw the steam coming from their nostrils and in her imagination she could hear their hooves crunching through the crusted top layer of snow. The buck raised his head and for a long moment looked directly at Jennifer. She sat motionless looking back. The buck tossed his head once and then walked slowly into the night's shadows. The two females followed. Jennifer looked down on the clearing where the deer had been and wondered how long they could keep the valley the same. It was her world now and she wanted it to last forever. But the octopus was coming. Gonna tangle y'all up in its arms. Can't never get away from the octopus. It's coming. Sure enough coming. It would be like the tentacles of her past. Once they closed about you, there was no escape. They squeezed and spread their jet black ink until you disappeared in the cloud.

Crazy Maggie's harsh cackle echoed in Jennifer's mind and through the dark night of Hidden Valley.

FOUR

Death accompanied the violin for nearly three centuries.

Some dedicated craftsman had finished the violin in 1717. The year was on a label that could be clearly read through one of the sound holes. The label also indicated that the violin was after the Stradivari style. The wood had been lovingly polished for weeks by an apprentice under the ever-watchful eye of his master. When finally the instrument had been deemed finished, it had played for kings and beggars, ladies in waiting and royal harlots, passing from one accomplished hand to another over the years.

It had survived two pogroms, those periodic massacres of Jews launched by rabid Cossacks and others, when terror filled the night and blood ran in the streets. Had the violin's owner lived to play after the first slaughter, the music could not be heard over the anguished funereal wails that followed. Both the violin and its next owner survived the second pogrom by cowering unnoticed in a deep hiding place, but no stomach remained for playing then.

And the years passed into decades.

Long after the anonymous artisan had finished his masterwork, the violin somehow made its way to America where it was carried into the Battle of Seven

Pines, an inconclusive fray fought in a swampy woodland near Richmond. Twelve thousand men died for skirmish lines that did not change despite the bloodshed. A painfully carved inscription formed an unpunctuated scrollwork around the edge of the violin's back. *H.C. albright was killed an uncle of mine serch the records and files and keep this instrument 702 Company B 26th Regiment 2nd Volunteers This violin found so sad after the battle at 7 Pines Virginia* There was more but time and use smoothed the letters until they were indecipherable. The battle had taken place in the uncomfortable humidity at the end of May 1862, a minor engagement that took up scarcely a page in the voluminous records of the epic struggle. The unknown nephew's testimonial spoke more eloquently than the Civil War histories.

The decades passed into centuries.

With its sadness intact, the violin somehow traveled to Arizona Territory to become an indelible part of the mythology of the Hidden Valley Feud, a prolonged ten year struggle over a way of life near the end of the nineteenth century. Its violence still tainted the valley a hundred years later. The long and bloody feud virtually destroyed two families and the scores of hired men who fought for one side or the other. And a woman, innocent of any crime save vengeance for a murdered lover, was taken from a tiny makeshift cell and hanged by men urged on by respectable wives.

No one knew how the violin came into the possession of Annie Potts or how a prostitute had learned to play the melancholy strains that echoed ethereally through the valley long after her death. Nor was it fiddle music, that heritage from the hill country of Appalachia. This music was strange and unfamiliar to the valley, marked by a sadness suitable to this particular violin.

But Annie Potts played the sorrowful music and brooded over the death of Billy Wilson for days after he was gunned down from behind in the dusty little main street of Hidden Valley. She played and played until the block of resin was worn and crumbling in her fingers, seeing no one, scarcely eating or drinking. Finally she took Billy's Navy revolver and waited in the alley until George Newton took his last arrogant stroll down the main street.

Annie did not ambush him, shoot him from behind as he had done her poor Billy, but neither did she give him warning. Annie simply walked up to him, pulled the revolver from beneath her shawl and shot the smirk off George Newton's face.

No one dared approach until Annie dropped the gun to her side and the silent tears streamed down her face. They took her then and locked her in the storage room of the saloon. Hidden Valley had no need of a jail. Few lived long enough to be charged and tried in Hidden Valley during the Feud.

Annie asked for her violin, but her request was refused.

"We've heard it enough, Annie, these last few days," they said, not unkindly. "Give it a rest now."

While Annie played her forbidden tunes in her mind, the women of the town debated and decided her fate and spent the night hours nagging their husbands to action.

They came for Annie with the first slight strains of the dawn over eastern mountains. They tied her hands, put her astride a borrowed horse, and led her out of town while their wives peeked through narrow curtain cracks. The horses snorted and labored up the steep trail to the tall stately pine.

No one met Annie's eyes when the lynch rope was thrown over the branch and the loose end wrapped around the trunk of the tree. No one met Annie's eyes when they tightened the noose around the soft white flesh of her neck.

The only words spoken that grim morning came from Annie's lips. "I wish you had let me play last night," she said. "I'm gonna miss my violin."

The horse reared from beneath Annie Potts and she fell and died.

The death of Annie Potts marked the end of the Feud. Shamefaced men rode home in silence where they drank and sullenly ignored their women, trying to forget Annie Potts twisting and turning beneath the branch of the hanging tree, her broken neck angling her face to the heavens. Afterwards, the valley seemed to close in on itself in self-imposed punishment, as though isolation and loneliness could atone for the sins committed in the beauty of the valley.

And so one century passed into another.

The violin grew dusty.

In the valley, it was surely winter now and a great change for Jennifer. Leaves had long ago changed colors and fallen to lie moldering. Dark swollen clouds hovered ponderously over the valley. Crusted snow spotted the ground and there would be more before the day was over. The ground was frozen. Even in the heavy blue parka, Jennifer shivered as she stood on the porch, sipping coffee, looking out at the vast expanse of the valley now shrouded in gloom beneath the gray overcast. Yet, little more than an hour's drive would take the traveler into the first wastes of the Sonoran desert; less than a hundred miles to the south were the busy suburbs of Phoenix and Scottsdale and Tempe, luxuriating in the bright sunny weather of mid-December, a winter in name only, like Santa Monica.

Smoke swirled from the chimney, drifting lazily away through the chilly morning. Oscar ventured tentatively off the porch, reaching out with one paw to touch the frozen snow in the shadow of the steps. He drew his paw back distastefully and looked up at Jennifer with large yellow eyes. He was quickly distracted by three sparrows that landed across the driveway and then flew to sit on the eave of the roof, chirping disdainfully as Oscar listened and watched them intently. The birds fell silent and Oscar turned to look at the thicket of trees to the left and beneath the house, swiveling his ears as he stared into the shadows of the pines.

"What do you see, Oscar?" Jennifer saw nothing there. "It's just some animal. A squirrel or something."

Oscar relaxed and returned to the porch.

"See, it's gone now," Jennifer said, reaching down to scratch behind Oscar's ears.

The voice startled them both.

"Jennifer Warren!"

The old woman appeared suddenly from the shadows in the stand of pines.

"Jennifer Warren," the old woman called again stepping into the clearing. She leaned on a cane.

Crazy Maggie. "You scared me," Jennifer said. Damn, she thought, I don't even know her last name. Just Crazy Maggie. I can't call her that.

"No reason to be afraid," Crazy Maggie said.

"Come on up. How'd you get here? I didn't hear a car."

"I'm old," Crazy Maggie said. "I ain't helpless. Ain't crazy neither, not like some folks think."

"I didn't think you were," Jennifer said defensively, truly seeing Crazy Maggie for the first time. Before, the old woman had simply been part of the ever-changing background of Hidden Valley, like the homeless in Santa Monica, or any city. After a time, it was easy to ignore them. They weren't there anymore. Unless they accosted you, begging spare change for their existence, they simply disappeared from conscious awareness. Like Maggie.

She was old, stooped, and walked with a limp, leaning heavily on the cane. Her wrinkled face was leathery from years of exposure to the elements of ranch life in the valley. But now, forced to recognize

53

her existence, Jennifer saw sharp blue eyes, clear and strong. There was nothing crazy about Maggie, not if you took the time to acknowledge her, to look into her eyes.

"I know what they call me," the old woman said looking around, down at Oscar. "Some folks don't like a black cat. Get scared."

"He's an orphan." Like me, Jennifer thought. We're both orphans.

"Beautiful cat. Don't matter none that he's black. Not to me. Somebody like Thad Murphy." She shrugged. "He wouldn't know no better. Sees bad luck in everything."

"Would you like some coffee?" Jennifer asked. "It's fresh."

"Is it strong?"

"I don't really know. I guess it's strong."

"I like strong coffee."

"Come on, Oscar. Let's have coffee."

"Oscar," the old woman said. "That's a good name for a black cat."

"I'm afraid I don't know your name," Jennifer said, opening the door for the old woman.

"You know what they call me."

"Well, I'm not calling you that."

Crazy Maggie smiled, approvingly. "Name's Henderson," she said. "But you call me Maggie."

Jennifer smiled. "All right, Maggie it is. And you call me Jennifer."

"Jennifer Warren," Maggie said, sitting at a kitchen table. She hung her cane over the back of the chair. "You married?"

Jennifer poured coffee. "Once. A long, long time ago."

"Children?"

"A daughter," Jennifer said. "You know all this. It's common knowledge in Hidden Valley."

"Wanted to hear it from you, not the town gossips.

54

They can never get anything straight. Good coffee."

"Strong enough?" Jennifer asked smiling again.

"Pretty near," Maggie said. "Pretty near. Another scoop or two and you would've made it."

"I'll remember that."

"Course you didn't know I was coming. Kind of invited myself. Make a bother of myself sometimes."

"It's no trouble," Jennifer said, "but I am curious . . . you didn't come all the way out here to see if my coffee was strong enough."

"Nope. Came to see if you were strong enough."

"For what?"

"To fight the octopus. Can't win. It's gonna eat you up, just like it's gonna eat this valley."

"That's what you said at the meeting."

"Nobody believed me then. You don't believe me now, but it's true. That big old octopus gonna destroy us."

"We have some recourse," Jennifer said, surprised to find herself defending the chosen course. "There are some things we can do."

"My daddy, he survived the Feud." Maggie looked away, out at the Valley, subdued beneath the gray clouds. "One of the lucky ones. But he had nightmares the rest of his life. When he wasn't drinking he was dreaming bad dreams. I never knew which was worst." Maggie's eyes emptied and grew distant as she looked into the past.

"What's all this have to do with Hidden Valley and the hotel?"

"I just don't want you having nightmares."

"I won't," Jennifer said. At least, not over this, she thought. I have enough nightmares of my own. "Would you like some more coffee?"

"Thank you, no, I've got to be getting along."

"I'll drive you back," Jennifer said.

"I got my little cart down at the bottom of the hill."

"That's why I didn't hear a car."

"Cart don't make much noise. Didn't mean to surprise you though."

"You startled me. And Oscar."

"No reason to be afraid of me," Crazy Maggie said. She scratched Oscar behind his ears. He offered his chin for more. "I got to go. I thank you for the coffee."

"Come again."

"I might do that."

The first delicate flakes of snow fell from the fat dark clouds as Maggie clumped down the steps of the porch. The snow swirled lazily, delicately.

Maggie stopped behind the red cab of the pickup truck and pointed at the gun rack with her cane. "You got something to put in that?" she asked.

Jennifer nodded. "I have a rifle."

"Can you use it?"

Again, Jennifer nodded. "Hank taught me how to shoot."

Maggie cackled the mad laugh Jennifer remembered from the town meeting. "Bet he sold it to you too."

"Sold me the truck as well."

"Don't surprise me none," Maggie said. "You get that gun out and put it where it belongs." She turned and limped down the hill. "Listen to me. I see things. You keep that gun handy."

Jennifer watched from the porch while Crazy Maggie hobbled down the road. When the old woman disappeared into the thickening snowstorm, Jennifer turned to Oscar and said, "My God, what was that all about?"

The snow continued sporadically all morning and into the afternoon, trifling with the valley, threatening an imminent storm, but then holding off, teasing and mocking the humans who went through their day with one eye cast at the sky. The heavily laden clouds hung low over the valley, solid and unmoving. Jennifer, like all the others, looked to the forbidding clouds often, wondering how long the storm would hold off. The

56

radio playing softly in the kitchen announced travel advisories frequently, warning of an impending blizzard that would curtail travel throughout northern Arizona. It was already snowing hard above the Rim, in Flag and in Winslow. Jennifer went through all the cupboards in the kitchen, taking stock of her supplies. Her shopping list grew with each cupboard examined. Cleaning supplies in one. Canned goods in another. Spices and other staples from another. Shopping and replenishing the supplies was usually a task Jennifer enjoyed. She could have brought everything from California where it was less expensive, but it was another ritual of being in the valley. It helped make her feel at home after the extended stays in California. She checked the weather again. Nothing had changed. Jennifer decided to do the shopping. *If it snows, I can get back before it's too bad.*

Jennifer was halfway to town when she remembered Crazy Maggie's warning that morning. *Get the rifle out and put it where it belongs.* Jennifer glanced in the rear view mirror and saw the empty gun rack and felt a sudden uneasiness. Her foot went to the brake. She slowed, nearly stopped to turn around and go back, and then stepped on the accelerator again. *This is silly,* she thought. *What am I doing?* Jennifer continued into town, telling herself that it was the leaden sky, the oppressive sky that bothered her. It was enough to depress anyone. *No, it wasn't the weather. There's nothing wrong with the weather. It's just a storm. It's winter. We're going to have a white Christmas. It'll be beautiful.* But the uneasiness persisted. *Who was that woman? What does she know?*

"Gonna be a hellish storm if it ever makes up its mind."

"Looks that way," Jennifer said, getting out her checkbook. She was the only one in the market. "Be a slow day for you if it snows like they expect."

"Slow anyway," Sam Evans said. "Gives us a chance to do some catching up though. Orders. Stuff like that." He rang up the last item. "That it for today?"

"Did you get the newspapers?"

"Sure did. A whole week's worth."

Jennifer looked at the total on the cash register. "Seems like I bought everything in sight." She wrote $117.19 in her check register.

Sam took Jennifer's check and slipped it into the cash drawer. "Jimmy," he called. "Need you to carry some groceries out."

"I can do it, Sam."

"Boy's gotta earn his keep somehow."

Jimmy Evans appeared suddenly from between two rows. "Hi, Miss Warren," he said shyly rubbing his hands on the white apron he wore.

Jennifer was reminded of the runner at the gas station in Barstow. Were all teenage boys so shy and gangling? Was I ever that young? "Hi, Jimmy," she said. "You glad to be on vacation?"

"Oh, I don't know. It's kinda boring."

"He'd rather be out hunting," Sam said. "Got himself a nice six point buck during the season," he added proudly. "You stop back, Jenny. Give you a nice piece of venison. Ain't nothing better."

"I'd like that, Sam. Thanks. And congratulations on the buck, Jimmy."

"Aw, I was lucky. Just kinda walked in front of me."

"I'm impressed no matter what happened," Jennifer said. "I'm going to run next door for a minute. Just stick the groceries in the truck."

"Yes, ma'am," Jimmy said.

In the hardware store, Jennifer bought a box of

58

twenty 30-30 cartridges for her lever action Winchester Model 94. Jennifer had learned from Hank that each bullet weighed 170 grains and had a velocity of 1895 feet per second at 100 yards. The smaller grain bullets had a greater velocity, but could be easily deflected by brush, and the 170 grain bullet had better stopping power.

"Whatever you're shooting at," Hank had said, "you want to knock the son-of-a-bitch down. Course it would be better if you had something bigger."

"Like that famous .44 magnum you're always talking about?"

"That'd be good, but it'd probably knock you on your pretty little bottom. No, this is gun enough for you right now. Just remember gun control is being able to hit your target."

And Jennifer discovered she was able to hit her target.

Clint Eastwood was demonstrating gun control on the TV screen when Jennifer walked into the bar at Hank's. Unshaven, a stub of a cigar held between clenched teeth, hard eyes shadowed by a wide-brimmed hat, the Eastwood persona fired a huge revolver and Hank hit the stop on his remote control. Eastwood disappeared and a soap flashed on the screen in its place.

"Aw, shit, Hank, we was watching that." The chorus of complaint came from two ranch hands at the end of the bar beneath the television set. They were the only customers in the bar.

"You ain't going anywhere," Hank said. "Exhibit a little patience. Pretend it's a commercial. Better yet, have another beer. I'll buy."

They were drinking from long neck bottles. "Okay," they said in unison again.

"Who'd he kill this time?" Jennifer asked.

"Bad guys," Hank said opening the beer bottles and sliding them down the bar. "Cleaning up the territory."

"Don't you ever get tired of those films?" Jennifer asked already knowing Hank's answer.

"Nope," he said. "Had a John Wayne festival once. Before your time. Watched John Wayne movies all day and all night. He was okay, I guess, but a goody two shoes. Always doing something noble at the end. Clint's real. It snowing yet?"

"Off and on. Off and on. Coffee fresh?" Again, Jennifer thought back to Crazy Maggie, asking if the coffee was strong.

"My coffee's always fresh," Hank said. "You want some of my fresh coffee?"

Jennifer nodded absently. "Hank, what do you know about Crazy Maggie?" she asked.

Hank slowly poured coffee into a thick ceramic mug. He brought it over and placed it on the bar in front of Jennifer. "Maggie's okay," he said. "She acts a little strange sometimes, but I never had no trouble with her."

"Meaning someone else did?"

"What's going on, Jennifer?"

Jennifer raised her eyebrows. Hank only called her by her full name when he wanted to be serious.

"She came up to my place this morning. I was just standing on the porch having coffee and all of a sudden, there she was. Came out of the woods calling my name. It was kind of spooky."

"What did she say?"

"Strange things. Started in about that octopus again. Wanted to see if I was strong enough to fight it. Told me to put the rifle in the gun rack."

"Did you?"

"No," Jennifer said. "I bought a box of shells just now though," she added sheepishly. "Hank, what did she want with me?"

"Aw, Maggie gets a little strange sometimes."

"Come on, Hank."

"All right. Maggie comes from one of the old families."

"She said her father was in the Feud."

"I reckon that's so. But the old timers say he was never quite right in the head after that. Crazy, like Maggie is now. I hear she wasn't always like that though. Way back now, she had a son, died of polio before there was any vaccine. Not long after, husband killed himself. Folks say she ain't been right since. Lives up in that old cabin by herself." Hank glanced up at the soap opera on the television and shut it off. "You want some more coffee?"

"Aw, shit, Hank," one of the regulars complained. "Now we was watching that."

Hank opened two more bottles of beer for the ranch hands without being asked. "That stuff'll pollute your mind. Drink instead."

"You're leaving something out, Hank. What is it?"

Hank took the coffee mug and refilled it anyway.

"Hank . . ."

"Some folks around here think she has the evil eye."

Jennifer laughed. "You don't believe that."

"Just tales they tell. You asked."

"Yes, I did. What kind of tales?"

"You really want to hear this? It's what people around here use to scare their kids. Get 'em to go to bed, make 'em eat their spinach."

"Hank, come on. What's the big deal?"

"They say if Maggie comes around somebody's going to die."

Oscar was on the window sill, pacing back and forth impatiently. He leaped down and swiped at Jennifer's ankles as she came through the door, arms filled with bags.

"Oscar, damn it. You know you don't like shopping."

61

The cat followed her into the kitchen and leaped to the counter. Jennifer stroked him gently. "When are you going to learn, I won't desert you?"

Still, Oscar persisted, following Jennifer back to the truck, batting at snowflakes with one paw. "You better get inside, Oscar. Get in front of the fire. It's going to come down now for sure."

Oscar leaped into the driver's seat and waited.

"I'm not going anywhere except into the house." Jennifer carried the last load of groceries and the newspapers into the house. Oscar was still sitting in the truck when Jennifer looked out the window. "Damn cat."

She went back and carried him inside. It was snowing harder now. One huge white flake stuck to his face. He brushed it away with his paw.

Again, Jennifer called her daughter's number. Again, there was no answer. Come on, Clea, where are you?

From long habit, Jennifer glanced through the personal ads first. She was relieved not to find a message from him. Always, when he placed an ad to her, it appeared in the San Francisco, Los Angeles, San Diego, and Orange County newspapers on the same day. Jennifer had checked. As long as nothing appeared in the Arizona newspapers, she was safe. It meant that he had not found her. Yet. Jennifer dreaded the day a message would appear in an Arizona paper. She would know then that he had discovered her hiding place.

Jennifer went into the bedroom closet on her hands and knees and pulled a hard rifle case from beneath her clothes. She placed it on the bed, opened it, and took the small rifle out, working the action to ensure that it was unloaded. While the action was open, she placed her thumbnail below the breech and peered down the barrel, adjusting the angle to catch the light's reflection from her thumbnail. The barrel was clear and clean. It had a slight residue of oil. She closed the action and put the rifle to her shoulder, sighting through the window at a ragged piece of bark hanging askew from a tree trunk. She inhaled, took up the slack on the trigger, exhaled half the breath and squeezed. Click. She carried the rifle into the living room and sat in front of the fireplace sliding cartridges into the loading port.

With the rifle still across her knees, Jennifer tried Clea's number again. Come on, Clea, please be there.

"Hello."

"Clea?" Thank God. "It's Mom. How are you?"

"Mom? Where are you?"

"I'm in Hidden Valley. Merry Christmas."

"Merry Christmas to you too."

"How have you been?"

"You know. Same old thing. How about you?"

"Nothing much changes with me either."

"You staying in Arizona for the holidays?"

"I'll go back to L.A. after New Year's. They're having the big party here as usual. What are you doing?"

"Nothing much. I've got a new boy friend. We're having Christmas dinner with his family."

"That'll be nice. I'm glad you won't be alone."

"Aren't you going to ask me what he does? You always do."

Please, don't let it start. "First, tell me his name."

"It's Bob."

"Okay. What does Bob do?"

"He's in his third year of law school. How's that?"

"I'm impressed." Thank God, he's not a dope dealer like the last one. "Where did you meet him?"

"At the restaurant. He came in for coffee after studying late for some big exam."

"Well, I'm happy for you."

"Thank you."

"Work going okay?"

"Yeah, I'm making pretty good tips, but I may look for another job soon. I'm not getting along with the manager. He plays favorites all the time. I'm making lots of jewelry though. Even selling some."

"That's great, Clea." Jennifer wanted to ask when she was going back to college.

"How's Bear?"

"Same old Bear. You should call him. He adores you."

"Maybe I will." Clea paused. "I sent you some earrings, but I mailed them to California. I should've known you'd be in Arizona."

"That's all right. They'll be there when I get back. I'm sure they're lovely. You'll be getting a package from me any day now."

"What did you get me?"

"You'll never change, will you?"

"You know me. I hate waiting until Christmas Day."

"Try. Just once. For me." Stop it, Jennifer. Don't nag her. It's going so well.

"We'll see."

Damn it. Jennifer heard the slight change in Clea's voice. "Hey, I didn't mean anything by it," Jennifer said hastily. "I was kidding."

Clea hesitated. "So was I," she said at last.

"Well, have a wonderful Christmas. I'll miss you. Maybe next year, you'll come home?"

"This is home now, Mom."

"Well, at least come for a visit. You know what I mean."

"Maybe."

"Merry Christmas. I love you."

"I love you too, Mom."

Jennifer hung up with a great sense of relief. They hadn't fought and argued. Perhaps we can start getting back together again.

FIVE

Jackson Holloway watched his wife sip her martini to give her courage. She posed provocatively, thrusting out her breasts, by the fireplace in the large family room with the huge window that overlooked the bay and the sailboat. Holloway knew she was trying to please him, hoping to avoid his wrath, because he used sex as a weapon, an excuse to mete out punishment and humiliation, the combination of pain and pleasure that kept her compliant to his wishes. Despite the times Holloway hurt her, he supposed he loved her, at least as much as he could love anyone.

Fifteen years his junior, Janice Holloway was statuesque with heavy breasts that were as firm and erect at the age of thirty-two as on their wedding day when she was only twenty. Other men found her face and figure stunning, staring openly at her as she moved gracefully through a room, undressing her, envying Holloway, and wishing that she belonged in their beds. She wore her blonde hair long, as he liked it, hanging almost to her slender waist. Today, she wore a simple dress belted at the waist. It accentuated her breasts. The bruises had almost disappeared and their traces were hidden now by makeup. Janice Holloway was a very beautiful woman, even to Holloway, even after twelve years of marriage.

But sometimes when Holloway looked at Janice, he saw another woman, the woman he hated, his child bride, the mother of his daughter, the progeny he had seen only in a photograph of a painting as she suckled at Kathleen's milk-swollen breast. Then he loathed all of them, his wife, his former wife, and the devil's bitch she had spawned.

When the obsessive mood came over him, Holloway addressed his wife as Kathleen, the whore's name, the name that spawned terror in Janice Holloway, the signal that heralded the torments that could last an hour—or days.

Janice had awakened that morning to find him staring at her ominously. But then he smiled and she relaxed.

"Good morning, darling," she said.

"Good morning, Kathleen."

Janice was filled with dread. But even with the fear that gripped her belly, Janice dared to hope as the alarming name was not repeated while they took turns showering, then dressing and going down for the breakfast prepared by their Spanish-speaking cook.

Jackson waited until they had finished breakfast before asking, "What are your plans for the day, Kathleen?"

Janice paled and licked at her lips before answering. "Lunch with Susan. That's all."

"Cancel it," he commanded. "Tell her you're going to be tied up," he said, smiling, looking at his watch. "And come to my office at ten."

"Yes, Jackson."

During the intervening forty-five minutes, Holloway had leafed through the taunting photographs that had arrived so long ago now, finding a pose that he liked before replacing the folder in his personal safe.

Janice knocked on the office door precisely at ten.

66

Again, Holloway smiled. He had taught her to be prompt. "Come in," he said.

Janice stood before his desk, waiting.

Once again, Holloway marveled at the remarkable resemblance between Janice and the slut in the photographs. Too bad for Janice. She shifted her weight anxiously, staring beyond her husband's head. Through the window, she could see the bay and the waterfront restaurant where she would have met her friend for lunch. A sailboat chugged under power slowly down the channel. She could see the people on board, two couples, normal people, going out for a day of fun, relaxation.

"What did you tell Susan?"

"That something had come up," Janice replied.

"Did you tell her you were going to be tied up?"

"Not in so many words."

"Call her back. Tell her exactly what is going to happen to you."

"Jackson . . ."

"Call her!"

Janice turned and started out of the office.

"Call her from here."

Janice froze.

"Use this telephone. Tell her you're being punished for lying to her."

"Jackson, please, don't make me do it."

Holloway took two clothes pins from the desk drawer.

Janice picked up the telephone and quickly called Susan, keeping her eyes on the clothes pins. He had put them on her nipples once. "Hi, it's me again." Janice hesitated. She did not want to experience the clothes pins again. The pain had been excruciating. "I have to tell you I'm going to be tied up today." Her face turned scarlet.

He picked up one of the pins and opened it, letting it snap shut.

"I'm being punished for lying to you."

I've been a naughty girl, he mouthed.

She repeated the words for Susan.

I'm going to be spanked, he mouthed.

Again, she repeated the words for Susan.

He nodded and put the clothes pins away.

"No, I'm all right. I want him to do it . . . You wouldn't like it . . . Perhaps tomorrow." She looked at Jackson. He nodded again. "Yes, tomorrow," she said. "I'll see you then."

"What did she say?"

"Susan thought it was exciting. She wants to hear all about it. I think she'd like to sleep with you."

"And is it exciting?"

"I hate it. You know that."

"Why don't you leave me?"

Janice didn't answer.

"You know I'd find you?"

"Yes."

"Do you love me?"

Slowly, Janice nodded her head.

"Despite everything?"

"Despite everything, I still love you." It was what he wanted to hear. She had no choice.

"Strip," he said.

Janice Holloway spent the day standing naked, wrists cuffed and drawn high above her head to the ring bolt imbedded in the wall, in darkness, locked in the tiny cork-lined closet of her husband's office. She never knew why he locked the door when he closed it, engulfing her in the terrifying darkness. She was helpless. She had learned not to cry out. Still, he closed her in the darkness of the coffin-like space, always carefully locking the door. The noise of the bolt sliding home was final, leaving Janice in despair.

It was not the first time she had been imprisoned in

68

the closet. She knew it would not be the last. He had forced her to aid in its construction, telling her all the while the use to which the closet would be put. It was Janice who had glued the cork to the walls. It was Janice who had stood on the small step ladder and twisted the bolt into the wall, straining with both hands to twist it into the wall. It was Janice who had begged him not to put her in the closet, not to close the door, not to torture her so. But he had only laughed and said, "Good night, Kathleen," as he closed the door and left her alone that first night.

Despite the cork insulation, faint sounds penetrated her prison. She heard Jackson talking on the telephone, initiating the calls because she had not heard the telephone ring. Once, she thought Consuela came into the room to ask instructions for lunch. And then it was quiet for a long time. There was no sense of time in her cocoon. She might have been in there for an hour or ten. The soles of her feet began to ache as she tried to ease the strain on her outstretched arms. Probably Jackson was at lunch, enjoying a glass of wine. She wondered if he thought of her during his day? Did he tell his business visitors that he locked his wife in the closet. Who was Kathleen?

The distant sound of the telephone startled her from mindless reveries. Jackson's voice murmured indistinctly from beyond the door. Silence again. Was he still there, seated at his desk? How long would he keep her shut away from the world? What would he do when he finally released her? It was better not to think. God, I hate him now. But I'm afraid of him too. One day, I will kill him. I swear I'll kill him. But she knew the threat was hollow, meaningless. Her life was ruled by her fear of him. Don't think. How long has it been now?

Janice heard the sound of the key sliding into the lock.

Thank God.

She closed her eyes against the light that would blind her.

It was almost over now.

The door opened.

"Janice, darling," Susan's voice said. "You look beautiful."

It couldn't be. Janice opened her eyes, blinking against the light. Susan stood beside Jackson. She was disheveled, hair falling into her eyes, blouse hanging free of her skirt. Her lipstick was smeared. Janice could see Jackson's erection bulging.

"Susan is joining us for cocktails," Jackson said.

Holloway took the martini away from Janice. She eyed the remains of the glass hungrily. "Please, Jackson," she said, "not in front of Susan." She dared not look at her friend.

"Strip," he said for the second time that day.

"I beg you. Fuck her if you want. I don't care. Do anything you want, but make her go away now."

"But, I've promised Susan that she could spank you. You don't want to disappoint Susan, do you?"

Oh, dear God in heaven, I swear I'll kill you. I'll kill both of you.

"Do you?" Holloway asked again.

"No," Janice whispered.

"Then, take off your clothes now. Susan has already seen your charms. She'd like to see them again. Wouldn't you, Susan?"

"This has gone far enough," Susan said. "I'm leaving now."

"No, you're not."

"I'll tell Harold you tried to rape me."

Holloway turned on Susan, advancing slowly, forcing her to back up until she was trapped against the fireplace. "No, Susan, you won't cry rape. You now belong to me too."

70

"Let me go. I was kidding. I won't say anything."

"I believe you, Susan." He reached out and touched her breast. "You know why I believe you, Susan?"

She shook her head, grimacing with pain as he pulled her to him by her breast.

"I believe you because I recorded that little scene in the office. 'Jackson,'" he mimicked. "'Jackson, I want you. Fuck me, Jackson.' Would you like Harold to have a copy of the tape, Susan?"

She shook her head again.

"No, I didn't think so. He'd throw your ass out without a cent. Now, go over there and sit down and shut up."

He turned back to Janice, seeing the face of the woman he hated. Suddenly, he was twenty-five years old, looking at the woman who had betrayed him. All of the old rage and anger flooded back, overwhelming him with hatred.

"Take it off, Kathleen, you worthless fucking whore."

Slowly, Janice unfastened the belt of her dress.

SIX

Sierra ran.

Through dark and twisted alleys filled with the stench of garbage and wine and human refuse, she ran. Looking back into the darkness and its invisible demons, she ran. Panting desperately, with the long blonde hair twisted and tangled in ugly strands, she ran. Past hissing cats with arched backs and bared claws and the dogs that snarled and growled, she ran. Stumbling, nearly falling, reaching for her baby, she ran.

Clea!

Where is Clea? she cried. Please, give her back to me, she pleaded with a voice that struggled for breath in the dank, foul-smelling night air.

She could not see the demons that pursued her. But they were behind her, reaching for her with long fingers covered with putrefying flesh. She felt their sulphurous breath on her naked back.

Clea! she screamed.

Sierra fell. She scrambled to regain her balance. Her breasts and knees and feet were bruised, bleeding from the abrasions and scratches. She twisted away, crying and begging, and knocked over a garbage can. The crash echoed and clanged in the dirty alleyway. Sierra cried out and put her hands up to fend off the devils.

Clea!

They were upon her.

The crash of the garbage can awakened Jennifer. She lay still in the night, listening. Oscar was beneath the covers, asleep on her legs. Jennifer slid from the warm bed quietly, into the chill of the bedroom. Oscar stirred, protesting with a brief sharp cry and then was asleep again. Jennifer took the rifle, reassured with the cold hard feel of the rifle's weight in her hand. Outside, the ground was covered with a blanket of snow. The moon reflected off the white. Jennifer crept silently, shivering, to the bedroom window, prepared to see alien footprints in the blanket of snow. Then, she heard the scratching of nails as the small animal, a raccoon or a possum, dug for food in the overturned garbage can. Beady red eyes glanced up at her. Jennifer exhaled with audible relief. A fox. She returned to the bed then, replacing the rifle in its place by the nightstand. Oscar crawled forward under the covers, snuggling close to her. She hugged him and listened to the creaks in the old house until she fell asleep again.

Harriet Spencer's ranch, the Double Bar, went all the way back to the mountains on the western edge of the valley, and stretched for miles along a dirt track, slippery and muddy during the winter, dusty and corrugated during the summer. The road followed the barbed wire boundary of the ranch. The only break in the wire was protected by a cattle guard.

Jennifer slowed, but still bounced as she turned her pickup truck across the heavy round rails of the guard. The sun sparkled off the snow as Jennifer drove into the ranch proper. Cattle watched lazily from both sides of the road as the truck slipped through puddles and mud. As Jennifer neared the big house and its outbuildings, two German shepherds barked and raced along the fence, kicking up the fresh snow with their back feet, escorting her, announcing her arrival. They circled the pickup when Jennifer parked in front of the house. They still barked, not with menace, but rather with joy at a welcome intrusion into the routine of their day.

"Samson! Delilah! You shut up all that noise."

The dogs immediately quieted and scampered over to Harriet Spencer who was coming down from the porch.

"Don't worry, Jennifer. They ain't got the good sense to bite anybody."

"They're beautiful," Jennifer said, petting each in turn.

"That's all they're good for. Eat and look pretty. But they're good friends. Ain't that right, Samson?"

The dog barked once in agreement. Delilah wagged her tail furiously.

"Am I early?" Jennifer asked.

"No," Harriet Spencer replied. "The others are late. They'll be along directly."

"You have a huge place here. I didn't realize it was so big."

"And it's a lot smaller than the original. One generation would sell off a piece to pay for something they thought they needed and then another generation would sell another piece for something else. There were a couple of frugal generations stuck in between there, otherwise there might not be anything left. Come on, I'll give you the five cent tour before the others get here."

Jennifer followed as Harriet Spencer led the way around the house to a complex of barns, sheds, and corrals. "There really isn't much to see," Harriet said. "Bunch of foul-smelling buildings. We could go have a drink if you'd rather."

"No, I find all this fascinating still."

"Well, it's the land that makes all this." Harriet gestured with her arm at the house, the barns, the

74

animals. "None of this means anything without the land. God, I love this land. I don't want to see anything happen to it."

"Your family goes back to the Feud, doesn't it?"

"The Hacklers do," Harriet said. "That's my maiden name. The family came in pretty near the end though. Joined up with old Sam Doughty and his crowd. Guess they got here in time to kill a couple of the Nelsons and get a couple of Hacklers shot."

"The last great Feud in the American west," Jennifer said.

"But they got this land out of it," Harriet said looking wistfully toward the mountains. "That's what the famous Hidden Valley Feud was all about. Land."

"Just like today," Jennifer said.

"It's our land now, Jennifer, we have to preserve it. Our little committee of five. It's our duty."

The committee of four argued through the afternoon as Jennifer listened.

Thad Murphy was petulant throughout. In his mid-fifties, Murphy's only passionate interest was the township council and the ever-swirling machinations of local and county politics.

Harriet Spencer rebuked Murphy sharply on several occasions. Each time, Murphy fell silent for awhile. He could not challenge Harriet's wealth, power, or prestige in the community.

Paul Sutter was quiet, explaining, "Until I know what I'm talking about, I'll just listen here. No use making a fool of myself."

Hank was Hank. Exuberant. Loud. Sometimes profane as in, "God damn it, Thad, we're trying to get some work done here." Energetic. Filled with ideas, some good, some bad, but always interesting.

Slowly, they made progress.

"We've got to pressure the members of the County

Board. Kendall still needs a lot of approvals."

"That means there's still lots of money to be handed out and Kendall's got a bagful of money that never seems to be empty. All he has to do is go door to door distributing it."

"We command votes. We can dry up the money bag."

"Take 'em to court. Question the Environmental Impact Report. Make 'em do another EIR."

"Put it on the ballot. Make the development outfit get voter approval. How many votes you think that hotel'll get in Hidden Valley? In the county."

"In Hidden Valley we can vote it down, although there are some supporters. You saw that last night. Still, we can win in Hidden Valley itself. But when you get into county territory, that's another question. Lotta folks out there see the hotel as growth in the economy, jobs, money in their pockets. It'll be hard to convince them."

"We need a political consultant."

"We should have started this a lot sooner. I tried to warn you."

"At least, we're doing something now, Thad."

"Oh, hell, Thad . . ."

"All right." He held his hands up in surrender. "All right."

Harriet said, "Before we adjourn, I think we should have a co-chairman. I can't do everything."

"I nominate Thad for vice-chairman," Hank said.

"Me, too," Paul said.

"Co-chairman," Harriet insisted.

"Co-chairman, then," Hank said. He leaned over and offered his hand to Thad. "I guess that makes it unanimous, Mr. Co-chairman. But let's you and me go hunting some of that vice real soon."

"I think this calls for a drink," Harriet said. "I'll take your orders now."

* * *

76

Jennifer drank another glass of white wine at Hank's while she waited for Jesus to prepare a take out order of spaghetti and garlic bread for her. His spaghetti was almost as good as his chili.

"That was a pretty shrewd move back at Harriet's," Hank said as he opened the bottle of chardonnay for Jennifer. Before Jennifer's arrival in Hidden Valley, Hank had served red wine and white wine. Now he kept bottles of chardonnay and cabernet sauvignon on hand.

"Which shrewd move was that?" Jennifer asked.

"Giving Thad a title. He's dumber than duck shit, but happy as hell with a title."

"He's not so bad. You rather did usurp his position and importance."

"Well, I don't trust him much."

"He'll make some contributions before this is over."

"Whatever you say, darling. I'm yours to command." Hank put a red shopping bag on the bar. "I got some reading material for you."

Jennifer groaned. "What's all that?"

"Everything we could lay our hands on. It's all the background on the proposed Hidden Valley Resort. Reports. All that. Feasibility. Economics. Jobs. Some real interesting reading."

"I suppose you've read it all."

"Every word."

"And now you want me to read it?"

"Every word."

"I guess I'd better."

"Reading between the lines is the most fun, darling. Makes you wonder how much they left out. Who got paid off."

"The good stuff."

"That's right, darling."

A cold breeze was blowing as Jennifer drove up the

hill to her house and parked the truck. She shivered as she dashed to the house and ran up the steps in the dark, purse in one hand, plastic bag of spaghetti and garlic bread in the other. She left the heavy shopping bag in the truck. It could wait until tomorrow. Oscar met her at the door, complaining loudly about the cold, his loneliness, and his dinner.

"Hey, you could have made a fire," Jennifer said, turning on lights and heading for the kitchen. "What stopped you?"

Oscar brushed against her legs, almost tripping her.

"Hey, Oscar, it's okay." She knelt and petted him. "I wish you'd understand I'm not going to leave you. You're just never going to get over being abandoned. I know. None of us do."

She continued stroking the soft black fur, trying to get him to purr, but without success. He would not purr. He was normal otherwise, but he could not be induced to purr. Jennifer gave up and poured fresh food into his nearly-empty bowl. Oscar stayed in the kitchen eating while Jennifer was there, fussing with her own meal that she would eat later after warming it in the microwave. But when she went into the living room, Oscar left the food and followed her, staying close, but not getting in her lap when she sat down. He looked up at her with the big yellow eyes, as though reassuring himself that she was there, but not yet forgiving her for leaving him behind.

Jennifer frowned. "I wish you wouldn't act like this, Oscar."

Jennifer cared little for the holiday season. She had long ago given up decorating a Christmas tree. Now, even wrapping Christmas presents each year was a task Jennifer disliked. It emphasized her loneliness and the lack of family. Clea's box had already been mailed. All that remained were the gifts for Kathy, Dave Mason, and Hank. And the celebration of the new year that followed was not a happier time. Where others looked forward to the sense of rebirth and the coming of spring and summer as an affirmation, a time when old mistakes could be rectified and lives altered for the better, Jennifer saw only the familiar pattern, another year of emptiness, the never-ending flight from the secrets of her past, and the constant telling of lies to conceal that past.

At times, Jennifer thought she must have committed some great error in another life, a grievous sin against another to have incurred such a karmic debt, such undying animosity directed against her. There were moments in the deathly cold chill before dawn when Jennifer felt his hatred directed at her, until his loathing was almost palpable, filling whatever room she occupied at the moment with a malice born of centuries. Her fear denied sleep. For a minute, an hour, Jennifer would suffocate from the evil around her, struggling to calm the irrational thoughts that took over her mind. Even the memory of those moments ignited the fear she had lived with for nearly twenty years now. Sometimes, Jennifer wanted it over and done with, no matter the outcome, and wondered how he could sustain his enmity for so long. She no longer hated him and what he had made her do with her life, but she could not quell the fear. She would always dread the day when he would reappear.

Oscar was having a fine time with the trappings of Christmas, frolicking with a bit of blue ribbon, burrowing beneath the sheets of brightly-colored wrapping paper, pausing long enough to knock a small roll of tape off the table, racing off again in pursuit of the elusive blue ribbon, returning to watch Jennifer with great interest as she wrapped another of her sparse offerings.

She took care with Hank's present, adding a special flourish of red, blue, and green ribbons, all intertwined into a large, almost floral display for the top of the box. Their relationship was changing—again. And why not? They had progressed over the years from Hank's natural suspicions of the stranger in the valley to casual friendship to a warm closeness, a shared kinship. He was kind, decent, older by five or six years, but Jennifer always felt that his easy, bantering way disguised secrets of his own. She had seen him brooding. He would be sitting in his accustomed place, seemingly in accord with everything around him, but his eyes became empty and distant, filled with an unfathomable coldness. She wondered about his secrets, but could never press him. She had no right, not unless she could share her own secrets. She could not do that. Jennifer had nothing to offer but deceptions, falsehoods, and distortions.

Others whispered of Hank's occasional disappearances, periods of three or four days when he left the valley, always driving south. He used to go with Billy Thomas, but Billy shot himself one Sunday morning, and now Hank went alone—two, three, sometimes four times a year. They said he went into Phoenix to raise a little hell, find solace and comfort in the arms of a long-legged whore. Before Jennifer had always hoped he might find a temporary love as well, even if he did purchase it. Now she was surprised to find a twinge of jealousy at the thought of Hank with another woman. Had he found love?

Love was as evasive as the blue ribbon Oscar chased. He could pin it to the floor, but quickly tired of a static victim, flicking at the ribbon, carrying it to the top of a chair until it fluttered and he could pursue it once more, inflicting feline cruelty upon it, growling as though in another cat life he had been the leader of a pride of lions on some African veldt, before a final abandonment, turning to another temporary amusement. Love was a fraud, a mean hoax perpetuated on Jennifer, on Hank, on too many others, an elusive and transient emotion, a dissatisfying and impermanent diversion.

Thick white cumulus clouds hung above the distant Mogollon Rim to the north, but the late afternoon sky above the valley was clear. The air was crisp and chilled. Oscar watched forlornly from the window sill as Jennifer stood on the porch admiring the clean view of the valley. He was still watching as she crunched through the snow, turning around the corner of the house to follow the path up the steep wooded slope.

The house was quickly lost from view, although smoke from the chimney twisted and curled above the bare trees for awhile. Then, too, the smoke was gone from sight and Jennifer was swallowed by the still and silent wilderness. She climbed the familiar trail, unafraid and confident. For those who took care not to violate natural laws and treated the wilderness with respect, there was little to fear. Mountain lions still prowled, but they avoided foul-smelling, foul-tasting man. In the spring, a black bear, grumpy and hungry after the winter's hibernation, or a female fiercely protecting a cub, might threaten the unwary. A frightened western diamondback in exile from the desert's upper reaches or a timber rattler might strike from ambush if suddenly surprised. More likely, however, the snake would steal away unnoticed. In the mountainous forests, there was always greater danger from man than the natural inhabitants.

Jennifer found serenity in the isolation, taking her pleasure from the quiet and solemn solitude of the forest that climbed the slopes high above her home. The house backed on government land, a part of the massive Tonto National Forest and the designated wilderness areas within it, where incursions by the machinery of man were forbidden. Man could go into the wilderness areas for play and sport, but to do so he had to meet the wilderness on its own terms, traveling by foot or horseback. No jeeps or whining dirt bikes were allowed to rut and violate the pristine floor of the forests or the slopes of the mountains.

Once, Hank had loaned her his copy of Conrad's *Heart of Darkness,* with its lush descriptions of Africa and the Congo River. After reading the short novel, one passage, in particular, had remained with Jennifer. Each time she climbed into the wilderness, Conrad's words returned to her. "Going up that river was like traveling back to the earliest beginnings of the world, when vegetation rioted on the earth and the big trees were kings. An empty stream, a great silence, an impenetrable forest."

Jennifer found peace in her impenetrable forest. She escaped the nightmares there and felt protected when the great silence enveloped her.

And upon reaching a certain height, there was a clearing where she always stopped and looked back on the valley spread out below her. Even the rudimentary elements of civilization found in Hidden Valley seemed tiny and insignificant when viewed from so far above. The snow that blanketed the valley obscured the wooden fences that marked boundaries carved out by man. The top of the world was still above her, but Jennifer could climb there if she wished—and beyond, to disappear into the wilderness of Hellsgate. She would be safe there. He would never find her then. But she always stopped at the clearing, savoring the wilderness, content to know that it existed, that she could go there if she wanted. It was her legacy to herself for tomorrow.

Then Jennifer found a small pile of cigarette butts. She felt betrayed by her wilderness. It had allowed another visitor, an outsider, a trespasser who did not understand its ways to come and stand in her spot, leaving behind a residue of the desecration. He had stood here long enough to smoke seven cigarettes, nearly down to the filter. He had been here for some time, virtually unmoving, waiting, looking down at the valley. Jennifer gathered the cigarette butts angrily, sticking them in the pocket of her windbreaker. Whoever had been here cared nothing for beauty. She circled the clearing, looking for other defilements, crushed beer cans, an empty wine bottle, the litter of a picnic. But there was nothing else.

Jennifer started back, walking down the path slowly, sadly. The mood had been spoiled by the careless intrusion of an unwanted visitor.

The winter dusk enshrouded the valley when Jennifer rounded the corner of the house. Hank's truck was parked behind her red pickup.

"Hank?"

He was sitting on the porch. Oscar was still in the window, looking out at Hank, waiting. He stood and stretched expectantly when he saw Jennifer.

"I just felt like stopping by," Hank said. "I hope you don't mind."

"Of course not," Jennifer replied. "Why didn't you go in?"

"I don't like to do that," Hank said.

"Don't be silly. You're always welcome. Come on in."

"You go ahead. I want to get something out of the truck."

Oscar rubbed against her feet. Jennifer nearly tripped over the cat twice as she went to the fireplace to throw a log on the glowing embers. Sparks flew and small flames immediately lapped at the new log.

"Merry Christmas," Hank said.

Jennifer turned. Hank stood there offering her a wrapped box. "Oh, Bear. It's not time yet. You're as bad as Clea."

"I wanted to give this to you now," he said shyly,

"not when there was a bunch of people around."

"That sounds suggestive," Jennifer teased. "Have you been ordering from Frederick's of Hollywood?"

Hank blushed. "I didn't, but maybe I should have. You look an awful lot like Amanda, you know. At least in the face." His blush grew deeper.

Jennifer laughed. "I wondered when you'd notice the resemblance."

"I've always noticed. I just didn't say anything."

"Bear, you're shy."

"I guess I am. Come on, Jenny, open it."

Jennifer took the box. It was large, but not very heavy. She noticed the care Hank had taken in wrapping it. A Santa Claus tag read, For Jenny, With Love. "All right. Let me get you a drink first. What would you like?"

"Scotch?"

"That sounds good. I think I'll have one too. It's a special occasion. We'll have our own little Christmas party. How would you like it?"

"On the rocks, please."

"I'll just be a minute," Jennifer said. "Your present is on the table. Why don't you take it over by the fire. I'll be right back."

When Jennifer returned with the drinks, Hank had settled on the couch. The fire was blazing now. Oscar had settled into Hank's lap. Coming up behind Hank, Jennifer noticed his thinning hair and a small bald spot in the back. She felt a warmth of affection for him.

They touched glasses.

"Merry Christmas," Jennifer said.

"And the very best new year for you," Hank said.

"For both of us," Jennifer said.

They sat quietly together on the couch, not touching, looking into the fire, feeling its crackling enchantment. Hank rubbed Oscar beneath his chin. The cat, eyes closed, stretched his neck and lifted his head back for Hank.

84

"Is he purring?" Jennifer asked.

Hank shook his head sadly. "We'll get him to purr one of these days," he said.

"He's a very melancholy kitty sometimes. But he likes you. I think he likes you better than me."

"He needs to talk cat-to-man. Women don't understand that."

"And what do you talk about in this cat-to-man nonsense?"

"Oh, you know, studly things." Hank smiled dreamily. "It isn't easy being a cat. Got to keep after the birds and mice all the time. Chase flies. Sleep. Eat. People don't realize. It's a tough occupation, this cat stuff. Clint's got to crowd a lot into his day." He looked down at Oscar. "Don't you, guy?"

"Go ahead and open your present."

"You first. Can't disturb Clint."

"His name is Oscar."

"Clint."

"You're impossible."

Jennifer took the box into her lap. She unwrapped it carefully, pulling the ribbons loose, setting them aside, running a finger beneath the paper, loosening it from the Christmas stickers, teddy bears in stocking caps, Santa's elves, wreaths of holly. Beneath the wrapping, was a plain white cardboard box. Jennifer lifted the cover. Inside was an old violin case, darkened by age. "Oh, Hank," Jennifer said. "Is it?"

He smiled. "Open the case and find out."

The violin was inside.

Jennifer's eyes filled with tears as she took the violin lovingly from its case, stroking the smooth wood.

"It's ready to play," Hank said. "I took it to Phoenix and had it worked on. The man said you could play a concert with it now."

"Hank, thank you. It's a lovely gift. Thank you so much."

Jennifer took the bow and put the instrument to her

chin. She played a classical piece from memory, softly, the delicate strains filling the room. It had been years since she last played. She was rusty, and her fingers were stiff on the strings, stumbling over the chords. But it would come back.

In Hank's lap, Oscar was alert, his ears turning, following the music. He looked at Jennifer as though astounded and delighted with her newly-demonstrated talent. Hank's eyes were closed now. There was a faint smile on his lips as he listened to Jennifer play.

When she stopped, Hank said, "You play beautifully."

"It's been a long time."

"It doesn't matter. Will you play more for me sometime?"

"Of course, but let me practice a little first. You didn't hear all my mistakes."

"I enjoyed it."

"Open your presents now," Jennifer said, wiping the tears away.

"Not me," Hank said. "I'm not the one who was so impatient she couldn't wait till Christmas."

"Hank, open the damn presents."

He tried to emulate Jennifer by opening the heavy box carefully, sliding the ribbon off. But it tightened. Then he tried to slip a finger beneath a corner of the paper. It tore.

Jennifer smiled and said, "Just open it, Bear."

He attacked the wrapping then, ripping the ribbon free, devastating the colored paper, opening the taped cover of the large box with force. But Jennifer saw the transformation come over him as he saw the Oxford Illustrated Edition of Charles Dickens neatly stacked within the box. He took *David Copperfield* from the box, caressing the smooth dust jacket. He opened it gently and turned the pages carefully. His eyes were bright with pleasure as he looked upon the original illustrations first done for the serial publication so many years ago.

"I hope you like them, Bear."

"I do," he said. "They're wonderful." He took another book out and leafed through it. He looked up at Jenny then, *Oliver Twist* still open in his lap. "It's the best present I've ever received."

"Better than your first rifle?"

"Anyone can shoot, but reading..." *Pickwick Papers* replaced *Oliver Twist* in his hand. Hank turned to the middle of the book and began reading aloud with his deep and melodious voice.

"'As brisk as bees, if not altogether as light as fairies, did the four Pickwickians assemble on the morning of the twenty-second day of December, in the year of grace in which these, their faithfully-recorded adventures, were undertaken and accomplished. Christmas was close at hand, in all his bluff and hearty honesty; it was the season of hospitality, merriment, and openheartedness; the old year was preparing, like an ancient philosopher, to call his friends around him, and amidst the sound of feasting and revelry to pass gently and calmly away. Gay and merry was the time, and gay and merry were at least four of the numerous hearts that were gladdened by its coming.'"

Hank closed the book.

"That's beautiful, Bear. You have a wonderful voice. Dickens could have been writing his words for you to read aloud." But the words evoked sadness, and an emptiness within that could not be filled with either the written or spoken word. Jennifer wished she could feel so joyous as the Pickwickians about the holiday season.

"Open the little one too."

Hank did, finding a bottle of cologne. "My favorite. Thank you, Jennifer Warren, for two wonderful presents. Thank you for making this a wonderful Christmas."

"And thank you, Bear. I'll play the violin as an

accompaniment to your reading." She reached out and squeezed his hand. "It is a great Christmas, one of the very best." And Jennifer suddenly realized it was true.

"Jenny?"

"Yes."

"I don't know how to say this, but I want to see you again."

"You see me almost every day when I'm here."

"Not like that. I'd like to take you out. On dates. Real dates, not just the Christmas party. I was thinking, maybe, well, maybe next time you come over, we could drive down to Phoenix, have dinner someplace nice, and go to the theater or a concert, but . . ."

"I'd love to do that, Hank."

"Really?"

"Honest."

"I was afraid there was someone else."

"There's no one else, Bear. Not now."

SEVEN

The banner above the auditorium entrance proclaimed, A COUNTRY CHRISTMAS, and was decorated with painted wreaths and sprigs of holly. The parking lot was already filled with the valley's assorted collection of transportation—pickups, jeeps, cars. Recorded Christmas music drifted through the open doors into the night. At the door, Ben Davis and Charley White were happily sipping from paper cups filled with whiskey as they greeted everyone, wishing all a Merry Christmas, collecting tickets from the men and a kiss from each of the women as they passed beneath the mistletoe.

Inside, the big room buzzed with joyous salutations, competing with the Christmas carols. Folding tables were covered with alternating red and green tablecloths. Homemade wreaths and pine cones served as centerpieces. The band, imported from Flagstaff for the night, unpacked their instruments and adjusted the microphones on the stage.

The bar was crowded. The two bartenders were sweating as they rushed to fill a multitude of orders. There was a crowd around the eggnog-filled punch bowl as well. A continuous clanging of pots and pans echoed in the adjoining kitchen where the dinner committee scurried busily, setting out large bowls of potato salad, cole slaw, and macaroni salad. A huge pot filled with beans simmered. The smell of frying chicken and barbecuing steaks escaped the kitchen.

Ben Davis and Charley White each kissed Jennifer as she and Hank entered the hall. "Don't let the other women know," Ben told Jennifer, "but you're the prettiest lady here tonight."

"Yeah, you can come back and stand under my mistletoe any time you want," Charley echoed.

"Why, thank you both," Jennifer said.

"Horny old devils," Hank commented. "You ought to be ashamed. Bet you kissed Crazy Maggie too."

"He did," Ben said pointing at Charley.

"Christmas time is the only loving I get," Charley said.

"Not surprised," Hank said. "Drinking on duty too."

"Save a dance for me, Jennifer," Ben called after them.

"Me too," Charley hollered. "One of them slow ones."

"They're sweet," Jennifer said to Hank.

"They're a couple of old fools."

"Why, Hank, I believe you're jealous."

"You haven't kissed *me,*" Hank said.

"Would you like to go back?"

"I brought my own mistletoe."

"You won't need it," Jennifer said flirtatiously, smiling at him, wanting him to kiss her, wanting his love. But suddenly she was frightened, regretting the loss of her protective barrier. But Hank only returned her smile shyly as he took her hand, leading her to an empty table away from the stage and the noisy bar.

"What would you like to drink, Jenny?"

"A glass of wine, I think."

Jennifer sat alone at their table and watched Hank cross the open dance floor, greeting and being greeted. She was envious of the easy way he fit into the community.

In looking at Hank now, Jennifer was still surprised by the transformation in their relationship after the years of friendship. There had been none of the sudden rush that came with an initial physical attraction to another individual, no instant revelation that this man would be important to her in love or sex. For too long now, she had associated love with pain and heartache. But her feelings for Hank were warm. She put her trust in him without fear. This kind and gentle man could not, would not, hurt her—not physically, not spiritually.

Jennifer had believed that before—once in her youth and inexperience she had thought it true of the man she had married, the man who fathered her daughter. She had expected to spend the rest of her life with him in love and companionship. Instead, she had spent her adult life in flight. And only a few days ago, she had thought Bennett Cameron was different, but outward appearances masked an inner cruelty that quickly surfaced, subtly at first, and then a swift degeneration into verbal abuse and potential violence. There had been others, not many, perhaps five relationships, in the two decades she had been running. Each had followed a pattern similar to that path taken by her husband. No, not Jackson. No one hated her so much as Jackson. It was more like Bennett, where an initial facade of love changed rapidly to dislike and hatred. Jennifer wondered what flaw she possessed to be so badly deceived each time, always attracted to men who were so mean and ultimately vicious, and so unappreciative of the deep reservoir of love she had to offer. Would Hank betray her too?

Please, God, I hope not. She smiled up at Hank as he returned.

"Chardonnay for the lady."

"Quality wines are making inroads everywhere in Hidden Valley," Jennifer commented wryly.

"Depends on who's appointed to the Christmas

91

party drinks committee," Hank said.

"Anyone I know?"

"Leave it to some of these people, we'd have nothing but bourbon and beer."

"Out of long-stemmed bottles."

"Long-necked, darling, long-necked bottles."

"I knew that."

"Course you did. Smart lawyer like you." He raised his glass. "Merry Christmas, again."

"To you and me," Jennifer said. "Everyone's looking at us."

"They want to see you."

"They're wondering what you're doing with me. We're going to start a lot of gossip."

"The matchmakers are already at work," Hank said. "Does that bother you?"

Jennifer shook her head. "No, let them talk."

"I'm happy to be here with you, Jenny."

"I'm glad you asked me."

The room came to them. Kathy and Dave stopped by to wish them Merry Christmas. Others straggled by, mostly Hank's friends. Harriet Spencer sat with them for a time. Paul Sutter and his wife joined them, pulling up extra chairs. Glasses and bottles covered the table. Thad Murphy and his wife stopped by. No one stayed long. It was as though everyone wanted to pay their respects to the king and queen of the ball, wanting to know the status of Jennifer and Hank without over-staying their welcome.

Thad Murphy was on the stage, speaking into a whistling microphone. "Testing. One, two, three, testing. Can everybody hear me? Charley, Ben, back there at the door."

"You bet, Thad," Ben hollered.

"Well, I want to welcome everyone tonight for the annual Hidden Valley Christmas and New Year's Party. Want everyone to have a real good time as usual. Also want to thank everyone who worked so hard to make this another big success. All the people on the food committee—smells good, don't it?"

"Let's eat," Crazy Maggie shouted.

"We'll get to that, Maggie. Got to dance a bit first. Want to thank Hank and his drinks committee. All the ladies who decorated the hall so nice. We're glad Pete Western and his band came down from Flag to be with us tonight. We're gonna have a good ole time, tonight. So Merry Christmas, Happy New Year, and let's have us some fun." Thad acknowledged the applause as he walked off the stage and the band broke into a medley of lively country western instrumentals.

"He's always got something to say."

"He's a politician, Hank."

"I suppose."

It was the last night of the Newport Beach boat parade and still a most festive and gala evening despite the fact that the parade had been going on each night for nearly two weeks. Two men met in the study of a lavish home on the bay. Dressed casually in expensive slacks and cashmere sweaters, they drank hundred year old cognac from crystal snifters nearly as expensive as the warm brown liquid they contained. Outside the double doors of the study, the murmur of muted conversations could be heard. They were punctuated with occasional exclamations of awe as a particularly impressive light display cruised down the bay.

"Jackson, why are you doing this?" Robert Shaw asked.

"Old times sake."

"She could be trouble," Shaw said. "She hasn't bothered you."

"That's the point. I don't want her bothering me." Holloway said. He swirled the cognac in his snifter. Light glinted from the diamond ring he wore. Holloway opened a folder on the desk and leafed

93

through a series of eight by ten color and black and white photographs. "Disgusting," he said, holding up one of the photos for display. It showed a naked woman kneeling. Her features were obscured by a mane of long blonde hair. "A minor porn star will not destroy my dreams."

"You don't know that it's her," Shaw said.

"If I say it's her," Holloway said, "why then it's her. Your job is to find her."

Shaw shrugged. "The trail is cold."

"The trail starts in San Francisco."

"And once I find her?" Shaw asked.

"I'll have a little talk with her."

"That'll be nice," Shaw said. He drained the remaining brandy. "Merry Christmas, Jackson."

"Yes, it is that joyous season. We should join my guests."

There was dancing after the buffet dinner. Hank taught Jennifer the stylized routines of country western dancing as couples paraded around the dance floor in set patterns. He held one of her hands and kept the other on her waist as he guided her through the intricate steps of one dance after another.

"You're getting real good at this," Hank said.

"I don't think so," Jennifer said laughing. "There's so much to remember. I'm a better dancer when it's rock. All I have to do is move."

"You move real nice. We'll be winning dance competitions soon."

During one of the band's breaks, Lucy Palmer, a music teacher at the elementary school led everyone in Christmas carols. They sang enthusiastically, working their way through "O, Come All Ye Faithful," "Silent Night," "White Christmas," "Rudolph," "Santa Claus Is Coming To Town," and others.

"And because this is our New Year's Party as well,"

94

Lucy Palmer said, "let's end our group sing with 'Auld Lang Syne.'"

People joined hands and sang, "Should old acquaintance be forgot . . ."

There were tears in Jennifer's eyes as she sang the familiar words. Always before, they had been meaningless for her, representing a desperate loneliness that could never be alleviated. Now, Jennifer looked around the crowded auditorium and felt friendship, knowing she was part of a community for the first time in her life. She had lowered her barriers with more people than just Hank. She had opened herself to others, allowed herself to be accepted. But they didn't know the terrible secrets she carried with her. What would they think if they learned of her past? She was vulnerable now in a way she had never been before.

"Why are you crying?" Hank whispered.

Jennifer shook her head and smiled up at him through the tears that filled her eyes. "I'm just happy, Bear," she said. "Very happy."

Jackson and Janice Holloway moved among their guests, holding hands, smiling, chatting with the rich, the powerful, the influential. They were all there. Many of the developers who had built the massive edifices of Orange County, the tracts of homes, the condominium complexes, were guests of Holloway. The politicians were there; three members of the Orange County Board of Supervisors, several mayors of the coastal towns, councilmen and councilwomen, a congressman or two, a state assemblyman. Old money was represented somewhat sparsely, but new money was present in a horde. They all laughed, drank, applauded the decorated boats cruising the channel. They were all eager for a word or two with their host, a pleasant and confident Jackson Holloway.

"Jack, let's get together for lunch soon. I'd like to

talk about the latest Kendall Enterprises project."

"That's fine, Steve, look forward to it."

"Jackson, how are you? Wonderful party. I always look forward to it."

"Thanks for coming, Congressman."

"You look lovely, Janice."

"That's a marvelous gown, Michele. You look stunning."

"What's the vote look like on AB 888?"

"It'll pass the Assembly easily and I think we have the votes in the senate. Everyone knows how important this is to Jackson Holloway."

"Great party, Jack. And Janice, you're more beautiful than ever."

Alone in his own den in the luxurious beach front condominium, Robert Shaw did not think the photographs were pornographic as he sat turning them over slowly. Not at all. To his eye, they were quite well done, very artistic. The photographer was good. And so was the artist who had painted the canvases, using the same woman as a model. In each, the woman had posed nude. Those photographs of the oil portraits were in color. Shaw wondered if the artist and the photographer were one and the same. He had a name for the photographer—Arthur Wilson was printed at the bottom of each photo—but it was impossible to make out the signature on the canvases, even with a magnifying glass.

Shaw's favorite was a painting of the woman with a baby—no more than three or four months old—held to her breast. The baby was not suckling the dark nipple. The eyes were shut and the tiny hands were closed in tight little fists. The woman's hair was arranged to envelope her face and fall to her breasts and on to the child. But enough of her features were visible to evoke a great sense of sadness. There was nothing of the erotic in the painting. It was simply a portrait of mother and child, a madonna and her baby.

The same aura of melancholy pervaded the other photos, even those meant to be starkly erotic: offering her breasts to an unseen lover, seated at a dressing table, applying perfume to the hollow between her breasts, lying on a rumpled bed, hair spread over the pillow. In some of the photos, the woman was bound or chained. She stood as a passive victim with her naked back to the camera, arms raised above her head, held there by a rope wrapped loosely around her wrists. In another, she was seated with the rope still about her wrists. Her imprisoned hands were raised, as though unpinning her hair. In still another, she knelt before the camera, blindfolded and hands cuffed behind her back. But no matter the pose in which he placed the woman, the photographer could not take her beyond the despondency.

Shaw closed the folder reluctantly and put it in the floor safe beneath his desk. There was no need for his wife or the cleaning women to see the photographs. They could only cause trouble with Darlene. She was already angry that he was flying to San Francisco without her. "Up and back in the same day," he had explained patiently. "It's business."

At least she blamed Holloway for sending him away during the holidays. He went to the window and looked out at the water, thinking that he had done all right with Holloway. This place was bought and paid for with Holloway money. God knows, he has enough of it. If the tasks Shaw performed for Holloway were sometimes unsavory, so be it. Shaw had spent a lifetime doing unpleasant jobs for others. At least, Holloway paid well for the occasional service. Shaw watched as the waves broke on the beach in a crashing white foam, a conspicuous contrast to the dark waters beyond, like the young woman's pale naked body in the photos. Shaw sighed and went to join Darlene in their bed where she lay awake, pouting and sulking.

Jennifer danced with others. Thad Murphy took her around the floor, moving enthusiastically. Paul Sutter danced with a slow deliberate grace. As promised, Ben and Charley each took her around the floor, returning her to the table with exaggerated politeness. In between, Jennifer and Hank danced. The trouble began when the cowboy invited Jennifer to dance for the third time.

There were four of them. Two were in the valley on occasion, hiring out periodically as extra hands on one or another of the outlying ranches. They showed up then in Hank's Place on Saturday nights to drink and play pool. The other two were strangers. They sat at a table near the bar, filling the surface with empty beer bottles, dropping cigarette butts down the long-necked bottles to sizzle out in the foam that remained.

"No, thank you," Jennifer said. "I'd prefer to sit this one out."

"Aw, come on, lady, you the only woman here worth dancing with," the cowboy said.

"No, thank you." Jennifer smiled up at him politely.

"Take it easy, friend," Bear said.

"You her husband or something?"

"We're friends."

"Well, till you're married, stay out of this. The lady can speak for herself."

"She already has," Hank said. He took a ten dollar bill from his pocket. "Go buy yourself and your friends another beer."

"I don't want your goddam money," the cowboy said. He turned abruptly and stalked back to the bar.

"I'm sorry," Hank said.

"It's not your fault."

"He was right," Hank said. "You're the best looking woman here tonight."

"Hank, I want you to dance with me," Crazy Maggie said, pulling him to his feet.

"See," he said helplessly.

"Go ahead," Jennifer said. "I'll be fine."

"Maggie, I want to sit this one out. I'm too tired."

"Too tired to dance," Maggie told Jennifer, "he'll be too tired to do anything else. Might as well shoot him then. Put him out of his misery."

"We'll be right back," Hank said.

"Maybe you will, maybe you won't. We'll just see about that. Besides, that cowboy ain't gonna do anything."

"You saw that?"

"I see everything," Crazy Maggie said dragging Hank to the dance floor.

But Maggie was wrong. When the band finished the song with a flourish, the cowboy intercepted Hank and Maggie as they walked back to the table. "I want to talk with you, asshole."

"You better go sit down, Maggie."

"I'll keep Jenny company," Maggie said. "But don't hurt 'em too bad, Hank."

"Crazy old woman. That's about your style."

"We don't want any trouble," Hank said. He backed off a step, raising his hands in a peaceful gesture.

"You got trouble. Where you come off treating me like the hired help? Try to buy me off with a beer. You just like all the rest of the assholes here. Too high and mighty to associate with the help. That bitch thinks she's too good to dance with me."

Jennifer shook off Maggie's restraining hand and started for the dance floor when she saw the confrontation.

"It's all right, Jenny," Hank said. He retreated another step without taking his eyes off the cowboy.

Jennifer had almost reached them when the cowboy

99

swung viciously at Hank. She barely saw Hank's hands move as he hit the man three times. The cowboy was on the floor groaning.

"Hank!" Jennifer shouted. "Watch out!"

Another cowboy was coming at Hank with a beer bottle in his hand. Hank crouched slightly, moving away as the man came after him, feinting with the bottle held by the neck. When he made his lunge, Hank again moved quickly, stepping inside the blow, flipping the cowboy to the floor.

It was over by the time other men in the room had arrived.

"Are you all right, Hank?" Jennifer asked. She had never seen his eyes so cold and distant, so filled with violence.

He nodded, still looking down at the two cowboys. Slowly, the warmth returned to his eyes.

"Sorry, Hank," one of their friends said. "He had too much to drink."

"Get them out of here," Hank said. "Bring them by sometime when they're sober. I'll buy them a beer."

"What happened?" Thad Murphy asked.

"Couldn't take no for an answer," Hank said.

"Wasn't much of a fight," Ben said. "You're slipping, Hank."

Hank smiled then. "Aw, I'm getting too old for this shit," he said. "Come on, Jenny. Let's have another drink."

The fight in no way lessened the festivities of the Christmas party. In fact, the party grew rowdier, as though the fight had signaled the end to formal politeness and allowed the people of Hidden Valley to send their inhibitions into the night. Crazy Maggie danced both Ben and Charley into submission, one after another, sending them packing to the bar gasping for breath.

She looked for new victims. "Thad Murphy, get your sorry butt over here," she cried. They led the way through a boot stomping dance. Faces were flushed. Voices were shrill, more insistent in argument with exaggerated claims about horses, pickups, motorcycles, anything that came to mind in conversation. Two cowboys argued inconclusively over whether Coors was better than Budweiser and finally had to be separated. Dave Wilson watched over Kathy protectively, cutting in on her whenever one or another of the high school boys held her too close in a dance. When Thad Murphy finally escaped Crazy Maggie, she went after Kathy's grandfather, dragging him to the center of the floor to wait impatiently for the next tune to begin. "Hurry it up, boys," Maggie hollered, "I'm an old woman. Don't have time for you to catch your breath."

Kathy came to Jennifer then, pulling a shy, gangling boy along behind her. "This is Mike," she said. "I got Maggie to dance with Gramps," she whispered delightedly. "He wouldn't leave us alone."

"It's nice to meet you, Mike," Jennifer called after them. Kathy led her boyfriend to a secluded corner where they sat whispering and holding hands while Maggie kept Dave occupied for three dances.

After the fight, Jennifer looked at Hank in a different way, with a new respect. She found it difficult to define. She had seen the coldness in his eyes, but she wasn't afraid of him. He had protected her. No one had ever done that before. Before, she had always been the target of violence. Not tonight. Everyone had closed around her protectively, ensuring that she was all right, making it known that she was one of the community now. No one, especially not an outsider, brought harm to one of the valley's own. Jennifer was one of them now. She had never been part of a community before. They were all her friends. For the second time that night, Jennifer thought she had never been happier.

At the end of the party, they danced to a country ballad of love. Hank drew Jennifer close, enveloping her in his arms. She rested her head on Hank's shoulder and moved slowly to the melancholy love ballad, feeling warm and protected in his arms.

"I don't want this evening to end, Hank, not ever."

"It's just beginning, darling."

"Yes," Jennifer whispered.

The band's lead vocalist sang, "I'm in love with you."

Jackson Holloway stood at the end of his dock, looking out at the lights across the channel. His 54 foot sailboat creaked and swayed against its moorings in the gentle swells of the dark water. Behind him, the house was nearly dark. The last of the boat parade guests had left an hour ago. Distant sounds of parade revelry drifted across the water. Holloway listened to drunken laughter and the lapping water, wondering which of the lights hid her disquieting presence. He drank directly from the cognac bottle. The fucking whore. She was out there. He remembered every detail of her. The sweet smell of her long hair, the soft swell of her breasts, the pressure of her thighs against his body. The whore. Who was she fucking now? Every time he thought of her the old rage swirled angrily, feeding his hatred of her. She had deserted him, running away from him, like he was someone common. He offered her everything and still she ran. But Shaw would find her. And then she would die, regretting every painful moment she had caused him, repenting the bitch she had spawned out of defiance. The agony of childbirth would be nothing in comparison to the suffering he planned for her. Holloway finished the cognac and threw the empty bottle at a distant light. The bottle disappeared with a faint splash.

PART II

EIGHT

The loft was in the Haight-Ashbury. Later, much later, Sierra would learn that Charles Manson and his family might have been there that night as she pushed her way down Haight Street toward Golden Gate Park and through the crowded sidewalks and the nightly parade of young and not-so-young hippies, flower children, tourists, bikers, runaway children, and undercover cops.

In her memories, it would always frighten Sierra to think that she might have brushed against Charles Manson that night, that his evil might have breathed upon her baby. Everything about that night and succeeding nights made her uncomfortable. Sometimes she would dream of those lost days and nights in the Haight and could almost smell the thick pungent aroma of the marijuana, hear the eerie shrill of flutes, see the frightened faces begging for spare change. Scattered images drifted through the dreams, appearing with clarity. She stood in the Haight-Ashbury precinct station huddled among the shadows of Golden Gate Park. The bulletin board was filled with pictures of children, yearbook pictures from junior high and high school, all missing. Sierra looked for her own picture, but her foster parents didn't care. They never had. "I'm looking for my sister," Sierra told the young

105

police officer before fleeing into the night. I'm looking for me, her mind screamed.

One night burly policemen wrestled a black youth into the police car, beating him with their night sticks as he cursed and raged and fought, coming down from some bad trip only when the door slammed behind him. He calmed then, smiling out at the officers. One of them asked, "How d'you feel?" Still smiling, the black youth replied pleasantly, "Feel like busting your motherfucking face in."

Another night an acid-tripping hippie smiled at her in a neighborhood grocery store as he tucked a jug of red wine beneath a dirty army greatcoat, only to wind up handcuffed as an even dirtier undercover cop arrested him for the shoplifting. The long-suppressed memories were never far from her consciousness.

The cordon of uniformed police officers sweeping down both sides of Haight Street looking for runaways passed Sierra through without asking for her identification. With Clea bundled in her arms, she could not be a runaway from the rigid confines of homelife in Kansas or Nebraska or Iowa looking for the glamorous mecca of San Francisco. In their eyes, they saw a young mother and the wedding ring she still wore. Although she seemed no older than many of the teenaged runaways and although they might not have approved of her long dress, her long hair, and her boots, they saw a married woman, probably a student, living with her husband in the Haight. There was no reason to throw her in the paddy wagon that followed slowly behind the officers, quickly filling up with the children too stoned to avoid the sweep. Sierra hurried off, cutting away from Haight Street at the edge of the park where Kezar Stadium loomed in the darkness.

The loft was chilly.

A radio was playing a Mamas and the Papas tune.

Sierra undressed behind the screen, slipping the terrycloth robe over her shoulders, pulling the belt

106

tight against her cold nakedness. She shivered and hugged herself tightly. The screen was flimsy but it would protect her for a few extra moments. It was only when Clea cried that Sierra emerged from behind the screen, hurrying to the nest of pillows she had made for Clea. She had twisted and thrown off the pink blanket. "There, there, baby," Sierra crooned, plumping at the pillows, digging a deep, safe burrow for the baby. She tucked the blanket around Clea. Her wide blue eyes stared up at Sierra.

The news came on the radio. "The polls are now closing in California. Early projections pick Bobby Kennedy in the presidential primary . . ."

"You ready to start, Sierra?"

"You have the money?"

"It's on the table."

Sierra saw the pile of bills on a folding table. It looked like all the money in the world to her. She nodded. "What do you want me to do?"

"First, take the robe off. I'll help you get the pose I'm looking for."

"There's no sex involved," Sierra said. "All I'm doing is posing for you."

"You don't have to worry about that. I just want you to model for me."

"All right," Sierra said. She walked over to the couch he indicated. She still clutched the robe tight around her.

"What's your real name?" he asked. "I'll bet it's something like Gertrude or Matilda, something really horrible."

"Just Sierra," she said.

"That's a pretty name. Better than Gertie anyway. How'd you pick it?"

The picture was clear in her mind. It was early spring in some faraway meadow with green grass and scattered trees and a clear stream of icy blue water. The valley was surrounded by snow-capped mountain

107

peaks. If I lived there, she thought, no one would ever find me.

"From a book," she said.

"Why don't you take the robe off now."

Sierra let the robe fall to the floor, covered her breasts and loins with her hands, and burst into tears.

NINE

Jennifer Warren Esq. stood at the windows of her corner office on the 27th floor, looking out at one of those rare Los Angeles days where the cloudless skies were a sharp and clear blue. Between the tall buildings of downtown L.A. Jennifer saw distant mountains with fingers of snow reaching down their slopes. They seemed close enough to reach out and touch. Window washers on the building across the street lowered their scaffold. To her right, an aircraft banked away as it turned to begin its long approach to LAX. It was a familiar view for Jennifer, although one that had altered over years as one new and modern skyscraper after another had been built, each climbing out of a deep pit in the earth, rising story by story, as workers scampered along steel girders, busy little worker ants industriously creating another steel and glass edifice to be filled ultimately with even more tribes of equally industrious creatures, droning their way through long work hours. But, although the view was familiar and sometimes spectacular, Jennifer enjoyed it only rarely.

She was always uneasy as she looked down and out into the city, knowing that he might be there, driving or walking one of the streets far below. There were times when Jennifer dreaded boarding a crowded elevator, fearing that the doors might open and he would be standing there. Would he recognize her?

How could he fail to identify her? Jennifer would never forget him, even if his photograph did not appear in the newspaper on occasion, even if she had not seen him on the odd television talk program over the years. Although she had altered her appearance as much as possible and was far different from the long-haired love child who had fled so many years ago wearing the bizarre fashions of the late nineteen-sixties, he had loved her once—at least pretended to love her. He would find something in the new woman that would ignite distant emotions, trigger recognition. Despite the threats, there was an occasional message professing his love for her.

Jennifer dismissed the thoughts as the usual morose hauntings she experienced every time she returned from the freedom of Hidden Valley to the confinements of Los Angeles and the law firm. At least she had survived the torments of another holiday season.

No, not survived. It was wonderful for a change, Jennifer thought, and leaving the valley had been more difficult than ever. Even Oscar had seemed reluctant to go, sulking all the way to the California state line. And now she had left someone behind, crying in his arms at the thought of how many days and weeks must be endured before she could break away again. Hank would come to visit her in Los Angeles, but that seemed far away. She missed him terribly already and it had only been three days. They talked each night with the euphoria of new lovers, but she longed for his presence, his humor, the strength of his arms when he embraced her, his gentle shyness as he made love to her, the way he held her breast afterwards as he shared his secrets.

He told her of leaving Hidden Valley the day after high school graduation, continuing his education at the Marine Corps Recruit Depot in San Diego where they made him a Marine forever more, at the Infantry Training Regiment at Camp Pendleton where he learned to fight in the mock Vietnamese village, in Force Recon where he parachuted from airplanes and fought the roiling surf in night landings from small rubber boats. Jennifer saw the same cold and hard glaze in his eyes that had been there after the Christmas party fight when he told her of long-range patrols in the Indian Territory of Vietnam's jungles and the rubble in the streets of Hue during the Tet offensive. He showed her ribbons and medals—the Purple Heart with a cluster, a Silver Star, the Navy Cross. He spoke softly, too, of the restless years after Vietnam, of intermittent spells of hard drinking and loneliness combined with harder work, saving money to buy the bar, something he could own, freeing him from the whims of others. He told her of his infrequent but mysterious disappearances from the Valley when he went whoring in Phoenix, buying a prostitute's time for a night or two or three. And then he said, "Now you know everything about me. I hope it doesn't change the way you feel about me."

"Of course not, Bear," Jennifer said, regretting her own inability to be completely truthful with him as she skimmed over the details of her life, not lying, but . . .

One day, she would tell him everything and hope he would not think any the less of her. For now, Jennifer could not tell him of Sierra, the girl she had been in another far and distant life. Some day soon, perhaps. For now, she only said, "I love you, Bear." It was enough for the moment.

Jennifer Warren Esq. turned to the files and memos on her desk. Since passing the California bar examination on the first try, Jennifer had labored in the anonymity of one of the largest and most prestigious law firms in Los Angeles. With three hundred attorneys handling the legal affairs of a multitude of conservative clients, the firm occupied five complete floors of the building. Jennifer's office was on the

111

midway floor. She would probably never make it to the 29th floor, not even the 28th. She had carved out her own special niche in the firm, preparing briefs for partners and other, more senior attorneys, analyzing the complexities of limited partnerships, making recommendations as to the proper course, deliberately choosing to remain in the background. She never appeared in court. She never attended client meetings. She worked long, hard hours, often serving the firm and its clients brilliantly, but she refused to partake fully in the practice of the law. Other, less-gifted attorneys, men and women alike, pushed and scrambled their way past the 27th floor on their way to the luxuries and greater remunerations of the 28th and 29th floors. Her kind and gentlemanly mentor, Leo Fowler, had long since given up asking, "Why, Jennifer, why?"

It was not a question Jennifer Warren Esq. could answer—not for Leo, not for anyone, not even for herself. The threat was always there. It was real, a factual promise, tangible and only awaiting fulfillment. It played constantly in her personal night track, drifting in and out through the memories, the one consistent never-changing refrain among a thousand melodies. No matter how high Jennifer turned the volume on the night track, the threat was always waiting there. She could not drown it out with volume. "This is my promise to you. I will kill you. . . ."

Jennifer believed him then. She believed him now.

"Welcome back."

Startled, Jennifer looked up. She had been totally engrossed in her work. She was nearly hidden behind a stack of law books, California codes, propped open to a series of precedents she was researching. "Leo, you scared me."

"Sorry, but you should have called. Said hello to an

112

old man. Then I wouldn't have to make the trek down here."

Jennifer smiled. "I apologize, but you know me. I get caught up in my work."

"Indeed," Leo said. "Hard work is an admirable trait if not carried to extremes."

"Not lecture number two," Jennifer said. "Again."

"I suppose I do go on at times."

"I know it by heart. Equal amounts of work and play. Keeps the mind sharp. Should I go on?"

"That will be unnecessary . . . if you'll join me for lunch."

"What's up?"

"Nothing is up, as you say. I simply would like the company of a beautiful woman. It impresses the doddering old fools at the club, keeps them wondering how I manage to attract beauty at my age."

"You're not old, Leo."

"Sixty-seven is hardly considered the prime of life."

"You'll still be going at ninety-seven," Jennifer said, "and I'll still love you, but I don't want to have lunch at the club. You know I hate that place."

"Still the feminist. We have women members now."

"Tokens," Jennifer said, keeping up the pretense. Her reluctance to go to Leo's club was not based on feminism. It was a place where Jackson Holloway might appear unexpectedly although he was not a member. Jennifer knew that from checking Leo's membership roster each year. Still . . . She would not take the chance, not even to please Leo.

"But powerful tokens. I would be happy to put your name in for membership."

"No, thank you, Leo."

"My dear, what am I to do with you?"

"Take me to lunch at that nice Japanese restaurant downstairs."

"I'm helpless when confronted with your charms. Japanese it is."

113

They took the elevator down to the shopping mall that occupied the two levels below the building's lobby. Office workers in the building could shop for virtually anything they needed, dine, use Federal Express, mail a package at the Post Office substation, order personal stationary or cards, or watch through a large plate glass window and listen as a radio disk jockey interviewed guests. The restaurant was large with separate dining areas for a number of Japanese specialties. Jennifer requested the back room where each booth was secluded and private, away from the greater luncheon traffic around the sushi bar.

Leo poured tea. "You look radiant, my dear. The holidays seem to have agreed with you."

Jennifer smiled. "Yes, I suppose they did. Did you have a nice Christmas?"

"A house filled with crying and screaming grand-children is hardly considered restful. But, yes, it was nice. And the nicest part was waving goodbye to cars laden with Pampers. Bye, bye, come again next year. When you're housebroken. Bah."

"You loved every minute of it. You play the benevolent patriarch very well."

"I was born to the role," Leo said smiling at her over the tiny cup of tea he cradled in both hands. "Unfortunately. But we stray from the subject at hand. Again."

"And what is that?"

"You are absolutely glowing. I've never seen you appear to be so happy. I want to know why. I want to know every delicious detail."

Jennifer was surprised to find that she wanted to talk about Hank, to share her happiness with someone. Why not Leo? He was her best friend. Her only friend really. Her world had been so isolated for so long, never allowing anyone to enter. It was safer that way. There could be no betrayals that way. Now there was Hank. Why not Leo?

"I met a man."

114

"Tell me about him."

"Well, I didn't just meet him. We've known each other for quite some time now, but . . . I always thought of him as just a friend. I thought that love had to happen suddenly."

She drifted off into memories. For a moment, she was nineteen again and wildly in love with the best man in the world. But he wasn't. He had turned out mean and cruel.

"I was too much of a romantic," Jennifer said. "Love at first sight and then it was just a short wait for everything to fall apart after that."

"I always knew you had been unhappy in love. I couldn't understand it. If I were thirty years younger . . ."

"You're sweet, Leo. I appreciate all you've done for me."

"Your gratitude was always unquestioned."

Jennifer blushed. "I guess I'm in love," she admitted.

"It becomes you."

"You know, I guess love did happen suddenly. Here we've known each other for years and everything changed, almost overnight. That's funny."

"When will I meet this friend of yours? Does he have a name?"

"Hank. Henry really. I call him Bear."

"And does he call you Cuddles?"

"Leo!"

"I'm just teasing you, my dear. Truly. I'm happy for you both. I want to meet him."

Sitting in a quiet restaurant with the delicate sounds of Japanese music playing in the background it almost seemed that Jennifer could lead a normal life. But she couldn't. Not now. Perhaps not ever. She knew she would have to tell Hank soon. They would never be able to have a normal life. There would always be the fear pervading every aspect of their life. "You can't," Jennifer said.

"Are you ashamed of me?"

115

"Of course not. But Hank doesn't live here."

"Ah," Leo said nodding his head. "That secret hideaway of yours."

"I'm afraid so."

"When are you going to tell me what you're hiding from?"

"I can't do that, Leo."

"Nothing could be so terrible that a friend couldn't help you."

"It's not like that. There's nothing anyone can do. I have to live with it."

"Alone?"

"Yes."

A slight Japanese woman wearing the traditional kimono weaved gracefully through the dining room to take their orders.

The view from the office window was like a kaleidoscope slowly turning, altering patterns on distant mountains and the cold lines of modern office buildings, transforming light and shadows through the morning into the afternoon and evening. As dusk and the approaching darkness tightened its hold on the cityscape, lights glowed from office windows, creating a variety of designs and configurations, hopscotching through the downtown buildings, adding a surreal cast to the mock winter's night. It was Jennifer's favorite time, those relaxing moments at day's end when she could move her chair to the window and watch as though the muted light show was created for her enjoyment and pleasure. In the past, she had left her balcony seat almost reluctantly, never hurrying to join the crush of commuters, never rushing to go home to the night track that haunted her evenings alone. But now the view was a distraction. She found herself eager to pull her car into the crowded streets and join the homeward bound traffic creeping along the Santa Monica Freeway. At journey's end Hank's telephone call waited. Instead of working late as usual, Jennifer filled her briefcase with work she could do at home and left the office.

Elevators from the upper reaches of the building and escalators from the shopping mall converged in the garage. As Jennifer went to the monthly parking area for her car, a tall man wearing a gray suit watched her as he waited for the attendant to bring his car. When his car—a black two-door Cadillac—arrived he tipped the attendant five dollars, carefully removed and folded his coat, laying it on the back seat. He started the CD player and waited for Wagner's Ride of the Valkyries to fill the car with sound before driving out. Robert Shaw smiled triumphantly as he circled up the ramp, tires squealing.

Oscar greeted Jennifer at the door, crying indignantly at her long absence. He had not yet adjusted to their return to the routine of work. It always took a week or more after a period in Hidden Valley before he finally acquiesced to her diminished presence. Until then, he expressed his disapproval by sulking and pouting for a short time each evening. Then his tactics changed and he clung to Jennifer, always underfoot, following her from door to bedroom to kitchen to living room.

As Jennifer changed her clothes, he perched at the end of the bed, watching each movement carefully. As she stood at the kitchen counter preparing a salad for dinner, he stretched out next to the coffee maker, occasionally sticking his nose dangerously close to the chopping knife to explore the smells of lettuce, radishes, a green onion, a wedge of tomato.

Later, he would sit in her lap as she worked at her desk or when she was in the chair that overlooked the

117

lights curving along the edge of Santa Monica Bay. If she got up, he followed her to her destination and back again, looking up at her with his wide yellow eyes, his pleading eyes. She often wondered what went through his mind during these moods and finally decided some tiny little instinct had instilled a fear of abandonment even as she tried to convince herself that it was impossible for a cat to remember being abandoned in an alley. But Oscar had not hardened himself, not yet, not like Jennifer. "Poor little orphan cat," Jennifer told him as she rubbed his chin. "I know what it's like to be unloved. I had the same kind of childhood. I won't leave you."

She played the violin—her violin—reaching out to Hank with the music, waiting for his call. And when the telephone rang and it was Hank, Oscar insisted on listening to his voice for a moment. Jennifer held the receiver to Oscar's ear and watched as the ears pointed and swiveled tracking in on Hank's distant voice. "Hey, Clint, how you doing today," Hank said. "Tough day at the office?" Bemused but satisfied, Oscar settled into Jennifer's lap to sleep out the duration of the telephone call.

"How are you, darling?"

"I miss you and I love you," Jennifer said.

"It's really empty here without you. I keep hearing your voice and I look up expecting to see you in the doorway or sitting in your spot at the end of the bar. It's not the same anymore. You've disrupted my life."

"Are you sorry?"

"Oh, no, darling. Never sorry. Just lonely. I was never lonely before."

"I was always lonely," Jennifer said, "but now I'm not, even with you so far away, I'm not lonely anymore. It's strange, but I feel like you're always with me."

They went on to talk of other things. Jennifer told him of returning to work, about Leo and their lunch, how the beautiful day did not match Hidden Valley. Hank told her of the mundane things in Hank's Place, the people who had been in, those who had asked about her and sent their regards, the latest gossip about the hotel project. It was easy for them to spend an hour or two on the telephone, chatting comfortably as the time passed unnoticed. But the conversation always turned back to their growing love for each other.

They felt transported back to their youth when love remained a wondrous and mysterious emotion, before either knew of the pain and heartache that all too often accompanied love, before they learned that love was fragile, that the physical delights passed quickly and bickering and arguments easily destroyed tenderness and devotion. For now, they were prince and princess wandering blissfully through a magical realm of enchanted forests and secret castles where harsh words were never spoken and each tingling caress carried with it promises of flight to all the pleasures offered by the senses.

They parted for the evening as reluctantly as they had parted after the Christmas party which marked the beginning of their love. That night, each had wanted to make love to the other, but with the sudden transformation in their relationship both were nervous and shy. They merely brushed lips, embraced quickly, and fled, spending the night alone, thinking of each other and what might be until sleep finally came.

Jennifer wandered out to the balcony after hanging up the telephone, letting her hand rest on the receiver for a time, as though the connection had not been broken, as though she could still feel Hank's presence. Standing there on the balcony, looking out at city lights and dark ocean waters, Jennifer was serene, thinking only of Hank and the unexpected pleasures that had come to her after so many years of waiting.

They had not rushed to intimacy, even though they spent their days and evenings together, driving up to the Rim to look out at the view, walking the wilderness trails. Hank took her to his home for the first time and she saw a neat clutter bestowed by the bachelor and the multitude of books that filled his cabin. He showed her around the small ranch he operated. They cooked dinner together and then sat in front of the fireplace. And finally it was right.

Hank kissed Jennifer, slowly, gently, prolonging the pleasure of that first intimacy, probing, exploring. Jennifer took his tongue, biting, nibbling at his lips, wanting the moment to last forever. She relaxed in his arms, taking comfort from his embrace, arching her body to meet his caress when he touched her breasts for the first time. Their breathing quickened and each felt the heartbeat of the other merging into a single pulse as they drew the warmth of the fire into their bodies. Her fingers played with the buttons on his shirt, unfastening them. She sat erect as he pulled the sweater over her head. She helped him with the clasp of her brassiere, letting it fall from her breasts.

"Ah, Jenny," he sighed. "You're so beautiful."

"As nice as Amanda?"

"Better. Much better."

She smiled and held his head as he suckled at her nipples, erect and swollen now, throbbing with urgency.

And then they were naked together on the rug before the fireplace. He cried out when she took him deep into her mouth for the first time, caressing him with her tongue, burning his flesh with hot fingertips. And then it was her turn to cry out as he turned her over on her back for the first time and burned her flesh with his lips, kissing her breasts, her belly, her thighs.

"Oh, God, Bear, it's wonderful. Please, I want you. Now."

He held her hips to the floor as she moaned with the sweet blissful torments of his touch.

Jennifer tried to draw him up, to enter her, but he

120

refused, staying with the slow rhythmic movements of her hips until she could hold back no longer and she exploded.

"Oh, oh, oh!" she cried. "Oh, Bear. Oh, God."

And when Jennifer thought she had experienced all the pleasures of the world, he started over, taking her to the heights once more.

"I can't stand it. Oh, Bear, you're so wonderful. I love you. I love you."

Finally she succeeded in bringing him to her. She kissed his lips frantically as they became one for the first time. She held him tightly, moving her body for him, drawing him deeper into her. And it was his turn to explode. She held him as he bucked and writhed, crying out with his own sweet agony.

And then it was over.

Exhausted they lay intertwined before the fire. Neither wanted to move. Neither wanted their first time together to end. He nuzzled her tangled hair and whispered, "I love you."

Jennifer replied, "And I love you. So very much."

Oscar interrupted the pleasant memories, brushing against her leg. She leaned down to scratch his ears, still remembering that first romantic time before the fireplace as they made love like a chapter from a romantic novel. "Are you happy? Are you as happy as me, Oscar?" He moved beneath her fingers, asking for more. I'm going to make you purr one of these days." The cat followed her inside as she went to her bed to fall asleep thinking of Hank and their love.

From his car on the street below, Robert Shaw watched her leave the balcony. When the lights in Jennifer Warren's unit were turned out, he started his car and drove slowly down the street.

TEN

Robert Shaw was in love with Jennifer Warren.

In the beginning, Robert Shaw didn't know he would come to love the image of the woman he would find living as Jennifer Warren. Jackson Holloway called her a slut. Shaw accepted his employer's judgment, took his substantial fee in cash and began the search for a woman who had disappeared. Now . . .

By the time Jennifer Warren fell asleep to dream sensuously of love, Robert Shaw had made the long drive from Santa Monica to Newport Beach, traversing three freeways, still crowded with cars and trucks though the rush hour had long since ended. Sometimes it seemed to Shaw—who was a frequent night traveler—as though people lived on the freeways, driving through purgatory in an endless glare of headlights. He sat in his study, drinking scotch, and looking yet another time at the photographs of the girl-woman who had called herself Sierra. He had fallen in love with a photograph, with the youthful woman portrayed. He longed to touch her full breasts, stroke her thighs, entangle his fingers in the hair that shrouded her face in most of the photos. There was an old movie like that, he remembered, where a police detective fell in love with a portrait of a murdered woman. But at the end of the film, she wasn't dead at all. What was the name of the film? A woman's name. Something like Sierra or Jennifer. She wasn't dead either. He had seen her, followed her, knew where she worked and where she lived. And the desire to possess her grew stronger.

Shaw found Jennifer Warren today even more seductive and enticing than in the collection of photographs he hoarded. She had scarcely aged, perhaps a few lines near her eyes. Her beauty had matured. She walked gracefully, distinctively, hips swaying beneath the stylish clothing, promising pleasures beyond his imagination. Jennifer Warren was not a slut, a whore. Holloway was wrong.

Shaw had not yet decided if he would tell his employer that he had found Sierra living in the guise of Jennifer Warren, an Attorney at Law. Holloway was insisting on daily progress reports, shouting and demanding results. "It takes time," Shaw told him. "God damn, give me a break, the woman's been missing for twenty years. You give me a few old photos and expect me to find her overnight. She might even be dead," Shaw lied.

"She's not dead!" Holloway yelled. "I know it. She's out there somewhere and I expect you to find her!"

"Calm down," Shaw said, "I'll find her, but it's going to take some time."

In reality, with persistence and footwork, it had been a relatively simple task to find Sierra, tracking her through the faint, obscure footprints she left, as though she had walked over a wet beach leaving behind minute traces of her passage in the sand that even the powerful surf could not obliterate totally. She was one of those women who, in all innocence, unaware of their sexuality and power, made an indelible impression on everyone who knew her, invoking either love or jealous hate. No one who met her ever forgot her. She had that same impact on Shaw, first from the photographs Holloway had provided, then from the additional

123

photographs he acquired, and finally from his surveillance of Jennifer Warren. Shaw felt the power and erotic passion emanating from Jennifer Warren as he watched her descend on the escalator to the parking garage. He felt that seductive lure again as he observed Jennifer's lonely vigil on the balcony of her condominium. It seemed to fill the quiet night, emanating outward from her presence and threatening to engulf him with an intoxication he could not control. He wanted Jennifer Warren for his own.

Shaw smiled as he sipped scotch. She had been living unnoticed in Los Angeles for years, practically in Holloway's back yard. Holloway was a fool for mistreating her, abusing her, letting her get away from him. Shaw didn't know what Holloway had done to her yet, but he would find out, just as he was learning about Sierra, who now called herself Jennifer Warren, Attorney at Law. She was no longer Sierra. That child no longer existed. Shaw knew only that Jennifer had been in love with Holloway, passionately devoted to him. But something had happened. Shit happened, Shaw thought, and Holloway lost her. Jennifer fled, disappearing from San Francisco entirely. It served the bastard right.

Arthur Wilson had loved her too. "I didn't know I was gay then," Wilson said. "I was still trying to make it in the straight world. But I never had a model, straight or gay, like Sierra." He closed his eyes and smiled as he remembered his model of so many years ago. Outside the photographer's studio on Castro Street, a passing parade of gay and lesbian couples strolled by, holding hands, talking animatedly as they enjoyed the brilliant sun-washed winter's afternoon.

Shaw figured that Wilson had to have been in his late twenties when he knew Sierra and wondered how the slender photographer with the effeminate mannerisms had gone so long without knowing of his own sexuality, but he said nothing, allowing Wilson to

124

ramble on, in his eagerness to talk of Sierra.

"I've often wondered what happened to Sierra. She just disappeared without a call or anything. We had a modeling session scheduled, but she didn't show up. Poof, she was gone." Wilson snapped his fingers. "Just poof, like that. I was distraught, as you can imagine."

Shaw could imagine. Sierra was a woman who could give Arthur Wilson an opportunity to question his sexual preference.

"Sierra used to talk about going down to L.A. to live among the barbarians. She wanted to go to law school."

"Did she say where?"

Wilson shook his head. "She didn't even finish college. Dropped out of Berkeley when she married that rich boy."

"What was he like?" Shaw asked.

"I never met him," Wilson replied. "All I know is that he ruined her life. Sierra was deathly afraid of him, terrified that he would track her down. She was such a sweet child too. And brilliant. She would have made a great lawyer. Such a waste." Arthur Wilson's eyes closed again and he drifted back to 1968.

Shaw waited patiently.

"I was in the Haight then, not on the Castro like now. We were all struggling, but I was beginning to sell my work and so I could afford to pay Sierra a little for the modeling. I think it was all she had to live on. For the two of them. The strength that woman possessed. She would have nothing to do with her foster parents. From what I was able to gather, they were just as bad as her husband. Little Clea. My God, she must be in her twenties now. Sierra was only eighteen or nineteen when she had Clea. Such a beautiful baby. If she's anything like her mother . . ." He drifted away again. "Remarkable," he said returning to the present.

"Do you know where the foster parents lived?"

"Somewhere in the East Bay with the Philistines.

125

Some ugly little place near Oakland."

Shaw made a mental note to contact the children services department or the child welfare authorities in Alameda County. The documents would probably be sealed, but Holloway would have a judge in his pocket somewhere who would subpoena the records. Holloway always had a judge or a councilman or a supervisor or a planning commissioner in his pocket somewhere.

"Would you like to see some old photographs of Sierra?" Wilson asked.

Shaw felt the longing come from deep within his stomach and his heart leaped at the thought of that magnificent body. He kept the tremor from his voice as he replied simply, "Yes."

Wilson took him into a back office adjoining a darkroom. Shaw waited impatiently as Wilson opened a drawer in a legal size metal cabinet. He removed two thick folders filled with photos and put them on a cluttered desk. "I still think this was some of my best work," Wilson said standing back to make room for Shaw.

It was the new shots of Sierra that Shaw pored over as he finished his drink and poured another from the bottle on the desk. He felt a voyeur's stirring as he studied the photographs yet again. He could not get enough of Jennifer Warren. There she was in the nude, reclining on a variety of props—a couch, a bed, next to a chair. But there were other shots, even more exciting to Shaw because the woman's charms were hidden beneath extravagant clothing styles—long dresses and prim Victorian blouses that buttoned to the neck—promising untold mysteries and pleasures for the gentle lover who persisted. And in those photographs her face was not hidden by shadows and long hair carefully arranged to obscure her features. Her beauty was so great that Shaw ached in his desire to possess her. In one photograph taken at ocean's edge, it was as though

126

Jennifer had emerged from a home beneath the waters. Her hair was blown by the wind and she looked at the camera with a forlorn and lost expression, as though she could be a wondrous creature from another world suddenly thrust into a harsh and frightening environment. The impact was of great sadness and loneliness. Another photograph focused on her face and shoulders. Again, the hair was tangled falling beneath her shoulders to the first gentle swell of her bosom, framing and enclosing the sorrow in her face and the haunted plea in her eyes. Shaw wanted to kiss the pain away.

He knew where some of it had originated. Holloway had come through with a tame judge who reluctantly signed the order opening the records of an orphaned child. Through the information in the records, Shaw had found the case worker, now retired, and the foster parents. The former case worker remembered the child vaguely. "There were so many children," she said. But she remembered the foster parents clearly and with bitterness. "They were the kind of people who lived off the children they took in. Used the money for themselves and provided the children with only the barest necessities."

"Why didn't you take them away?" Shaw asked.

"There were so many . . ."

Jennifer's foster mother, a dowdy and embittered woman in her sixties, had called her an ungrateful bitch. "Went away to college and never said another word to us. That was the last we heard of her. After all we done for her too."

Her foster father was drunk when Shaw paid the visit, but his eyes focused momentarily and flashed with some hidden memory. Shaw saw the expression and wanted to pound his fist into the leering grin, suspecting the old man had molested the blossoming child, making her life a hell. But the moment passed quickly as the old man sank back into his gin-induced stupor.

So a hellish foster home contributed to the great sadness so evident in the photographs, but that was not the complete story. Holloway had played some terrible role as well. Shaw sighed. It would come out in time.

There was one more photograph, a small portrait ripped from a law school yearbook. Shaw found Jennifer Warren by following the ambition she had expressed in passing to the photographer. With the collection of photographs firmly in mind, Shaw simply went to all of the law schools in the Los Angeles area, starting with the major university law schools at UCLA and USC and working his way through the private schools. He spent a week leafing through all of the old yearbooks until he found her face staring out at the camera with that now familiar sadness. Jennifer Warren, Class of 1981. Had Jennifer Warren been a different woman, one with less resolve and determination, she might have disappeared for all time. Her ambition betrayed her. Robert Shaw stroked the photograph tenderly, as though he were caressing the naked flesh of Jennifer Warren.

Laura. That was the name of the old film. Clifton Webb had been in it. Who played Laura? Shaw wondered.

ELEVEN

Jennifer and Hank went to a restaurant perfect for lovers on an afternoon when a chilling early February rain fell against the window and gray clouds obscured the ocean horizon. A blaze in the stone fireplace warmed the intimate dining room. Outside the window, a lone sea gull sat upon a railing, head tucked beneath its wing, huddling against the cold. Below, dark waves rushed the shoreline, breaking early over black rocks. The surf swirled angrily around the pilings and then surged away, leaving the ripples of a vicious riptide in its wake, as though trying to draw man's puny edifice into the depths of the malevolent ocean waters.

Jennifer stared through the rain-streaked window. She was dressed simply, wearing a long woolen skirt, boots, and a bulky-knit red sweater that could not hide the swell of her breasts. Her raincoat was draped over her shoulders. Soft blonde hair was pulled up and tied with a red ribbon that matched her sweater. Her face was beautiful with fine and delicate features, marred only by the tinge of sadness clouding blue eyes as she looked out the window at something only she could see.

The restaurant was nearly empty. Their waiter, a young man, probably an aspiring actor or screen writer, hovered nearby, looking at her with that mixture of awe and lust and intimidation she was accustomed to seeing in a man's eyes. It had always been like that. Men saw her and wanted to take her to bed first and later use her as a decoration for their arm. Jennifer knew men found her stunning, accepted it, but sometimes longed for the peace that would come with unattractiveness. It would happen soon enough now. The first lines around her eyes had come with her fortieth birthday. Others would follow. Perhaps, she thought, perhaps then I can trust again, love again.

The waiter was there, protectively, a disappointment in his eyes that said, He's too old for you. Take me. I can make you happy.

Jennifer smiled and said, "I'll have another glass of chardonnay now, please."

The young man beamed. His goddess had spoken to him alone.

"Something for you?" he asked of Hank curtly.

"Make it two."

The waiter left for the bar, looking back at Jennifer over his shoulder.

"He doesn't like me," Hank said.

"He's jealous of you."

"I thought it was my cowboy boots."

"That too," Jennifer said smiling.

Hank looked out at the seething water. "I like the rain," he said.

"I don't," Jennifer replied. "It's depressing." It had rained then too. It always rained then.

Clea cried steadily.

The tiny apartment was cold, but Clea remained hot and feverish. Outside, the rain, driven by harsh winds off the bay, fell steadily. There had been no let up for days. Sierra shivered as she bared her breast for Clea, begging her to nurse. "Please, little one, try." Clea only cried harder, coughing wretchedly. Sierra shifted the baby and lifted her sweater even more, exposing her other breast. Clea clutched at her mother's nipple with tiny fingers and cried. Sierra pressed her close and

130

hummed and sang nonsense little phrases. "Please, little baby, please."

They had spent hours waiting at a free medical clinic. The waiting room was overheated and each time the door opened to admit another suffering runaway or addict the cold rushed in, clearing the air momentarily before the heat built up again, stifling breath. One girl, no more than fifteen, cowered in a corner of the waiting room, struggling to come down from a bad trip where spiders threatened to devour her. She had been brought in and left by a boyfriend with a straggly eighteen year old's beard.

When Sierra had finally been called, the audience with the harassed young doctor had been brief, almost cursory. "She'll be fine in a few days," the doctor said. "It's just a cold." A nurse smiled at Sierra sympathetically.

Arthur, dear Arthur, who thought he loved her, came for Sierra and Clea in his old and battered Volkswagen, driving them through the gloomy, rainswept streets back to North Beach, stopping briefly at a market to pick up a few things for Sierra while she waited in the car, hugging Clea to her.

She gave up on trying to entice Clea to suckle and took her to the crib, wiping her nose, wrapping her in blankets. She stood over the crib, looking down, fighting back her own tears.

Finally, Sierra cried.

Jennifer looked down at the raging surf. A lone sandpiper scurried along the edge of the foaming water. Hank reached across the table and took her hand. "Don't be sad," he said. "It's only rain."

"The angels are crying," Jennifer said.

"Why?" Hank asked.

"Because they're unhappy. They look down and see what we do to one another and they cry. They can't help it." She looked back at the sandpiper, still following an aimless path along water's edge, tempting its fate, hurrying away when a larger wave crashed to shore.

131

"I have a wonderful idea," Hank said.

"And what's this wonderful idea."

"After lunch, let's go home and make love."

"What! And skip the Clint Eastwood film festival?"

"We'll make our own movie. Love on a Rainy Afternoon."

Sierra fled the hot burning lights, rushing from the makeshift studio in tears. The director's outraged cry followed her. "Stupid cunt," he yelled.

"That is a wonderful idea," Jennifer said quietly.

Neither Hank nor Jennifer noticed the black car parked midway down the street when they dashed through the rain into her building. After they had disappeared into the lobby, the man sitting in the black car behind steamed windows wrote down the number of the license plate on Hank's truck.

He undressed her slowly, his hands roaming over the softness of her belly, caressing the warmth of her back, as he lifted the sweater, lingering in the ritual disrobing of his goddess, pausing to kiss her lips, burrowing beneath the strands of her hair to kiss her white slender neck. She stood before the bed, following his silent directions, arching her head back, exposing her throat for his gentle touch, lifting her arms as he pulled the sweater over her head, willing him all the while to go faster, already wanting him inside her, but enjoying the slow rise of desire within. His lips and fingers played over her body, worshipping his goddess before her altar. She drew him close with her arms, cradling his head as he bent to kiss her breasts swelling from their black lace covering.

They both sighed when her breasts fell free of the enveloping lace. His sigh was engendered by awe as though it were the first time he had seen those precious

132

mounds of soft white flesh decorated with dark swollen tips. Jennifer sighed with increased yearning as she lifted her breasts, offering them to his lips, shuddering when he drew one hard nipple into his mouth.

"Oh, God, darling," Jennifer whispered impatiently.

He took little heed of her eagerness as he left one nipple wet and glistening and turned to her other breast, biting gently with delicate and precise pressure.

Outside the wind gusted and the rain rattled against the window panes.

Her woolen skirt and the half slip beneath fell in folds about her ankles. Kneeling, he stroked her hips and thighs and kissed her belly as she tangled her fingers in his hair.

The chilling rain, driven by the wind, demanded entrance.

Jennifer fell to her knees, frantically pulling at the buttons of his shirt. She smothered his face with kisses and probed his mouth with her tongue. She pulled away at last and pushed him to the floor. "Now, darling," she said.

Making him the prisoner of her attentions, she tortured him relentlessly, feeling him grow beneath her caresses and within the warmth of her lips and mouth. She heard his cries of pleasure and renewed her exploration of his body, driving him to greater heights of exquisite pain until they were both maddened with desire and nothing remained.

They joined and exploded simultaneously into helpless throes, each striving to give the other greater pleasure.

They remained as one for a long time afterwards, holding each other tightly, limbs intertwined, as the warmth of their passion ebbed, slowly draining from their bodies. Even then, they were reluctant to part.

"I love you, darling."

"And I love you," Jennifer answered. "I'm so happy you're here, Hank."

133

Outside, the black car drove slowly through the cold rain, headlights burning angrily in a futile effort to pierce the drab gloom of the afternoon. The driver pounded his steering wheel with jealous rage.

The rain fell steadily. Jennifer and Hank watched the gray mist swirl through the streets, obscuring the view. They were both quiet and subdued, finally drained of passion, content to be close to one another. Oscar sat in Hank's lap, eyes slowly closing, nodding, jerking awake to stare up at Jennifer with his large yellow eyes.

"He's wondering what's going on," Jennifer said.

"What is going on?" Hank asked.

"What do you mean?"

"I'm worried, Jenny."

"Why?"

"I want us to be together."

"We are together. We will be together."

"It seemed fine in Hidden Valley. But now that I'm here . . . See how you live . . . What your life is really like . . . Everything seems different somehow . : . I don't know anymore."

"Nothing's changed, Hank. I still love you. I want to be with you."

"I don't have much to offer. Christ, I own a bar and a restaurant. What are you going to do in Hidden Valley? Be a barmaid?"

"I'll do what I've always done, Hank."

"Come and go?"

"Not forever. I'll take the Arizona bar exam. Practice law."

"Jenny, I want to marry you."

Oh, God, Hank. Not now. Not yet. We were so happy. Jennifer turned away from him and looked out at the rain. Sometimes I see me dead in the rain. Is that

134

a line from *A Farewell to Arms?* she wondered. If it wasn't, it should be, she thought. She remembered Frederick Henry walking back to his hotel in the rain after Catherine died. It was so sad. Will Hank leave me now? Will he drive back to Arizona in the rain? Oh, Hank, you should not have asked me to marry you. It might have been all right with time.

"Please, Jenny, will you marry me?"

Jennifer wanted to flee, to disappear into the rain, the cold chilling sad rain. She turned away from the window and the rain. "Hank, I love you very much," she said. "But you don't know me, Hank. I'm not the woman you think I am."

"You're the woman I want to spend the rest of my life with."

"You're stubborn," Jennifer said, "a stubborn wonderful bear." She reached out and touched his cheek gently. I have to tell him the truth. I should have told him before. "I have a history, Hank, a past I'm not very proud of . . ."

"That doesn't matter," Hank interrupted. "We have our own history. We're making our own home movies now . . ."

Stupid cunt!

The words echoed over the years, filling her mind with the pain of memories that threatened to overwhelm her, suffocate her. It had rained then too . . .

"Wait here," Jennifer said. She got up and went into the bedroom. Oscar leaped from Hank's lap and followed her. Jennifer opened the door of the walk-in closet. She knelt and pushed aside the tight folds of dresses and coats and slacks. A portable safe was hidden behind the clothes. She paused with tears welling up in her eyes. Oh, Christ, it's all over now. She twirled the dial, setting the combination in place. Again, she paused. Oscar nuzzled against her. She pushed him away and brushed at the tears in her eyes. It could have been so perfect. She opened the safe and

135

looked in at the large envelope, nearly buried beneath the collection of personal columns, the twenty years of threats. She took the envelope out. It was crammed with the evidence that would destroy love, destroy happiness. It's not too late. Put them back. He'll never know. And when he's gone . . . Burn them. Why did I keep them?

Jennifer returned to the living room and handed the envelope to Hank. "Look at these and then ask me to marry you," she said angrily.

She left Hank alone and went across the hall and knocked on Jerome's door. "Give me a cigarette," she said when he answered.

"Jennifer, what's wrong?"

"Just give me a fucking cigarette."

Holloway was right. Jennifer Warren, Sierra, whatever she called herself, was a bitch. The jealous rage had built throughout the long and arduous drive from Santa Monica to Newport. There had been one accident after another on the rain-slick freeways. Visibility had been gravely impaired and speeding cars and trucks showered the windshield with water and oil. Now he had a blinding headache and the scotch did not alleviate either the headache or the jealous fury. She had betrayed him for a God damned, red necked, beer guzzling cowboy. The bitch would pay for that.

Jennifer could not look at Hank. She stood on the balcony, smoking and watching the rain dissipate her dreams and hopes. It had been years since she smoked and the vile taste only served to remind her of how far she had come and how far she had to fall. Behind her, Oscar sensed her pain and cried piteously, but did not dare to venture into the rain with her. Jennifer ignored him and waited for Hank to walk out of her life.

He can have the violin. It would be too much to keep it, a mocking reminder of what she had lost. And Hidden Valley would be lost too. I can't go back there now. I'll have to find someplace else to go when Jackson comes for me. Where will I go this time? Texas? Utah? New Mexico? Oh, God, why? I don't want to run anymore. I want to be happy. I want to die.

Jennifer threw the cigarette into the rain and watched the last glowing ember fall. It died on the wet ground along with her hopes and dreams.

Jennifer heard the night track then, drumming, rising, building to a hideous crescendo that careened through her mind approaching madness, an explosion. She wanted to turn it off, but she could not reach the controls. They were too far away, buried in the distant past. Below her, she saw the black shapes slipping through the darkness, searching for her. There was no escape. Someday, they would find her. Soon, soon now, they must find her.

Please, Clea, don't cry. Please, baby, don't cry. Don't let them know we're here. She crouched in the dumpster, sheltered beneath its lid from the rain and the shapes drifting through the dark alley looking for her. She held the child tight to her breast, fighting against the awful stench of garbage and the bile that rose in her throat. Outside, they were looking for her. Please, God, don't let them look in here. Oh, dear, Jesus, God, don't let them find us. They were close now, standing next to the dumpster, talking softly. Their footsteps moved away and the night was quiet. Sierra listened. Clea stirred against her breast. Please, no, not now, not yet. She was sinking into the garbage. It was like quicksand, clutching at her, drawing her down into the filth and rank foulness. Sierra held her breath, not daring to move, not daring to hope. She heard something move in the dumpster. Oh, Christ. She fought hysteria when she heard the rat squeak, biting hard into the filthy cloth of her sleeve to stifle the scream coming from deep within her soul.

Hank was beside her then, looking out at the dreary dusk of the approaching night. "You were beautiful then," he said softly. "You still are."

Jennifer fought against the old scream and shook off the touch of his hand on her arm.

Hank persisted. "Come inside now," he said.

Jennifer allowed him to guide her inside, but she avoided his eyes, knowing they would be filled with accusations and the pain of her betrayal. She would never be able to face him again. Her past had destroyed her. Again. She glanced quickly at the coffee table. He had replaced all of the photographs neatly in the large brown envelope.

"You said I should look at the pictures and then ask you to marry me. Well, I've looked, and I still want you to marry me, if you think I'm worthy of you."

"Oh, Jesus, Hank, how can you even think of marrying me now?" Jennifer exclaimed. "I've shown you what kind of woman I was then."

"You showed me pictures taken of an artist's model. There's nothing wrong with that."

"Do you know where some of those pictures appeared? For Christ's sake, I was in half-a-dozen different smutty magazines. Old men and perverts used photographs of me to get excited so they could masturbate." Jennifer shuddered. "It's like they used my body and I let them. I was their whore. Sometimes, I can feel it on me. Why do you think Clea hates me so? She found those pictures. She calls them her baby pictures. Some legacy for my own daughter."

"We're not talking about Clea," Hank said. "She'll have to come to terms with her mother on her own. We're talking about you and me. I don't care what you did in the past. Our lives together started last Christmas. Jesus Christ, do you think I'm pure? I've killed people. Poor fucking little people who just wanted to be left alone in their fucking rice paddies.

138

But they wore black pajamas so I killed them. And I liked it. I liked killing people who never did anything to me. I've been with whores and I liked that too, because they didn't expect anything from me. They didn't care if I was a killer. All they wanted was my money and I gave it to them because I didn't have to give them anything else."

"Hank . . ."

He interrupted her. "If you don't want to marry me now, I'll understand. But if you don't, let it be because of what I was and what I am. Don't try and use some old photographs as an excuse to get rid of me."

"Hank, please . . ."

Again, Hank interrupted her.

"I love you, Jennifer, and I don't give a good God damn about anything else."

Jennifer paced the room, wishing she had another cigarette. "I tried to tell myself I was doing it for Clea," she said. "I still try to say that. I had to tell myself something to save my self respect. But I don't believe it. I could have done something else. Anything. But I didn't."

"You thought you had no choice. You had a baby. You had to survive. You did what you could at the time. No one can blame you for that. I don't."

"Oh, Christ, Hank, what about Clea? What about me?"

"I don't know about Clea," Hank said. "As for you, it happened a long time ago in another life. You have to put it behind you. You can't let it affect the rest of your life."

"Have you put Vietnam behind you?" Jennifer asked quietly.

"That pisses me off, Jennifer. You posed for a few pictures without any clothes on. Big fucking deal. We were kids. They told us we were fighting for democracy. What a bunch of bullshit. The only thing we fought for after awhile was ourselves. We wanted to stay alive and we killed a lot of other kids who just wanted to stay alive."

"I'm sorry," Jennifer said angrily. "I didn't mean to cheapen what you did, but I was a kid too, and I didn't have anyone to rely on. I was alone, damn it, and I don't like what I did. And nothing you say can change that."

"So," Hank said, "you think you're suffering post pornography syndrome?"

Despite herself, Jennifer laughed. She couldn't help it. "I guess I am," she admitted.

The tension left the room. Jennifer sat beside Hank on the couch, looking down at the envelope filled with the accusations from the past for a long while. Finally, she turned and looked up at Hank. "I lied to you, Hank, when I said I didn't like it. There were times I *did* like it. It was a way of getting back at him. He hurt me. And I could hurt him back. Later, much later, I sent him the photos. He was insanely jealous of me. I wanted him to hurt. It was a stupid thing to do."

"That's what youth is for," Hank said. "We have to get all the stupid things out of our system." He paused. "Are you ready to tell me about him?"

"I guess I better. You know everything else now." Jennifer paused, gathering courage, wondering how much she could reveal before Hank left her, wondering which secret would be the final destructive blow to their relationship.

"I met him at Berkeley. He was a graduate student, staying in school to avoid the draft. He was so handsome and confident. He had money. Everything. I fell in love with him the first time he talked to me. He made love to me that first night and I moved in with him the next day. He was involved in the anti-war movement in a big way, SDS, civil rights, all the protest things. He knew Black Panthers. Bikers. But he wouldn't burn his draft card. He didn't want to lose his student deferment, you see. We got married three months after we met. I was already pregnant, but he didn't know that. Everything had been so wonderful, but he went berserk when he found out I was pregnant. Wanted me to get an abortion. Claimed that Clea wasn't his child. He beat me. Badly. Kept me locked up for a time. As soon as I could escape, I ran. Disappeared in San Francisco. I had Clea in the Haight with a midwife in attendance. I was afraid to go to a hospital, afraid he might find me. After that, I started posing and as soon as I had enough money, I came to L.A. That's when I changed my name and became Jennifer Warren." She paused, looking back into the hated memories. "It was difficult. I worked. Two jobs sometimes. Secretary. Waitress. Went to classes. Took out student loans. Sometimes I took Clea to classes when I couldn't afford any kind of day care for her. We made it. Somehow . . ."

Again, Jennifer paused. She turned to Hank finally. "That's it. Now you know everything about me," she lied. She couldn't tell him everything, not yet. Perhaps someday. Perhaps never. Please, God, don't make me tell him everything. Please let us be happy.

"What a bastard."

"Yes."

"None of it makes any difference. I don't know anyone named Sierra. I only know Jennifer Warren and I love her and I want her to marry me. Will you?"

"Yes. If you still want me after all this, I'll marry you."

"Thank God," Hank said. "I couldn't stand to lose you." He leaned over to kiss her, but stopped when the doorbell rang.

Jennifer looked at him and shrugged. "I don't know," she said getting up and going to the door.

"Are you all right?" Jerome asked. "I was worried about you." He held a baseball bat in his hand.

"Oh, Jerome," Jennifer cried. "I'm sorry. You must have thought I was crazy. I'm fine. Really, I am."

141

"I've never seen you like that."

"I was upset, but everything's great now. Come on in. I want you to meet someone."

The envelope was no longer on the coffee table.

"Hank, this is Jerome. He's a good friend from across the hall and supplies the occasional cigarette."

"I'm glad to meet you, Jerome."

Jerome shifted the bat to his left hand. "It's nice to meet you. I feel a little silly now . . ." He held the baseball bat up. "But Jennifer seemed so upset."

"I appreciate your concern," Hank said. "I'm glad to know she has a good friend in the building to look out for her."

"Is it all right if I tell him?" Jennifer asked.

"If you don't, I will. I don't want him to think I'm some monster."

"We're going to be married, Jerome."

"Well, that's wonderful. Now I really feel silly. I wanted to be the white knight riding to the rescue."

"It was the cigarette that did it."

"I want to be a bridesmaid," Jerome said. "I'll wear my blue chiffon."

"You can be a bridesmaid, Jerome, but not the blue chiffon."

"He's a big one, isn't he?" Jerome said arching an eyebrow at Jennifer.

"Yes," Jennifer said, "and he's mine."

"I'll give you two cigarettes."

"I'll take one of those cigarettes," Hank said. "If you don't mind."

"I didn't know you smoked," Jennifer said.

"I didn't know you did."

"I'll leave the pack," Jerome said. He took Jennifer in his arms. "I'm so happy for you, sweetie."

"Thank you, Jerome. I am happy. Very happy."

But Jennifer wondered if happiness would betray her, make her complacent, and ultimately destroy her dreams.

TWELVE

Darkness had always been her friend, closing in around her, enveloping and sheltering her in its protective cloak, hiding her from the demons who prowled the unlit alleys and murky corridors of the night—and her mind. Beside her, Hank slept easily, snoring only slightly. His hand rested lightly on her breast. She smiled in the darkness of the bedroom they shared, would now share for the rest of their lives, hoping his dreams were pleasant. But her smile was brief and sleep would not rescue her from somber thoughts and memories. She wanted to dream with him, to become one with him, to merge their senses in a nocturnal fusion of minds and souls, instead of always wandering alone and friendless with the hateful reminders provided by her night track.

Would that not be the truest love of all? To be together always, day and night, sharing everything, knowing everything, protecting one another with their love. But that required honesty, total and complete, with nothing held back. He would see her soul naked and unadorned as he had seen her body. But with cosmetics and frilly decorations, the frailties of her body could be disguised, distracting him. Could she hide her soul? No. Once, the lies were exposed . . . Then, *then,* he would know her for what she truly had been and run from her, taking her fleeting happiness with him.

The aftermath of her bitter and humiliating revelation had been a brief euphoria that came with the knowledge that he would not desert her, that he still wanted her for his wife and mate. Now, with the darkness, that joy and bliss had been all too quickly replaced by the recurring pain and sadness that haunted her memories. The chains and ropes that had once bound her for the camera's unrelenting eye now held her motionless in the bed where her savior slept passively beside her, unable to rescue her. The black night, that old and faithful friend for so long, had turned against her, given her up to the voices of the past.

Sierra prayed beneath the psychedelic posters. She prayed that she wouldn't lose the baby that was growing within her womb. She didn't know what time it was. She didn't know how many days had passed since her husband had beaten her and locked her in the small bedroom they had once shared with love. Stiff, sore, and lacking the will to move, Sierra prayed—and plotted her escape. Her face was swollen and disfigured by black bruises turning yellow and ugly. In the next room, there was laughter and muted voices. Portions of conversations drifted to her, as Jackson and his friends planned their demonstrations against a racist and imperialist government. An explosion. Something was going to explode. A building? Sierra no longer cared. Idealism had been shattered with his first blow. There was nothing left for her but prayer. Please, God, don't let me lose the baby.

Sometime during the night, the rain stopped, leaving behind a wicked chill and a penetrating dampness, but Jennifer had drifted off into troubled sleep and nagging nightmares. As foghorns echoed eerily up and down the coast, others shared the spectral night with Jennifer.

144

The architect's model of Hidden Valley Resort reminded the night security guard of a train set he had received one long-ago Christmas. The model filled the center of the large well-lit lobby of Kendall Enterprises. In another time, it might have been an elaborate electric train layout, the creation of a wealthy and eccentric hobbyist, someone used to creating empires. But this model was static, without the life of miniature trains following their ordained paths through villages, puffing smoke, clattering imperiously through the arms of the rail guards lowering automatically, going into mountains, through tunnels and over bridges, all the while with a master sitting at the controls, tooting the mournful replica of the lonely train whistle.

The model was complete in every detail. The centerpiece was the hotel itself, nestled against green foothills covered with tall pine trees. A long curving driveway was lined with multi-colored flowers and shrubbery. Expensive cars were arriving and departing. There was a large sprawling main building with adjacent wings and walkways leading to secluded and rustic bungalows amidst the pines. There was an olympic size swimming pool and diving area behind the hotel. Small figurines wearing brightly colored bikinis lay on lounge chairs. Another group of figurines stood at the poolside bar. There were couples playing singles and doubles matches on nearby tennis courts. Other couples were just starting out on a trail ride from the hotel's stable. Their horses were sleek, prancing. Two championship golf courses wound through wooded hills and valleys. The greens and fairways would be immaculate if the model was any indication. Dozens of tiny sandtraps guarded the greens and there were immense water hazards. The golf courses, like the swimming pool, were populated with figures of men and women on the tee, on the putting greens, riding golf carts on their approaches. One female figure with pointed breasts was poised on the first tee at the height of a perfect backswing, a red skirt swirling around her long tanned legs. For children, there was a small amusement park with carnival rides and ponies.

Night after night, the security guard stared at the architect's model of Kendall's most ambitious project ever, wishing he could go someplace like that on a vacation. Just once, he thought, I'd like to live like that for awhile. Get me a woman with one of those bikinis. Sit around the pool and drink for awhile and later. Yeah, there'd be a lot of later with a woman like that. Shit, forget it. I don't even know where it is, someplace in Arizona. Hidden Valley, Arizona, a plaque at the front of the model proclaimed. He'd looked for it in his road atlas, but couldn't find it anywhere on the Arizona map.

As he examined the model, something about it bothered him. Something was wrong with the model, the concept. Sometimes he walked around the model, examining every detail. Once he even tried to look up the swirling skirt of the woman golfer on the first tee, wondering idly whether the architect had given her panties to wear. Then, the guard thought he had figured it out. The model was bathed in perpetual sunlight. The sun never set on this model. He turned the lobby lights out and stood there in the darkness looking down at the architect's impression of the resort feeling uncomfortable, like he had disturbed the ordered world of the model, casting it into an apocalyptic gloom. He imagined cries of terror from the little people whose pleasures he had disturbed. The guard ran to the bank of switches and hurriedly threw the lights on again. He was sweating when the lobby was fully lit. He avoided the model for the rest of that night.

It was only after many long nights of circling the model that the guard realized what was wrong. It was so simple. The model made him think of what the world must have looked like before God breathed life into His tiny creations. The model and its people were waiting for Stephen Kendall to breathe life. The guard smiled and chuckled then. Stephen Kendall was just the person to give it life. The son-of-a-bitch thought he was God anyway.

Robert Shaw continued to brood about Jennifer Warren and the man she had been with, the big hulking man in jeans and a thick wool-lined windbreaker. A fucking cowboy from Arizona. Shaw wanted to kill him. And her. The bitch. It had been years since he had felt a jealous rage over a woman. She had turned out to be a whore too. Susie, dear sweet Susie, with her big tits, willing to wrap her long legs around anyone who wore pants and some who didn't, playing with him, fucking him passionately, professing love all the while, and then taunting him finally with her many infidelities. Shaw wondered idly if she had ever had her nose straightened after he had broken it. Susie had a daughter too. Where was Jennifer Warren's daughter? Clea. Shaw hoped she took after her mother and not Holloway. Christ, if she was anything like her mother, she'd be a heart breaker. God damn that woman.

The letter still mocked Jackson Holloway, even after two weeks. Thank you for your application, it read. Your application will be kept on file and you will be notified if a suitable vacancy occurs, it read. The sons-of-bitches. After three months of telephone calls and reassurances that everything was proceeding normally, he received a fucking form letter, not even a telephone call from the man. Now, Holloway's calls went unanswered. After all he had done for the man. He had promised the appointment, God damn it!

It was the background check. It had to be. The FBI had found something in the past. But there were no traces left, nothing to be discovered after twenty years. He had made sure of that. Except for her. It had to be her. Somehow, the FBI had found her and she had talked. The bitch. Shaw. He should have found her and then none of this would have happened. God damn Shaw anyway. All this time and he's still working on it. Well, he better find her. And soon. Time was running out for Shaw and the bitch. He took a yellow legal pad and began composing an ad for the personal columns.

THIRTEEN

Like a bad dream, the storm had passed through during the night. Dawn glowed faintly at the horizon, outlining distant dark mountains with a faint pink border, as though timidly peering over mountaintops, ensuring the anger of the furious storm had abated before venturing further. To the east, over the California and Arizona deserts, the sun still battled the storm, its soft rays retreating before the raging onslaught. But in the vast Los Angeles basin, the storm had left the early morning cleansed beneath a shining sun that edged higher, slowly warming the brisk and clear morning. Bright blue skies matched the ocean's icy crystalline surface and the ragged edge of the water was marked by a gentle surf breaking on the newly washed sands of the beaches. It seemed as though nature, her aggressions finally spent, was in a forgiving mood after punishing man's transgressions.

Oscar crawled from beneath the covers where he had slept in a tight ball at Jennifer's feet. His furry whiskered snout emerged and his large yellow eyes looked quizzically at Jennifer. He put his paw forward to rest delicately on Jennifer's arm. He meowed once.

"Hungry, babe?" Jennifer whispered.

Another soft cry. A second paw snaked forward. The large eyes stared at her.

"In a minute."

She looked at Hank. He was turned away from her, brown hair rumpled in wild tangles. He's going to be my husband, Jennifer remembered. The reality of it amazed her and filled her with serenity. He truly did not care about the past. Still, she regretted not telling him everything last night when the opportunity was right. Now it was too late. But perhaps she would never have to tell him. Perhaps God would be kind to her this time. She eased quietly from the bed so as not to disturb him and slipped into her robe. Hank did not stir, breathing regularly, sleeping undisturbed by his dreams.

Oscar followed her into the kitchen and danced around her feet while she put the coffee on to brew. He twirled in ecstasy at the whir of the electric opener and when Jennifer put the bowl of mixed grill on the floor, he attacked it, growling happily.

"I hope Hank's as easy to please as you. I haven't told him I'm not a very good cook." She went to the front door and retrieved the morning newspaper from the hallway.

Jennifer took the half-filled coffee pot from beneath the spout, replacing it with her cup, waiting impatiently until the cup filled with a couple of inches of the hot black life-giving liquid. She sipped the coffee and, as she had done ever since that first message so long ago, opened the newspaper to the classifieds first. She skimmed down the personal column and sighed gratefully when there was nothing addressed to Kathleen. Jennifer hated looking at the personal column and not just because of the instant fear provoked by one of his hate-filled messages. It wasn't just the personals, although they were depressing enough. The front page of the classifieds was filled with all the sadness and tragedy of the human condition. Each morning, Jennifer was drawn to the agony. She could not escape it. It was another of his legacies to her.

Contestants were always needed for game shows, promising huge sums of money and prizes for the bright, the bubbling, the effervescent. There were multitudes of lost dogs and cats. Collectors wanted Barbie dolls and Elvis Presley memorabilia. Someone was searching for the beautiful blonde vision encountered and lost in a supermarket line. Lonely people sought companionship and pen pals. SWF, fortyish, seeks adventure with SWM. There were numbers for Asians and Latins and Pacific Islanders to call for introductions. Other ads promised happiness for the overweight, for Christians, for Gays. Ads thanked St. Jude for "prayers answered." A brochure promised the truth about homosexuality. Another ad said that Jesus would return in October. Marry today without a blood test. There were ads for cheap divorces and bankruptcies, cable descramblers and free Bibles, the depressed and the anxiety-ridden, health insurance and credit repair, concert tickets and loans, dream fulfillment and background checks for future spouses. The front page of the classifieds and the personal columns were always a litany of human misery. They were also filled with the solutions for the endless catalog of travail. One stop shopping to earn money, control weight, smoking, pain, depression, alcohol, drugs—all in a free session of mind control.

Jennifer looked back at the private investigator's ad. Very discreet. Very professional. Call 24 hours. Jennifer wondered if the licensed P.I. could find the traces of her trail, knowing the care she had taken to disappear completely, changing names, living quietly in obscurity and anonymity for so many years. Despite her many elaborate steps, Jennifer did not feel secure, not while Jack was out there waiting, feeding on his hatred of her and Clea. Perhaps he already knew where she lived and was only toying with her, waiting for the precise moment that would destroy her happiness most completely. Despite the passage of time, Jennifer still

151

shared a kinship with Jackson Holloway. There were moments—often months, sometimes years apart—when his voice, his overwhelming presence drifted to her across the chasm. When Jennifer felt that strange power transfixed on her, she dreaded the morning more and more with each passing day, forcing herself to go for the newspaper, opening it with apprehension and uneasiness. She knew when another message would come, not precisely, but she knew when his rage was building and she turned to the personals each day, knowing that it would appear soon. Jennifer knew for a certainty that another personal would be addressed to her soon. There had been nothing since before Christmas and she knew that Jack would sense her happiness and seek to destroy it once more. When that feeling came over her, she was rarely disappointed and always filled with fear when she saw her name of old. Kathleen: I hate you. Let me count the ways. I hate you. I hate you. I'm going to kill you. Bitch. Cunt. Whore. I hate you.

And then the brewer hissed and spat and the coffee was done finally. Jennifer put the classified section aside and filled her cup and another for Hank. She started for the bedroom and then stopped. What if he's changed his mind? What if he has buyer's remorse? Reluctantly now, she went into the bedroom, wishing that she had left the newspaper lying on the corridor floor. It was such a depressing way to start every morning of your life.

Jennifer sat on the edge of the bed next to Hank and put his coffee on the bedside stand. Reaching out hesitantly, she touched his shoulder, stroking it gently until his eyes opened.

He looked up at her and smiled. "I love you," he said.

Jennifer felt the relief flood through her. "Still?"

"Always."

"No regrets?"

"None. You?"

152

"No. I'm very happy," Jennifer said. Now, she thought. Now, I'm happy. At last.

"You know what we should do," Hank said. He sat up in bed.

"No, what should we do?" She reached out and stroked the tangle of graying hairs on his massive chest.

"Let's go to Las Vegas and get married," Hank said. "Right now."

"We can't do that, silly."

"Why not? What's to stop us? We can be there in what? Five, six hours? We don't have anybody in particular to come to the wedding. It's not like we're overrun with family and friends."

"What about Clea? I'd like her to be at my wedding. If she'll come."

"We'll call her. Tell her to get on a plane. Come on. What do you say?"

"Let's wait, Hank. There's no hurry. We have all the time in the world. I want to enjoy this wedding."

"What was your other one like?"

"I was a child . . ."

It was warm in the meadow high in the Berkeley hills. Across the bay, San Francisco was white and gleaming. The child bride was beautiful and barefoot. She wore white, a simple long dress. There was a garland of fresh flowers adorning her hair. Her voice was strong and clear, carrying across the meadow, as she recited the simple words of the vow she had written. "I, Kathleen, pledge my undying love and devotion to you, Jackson, my friend, helpmate, and husband, now and for all the days and nights to come."

". . . a young and foolish child," Jennifer said.

"And now?"

Jennifer smiled. "I feel like a girl again, with my whole life before me. A wonderful life, with a wonderful man."

"I guess I can wait then," Hank said.

"I'm worth it," Jennifer said with a lightness she did

153

not truly feel. Will you still love me when you know everything?

The tires on Hank's truck were slashed.

"The son-of-a-bitch," Hank said quietly. He looked at Jennifer. "Things like this happen a lot around here?" he asked.

"Occasionally," Jennifer said. "Probably some gang, or one of the homeless making a statement on society. Saw your Arizona plates and wanted to welcome you to California." Jennifer was not as confident as she hoped she sounded for Hank. What if this was a warning to her? But it couldn't be. It had to be one of those random, senseless occurrences that came with a society in agonized turmoil, an individual or two or three lashing out in violent despair. It happened all too often. The newspaper headlines and the television newscasts were as grim as the classified section.

". . . Sacred Heart of Jesus, have mercy on us, St. Jude, worker of miracles, pray for us St. Jude, help of the hopeless, pray for us.

"Say this prayer 9 times a day, by the 8th day your prayers will be answered. It has never been known to fail."

"City life," Hank said. He poked at a tire with the toe of a boot. "I don't suppose I could shoot them if I catch them."

"Not a good move," Jennifer replied. "Besides, if it was a gang, they'd shoot back. I don't want to lose you now." She squeezed his hand. "I'll go in and call the auto club."

Robert Shaw watched from two blocks away as the tow truck arrived. He still regretted the loss of the knife. The blade had snapped on the last tire. But his friend on the police department would get him another switchblade, a dozen if he wanted them. Still, it had been a good knife. Shaw stirred uncomfortably in the cramped seat of his wife's Corvette. He was sorry now he'd insisted on trading cars for the day. Darlene hadn't been happy about it either, but he didn't want the Cadillac sitting in the neighborhood again. Someone might notice. It was a small risk, but unacceptable. It was always the small risks that fucked you up. Down the street, the cowboy kicked one of the tires again in frustration, anger. Shaw laughed. "Fuck you, cowboy."

Shaw followed when the cowboy and Jennifer climbed into the cab of the tow truck. Shaw waited while new tires were put on the truck. He followed when the cowboy drove to the Santa Monica Police Station. He waited, unconcerned, while the cowboy and Jennifer were inside. They were making a police report for insurance purposes. The cops were too busy to respond to a vandalism complaint. Shaw followed when the cowboy and Jennifer took the Santa Monica Freeway to the interchange with the San Diego Freeway and headed south. "Shit," he said. "I could have waited for them to come to me."

Going to Newport Beach made Jennifer nervous. She knew that Jackson Holloway lived there. But Hank wanted to see Kendall Enterprises. "Make a little reconnaissance," he said. "See the enemy on his home territory." So Jennifer acquiesced hesitantly, telling herself that she had nothing to worry about, that her fears were groundless. Any chance of suddenly colliding with Jackson was extremely remote. Still, she worried, and grew increasingly anxious as they neared the luxurious beach community.

Driving down Pacific Coast Highway, Hank passed a white limousine. The dark smoked windows hid the passengers. Jennifer averted her face. He might be in

155

the limousine, staring up at her. The limo turned slowly into the Bay Club entrance. Jennifer sighed with relief. And then another white limo appeared suddenly and again she turned away from the dark evil windows that might hide Jackson Holloway. She felt naked and exposed. She wanted to hide on the floor. Curl up out of sight of the prying eyes. The limo continued serenely down Pacific Coast Highway.

Jennifer took a deep breath and tried to relax. Only once in all her years in Los Angeles had she seen an acquaintance on the crowded freeways. And that person had not seen her, passing her several lanes away. There were too many cars on the freeways and streets of the greater metropolitan Los Angeles area. Humanity had massed—eight million, ten million, and growing larger every day—in L.A. where they were swallowed by sheer size and magnitude, to live anonymously as they plodded through daily routines, never looking right or left. It was not a small town like San Francisco was still a small town with distinct neighborhoods and individual communities where long-time residents lived and shopped and worked among neighbors. That was why Jennifer had chosen Los Angeles so many years before. She could disappear into the smog with Clea, to be devoured whole by the murky gargantuan.

"Pray for me, St. Jude," Jennifer whispered, her lips scarcely moving. "St. Jude, help of the hopeless, pray for me."

"Are we getting close?" Hank asked.

"Follow the signs to Fashion Island," Jennifer replied, interrupting the prayer she'd read in the newspaper. "We'll turn left."

Hank slowed as they passed an auto dealership. The lot was filled with luxury cars—Corvettes, Porsches, Ferraris. "Lots of big money down here," he commented.

"Very big money," Jennifer said. "And very big power."

156

"I don't know which irritates me the most," Hank said, "the money or the power. I guess it doesn't really matter. Either way, Kendall thinks he can come in and buy Hidden Valley. Do what he wants with it."

"This is a bad idea, Hank. There's nothing we can do here," Jennifer said.

"I just want to see what his operation looks like. I'm not going to barge into his office and threaten him or beg him not to destroy the Valley. I just want to see where the bastard hangs out."

They passed a country club on the left and then followed a wide palm-lined avenue into the complex known as Fashion Island. The lawns were well-kept and manicured. The shopping complex—with its Neiman Marcus and Brooks Brothers and Bullock's Wilshire—that formed the island was surrounded by modern office buildings that housed developers, huge land owners, financial organizations, presidential political consultants, and Kendall Enterprises. The Irvine Company, modern heir to one of the largest of the old Spanish land grants, had its offices in one of the buildings.

They circled Fashion Island until Hank spotted a modest sign identifying Kendall Enterprises and pulled into the underground parking lot. Following Hank reluctantly to the elevator, Jennifer sought the shadows and was thankful that the elevator and the lobby were empty except for a receptionist seated at a desk. A huge model dominated the brightly-lit lobby.

"May I help you," the young woman said, smiling at Hank.

"No thanks," Hank said. "Just wanted to take a look at this model."

"We're very proud of it," the receptionist said, leaving her desk to join them. "It's the largest project we've ever done here at Kendall Enterprises." She handed him a brochure.

"Yes, I'll bet you are proud," Hank replied, taking

157

the large and slick color brochure, walking around the model.

Jennifer felt faint, but forced herself to smile at the receptionist. She felt exposed again, like a frightened animal trapped in the poaching light of the hunter. She felt the crosshairs of his rifle centered on her body. St. Jude, help of the hopeless . . . An elevator door opened and several men in suits entered the lobby. Jennifer turned aside to study the hotel model, hoping they would not stop. She felt their eyes staring at her back. Was Jackson with them? The men left the building engrossed in a conversation about financing for a project.

Jennifer tried to concentrate on the model in front of her, imagine herself as one of the tiny figurines playing tennis with her skirt swirling or walking a long green fairway without care, without the haunting memories and the fear that had been her constant companion for so many years. Jackson Holloway had deprived her of normalcy. She had done nothing that could be considered usual for a woman of her age. She was without husband for herself or father for Clea. Instead of playing tennis or golf, serving in the PTA, attending concerts, going to parties, socializing with others, her life had been sequestered between home and office, always hiding, always looking over her shoulder for Jackson, a shallow existence spent working, reading, and replaying the night track of an empty life. Instead of proudly attending her daughter's high school graduation, Jennifer suffered when Clea had chosen to ignore the ceremonies, running away from her mother as quickly as possible. Jennifer wondered if the breach between them could ever be bridged by healing words. Was it too late? Had it always been too late? Would Clea come to the wedding?

Jennifer looked across the model at Hank. He was listening intently as the receptionist chattered knowledgeably about developer fees, sales tax revenues, and creating 500 local jobs and several million dollars a year in local revenues with the resort hotel. Hank nodded pleasantly, smiling with each new fact revealed, easily disguising his hatred of the project. Doubt entered Jennifer's mind. Was he disguising his true feelings about her. Was he going to be like the other men who had come into her life, professed love for a time, and then left shouting hateful obscenities at her? Was he another Bennett Cameron? He couldn't be, not Hank, not dear gentle Hank. It was impossible. He could not fool her that much. But Jackson had deceived her, leading her into the Age of Aquarius with promises of everlasting love and turning against her with an implacable hatred that had festered now for two decades. How would it end finally? Would it ever end?

"It's a championship golf course," the receptionist told Hank, parroting the advertising platitudes of the brochure, "and will be designed by Jack Nicklaus. Do you play golf?"

Jennifer looked down once more at the vast model, designed as a retreat for the wealthy and the privileged, the people like Jackson. Jennifer was suddenly nauseous. "Is there a rest room?" she interrupted.

"To the left of the elevators."

In the rest room, Jennifer put her purse carefully on the counter next to the gleaming porcelain sink. She took a paper towel from the dispenser and let cold water saturate it before squeezing the moisture out and holding the damp towel to her forehead. Although she closed her eyes, the model of the hotel was vivid in her mind. It seemed that Kendall Enterprises had entered the conspiracy against her. Hidden Valley, so aptly named for her hideaway, would fill with strangers. The freedom she knew only in the Valley would disappear with the first bull dozers rumbling and growling as they cut into the earth, razing trees, destroying the natural contours of the land, rearranging the defenseless land to suit one man's greedy vision. What will we do then?

When Jennifer left the rest room, she stopped to ensure that Jackson Holloway had not entered the lobby during her absence. Hank and the receptionist were alone.

Hank turned to Jennifer at the sound of her soft footsteps crossing the tiled floor. "I'm ready, if you are," he said.

Thank God. Jennifer nodded and turned immediately for the elevator.

"We're taking reservations for the opening week," the receptionist said brightly, hopefully. "It's going to be quite an event."

"No, thanks," Hank said. "That's still three years away. Too far in advance for us. A lot of things can happen between now and then. But thanks for the offer. We'll sure keep it in mind."

Jennifer climbed into the truck and leaned back against the seat. She sighed with relief.

"You know what I'd like to do now?" Hank said.

Anything. Just get me out of here. "Las Vegas again?"

"Nope. Something even better. Well, at least for the moment."

"What's that, cowboy?"

"Let's drive on up the beach aways. Get away from all this and stop, get a chili dog, go for a walk along the water. Always wanted to kiss a pretty girl with the waves pounding away. Just like Burt Lancaster and Deborah Kerr in *From Here to Eternity.*"

"Got anyone in mind?"

"Oh, yeah."

"That water looks pretty, but it's damned cold. You're not rolling me around in it."

"That's the trouble with you, darling. Got no sense of adventure."

I've had enough adventure today, Jennifer thought.

160

"All right," she said, "let's go ravish me on the beach."

Jennifer calmed once they were away from Newport Beach. They stopped in Huntington Beach and, while Jennifer ordered hot dogs and french fries, Hank dashed into a liquor store and bought a six pack of beer. Further north, they parked in a nearly deserted lot and ate in the truck. Then, they each took a can of beer and strolled across a wide expanse of sand to the water's edge. A gull swooped, circled and landed, waddling up to them, screeching for a handout. Hank tossed a french fry. The bird grabbed it from the sand with its beak and flew away.

"How'd you know to save a french fry?" Jennifer asked.

"Always keep a little something for a stray dog."

"Or bird?"

"You never know when a bird'll stop by needing a little something."

"You're strange," Jennifer said, "but I love you very much."

The beach was nearly secluded. A few dark spots, surfers in their black wet suits, bobbed and danced off shore, waiting for the perfect wave. At the horizon, an oil tanker slowly sailed north toward the Long Beach or Los Angeles ports. Closer in, there was a lone sailboat with sails standing full. In the distance along the beach, a dog crashed into the surf chasing after something thrown by its master. Santa Catalina stood out in the clear day, the two segments of the island appearing like a broken-backed whale. To the north, they could see Long Beach and the Palos Verdes Peninsula and beyond to Santa Monica and Malibu. In the other direction was Newport and Laguna and Dana Point. Jennifer turned her back on Newport and walked slowly along the water's edge, sipping beer, dancing away as rivulets of the cold salty water, the residue of waves, their energy spent, reached for her feet with a last dying grasp.

Hank caught up with her and took her hand. "It's nice out here. Peaceful."

"It's lovely."

Hank held his beer can up. "Here's to us," he said. Jennifer clinked her can against his. "To us."

They walked on, quietly. Jennifer tugged her windbreaker tight against a chilly breeze. "Will we always be this happy, Bear?" she asked suddenly.

"Always," he replied.

"Promise?"

"I promise."

Jennifer smiled. "Will you ravish me now?"

"I'm horny, but I'm no fool. It's cold out here, woman."

"I can warm you up."

"You always do." He put his arm around her shoulders as they walked. "What took us so long to get together, Jenny?"

"I don't know. The time wasn't right, I guess."

"But it is now."

"Oh, yes."

A flight of gulls flew overhead as Hank took her in his arms and they kissed.

The couple stood out sharp and clear in the telephoto lens. His hand slipped beneath her jacket to fondle her breast. Shaw swore jealously as he snapped the picture. "You fucking whore." He took additional pictures as they walked hand in hand back to the pickup truck with the brand new tires. Then he put the camera on the seat next to him and started the Corvette, made a tight circle, and drove south on PCH. "Let's go see what you were doing at Fashion Island," Shaw said.

* * *

Jennifer let the telephone ring for a long time. Finally, just as she was about to hang up, Clea answered breathlessly.

"Hello?"

"Clea, it's Mom."

"Mom, hi. I just got in and couldn't get the damn key to work in the lock. I hate that. It seems like every time the phone rings I'm on the other side of the damned door. How are you?"

Hank was next to Jennifer on the couch. She squeezed his hand nervously. "I'm fine," she told Clea.

"Where are you?"

"At home. How have you been, honey?"

"Oh, fine, busy." Clea paused. "I've got some news."

"What's that?"

"I'm tired of being a waitress. I'll have fallen arches before I'm twenty-one. So I'm going back to school in the fall. I've already sent in the application and everything."

"Clea, that's terrific. You know I'm pleased."

"Yeah, I know. But please don't make a big deal out of it or anything. You know I hate that."

"I won't, but if you want any help . . ."

"I know, Mom, thanks."

"I have some news too," Jennifer said. "I'm getting married."

"You're what?" Clea exclaimed. "Really?"

"Yes, really," Jennifer said, smiling at Hank, holding his hand for reassurance.

"Tell me everything. Wait, it's not that last creep you were dating. The young stud?"

Jennifer laughed. "No, this is an old stud. It's Hank."

"Bear?" Clea shouted. "Big old Bear."

"The very same."

"Mom, that's terrific. I think it's really great."

"We want you to come to the wedding. Will you?"

"Of course, I will," Clea said. "I wouldn't miss it for

163

anything. When is it?"

"We don't know yet. Sometime this spring probably. I'll let you know as soon as we set a date."

"Mom?"

"Yes, honey?"

"Mom, I hope you'll be very happy," Clea said. "You deserve it."

FOURTEEN

Robert Shaw's jealousy grew as he followed the lovers, watching them cling to each other, embrace, kiss, stroll along holding hands. For a week, he followed them through shopping malls as they window-shopped or browsed through bookstores, to restaurants where he waited outside, fuming and raging at Jennifer Warren's infidelity, to a real estate office where he waited for more than two hours before they emerged. Once, he stood boldly in line behind them at a complex of six movie theaters, purchasing a ticket to the same film, and sat three rows behind them, agonizing as they touched briefly, whispering to each other. She was an enchantress, a diabolic witch, who dressed provocatively, seducing him with her every movement, the sway of her hips, the swell of her breast, a casual tossing of her hair, the bright, adoring gleam in her eyes as she looked at the fucking cowboy.

He knew the cowboy's name now. A friend in Phoenix had traced the license plate on the pickup truck. Registered to Henry Moore at a rural route number in Hidden Valley, someplace way to hell and gone where some fool of a developer planned a resort hotel. That much he had learned from the developer's receptionist. He wondered how Jennifer Warren had ever met the guy, living in some place like that.

165

The nights were the worst. Shaw parked outside the condominium, staring up at the lighted window behind her balcony, watching as they stood looking out at the lights and the dark ocean, watching as they kissed, dying inwardly as they went inside, extinguishing the lights. In his mind, he saw the whore wrapping her legs around her lover, heard her cries and whimpers and moans of pleasure, and despised her, wanting her all the while for his own. Violent fantasies flared vividly then as Shaw imagined what he would do to her once she belonged to him. But it was her choice. She could have it either way. He would be a kind lover or . . . The bitch liked to be tied up. Just look at those pictures. She liked it. Jennifer, he pleaded, I love you.

One evening before returning home, Shaw stopped at a hardware store and bought a coil of braided rope and then went back to sit in his study tying and untying knots as he looked at the pictures of the woman he loved. Engrossed, Shaw didn't hear his wife enter the house. He thought she was out for the evening with a friend. Suddenly, Darlene was next to his desk looking down at Jennifer Warren.

"What's all this?" she asked.

Embarrassed, Shaw fumbled with the rope, trying to hide it beneath the desk.

Darlene turned over a photograph to look at the next. "Stunning," she said, "if you like that sort of thing."

"A woman I'm looking for."

Darlene raised her eyebrows. "For yourself?"

"Of course not," Shaw said. "She's someone who disappeared twenty years ago."

"And now Jackson wants her back?"

"You don't know anything about this, Darlene," he warned. "He's crazy sometimes. Just forget about these." Shaw closed the folder. "Forget about the woman."

"Have you found her?"

"Not yet," Shaw lied, putting her off just as he had done with Jackson Holloway almost every day for weeks now. "I don't know if I want to find her."

Darlene stood behind her husband and rubbed his shoulders. "I wish you'd quit working for him. It's not worth it."

"He pays well."

"I don't like him. He's evil."

"That feels good."

"Why don't you come to bed? I'll relax you." At the door, she turned and smiled. "Bring the rope if you want."

Feeling foolish now, Shaw tossed the rope aside and followed his wife to make love to her while he thought of Jennifer Warren.

His obsession, momentarily satiated by sex and guilt, returned as soon as Shaw watched Jennifer walk from the building the next morning. She had a distinctive walk, feminine and enticing to the male. The cowboy walked with his hand possessively on her hip, broadcasting familiarity with his woman's body. And Shaw was instantly filled with jealousy again. "God damn that woman," he said, tightening his grip on the steering wheel.

The memory of Darlene's efforts to please him and her frantic cries of pleasure faded as Shaw watched Jennifer climb into the pickup. Robert Shaw wished he had never seen or heard of Jennifer Warren. But he wanted her for his own.

Jackson Holloway was in his most dangerous state. Shaw recognized the ominous mood immediately. When Holloway blustered angrily, stormed around the room, swearing and shouting demands, he could be controlled, easily maneuvered. But when he sat calmly behind his desk in the large study overlooking Newport Bay, scarcely speaking, staring with cold, unemotional eyes, he was menacing.

"Where is she?" Holloway asked.

"I don't know, Jackson."

"You've had months."

"She's been missing for two decades," Shaw said.

Holloway waited.

Shaw resisted the urge to continue speaking. Talking got you into trouble. He had seen Holloway use his silence as a weapon before, waiting until an aide, unnerved by the quiet malevolence, started babbling, eventually saying something that Holloway could target for a relentless attack.

Shaw waited, but he was beginning to sweat. The room was too hot, he told himself. The bastard does it deliberately.

Holloway waited.

The silence in the room was unbearable.

Shaw concentrated on maintaining a calm, unconcerned demeanor. Fuck it, he thought, no woman's worth this. Not Jennifer Warren or Sierra or Kathleen or whatever she calls herself. Raquel fucking Welch isn't worth this. Give her up. Let the bastard have her. Darlene isn't so bad. She's still a good looking woman. Takes care of herself. Loves you. Who's Jennifer Warren anyway? Some bimbo Jackson wants. Let him do what he wants with her. Get out of it. Let him have her. Now. Can't do it now. He'll know I've been lying to him. In a day or two. Make a phone call. Jackson, I've got her. Here's her address. See ya. Take Darlene to Bermuda for a few days. Get away from the son-of-a-bitch. Do a disappearing act of my own. No wonder she ran away from him. Can't blame her for that.

"I have a new pet," Jackson Holloway said.

I did it, Shaw thought triumphantly. I outwaited the bastard. "Oh," he said cautiously.

"Yes," Holloway said. "Cute little thing." He reached down and brought a covered carrying case to the polished desk top.

What the hell's he got? Hamsters? Fucking bunny rabbit?

Holloway removed the cover dramatically.

The chilling rattle filled the room. The snake was coiled in a corner of the glass cage.

Shaw leaped to his feet. "Jesus fucking Christ, Jackson!"

Holloway leaned back in his chair and laughed. "Why, Robert, I do believe you're afraid of Clarence."

"This isn't funny, Jackson. I hate snakes."

"He can't get out. Besides, he's certainly more afraid of you than you are of him."

"I doubt that. Look at the fucker."

The rattlesnake was small, no more than eighteen inches long. Sand covered the bottom of the cage. A wire mesh covered the top of the cage. Again, the snake sent its warning echoing through the room. Shaw saw the tiny fangs extend as the snake opened its mouth.

"His name is Clarence, Robert. He's a sidewinder. He'll never get any bigger than this. And his bite isn't really deadly. Oh, I suppose if he got you in the right spot, and if you went untreated, I guess you could die."

"I almost died when you opened that up."

Holloway smiled. "Go back to sleep, Clarence." He replaced the cover and put the cage back on the floor.

"Don't do that to me again. I almost had a heart attack."

"Rattlesnakes are very interesting," Holloway said. "I've been reading up on them. Did you know that they are only found in the Americas?"

"That's enough to make you want to move to Europe."

"Like you, Robert, man thinks of the rattlesnake as an enemy and kills a great many each year, particularly on highways."

169

"That's good," Shaw said.

Holloway smiled. "The rattler has a great many other enemies, as well. Other snakes, coyotes, foxes, wildcats, badgers, hawks, even the funny little roadrunner, all prey on rattlesnakes."

"I feel sorry for them."

"You should, Robert, you should. How is Darlene?"

Jesus, he's off the wall today. "Darlene's fine."

"That's nice. She's a wonderful woman. Always so gracious."

And she hates your fucking guts. "Yes, she is," Shaw said.

"We go back a long ways together, Robert. We each know some things about the other. That makes for a good working relationship, doesn't it? Keeps everyone honest. I've had the feeling you've been avoiding me lately. Have you been avoiding me, Robert?"

"Of course not. It just didn't seem worthwhile wasting your time until I had something tangible to report. I've been making some progress, I think."

"Good. You will find her for me, won't you?"

"If she's still alive, I'll find her."

"Oh, she's alive. I feel that very strongly. Yes, she is most certainly alive. For the moment. Go and find her for me."

"I said I'd find her." Shaw stood.

"And stay in touch."

"Oh, I will."

After Shaw left the study, another man entered. He was young and tall, very muscular. He worked out with weights frequently and liked to wear tailored shirts that were stretched taut across his chest.

"Well?" Holloway asked.

"He's lying."

"Perhaps," Holloway said. "We'll give him a little more time."

170

Badly shaken by the rattlesnake named Clarence, Robert Shaw went back to following the lovers. That Holloway motherfucker is one crazy dude, he thought. At least, you've got a few more days, Shaw told Jennifer Warren.

FIFTEEN

Jennifer awakened, cold and lonely in her bed, reaching out to where Hank should have been, but he was gone now. He had left that day, driving back to Arizona. Already, she missed him terribly. She had cried after watching him drive down the street, waving until he turned the corner and was out of sight. She had cried again after his call to let her know that he had arrived home safely. Jennifer wondered if he missed her as much. She flipped on the bedside lamp and went to the wall thermostat and turned the heat higher, running back to bed, drawing the covers close, shivering in the vast emptiness of her bed. Oh, Hank, I wish you were here. I was never cold when you were sleeping beside me. I wish you were here to hold me and love me. Are you cold, my darling, with nothing but photographs to remind you of me?

Shyly, oh so shyly, and blushing, Hank had asked to take a photograph or two home with him. Trembling, she gave him all of the photographs. He answered her question before she could ask.

"Because I love you," he said. "Because I find the photographs incredibly erotic. And because you were posing for me, although you didn't know it. If I were an artist, I would want only you for my model. If I were a photographer, all of the film in the world would not be

172

enough to capture your beauty. And, if I were a writer, I would describe you endlessly, always weeping because my words were so inadequate. Someday, I will build a private gallery and frame your beauty. We will grow old together and remember how we were."

"Oh, Bear," Jennifer said, offering the photographs to him.

Sometimes now when Hank made love to her, he pinned her wrists to the bed, holding her with a gentle pressure, never hurting her. Jennifer always gave herself up to him in that moment, enjoying the pleasurable sensation of his mastery. He played her body as she played the violin, drawing one passionate response from her after another until she grew weak and thought she could not endure another tingling excitement. Did he find the old photographs of her body wrapped in ropes and chains exciting? Did he want to tie her before making love to her? She didn't care. I'll do anything for you, darling, if only you love me as I love you.

Arthur, who loved her but didn't yet acknowledge his homosexuality, was always kind and considerate. His ropes were ivory white, soft and silken, and he never tied her tightly and only after he was satisfied with the lighting. Sierra sat on the tall kitchen stool, carefully placed against the black curtain that served as a backdrop in his makeshift studio, watching as he selected several lengths of rope. This afternoon, she wore boots and the long brown corduroy skirt, but she was nude to the waist. It was cold outside, but the lights and the space heater warmed her. When Arthur approached, Sierra obediently placed her hands behind her back, allowing him to begin circling her wrists with strand after strand. Although the ropes were not tight, Sierra felt a prisoner when he had finished. And then he knelt before her. She lifted her legs while he placed the ropes carefully around her knees and then her ankles. "The kinky old bastards like to see a lot of rope," he had explained to her the first time he photographed her. Sierra didn't care now, shutting her mind to everything but the money Arthur paid her, the money that allowed her to survive, allowed her to pay rent, buy food and warm baby clothing for Clea. Nothing else mattered.

Not until now. Jennifer thought of Hank looking at the photos two decades later, telling her she was a model that any artist would feel compelled to paint or photograph, until finally her embarrassment eased and she began to believe him. He helped put those demons to rest in the deepest recesses of her mind. You're wonderful, darling. Dress me in chains and ropes, if you want, darling. I'll be your little sex slave. God, you turn me on. God, I miss you and want you. If only he could help with the rest, but no one could do that. Who could erase conspiracy, murder?

"I'd like to try something a little different today," Arthur said. "Do you mind?"

Sierra felt a moment of panic, tugging at her bound wrists. The rope did not give. She was helpless.

"What?"

"I'd like to place a rope around your breasts," Arthur said. He was blushing. "I'll try not to touch you too much. I've been thinking about it. If you just lean forward a little, I think I could do it without touching you at all. I'd pay extra."

I could get a stroller for Clea. She's getting so heavy. *Sierra nodded.*

Later, looking down at the single strand of rope that encircled each breast with its erect nipple, and criss-crossed her chest, Sierra saw the powerful eroticism the photograph would have. Sierra closed her eyes as Arthur shot an entire roll of film.

He untied her hands and gave her the bulky knit sweater. Sierra slipped it over her head gratefully as Arthur knelt in front of her again, unfastening the knots that held her knees and ankles together. Sierra rubbed her wrists. Despite his care with the ropes, there were tiny indentations in her delicate flesh. She rubbed them softly. The ligatures would disappear quickly.

When she was free, Sierra checked Clea. Her baby was awake, cooing, reaching for her. Sierra picked her up, uncovered her breast, and let Clea nurse.

Sometimes, Sierra waited while Arthur developed the film, watching as her images appeared, dancing and shimmering in the trays filled with liquid. "Beautiful," Arthur always said. "Beautiful."

Hank thinks I was beautiful then. He thinks I'm still beautiful. Again, Jennifer turned on the bedside lamp, took the telephone and quickly pressed the numbers.

"I'm sorry to wake you," she said when Hank answered, "but I couldn't sleep. I've just been lying here thinking of you and I wanted to hear your voice again."

"I'm glad you called, darling. I miss you very much."

"I've decided something," Jennifer said, although she had not made a conscious decision until the words left her mouth.

"And what have you decided in the middle of the night?"

"I don't want to be away from you any longer than I have to. I'm going to give three months notice. I have to give Leo at least that much time. I'll start closing things down here. The realtor has already listed the condo. The sign is already up. By May, I'll be able to leave one way or another. Is that all right with you?"

There was silence. Oh, God, he hasn't changed his mind? "Hank?"

"I was just thinking about a honeymoon. Where would you like to go?"

"Oh, I don't care. Someplace romantic. We don't have to go anywhere. As long as we're together."

"We'll get married in May," Hank said. "How about the Red Light Motel in Nogales."

"Nogales would be fine. But Oscar can't go. He doesn't speak Spanish."

"How about Paris? I've always wanted to walk along

the Seine holding hands with a beautiful woman."

"Paris would be lovely. Can we drink wine in a sidewalk cafe?"

"Whenever we're not in bed, we'll be in a sidewalk cafe."

"Promise?"

"Bed or cafe?"

"Both."

"Both it is."

"Oh, Hank," Jennifer said softly.

"I know, darling. We're going to spend the rest of our lives together."

"Isn't that a nice thought?"

Jennifer called Leo Fowler's private line, but there was no answer. It was too early for a partner to be in his office, even a hard-working partner like Leo. She hung up and called his voice mail instead. "Leo, this is Jennifer, I'd like to see you, this morning if possible. It's important." She hung up a second time and stared at the files on her desk. My God, I'll never be able to get out of here in three months. But I will. Somehow. She took one of the files and opened it.

Robert Shaw made the connection with the for sale sign immediately. That's why they were in that real estate office. She was going to Arizona with the fucking Cowboy. Christ, I've got to stop this. Tell Holloway what I've got and get out. Except Holloway won't let me out. Not now. Not ever. We're asshole buddies. Too much has happened to get out. Too many dirty little jobs for Holloway. Ask for Marcie, the sign read. Shaw called the number on his cellular phone and asked to speak with Marcie.

*   *   *

176

"I have meetings until lunch, Jennifer. Can it wait until then?"

"Sure, Leo. I'll even buy."

"Japanese, I'll bet."

"What else?"

Marcie Coleman was eager to please. She left her office immediately to meet the man who introduced himself as Clarence Thompson and talked non-stop as she dialed the combination into the lockbox attached to a railing outside the building. "This property just went on the market," she said. "It's a real steal and it won't last long. Two bedrooms and a den. Great location. Quiet neighborhood. Good schools. An ocean view. Easy access to freeways. It speaks for itself."

As he memorized the lockbox combination, Shaw wondered why Marcie didn't shut up if the condominium spoke for itself.

"There we are," Marcie said brightly as the lockbox popped open and she removed two keys, leaving the lockbox open. She smiled at Shaw. "Are you married?"

"Yes."

"Any children?"

"No."

"Then I guess you wouldn't be interested in the schools."

"Not really." Jesus, get on with it, woman.

Marcie turned to the door, fumbling with the keys. "You can pick a four number code for the entry system in case you forget your keys."

"How does it work?" Shaw asked.

"Just press the pound key and then any four numbers you choose. Like this." Marcie pressed the pound key on the dial pad followed by the number eight four times. The door buzzed and she pushed it open.

"Power numbers," Marcie said. "She must be

177

interested in the metaphysical. Are you interested in New Age things, Mr. Thompson? So many people are these days."

"No, I was a peasant in previous lives. I lost interest when I discovered that." Fucking woman. He followed her to the lobby elevator.

She talked all the way to Jennifer Warren's top floor, extolling one virtue after another of the condominium complex. As she inserted the key into the deadbolt and the doorknob, Marcie said, "I have to be careful not to let the cat out. His name's Oscar." She opened the door cautiously, peering through a crack. "No Oscar," she said and opened the door wide. "Well, here we are. Isn't this lovely?"

A black cat sat on the back of a couch, staring at them with intense yellow eyes. "Oh, aren't you pretty, Oscar," Marcie said going up to the cat. The animal fled down a hallway.

Oscar, I don't blame you a bit, Shaw thought.

"Well, I'll just leave you to look around quietly," Marcie said.

"Thank you."

Of course, the real estate agent proceeded to follow Shaw from room to room, talking all the while. Shaw didn't care. He'd be back later. As soon as he made copies of the keys. So he worked his way from the living room and the balcony ("Lovely view," Marcie said) through the kitchen ("Lots of counter space and cabinets," Marcie said) and down a hallway into the bedrooms ("Big master suite," Marcie said), opening closet doors ("Aren't they nice and large," Marcie said), peering in with what he hoped to be interest. Oscar the cat sat on the pillows of the neatly made bed staring at the intruders. Again, Marcie tried to pet him. This time, Oscar hissed and Marcie pulled her hand back quickly. "Brute," she whispered, thinking Mr. Thompson could not hear her.

Way to go, Oscar, Shaw thought, going into the den

abruptly, losing the bitch for a moment, but she quickly caught up to him.

"What kind of work do you do, Clarence? May I call you, Clarence?"

Shaw nodded, smiling, wondering what Miss Prissy would think if she knew his namesake was a fucking snake. "I'm in investments," he said.

"That's nice. And the den would be a wonderful home office for you."

"Yes, well, Miss Coleman . . ."

"Mrs. Coleman, but please, call me Marcie. Everyone does."

"All right, Marcie, I think what I'd like to do is come back with my wife and see what she thinks."

"That'll be fine. Would you like to make an appointment?"

"No, let me call you."

"I'll give you my card. Do you have a card?"

"Not with me, but I'll give you a call in the next day or so as soon as I know our schedule."

"By then, we'll have the flyers printed up. As I said, this is a new listing and we haven't had a chance yet. We like to have photographs for all our flyers. But don't wait too long. This is a choice property and I really don't think it'll stay on the market long."

"Oh, I'll be back soon," Shaw said. "Very soon."

"Did you have a nice vacation?" Leo asked as they waited for the elevator.

"Very nice," Jennifer said thinking of Hank.

"I always miss you when you're away from the office," Leo said.

The elevator doors opened. The car was crowded, but they managed to squeeze in. The elevator stopped once more and then began the express descent to the lobby.

They were silent until they had ridden the escalator

from the lobby to the shopping and dining levels below. Then Leo said, "Actually, I'm looking forward to a little Japanese food. I haven't been here since the last time we had lunch. You know, you're very predictable, Jennifer."

She smiled at her friend and mentor. "I suppose I am," she said. "At least when it comes to lunch."

"And what is that supposed to mean?"

Jennifer smiled again. "Wait until we're in the restaurant."

Again, Jennifer chose the more secluded back room of the restaurant. Tea appeared almost immediately after they were seated. Jennifer poured for both of them.

"Now, what's this important matter you have to discuss?" Leo asked.

"I'm getting married," Jennifer said.

"That's wonderful," Leo said, taking both her hands in his, clasping them warmly. "I'm so happy for you. Is your Bear person the lucky man?"

"Yes, it's Hank and I've been waiting for him all my life."

"I hope and pray you'll be very happy together. You deserve every happiness. And I hope Hank's smart enough to appreciate you."

"Oh, I think he does," Jennifer said. She paused to sip her tea, dreading what must come next. Leo had been good to her, almost like a father. She did not want to hurt him with an abrupt announcement that she was leaving the firm, but there was no other way to do it. "There's something else, Leo."

"And what is that, my dear?"

"I'm moving out-of-state after we're married. I'll be leaving the firm. I want to give you as much notice as possible. Is three months enough?"

Shaw studied the contents of each of Jennifer

Warren's dresser drawers carefully before going through them. He wanted to replace everything exactly as he found it. But there was nothing of interest in any of the drawers. Neatly folded panties in one. Brassieres in several colors in another. Panty hose in another. Shaw lifted her underwear to his face, inhaling deeply, smelling her scent. He took a black lace brassiere and let it fall open, searching for the tag. Thirty-six C. But he knew she had big tits. He could see that for himself. Sometimes, when the cowboy had been here, she had gone without a bra, driving Shaw crazy with desire as he watched her breasts through the binoculars as they jiggled provocatively beneath a thin blouse. He wanted to cup those breasts in his hands, feel the nipples grow with desire for his touch. He refolded the brassiere and replaced it. He went to the nightstand and opened a Dickens novel, *David Copperfield*. Her bookmark was at page 447. Old illustrations adorned the pages. He found an inscription on the title page in her handwriting, clear and feminine. *For Hank, Our first Christmas together, with all my love, Jennifer*. Hank. A good fucking cowboy name. Shaw was at least pleased that she didn't dot her i's with a smiling face.

The spermicide was in a nightstand drawer, a contraceptive foam. He fingered the tube that had been inside her. Did she do it herself? Did the cowboy do it for her? The nightstand on the cowboy's side of the bed was empty. With a Gideon Bible, the place might have been a God damned hotel suite, devoid of all personality.

In the closet, he went through her clothing, jackets, skirts, blouses, sweaters, jeans, picking a piece at random to smell. He couldn't get enough of her smell. It intoxicated him, inflaming him with jealousy again. He got on his hands and knees and looked through a collection of high-heeled pumps, casual shoes, slippers and loafers, and boots. Pushing through a thick collection of business suits, he discovered the portable safe. Important papers, jewelry, or is she hiding something? Shaw noted the number beneath the combination dial. Thirty-six, like her tits. He moved the dial one number at a time. Thirty-five, thirty-four, thirty-three, pulling at the handle at each stop. The door would not open. Slowly, he went to the higher numbers. Still, the door would not open. Shaw was proud of Jennifer. No laziness here. She's a very meticulous and wary woman, dialing the entire number each time she opens it. Shaw pushed the clothes together again. How did women manage to cram so much into a closet? He stood and went into the bathroom.

Jennifer Warren had expensive tastes in cosmetics and perfumes. Chanel Number Five. Did the cowboy give it to her? No fucking way. He wouldn't know how to lavish her with the gifts she deserved. Beer and cheap restaurants. That would be his style. The cupboard beneath the vanity sink was nearly empty. There was a box of super plus tampons. He opened it. Twelve of the original forty remained. He closed the box and returned it. He started through the vanity drawers, finding a dual container for contact lenses, brushes and combs, eye shadow, and tubes of lipstick. He took the cap off the lipstick and put it to his own upper lip, feeling her lips brush against his, tasting it with his tongue, wanting her all the more.

There were strands of long blonde hair entangled in the brushes and tines of the combs. Shaw carefully removed them and made a tiny locket of Jennifer's hair. He had read somewhere that possessing such a locket took a part of the soul, gave power over the individual and that a sorceress could use strands of hair or parings from fingernails to bewitch and enchant, making the individual a prisoner, controlling and dominating emotions and actions. Shaw smiled. That's what I need. Find a fucking witch and have her make Jennifer fall in love with me.

Shaw stood at the bathroom door and looked around.

There was nothing in the condominium to suggest anyone lived there, truly lived there. Oh, there were art prints on the walls, cooking utensils in the kitchen, towels and sheets in the linen closet, frozen dinners in the freezer compartment of the refrigerator. There was a stack of magazines on the desk in the den, professional publications like *LA Lawyer* and *California Lawyer*. No photographs or albums of a family, not even her daughter. No collections of letters. There was nothing to suggest anything more than a temporary stay, although a trip to the County Recorder's office downtown had rewarded Shaw with the knowledge that she had lived there for eight years. Eight fucking years and it still looks like a hotel room. Who the hell was this woman?

"I take it all back," Leo said. "You're not predictable at all. Two bombshells in one luncheon. It's enough to make an old man cry. Getting married is one thing. I'm truly happy for you, but to leave the firm . . . What will I do without you?"

"The same thing you did before I came."

"Perhaps I'll retire as well. Who wants to deal with brash young people right out of law school? All they're interested in is the starting salary and how soon they can become a partner. They have no interest in or love for the intricacies of the law. They give validity to Shakespeare's dictum."

"The first thing we do, let's kill all the lawyers."

"*Henry VI.* I have it on a sweatshirt, a souvenir from the Folger Library. I wear it while gardening."

"Oh, Leo, I'm going to miss you."

"And to what end of the earth is this Hank taking you?"

183

Jennifer hesitated. What could it matter now? "We're going to live in Arizona."

"Of course, your mysterious Arizona hideaway?"

"You knew?"

"I suspected. Once, I came searching for you. Your office was open. I could not help but see the study guide for the Arizona bar examination."

"That was careless of me." Have I made other mistakes? Jennifer wondered. Have I slipped up in other ways? Impossible. I've been too careful. No one knows who I am. What I've been. Where I'm going. If I don't know, how can anyone else.

"I wish you all the luck in the world," Leo said. "But I will miss you too."

"Am I going with your blessing, Leo?"

"With every blessing I can muster."

"Thank you, Leo. I appreciate it more than you can ever know."

Oscar watched as Shaw copied the telephone number on the back of Marcie Coleman's card. He took another brief tour through the rooms, double checking that everything he had touched had been replaced exactly. The violin case, each drawer, clothing in the closet, cupboards in the kitchen, magazines in the den—he was satisfied that all was as he had found it. She would never know that he had been here.

Jennifer found Marcie Coleman's card on the kitchen counter, indicating she had shown the place to a prospective buyer. Oscar leaped to the counter and paced restlessly back and forth, hair raised slightly, aggravated, complaining. Jennifer stroked his fur. "Did you have strangers interrupt your day? Hopefully, it won't last long, Oscar. Soon, we'll be in Arizona and you can chase birds and squirrels

184

forever." Jennifer opened a new can of cat food, but Oscar seemed uninterested in the electric can opener. The sound usually drove him into a Pavlovian dance of anticipation. Jennifer placed the food on the floor. Oscar sniffed at it and turned away disdainfully to follow Jennifer into the bedroom.

Jennifer had undressed to bra and panties and was putting her dress on a hanger when the telephone rang. She ran to the bedside telephone, dropping the dress on the bed. She picked up the telephone receiver, brushing her hair back from her ear.

"Hello."

Silence.

"Hello? Hank?"

Jennifer heard nothing, not even the usual crackle of an imperfect connection. A chill came over her as she envisioned a telephone line running into a vast emptiness.

SIXTEEN

Kathleen: The shadows are restless, slowly creeping from the past. The shadows are looking for you. J.H.

The message was disruptive as always, shattering the calm order imposed on her troubled world. Weeks, months, even years, passed without incident, until a message appeared, forcing her to panicked confrontation with her tenuous reality. Again. How many times had it happened over the years? Jackson always seemed to know the exact moment to place the messages, when she was frail and vulnerable or, like now, nearing happiness. Dear, God, please make him leave me alone. Jackson, why won't you let me go? Please, please, just a little longer and I'll be in Arizona with Hank. I'm safe there. No one will ever find me. I'll never look at another personal column ever again in my life. I'll be dead. Jackson Holloway will be dead. He doesn't know where I am. The shadows are looking. He doesn't know. He's never known. There is nothing to fear. Go about your life and ignore Jackson Holloway. It will be over soon now. Just a little longer. Only three months. There is nothing to worry about. He's striking out blindly. He doesn't even know I look for the messages. There is absolutely nothing to worry about.

Jennifer called in sick.

The headache was already building. It happened like

186

that sometimes, a message to Kathleen from J.H. triggering the pain that slowly built to enclose her head in a maddening vice. Jennifer opened the aspirin and poured four white tablets into her hand. She drank the entire glass of water. Breathing deeply, methodically, Jennifer pressed her temples, willing the first awful throbs to go away. The pain subsided slightly. Perhaps it wouldn't happen this time. Forget Jackson. Think of Hank. Think of the wedding. Clea wants to come to the wedding. That's wonderful. Forget Jackson. Forget Jackson. Forget Jackson.

He dragged her into the living room, twisting her hair, hurting her. "Were you listening at the door?" he shouted, throwing her on the floor. "Were you?"

"I wasn't listening. I swear. I didn't hear anything."

"Ain't you got no control over your woman, man?" the biker asked.

Kathleen looked up at the two bikers in their greasy denims. Big Mikey wore the one percent symbol of the outlaw. But the woman frightened her more. She could see the handle of the knife protruding from the woman's boot. She was the one they called Maureen. Maureen looked down at her. There was no sympathy or pity in her eyes. She smiled cruelly at Kathleen.

"Yeah, I can control her," Jackson said. "I can control her," he said unzipping his trousers.

"Please, Jack, don't do this," she pleaded. "Not in front of them." Kathleen looked around wildly for a way of escape. They surrounded her. The woman called Maureen laughed. "Show us your technique, honey," Maureen said. "Maybe I can learn something. I doubt it, but I'm always willing to give it a try."

Jack pulled her to the chair by her hair. Kathleen crawled after him, trying to escape the pain. "No, Jack, please don't."

Maureen leered down at Kathleen. Her boyfriend was squeezing her breasts beneath the dirty denim jacket. "You see anything you like, Mikey, let me know," Maureen said.

Jackson forced her down, pulling her hair again.

Oh, God, he's going to make me do it in front of them. Jackson, I loved you. Why? Sobbing, Kathleen took him in her mouth.

"Way to go, honey," Maureen cheered.

Oh, God, at least you could have washed.

Kathleen lay on the floor crying when it was over.

"You want her now, Mikey?" Maureen asked. *"I don't mind."*

"Sure," Big Mikey said. *"Why not?"*

Kathleen heard the rasp of a zipper. No, her mind screamed.

Jennifer Warren pressed her temples harder, trying to kill memory.

Shaw was puzzled as he followed Jennifer's car down Pico Boulevard. She never took surface streets. And, as she turned out of the driveway, he caught a glimpse of her. She wasn't dressed for work today, unless the windbreaker covered her usual suit. Shaw doubted that. "Not my Jennifer," Shaw said as he accelerated through a yellow light a block behind her.

Jennifer drove in the right hand lane. Shaw followed from the left lane, not wanting to get trapped in case she suddenly moved over and turned left. But she wouldn't do that," Shaw thought. She doesn't know I'm here. He shrugged and moved over a lane when her turn indicator started blinking. She turned right.

"Shit!" Shaw braked to keep from slamming into Jennifer's rear bumper. Jennifer was stopped at a newsstand that sold out of town papers and a variety of magazines. The old newsman was just passing a thick pile of newspapers through her window. She drove off.

"Give me the same papers you gave that woman," Shaw yelled at the old man.

"I ain't supposed to sell papers to cars," the old man

complained. "Cops don't like it. You're supposed to park."

Jesus Christ! Jennifer's car was already turning the corner. "You did it for her."

"She's a lady."

Shaw gave him the ten dollar bill. "Keep the change. Just get me the papers."

The old man limped back to the newsstand, slowly taking papers from several different stacks. He hobbled back to the open window. "Ain't supposed to do this," he complained again.

"Just give me the fucking papers," Shaw said, grabbing them from the old man's hand. His tires screeched as he raced after Jennifer. He turned the corner. She had disappeared. He turned another corner. She was making a left hand turn on Pico. She went through the yellow light. Shaw relaxed. She was going back to Santa Monica. As he waited through the red light, Shaw looked down at the assortment of newspapers, all from that morning. San Diego, Orange County, San Francisco. "What the fuck does she want with all these?"

Jennifer went through the collection of papers quickly, separating the classified sections from the other sections. She went down the personal column, easily picking out Jackson's message with a practiced eye. She had done it often enough. The message was in each paper. Creeping shadows. Jennifer sighed, already feeling the pain of the headache receding, the tension easing. Jackson still did not know where she lived. He was still striking out blindly, placing the ads in the newspapers of all the cities where he thought she might be. Jennifer went to the couch and put her feet up, leaned back against the pillow and closed her eyes, waiting for the pain to vanish entirely. The sense of helplessness was the worst part. Jennifer always wished she could do something, anything. But she was power-less. All she could do was wait for the next disturb-ing threat. Jackson would send it soon. He always did.

Parked down the street, Shaw leafed through the newspapers wondering what Jennifer hoped to find in the assortment. Maybe she was just a newspaper freak and liked to keep up on what was happening in other parts of California. Why? She was selling the condo-minium. Why? Presumably she was moving to Butt Fuck, Arizona, to live with the cowboy. Shaw went through the real estate ads in each paper. Sparse. Weekends. That's when the realtors put their ads in. Who wanted to move to fucking Oakland anyway? "Jennifer, Jennifer, Jennifer," Shaw said. "What are you up to?" He tossed the last of the papers in the back seat and started day dreaming about Jennifer wrapping her big tits around his dick. The tantalizing smells of her perfumes and clothing lingered in his memory. He thought briefly about taking the key to her unit. He could be in before she knew what was happening. Take her for his own. Instead, he touched himself and pretended it was Jennifer.

Jennifer Warren stayed home from work for two days. While she stayed inside the condominium, doing housework, sleeping, watching old movies on cable channels, talking to the office by telephone, watching frozen dinners heat in the microwave, and waiting for Hank's nightly calls, Shaw waited, alternating between fantasies of Jennifer doing imaginative things to his body and trying to figure out what she was up to. Several times, he dialed her number on his car phone, hanging up after hearing her voice. He thought it was deep, sexy, alluring. At home each night, Darlene was both puzzled and pleased by the newly rediscovered sexual activity. "Are you taking hormone pills, darling?" she asked.

On the morning of the third day, Shaw was driving the Newport Freeway toward the 405 when he spotted a familiar car in the rear view mirror, a black Lexus sport coupe with dark tinted windows. He had noticed it earlier on PCH, admired its lines. Probably it was some old fart of a stockbroker, trying to reclaim his youth with a fast car that would impress the young women at the office. Shaw changed lanes. The Lexus, several car lengths behind, moved over. Shaw slowed, forcing the cars behind him to pass. The Lexus stayed behind. Instead of taking the 405 north, toward Santa Monica and Jennifer, Shaw joined the crush of automobiles on the freeway heading south, moving over to the fast lane as soon as he could, nosing the Cadillac between cars. The Lexus stayed with him. "Christ, how long have you been there?" Shaw reached beneath the seat and pulled the Colt .357 magnum with the four inch barrel from its concealed holster. He put it on the seat beside him.

The early morning traffic eased once Shaw passed Orange County's John Wayne Airport and he was able to cruise easily at sixty-five. The Lexus was in his rear view mirror all the way. Shaw stayed in the fast lane through Irvine and past some of the only remaining open space in Orange County, brown scrub-covered hills. The northbound lanes of the freeway were jammed. But Shaw and his companion made it to Mission Viejo in less than thirty minutes. When the 405 merged into Interstate 5 at El Toro, Shaw stayed to the right and began searching for a restaurant. "Might as well have some coffee," he said, glancing in the mirror to make sure he hadn't lost the black Lexus. Then he leaned forward to watch a fighter plane, wheels and flaps down, circle in its approach to the El Toro Marine Corps Air Station runway.

Jennifer left for her office feeling good, happy to get away from her self-imposed confinement, even looking forward to dealing with the files on her desk. The fear engendered by Jackson's latest message had long since turned to anger. Twice, during her stay at home, Jennifer had composed an answering ad. J.H. Leave me alone. I won't hurt you. Kathleen. Both times she had torn the page from the legal tablet in tiny pieces. She knew it was a foolish idea. He didn't know where she was. He couldn't be sure she was even in California. For that matter, he couldn't be sure she was still alive. The telephone calls were vaguely disturbing, but it happened sometimes. A wrong number would be called several times, the caller discourteously refusing to accept that the number was incorrect, refusing to acknowledge her presence on the line. If it kept up, she would have the number changed. There was no use complaining to the police or the telephone company. They couldn't do anything. She was determined not to let it worry her. Jackson had disturbed her enough for one week.

Shaw slipped the revolver into his jacket pocket before he got out of the car. He walked across the parking lot, watching the reflections in the coffee shop windows. By the time he reached the newspaper machines, the Lexus had parked in the last row, backing into the slot. Shaw fumbled through the change in his pocket and dropped a quarter and a dime into the slots and pulled the *Orange County Register* from the machine. He glanced idly at the headlines as he pushed through the door into the restaurant.

A girl standing behind a podium stared blankly at him.

Christ, what happened to good morning, Shaw thought. "One, please," he said. "A window booth."

She took a menu from within the podium. "Right this way."

Terrific. She can talk. Shaw followed her to a booth. "Is this all right?"

Shaw could see the black Lexus. "It's fine," he said.

"Enjoy your breakfast."

Shaw ordered coffee and an English muffin. Darlene had already fixed scrambled eggs and bacon for him. He looked out the window. Whoever was in the black Lexus was content to wait out there. Shaw turned to the sports pages. A baseball holdout he had never heard of had just agreed to a five million dollar contract. Probably a .220 hitter, Shaw thought. The Angels still hadn't won a spring training game. The Detroit Tigers hadn't lost yet. The Dodgers were in the middle of the standings. Shaw hated baseball. He ate the English muffin and finished a second cup of coffee before he called his waitress over and asked where the telephone was located. She pointed. Perfect, Shaw thought. He slipped a five dollar bill on the table and headed to the back of the restaurant. "Let's see who you are, boyo."

Shaw went past the pay telephones into the kitchen and out the back door before anyone could protest. He trotted down an alley and circled behind several shops, emerging on the sidewalk. Black Lexus wouldn't expect him to approach from the street. He took the revolver out and held it against his leg. Shaw smiled as he approached the car. Both windows were down. A young man with blonde hair was watching the restaurant intently.

"Good morning, motherfucker," Shaw said pleasantly, pointing the revolver through the open window. "Put your hands on the steering wheel."

The man complied, slowly turning his head to stare at Shaw through mirrored sunglasses.

Shaw slipped into the seat. His knee bumped against

a car phone.

"Nice car," Shaw said. "What's it cost?"

"Is this a robbery?"

"Forget it, asshole. I've been watching you in my rear view mirror for fifty miles."

The young man shrugged.

"You carrying?" Shaw asked.

"No."

"No, you wouldn't be," Shaw said. "Pretty well built. You'd think you could handle anything with muscle. Work out much?"

"Some."

Shaw nodded. "Who sent you?"

"I'm in private eye school. This is the course in tailing. Just practicing on you." He smiled arrogantly.

"Don't be a smart ass," Shaw said, cocking the revolver. "You don't want to piss me off."

"Be cool."

Shaw heard just the slightest touch of fear in his voice. That's better, he thought. "Who sent you?" he asked again.

No answer.

"That's okay," Shaw said. "I admire loyalty. To a point." He glanced down at the telephone. "You have some numbers programmed, sport?"

"Some."

"Let's see who's in there." Shaw hit the numbers 01 and the send button, listening to the melodious chimes as the number dialed automatically. The answering machine picked up after the first ring. "Hi, this is William," an effeminate voice said. "I'm not in right now, sweetie, but leave your name and number and I'll call you back ever so soon."

Shaw raised his eyebrows. "You don't look queer. Just goes to show."

"Fuck you."

"Now, now. I'll keep your little secret. It is a secret, isn't it?" Shaw pushed 02. No answer. "Too cheap to buy an answering machine?" Shaw asked. "It's the twentieth fucking century. What kind of cheap friends do you have anyway?" Shaw pushed 03.

"Hello."

Bingo!

Shaw picked the telephone up. "Hey, Jackson, how they hanging?"

"Robert?"

"The very same."

"Where are you?"

"Mission Viejo if you can believe that shit. I'm sitting here with a friend of yours."

"And who is that?"

"I forgot to ask his name. Young stud. Drives a black Lexus. Know him?"

"Yes, that would be James."

"Did you know he's a faggot?"

"No, I didn't know that."

"Well, he is."

"Did you call to discuss his sexual preference?"

"Actually, no. I was just playing with his telephone and you answered. Don't you trust me, Jackson?"

"I was merely taking a precaution."

"I'm disappointed in you, Jackson. I told you I'd find the woman."

"I'm a little disappointed in your lack of progress."

"You should trust me more," Shaw said. "I've got her."

There was a long pause. "We should talk," Holloway said finally.

"I agree," Shaw said. "I'll drop by. What should I do with James?"

"I'll deal with him later."

"I think he should walk home."

"Serves the dumb bastard right."

Shaw laughed. "I'll see you later." He replaced the telephone and turned to James. "You know where the distributor cap is?"

195

James laughed. "It's all electronic, asshole. There is no distributor cap."

"Imagine that. We'll just have to let the air out of your tires then."

Jennifer was surprised by the number of people who dropped by her office, stopped her in the corridor, joined her in the coffee room for a few minutes, or chatted casually in the library. Her colleagues among the attorneys, partners, secretaries, clerks, interns, even the men from the mail room, all had heard she was leaving the firm and expressed their regrets and their best wishes. For Jennifer, her work and the huge law firm had always been an impersonal bureaucracy, a place to hide and earn decent money. Except for Leo in the firm and Jerome, her neighbor across the hall at home, Jennifer had no personal friends in Los Angeles. Her fear of Jackson Holloway had deprived her of friendships. Her relationships in the firm were few and those were largely indifferent—a shared luncheon, an informal conversation, a perfunctory sharing of personal details with Jennifer always weaving through the web of anonymity she had cast for herself. Now it was all drawing to a close and Jennifer was astonished by the revelation that people liked her, looked upon her as a friend and a valued colleague. She was touched by the expressions of regret about the news of her departure from the firm that had been her home for so long.

And Jennifer was equally startled by her own realization that these people were her friends, that she would miss them. She would miss the easygoing banter with Jeff who pushed the mail truck from office to office, playing small practical jokes by putting his favorite attorneys on mailing lists. For a year, Jennifer had received catalogs advertising flimsy lingerie from Frederick's of Hollywood. Each time Jeff delivered a new edition of the catalog he announced it loudly, bringing a crimson blush to Jennifer's face. He confessed to the prank only after the catalog subscription ceased. Jennifer would particularly miss Bea, her crusty secretary who took no nonsense from anyone. Even partners like Leo went out of their way to remain on Her Beaship's good list. There were others too. As Jennifer thought about leaving, there were tears in her eyes. A portion of her life was nearing an end, a segment of her existence that represented what little happiness she had known during the past two decades. The rest had been a twenty year nightmare. It, too, was drawing to a close. In Arizona, with Hank, she would finally be safe from Jackson Holloway.

Shaw's mind was made up by the time he reached Alicia Parkway on his way to the ocean and the drive through Laguna Beach and Corona del Mar to Newport. The game was out of hand. Even Shaw's conversation with Holloway had been too insolent. Holloway had no sense of humor and Shaw knew he had crossed him. It was time to make amends before it was too late. Holloway could have Jennifer Warren. Let him do what he wanted with her. I don't want to know anymore. I don't care what he does to her. Already, Shaw could hear her screams. He shuddered.

Jennifer had lunch with another attorney, Lora Elizabeth Elliott, one of those acquaintances from the office who suddenly turned out to be a friend. They ordered soup and salad at an imitation sidewalk cafe in the shopping area below and watched their fellow inmates from the building pass by on lunchtime errands.

"We should have done this more often," Lora said.

"I'm not leaving for months yet," Jennifer replied. "We'll have other opportunities."

"I hope so, but I'm afraid it'll be like all the other times. Too busy, too much work, lunch meetings. We never seem to have time for our friends until it's too late." Lora smiled at Jennifer. "I will miss you," she said.

Holloway was on the patio when Shaw arrived. The revolver was a comfortable weight in his jacket pocket. A fresh legal tablet and gold pen were on the table in front of Holloway. The legal pad was gray. Everyone else in the world uses yellow, Shaw thought, but Holloway has to be different and use gray. At least he didn't have the fucking rattlesnake today.

Holloway smiled as Shaw approached the table. "I knew you wouldn't fail me, Robert."

Don't trust the fucking smile. Shaw shrugged. "These things take time."

"I apologize for James. I admit impatience. Where is she?"

"I apologize for my attitude this morning. I was a little upset to find muscle boy on my tail."

"We can forget all that now," Holloway said. "Where is Kathleen?"

"Santa Monica," Shaw answered. "Her name is Jennifer Warren now." He recited her home and office addresses and the telephone numbers for each, tossing a set of keys on the table as he spoke. He had stopped on the way and had an extra pair of keys made. They were safely locked in the glove compartment of the Cadillac. "One for the front door," Shaw said. "One for her unit."

"A remarkably thorough piece of work, Robert. I'm pleased. How did you find her?"

"I tracked down the photographer in San Francisco. He gave me a clue that worked out. Said she intended to go to law school. I went to all the law schools and looked through old yearbooks until I found her picture."

Holloway laughed. "Photography would seem to be her undoing. So, Kathleen's a lawyer now. I'm not surprised. She had a good mind and she always was ambitious. Have you seen her?"

"She's still a very beautiful woman, Jackson."

"Is there anything else to tell me?"

Shaw shook his head. "That's everything, Jackson," he lied. He had done his job and found the woman. He would keep the Arizona information to himself for a safeguard.

"I'm grateful for your work. I won't forget this, Robert."

"Jackson, I have a question before I go."

"Yes."

"What did Jennifer—Kathleen—do to you?"

Holloway waited a long moment before he answered. "She was my wife," he said finally.

After Shaw left, Holloway walked to the end of the pier and stood looking out over the bright blue water of the bay, savoring the information, trying to imagine Kathleen as she appeared today, and trying to remember the girl he loved, the woman he hated, and the satin feel of her skin, the warmth of her youthful body, the pleasure of her smile, and the pain she had caused. "Oh, Kathleen, you should not have betrayed me," he said. "You will have to pay for that now. Retribution is at hand and I'm afraid you will not like what I have planned for you. But there is time. There is no hurry now." Holloway turned and walked back to the house, looking forward to a glass of celebratory champagne with his lunch.

He was watched by the Japanese gardener who thought it odd that the man talked to the breeze.

That night, Shaw sat at his desk, looking at the photographs again. He regretted turning Jennifer over to Jackson Holloway, but it was time. He had been playing a dangerous game with Holloway. Still, a sadness remained as he looked upon Jennifer's images. He sighed and reached for the telephone. He thought about warning her and dismissed the idea immediately. All he could do now was listen to her voice for the last time.

"Hello?"
Silence.
"Who are you? Why are you calling me?"
Silence.
"Don't call me again." She slammed the receiver down.

Jesus, Shaw thought, she's scared. I can't do it. I love her. I've got to warn her. Let her know that she's in danger. Who knows what Holloway will do to her? Fuck him. She deserves better. He pushed the redial button on the telephone.

Jennifer sat in the darkness, watching as the shadows closed in upon her again, creeping slowly across the now desolate landscape to close about her, enveloping her in a suffocating cloak. She was alone and helpless in the darkness.
The telephone rang again.
"Leave me alone," she whispered. "Leave me alone, you bastard."
Jennifer let the telephone ring for a long time. Finally it stopped.

SEVENTEEN

The rattlesnake coiled and buzzed angrily when it was released. The snake saw the man moving away before he went out of its limited range of vision. The tremors in the floor ceased. But the snake did not relax in the alien and dangerous surroundings. Its tongue flicked constantly, carrying a foreign odor to the sensing organs in the roof of its mouth. The odor was reinforced through the olfactory nerves in the snake's tiny nostrils. The organs in the snake's facial pits were acutely sensitive to a change in temperature, allowing it to focus on the small warm-blooded mammals that were its prey. The snake was growing hungry. It hadn't been fed for more than a week. It remained coiled as it felt a change in temperature nearby. The snake waited.

The cat had been sleeping in the bedroom when it was awakened by the sound of the door and the stranger entering the apartment, another intruder. The cat listened, waiting for the stranger to explore like the others had done. Then, there was another sound and the cat's hair stood up all along its back. Sharp pointed ears swiveled like small radar antennas as it listened for the sound, waiting for it to repeat. The cat heard the door close again and the scratch of the key in the lock.

The cat strained for another of the strange sounds, a smell. Then it drifted to him, very faint at first and then stronger, a human odor, pungent with an irritating cologne. But there was something else. The cat sniffed, wrinkling its nose. It was in the living space, something new, something dangerous. The cat dropped noiselessly to the floor and began its stalk, taking one careful step after another, entering the hallway, using all of its senses to focus on the trespasser. The cat inched forward patiently, cautiously, its primeval instincts, tamed by plentiful food, water, and affection, seizing control.

Jennifer left her office, took the elevator to the garage level, and soon joined the crush of automobiles crawling up the on-ramp to the lights that regulated freeway access. The pause between the red and green flashing lights was longer than usual. Jennifer timed the red light and sighed when the second hand on her watch reached forty-five seconds. It was going to take forever to get home and she still had to stop for cat food. She passed the man, perhaps her age, standing at his usual spot, holding up the hand-lettered sign that read "Homeless Veteran. Will work for Food." She had the dollar bill ready and handed it to him through the window. "God bless, ma'am," he said as usual. He had been at the same place for several weeks now and Jennifer had never seen anyone else acknowledge his presence, much less give him money. It was another sign of life in Los Angeles. They were at so many corners and on-ramps now. Again, Jennifer sighed. At least in Hidden Valley, she thought, we'd take care of our own. Finally, she reached the light and waited for it to turn green. Ten minutes, just to get on the freeway.

The rattlesnake's initial agitation had subsided. It

remained coiled and alert, but it was no longer alarmed. The rug was warm and the lengthening shadows dulled its instincts. It did not seek a den beneath the couch. The evening and the night were allies of the snake and its sensors were at work, tracking the slightest perception of warmth in the prey that slowly approached.

When the cat reached the end of the long hallway, it peered intently into the darkening living room and saw its adversary for the first time. The cat settled into a crouch and watched, waiting for some slight movement, an opportunity to attack. It was in no hurry, its traverse of the hallway had taken nearly an hour as it paused to sniff and listen before taking each careful step forward. Now, it was content to remain in place for a time.

Jennifer made a mistake in judgement on the freeway. Her mind had been filled with thoughts of Hank and the house in Hidden Valley, her friends, idle plans for a springtime wedding, Clea, and she had missed one of those small indicators that long-time freeway commuters learn to recognize. Long ago, Jennifer had plotted the quickest routes home through the ever-changing currents on the rivers of the freeways. There was one place on the Santa Monica where an instant decision was necessary. Her normal route took her along a feeder road where thru-traffic was allowed. But she had to make a decision as to the exact moment to access the freeway or remain on the feeder route. The indicator was brake lights. If brake lights flashed on a mile ahead, it was best to access the freeway. No brake lights meant it was faster to stay on the feeder road. Jennifer missed the indicator and fumed as the freeway lanes to her right opened up while she remained stalled in traffic. "Damn, damn, damn."

The rattlesnake saw the movement, a black shadow moving slowly through lighter shades of gray. Its tiny tongue flicked nervously, instincts warning of danger.

The cat crept forward warily, ears erect, still listening for the slightest sound. Its tail twitched slightly, eagerly, as it continued the hunt.

Jennifer's wait in the checkout line was interminable. The clerk kept chatting with the bagger about her impending date with a new young man, met over the weekend. Jennifer had stopped for cat food only, but decided to pick up a few other things as long as she was in the store. The few things had quickly grown to fifteen items, more than allowed at the express line. And now she waited. It's as bad as the freeway, Jennifer thought, as she learned more about the clerk's new young man than she could possibly want to know. She glanced at her watch. Two hours from the time she had closed her office door. The office was almost exactly 14 miles from her home. So much for leaving early, Jennifer thought as she finally pushed her cart close enough to begin unloading the fifteen wretched items.

The rattlesnake struck. The cat leaped in the air, twisting sideways, its razor sharp claws raking the snake's body, drawing blood, as it flashed by in a blur. The snake coiled again and rattled, the sound filling the room. The cat retreated, whimpering, not from fear, but from the smell of blood. The stalk began again.

Jennifer, purse slung by its shoulder strap, bag of

groceries cradled in her arm, stopped at the door, to untangle the house key from the other keys on the ring.

The rattlesnake, wounded and bleeding from the razored slashes along its back, sensed the tremors in the floor as another creature approached. The cat heard Jennifer, but the blood lust was on it and it did not relax its focus on the strange creature.

The door opened and the room flooded with light. The snake uncoiled and fled for cover, slithering quickly across the rug.

The cat pounced.

Jennifer heard the rattle and froze, chills crawling along her back, her arms. She saw the snake then and dropped the bag of groceries, gasping out at the sound of the rattles and the furious battle taking place on her living room rug.

Oscar had the snake at full length, claws buried in its back, fangs snapped at the flailing neck of the snake, missed, snapped again, bit deep.

"Oscar," Jennifer cried.

He shook the snake furiously, snapping the vertebrae in its neck. The rattlesnake died instantly, but nervous reflexes in its body reacted and the ominous whir of its rattles still filled the living room with a deadly sound.

Jennifer rushed to a kitchen closet, grabbing a long-handled mop and returned to the living room. The rattlesnake hung limply from Oscar's jaws. Jennifer advanced cautiously, the mop reversed in her hand like a spear. "Oscar, put it down," she said. "Drop it, Oscar."

He looked up at her triumphantly, his yellow eyes bright with victory. He walked toward her splay-legged, the snake's body trailing beneath his belly.

"Drop it, Oscar!"

He looked up at her, confused by the sharp tone in her voice. He dropped the snake. The tail whirred and he leaped backwards. Jennifer crushed the snake's head with the mop handle and stepped back to lean against the wall for support. Her legs were suddenly weak and shaking. "Jesus Christ," she said.

Oscar sat looking at the creature he had killed with interest and then lifted one paw and began washing the blood away.

"God, I'm glad I didn't have you de-clawed," Jennifer said.

Jennifer was suddenly filled with fear. Had the snake struck Oscar? Oh, God, would he collapse and die in front of her? "Oscar, are you okay?" She scooped him up in her arms, giving the snake a wide berth.

The vet in the animal emergency room looked at Jennifer cautiously. Oscar sat quietly on the table in the examining room. "I can't find any evidence that he was bitten," the vet said. "How long ago did this happen?"

He doesn't believe me, Jennifer thought. "I don't know," she said. "Twenty minutes, half-an-hour. Maybe a little longer. I wasn't keeping track of the time."

The vet stroked Oscar behind the ears. "I think he's fine. If he'd been bitten, he should be exhibiting some of the symptoms by now, restlessness, panting, drooling, swelling. He'd be weak. I don't think he's been bitten. I'd be glad to keep him overnight for observation."

Jennifer shook her head. "I can keep him under observation myself."

"Where was this snake?"

"In my living room," Jennifer replied.

"How did it get there?"

"Jesus Christ," Jennifer snapped. "I don't know how it got there. It was just there."

"Highly unusual," he said.

No shit. I'd say it was highly unusual, Jennifer

thought. A rattlesnake that should be hibernating in February manages to get into a third floor condominium. "How much do I owe you?" she asked.

"You can pay at the desk out front. Take it easy, Oscar."

"Thank you," Jennifer said. "I'm sorry if I was short with you."

The vet shrugged his shoulders. "I'd call the police if I were you. You can do it from here, if you like."

"When I get home," Jennifer said. "They'll want to see the snake."

The vet nodded. It takes all kinds, he thought, thinking there must be a full moon. That always brought the crazies out.

The rattlesnake was gone.

Jennifer unlocked the door and stepped inside carrying Oscar in his traveling case.

The snake was gone.

The chills crawled up and down her back. She froze. Oh, God, it's still alive. It can't be alive. I crushed its head. She could see the bloody pulp. The mop handle was still there where she had dropped it. It's dead. I know it's dead. Oh, Christ, the door was locked. She tried to think back. Did I lock it when I left? I don't think so. I just ran for the car with Oscar.

Jackson! He's been here. Maybe he's still here.

"Hello, Jennifer." He was behind her in the hallway.

She jumped, nearly dropping Oscar. "Oh, Jerome, you scared me to death."

"Sorry, sweetie. Is Oscar all right?"

What am I going to do? Think, Jennifer, think. Call the police. Right now. What are they going to do? They'll think I'm crazy too, just like the vet. No one's going to believe me. I don't even believe me now.

"Is Oscar okay?"

"He's fine, Jerome. I took him to the vet for his

shots," she lied. "Would you watch him for a minute, please?" She put the carrying case down and went into the bedroom, turning on lights as she went, going straight to the closet. She took down her other purse, her traveling purse and reached into the folds of the concealed holster, feeling the reassuring presence of the revolver. Keeping her hand on the grip, she carried the purse from room to room. The place was empty. Jackson, whoever had been there, was gone.

Still carrying the purse, she went back to the front room and put the purse on the dining table. The palm of her hand was sweaty. "Thanks, Jerome."

"What's up?" he asked.

"Nothing," she said, blocking his view of the living room and the mop. "Just being nervous. Woman living alone. That sort of thing."

"Somehow, I don't picture you as a frightened woman."

"I'm not, usually, but . . . you know. I've been watching too much television news, I guess."

"Okay. See you later?"

"Sure." Jennifer closed the door behind him and quickly locked it.

She left Oscar complaining in his box and took the purse with the gun into the bedroom and quickly started throwing things into her suitcase.

James expected the quiet residential street to fill with police cars, sirens screaming, red lights flashing. But nothing happened, except that lights went on in every room of her apartment, at least those that he could see from the street. He squeezed the hard rubber ball with his right hand. Holloway was right, he thought, she'll be going crazy. She sure made a mess of the snake. Poor Clarence. But why didn't she call the police? She must be crazier than Holloway. Come home and find a fucking rattlesnake. He laughed. I'll bet she wet her pants. Took a chance going back in there after she went tearing out in her car, running the stop sign at the corner. Jackson would have been pissed if she hadn't come back. But she did. And now she thinks . . . who knows what she's thinking. James heard a siren in the distance. Finally. He looked in the rear view mirror and saw red lights flashing briefly as an ambulance streaked across an intersection. Shit. What's she up to? Should have just gone in and grabbed her. Take her to Holloway. Get it over with. But no. He wants to fuck with her mind first. Crazy bastard. He shifted the ball to his left hand.

Jennifer left the lights burning, locked the door, and took the elevator to the garage, hoping that she wouldn't run into Jerome again. She didn't want to have to explain her sudden departure. I'll call him so he doesn't worry. God, the real estate woman. She's not going to like blood on the carpet. I'll call her. Get the cleaning service in. There's no time for any of this now.

She is one fucked up lady.

James followed her through the night streets as she turned corners suddenly, doubled back with quick U-turns in the middle of a block, got on the freeway only to exit at the next off-ramp, turned again. Finally, her course straightened.

She doesn't know I'm here.

She made another turn.

James cruised slowly to the corner, came to a complete stop, and followed her.

The street ahead was empty.

"Shit!"

James stepped on it, stopping briefly at intersections, looking both ways, speeding to the next corner, turning, repeating the process.

"God damn it."

He widened the search, grid-locking the area, swearing, worrying. Holloway is going to be very pissed. "Shit, shit, shit!"

He saw her car, turning slowly into a storage compound. He sighed with relief and pulled to a stop. The compound backed on the freeway. There was no other way out. "Gotcha," James said.

The truck wouldn't start.

Jennifer pumped the accelerator, waited, turned the key, listened to the starter grind ineffectually, stopped, tried again. Oscar cried in his box. "It's okay, baby. It's okay."

"Don't cry, baby, honey," Sierra whispered. *"Please, Clea, don't cry. They're looking for us. They'll find us if you cry."*

Jennifer turned the key again. The battery, weak to start with, was draining quickly. The engine coughed, struggled, died. "Please, God, let it start."

Please, God, don't let them find us.

The engine caught, sputtered. Jennifer pumped the accelerator in time with the tortured wheezes. It roared to life. "Thank you, dear God, thank you."

Jennifer let the engine run at full speed for several minutes, afraid to ease off on the gas, afraid it would die and she would never get it started again. Finally, she pulled out of the storage space and pulled the emergency brake. Tentatively, she lifted her foot from the pedal. The engine continued to hum as though nothing had ever been the matter. Jennifer raced to the car and backed it in, pulled the door down, locked it. Then, she was in the pickup, driving slowly through the deserted rows of garages and walk-in lockers.

"Thank you, God."

Jennifer looked both ways and drove slowly into the street, turning toward the freeway.

                            *   *   *

James waited, squeezing the hard ball, growing impatient. What the fuck is she doing in there? No one in, no one out. What the hell is she doing? He couldn't stand it any longer. He started the Lexus and drove into the storage compound past boats and RV's to the rows of corrugated sliding doors and down one narrow street into another. Signs warned of guard dogs after nine o'clock. The fucking place was empty. But there was no other way out. Where did she go? Christ, is she going to live in one of these dumps?

"Shit!"

The pickup.

How long ago? Ten minutes. Fifteen?

What's she doing with a pickup? I'll never find her now. Unless she goes back to her place. Would she be that stupid? She's been a smart fucking bitch so far. Who would have thought about the pickup? Fuck me. Holloway is not going to like this. James raced the Lexus out of the storage compound and headed for Jennifer Warren's condominium complex.

The violin.

I forgot the violin.

It'll be all right. Don't go back for it. It'll be fine. Leave it. Hank will understand. Oscar still cried in his box. He wanted out. "In a minute," Jennifer said. "In a minute." He clawed at the rungs on the top.

Don't go back. It's just a violin.

Jennifer slowed the truck and turned back.

The street was quiet, normal. An elderly couple walked down the sidewalk, watching their small Yorkshire Terrier scamper ahead of them. The street lights were on.

Jennifer parked in the red zone in front of the condominium, hesitated briefly before shutting the engine off. It'll be all right, she told herself, reaching for the purse with the concealed weapon. "I'll be right back, Oscar."

She kept her hand on the butt of the revolver as she took the elevator to the third floor. The hallway was empty. The condominium was empty. The violin case was in her hand. Jennifer was at the door, ready to flip the switch turning the living room lights off. On an impulse, she left the lights burning and closed and locked the door behind her. The hallway was still empty. She heard faint music seeping beneath a neighbor's door.

Jennifer paused in the lobby, looking up and down the street. Normal. Everything is normal. None of these people come home to find a rattlesnake in their living room. None of these people were ever married to Jackson Holloway. She dashed to the truck and slid the violin case to the floor on the passenger side.

The truck started without complaint.

Jennifer drove down the street, turned the corner, and drove toward the freeway once more.

James turned into the street and immediately looked up at the third floor. The lights were on. He looked for a parking place. She was back. He leaned back in the leather seats and tried to ease the tension from his body. He started squeezing the rubber ball, looking up at the lights in Jennifer Warren's apartment through the sun roof of the Lexus.

She was back.

"The stupid bitch."

PART III

EIGHTEEN

Once Sierra grew accustomed to being naked in front of a stranger, she found that the hardest part of posing for Arthur Wilson was remaining still while he worked, holding the exact position he wanted, the same expression. That, and staying awake, fighting off the fatigue, the worry, and ignoring her hunger pangs. She had been going without a break for the greater part of the day on her abortive attempt to panhandle spare change for food. Now she had to fight off yawns, biting her tongue, as she struggled to remain alert. She needed this job—she forced herself to look upon it as a job—and the five dollars an hour Arthur was paying her. It was all the money she had in the world. In her mind, she noted the hours as they slowly passed and itemized the things she would be able to buy for Clea, for herself. It helped dilute the shame she felt. Keeping an eye on Clea helped too. The baby slept peacefully in the make-shift crib Arthur had helped her put together. Sierra smiled at Clea with her eyes, ignoring her naked body. It's a job, she said to herself. It's a job. Twenty dollars so far. And more to come.

Arthur had been considerate, waiting until Clea was asleep before starting. He gave her frequent breaks to ease aching muscles, letting her see the progress of his work as he transferred the lines and curves of her body to canvas in dark bold strokes of his drawing pencil. He made coffee for her. He turned the radio to her favorite station, and hummed along with the Fifth Dimension as he sketched.

"And now we are going live to the Ambassador Hotel," the announcer said, "where Senator Robert F. Kennedy is speaking to his campaign workers."

The now familiar accent filled the room. "So my thanks to all of you and it's on to Chicago, and let's win there."

"That was Senator Robert F. Kennedy who today won the California presidential primary."

"I'm hungry," Arthur said. "How about you?"

"I could eat a little something," Sierra said cautiously, not wanting to appear eager. She was too proud for that.

"How about some soup?"

"Soup sounds good." Sierra slipped into the robe and tied it tightly around her waist. Sierra went to check on Clea. The baby was still sleeping soundly. Sierra turned to the easel, standing back to look upon her likeness. "You're very good," she said.

Arthur smiled, pleased at the compliment. "I have a good model. You make me seem better than I really am." He went into his small kitchen and started rattling pots and silverware.

"We interrupt our program to bring you this news bulletin. Senator Robert F. Kennedy has been shot. We repeat, Senator Robert F. Kennedy has been shot. No further details are available at this time. We will bring you additional bulletins as soon as possible."

"Did you hear that?" Sierra cried.

"What?"

"Bobby Kennedy's been shot."

"Oh, no. Not him too."

They sat then for a long time into the morning, stunned and listening to the details of the assassination attempt as they came in. "The Senator has been transferred to Cedars Sinai Hospital in Los Angeles . . . Doctors are operating at this time . . . Kennedy's condition remains critical . . . The gunman is in custody . . . In other news, a bomb exploded at an ROTC office complex on the campus at . . . Three people were killed in the explosion . . . This just in. Apparently, the Senator was struck by two shots from a .22 caliber pistol. Members of the Senator's entourage wrestled the pistol away from the gunman who has not been identified at this point . . . The Senator is believed to be in critical condition . . ."

Sierra's prayers turned to tears. She cried for Kennedy and the loss of the dream he represented. She cried, too, for the three people who were killed in a bomb explosion, their deaths virtually unnoticed, greatly overshadowed by a dying presidential candidate.

Many years later, Sierra—by then she called herself Jennifer Warren—would read that there were more than 200 major demonstrations on more than 100 American university campuses during the first six months of 1968. Through all that turmoil, bombs were planted, university officials were beaten and reviled with obscenities, students burned their draft cards, confronted the police and the National Guard, were beaten, in turn, and went to jail. And nothing changed. The years of love had turned to hate. Young men died in Vietnam. The bombings continued. The police rioted in Chicago. Nixon defeated Humphrey. And three people died in an obscure explosion. The people who planted the bomb were never caught.

But in those early morning hours of June 5, 1968, as Arthur Wilson held her and tried to comfort her, Sierra cried for the dying Robert F. Kennedy, for three people whose names she did not know, and for herself.

Sierra knew who had planted that bomb. Jack had done it. Jack and his friends. She had overheard bits of conversation when they planned it.

She was an accessory to murder.

Her husband, Jackson Holloway, and his self-styled revolutionaries, would kill her too.

217

NINETEEN

He had found her.

When the adrenalin engendered by fear and flight wore off, Jennifer realized the enormity, the terrible truth, of that evening's events. Jackson Holloway, the only person she had ever known who possessed a mind twisted enough to put a rattlesnake in her home, had somehow found her.

Jackson, who had pretended, for whatever sick reason of his own, to love her, seducing her with whispered promises of the home and family she had never known as she had been passed from one foster home to the next, presenting her with gifts, making each of her days a Christmas, filling her belly with his seed, creating their child, a child of love, only to turn viciously upon her, replacing love with a sudden malignity, abusing her with hateful words, and later, beating her until her body was covered with yellowing bruises, keeping her locked up, passing her from one person to another . . .

Until she ran . . .

Taking the first opportunity, she fled his evil embrace. Running, hiding, running . . .

Four months pregnant. Just beginning to show. Living from hand to mouth on the streets and in dingy rooms during the interminable months until she came to term and Clea was born with only a midwife in attendance. Lovely Clea.

Jackson, dear, sweet, mean, evil Jackson.

Sierra climbed down the fire escape with Clea in one arm and a knapsack, hastily packed with a few clothes, baby bottles, and the cache of money she had accumulated posing for Arthur Wilson and the others. She jumped into the huge trash container, covering herself with filth, listening, terror-stricken, while they searched the apartment, the alley.

He had found her again.

After all the thinly-disguised threats in the messages he sent over the twenty-odd years, he had found her.

It was the moment she had dreaded, the moment she had prepared for over so many years now, forsaking Arthur Wilson without a word, the only person who had befriended her, carefully hiding every trace, every clue, anything that might provide Jackson Holloway with the slightest hint of Kathleen's, Sierra's, Jennifer's, whereabouts. And it still hadn't worked. He knew where she lived. Where she used to live. Only a few more months. That was all I needed. A few months, weeks even. Too late.

Running.

Driving aimlessly through streets with her eyes pinned to rear view mirrors until she was positive that she was not being followed. Driving east on one interstate, turning south instead of north, taking a different and strange route. On each side of the freeway, peaceful residential communities sprawled, their inhabitants just going to bed, turning out lights, letting the dog out for a last run, allowing the cat to prowl contentedly through the night hours, checking on their children sleeping quietly without threat in upstairs bedrooms, perhaps making love, perhaps only curling next to the warm body that shared the bed, taking comfort in the presence of another, together.

Not alone. Never alone.

Not running. Never running with a madman snapping at their heels.

The glare from on-rushing headlights danced and twinkled on the windshield. The windshield was dirty, neglected too long, like the battery. Happiness had made her complacent. She had ignored the pickup truck. Jennifer wondered what else she had ignored, what mistake she had made, what tiny error had been committed, allowing Jackson Holloway to track her down. If you love something, set it free. If it doesn't come back, track it down and kill it. She had seen the bumper strip on a pickup parked outside Hank's bar. Had he ever loved her? He hadn't set her free. She had seized her freedom, but now he had tracked her down. He would kill her.

The constant flare of headlights brought on the headache. She fought the pain, concentrating, too hard, on her driving. Beside her, Oscar slept on the seat, happy in his liberation from the traveling case, perhaps dreaming of his triumph over the snake. "Thank God, I didn't have you de-clawed," Jennifer said again. "Wait until I tell Hank." But I can't tell Hank. What am I going to say now? It's too late. I've got to call him. Tell him I'm coming. He'll wonder where I am tonight. Why I'm not answering the telephone. Why I'm running.

Running, hiding in the night, fleeing the creeping shadows of Jackson's mind, going the only place I know with a cat, a gun, and a violin with a sad and tortured history etched into its smooth wood. Jennifer thought of poor Annie Potts, denied the pleasure of her music during her last hours, taken instead by the vigilantes and hanged from the lonely tree for killing her lover's assassin. Poor Annie Potts, poor wretched whore. Your tale was the last pitiful chapter written in the violin's history. Until now. Until Jennifer Warren. Her lover had presented the violin reluctantly, and only then as a gift of love. But death had followed the violin

220

for centuries. Would a former lover, a former husband, add another chapter of sorrow to the violin's lamentable history?

And Maggie, Crazy Maggie, visiting suddenly, unexpectedly. Death followed Maggie through the Valley. That was the legend in Hidden Valley, a nightmare story told to unruly children. It was an old wives' tale, meaningless superstition.

What will he do to me? Kill me, surely. But not quickly. Not Jackson. He would find some perversity to torment her with. Jennifer saw Annie Potts hanging from the death tree, her body twisting slowly. Did the breeze ruffle her skirts? It wasn't Annie. It was Kathleen hanging from the tree, eyes and tongue protruding grotesquely in death. Will he take pictures? I should never have sent those photos to taunt him, to fuel his hatred, jealousy, revenge. How did he find me?

James finally lost all patience with waiting. He had squeezed the hard rubber ball five hundred times with each hand, fiddled with the CD controls, searched without success through the stack of disks for music that would help him pass the time, and stared up at Jennifer Warren's lighted windows until his eyes bulged, watching intently for some movement, a passing shadow, anything that would indicate she was there.

At nine, James slowly began to realize she had deceived him.

At ten, he said, "Fuck it." He took the keys to her condominium and marched boldly across the street, entered the building and took the elevator up to her floor. Without hesitating, he opened her door and stepped inside.

Silent.

The blood on the rug had turned nearly black.

He went from room to room.

221

Empty.

She had packed hastily, leaving drawers open.

"God damn it," James said, looking around. He hated women sometimes. He particularly hated women who fooled him so badly.

The telephone rang. He looked at it with interest. He picked it up and listened.

"Jennifer? Jennifer?"

It was a man's voice, deep, husky.

"Jennifer? Who's there?"

James replaced the telephone carefully in its cradle.

He left without bothering to lock the door. The elevator was still at the third floor. As he pushed the lobby button, James began wondering what he could tell Jackson Holloway.

It was nearly midnight when Jennifer pulled off the freeway at someplace called El Cajon. It was fifteen or twenty miles east of San Diego, another suburban community with normal people following normal routines. At least, I'm pointed in the right direction now, she thought. Jennifer pulled into the gas station and went into the mini-mart, leaving a credit card. "Number ten," she told the clerk.

As she filled the truck's tank at a self-serve pump, she stared at the pay telephones. I've got to call Hank. What am I going to tell him? God, I don't want to explain all this, but I have to call. He's probably been calling me all night and he'll be worried.

Jennifer topped the tank off, replaced the hose, and went back inside to sign the slip and retrieve her card. The clerk heated two hamburgers in a microwave for her. She added a bag of potato chips and poured coffee into the largest cup she could find. Returning to the truck, she pushed Oscar out of the driver's seat and pulled the truck forward and parked by the telephones. Just call. Oscar wanted to sit in her lap. "No," she said sharply. She felt guilt for not having anything for Oscar. Christ, I can't even take care of my cat right. Irritated, Oscar went back to his side of the cab and licked at one paw, as he eyed the bag with the hamburgers. Jennifer climbed down from the truck again and placed the call with her credit card number. The two dimes fell into the coin return. She found four dimes when she went to retrieve them. Maybe my luck is changing, she thought. Finally.

"Hello, Hank." She was suddenly weary, tired of driving, sick of running. She wanted to be at home with Hank. She wanted his arms around her. She wanted him to say that everything would be all right.

"Jennifer, Christ, where have you been? We've been calling you for hours."

"Who's we?"

"Clea's here. We were going to fly over for the weekend. Surprise you."

Oh, God, not Clea. Not now.

"What is she doing there?"

"She broke up with her boyfriend and wanted to get away for a few days. She called me and asked if she could stay here."

Clea called Hank, not her mother. God, where did I go so wrong with her, with everything? I've made a mess of her life and mine.

"I put her in your place. I thought that would be all right."

"Of course, it is. I'll be glad to see her." Oh, God, tell her to go home.

"Where are you?"

"I'm on my way to Hidden Valley. I'll be there in the morning. Have Jesus fix breakfast for me."

"I was worried. I called and called. I finally sent Clea up to your place." Hank paused.

Jennifer waited, holding on to the telephone booth for support.

"The last time I called, someone picked up the

223

phone, but didn't say anything. I called the police and asked them to check. No one answered and the door was unlocked, so they went in. It was empty."

"Probably just a telephone screw-up," Jennifer said. I locked the door. I know I did.

"Jennifer, what's going on?"

She sighed. "I'll tell you in the morning. I've got to go now. I love you." She hung the telephone up quickly, before he could ask more questions that she could not answer. There were no answers, only the truth.

Jennifer went back into the store and found a can of overpriced tuna. "Would you open this, please," she asked the clerk.

"Still hungry?"

"It's for my cat," Jennifer said.

The clerk shrugged and reached under the counter for a can opener.

"Thanks."

Jennifer used her finger to stir the tuna into bite-sized chunks for Oscar. He nibbled greedily and licked at the oil in the can, while Jennifer ate her hamburgers and sipped coffee.

Then, Jennifer was back on the freeway, driving into the night.

Two hours later, she was descending out of the mountains into the desert. In the distance, she could see the lights of El Centro, a farming community fueled by Colorado River water and the cheap labor provided by illegal immigrants who crossed the border to work. They'd be getting up soon to be in the fields at first light, spending another back-breaking working day stooped over endless rows of tomatoes, lettuce, cabbage.

Jennifer exited the freeway, pulling into an all-night diner and truck stop. It was cold in the desert and Jennifer zipped her windbreaker before stepping out of the heated cab. She yawned and stretched. The last hour had been difficult as she struggled to stay awake. A truck engine rumbled nearby. A police car was parked near the door to the restaurant and she debated briefly about going back, leaving her purse with its concealed revolver in the truck. Forget it. Just act normal. The cop was sitting near the cash register, talking quietly with a young waitress. His cap was on the counter. He glanced at Jennifer only briefly, smiling hesitantly, and then looking away shyly. He was young too. He sipped his coffee as he waited for the waitress to return with Jennifer's coffee container to go. Several booths were filled with truck drivers who fell silent at Jennifer's entrance. They looked at her admiringly.

"Can I getcha anything else?" the waitress asked. "Got some nice Danish. Fresh."

"No thanks," Jennifer replied. "Just the coffee." She set the purse carefully on the counter.

The policeman worked up his nerve. "Traveling far?" he asked.

"Phoenix," Jennifer said.

"Have a safe trip," he called after her as she turned to leave.

"Thanks."

The lights of the small community fell behind as Jennifer drove back into the night.

The respite from driving and the coffee helped only for an hour and then Jennifer had to renew the fight to stay awake. By then she had passed through the closed agricultural checkpoint at the Arizona border, wondering if she could ever return to California. There was a rest stop two miles ahead. Jennifer slowed. I've got to sleep, just for a little while.

The rest stop was crowded. There were a couple of RV's, several cars, two big trucks, a pickup with a camper. Jennifer turned the engine off and leaned back, closing her eyes. She sat up suddenly and checked to

225

make sure the doors were locked. She pulled her purse closer and leaned back again. Her body vibrated from too many hours on the road and she couldn't turn her racing mind off. It was perverse. First, she couldn't stay awake and now she couldn't sleep. Too much had happened. Too much had yet to happen.

She thought of Hank, alone in his big bed, and longed to be with him. Only a few more hours and we'll be together. And Clea. God, what a time to visit. It's been more than a year since I've seen her. She has to go back. She has to stay away until this is resolved. Resolution, tis a desire devoutly to be wished. That's not right. What is the quote? Consummation. That's it. " 'Tis a consummation devoutly to be wished. To die, to sleep. And by a sleep to say we end the heartache and the thousand natural shocks that flesh is heir to." Poor Hamlet. Poor Clea. Her father a murderer. The father she's never known. Her mother a murderess. By complicity, if not in deed. Her hand slipped between the folds of the purse. She felt the cold butt of the revolver. Her fingers closed around it.

A truck crept into the rest stop. Its headlights flashed across Jennifer, illuminating the cab of the truck momentarily. They were cut off. The rest stop was dark again, except for the lights over the rest rooms.

Gently, Jennifer lifted Oscar from her lap. He resisted, stirring in her hands. She started to put him down when she felt a tiny reverberation in his body. She put her head close to him and listened. He was purring. "Oscar," she exclaimed, "you're purring." She listened again and flattened her hand against his fur. It was there. Weak, but growing stronger. He was purring.

"Maybe that's a good omen," Jennifer said. She started the truck. There were faint streaks of light at the horizon.

*   *   *

226

It was mid-morning before Jennifer approached Hidden Valley from the south. She had become embroiled in the morning rush hour in Phoenix but when she reached Scottsdale she was going against the traffic rather than with it. Another stop for gas in Mesa and then she was at Apache Junction, turning north toward home, following the old Apache Trail, skirting the Superstition Mountains with their murderous legends. She could see Weaver's Needle jutting into the sky. The gold was supposed to be near Weaver's Needle. And then the Superstitions were behind her, lost in the endless bleak landscape of the Sonoran desert. A black range of mountains seemingly blocked her path to the north, but the pass appeared, as if by magic, opening up to let her through, closing behind her. Jennifer wished she could close the pass forever, like an enchanted castle's drawbridge, keeping outsiders and Jackson Holloway away from those she loved.

He can't find me here. He can't track me through the desert and the mountains into Hidden Valley. I've planned all this too carefully. But you planned everything else too and he found you anyway. What if he's waiting for you? He can't be. He just can't.

And if he is?

I'll kill him, Jennifer thought. I'll be a murderess for real. Like Annie Potts. Give them a reason to hang me. Do they have the death penalty in Arizona? They must. Do they hang you? Firing squad? No, that was Utah. Lethal injection, gas chamber, electric chair. I don't care. I'll kill him before I'll let him hurt Hank and Clea. I have to kill him. If he comes for me, I swear I'll shoot him dead and never regret it, no matter what they do to me after.

And then she was home. Exhausted, stiff, and feeling dirty and grimy, she carried Oscar into Hank's place.

He was behind the bar. He looked up at the sound of the door and just stood there, staring for a minute. "Hello, darling," he said finally.

227

A young woman was seated on a bar stool in front of Hank. She turned and said, "Hi, Mom."

"Hi, guys," Jennifer said. Then she fainted, falling into a huge black hole, screaming silently, twisting and swirling into the dark void where Jackson Holloway waited for her.

Jennifer flailed, fighting, struggling, pushing away the hands that held her prisoner. He was trying to poison her. She could smell the vile poison. She heard Clea crying out. Oh, God, he had her too. Now he had both of them. He was holding her hands. She couldn't escape the strong grasp. She jerked awake.

It was Hank.

"God damn, woman, you scared me."

"Mom, are you all right?" Clea was holding a vial to Jennifer's nose.

Ammonia. That's all it was, ammonia.

"What happened?" Jennifer asked.

Clea was hugging her, crying. "You passed out. I thought you'd died."

There was a ring of faces standing over her, staring down.

"She okay, Hank?"

"What happened?"

"You all right, Jennifer?"

Jennifer took a deep breath. "God, I don't know what happened. I was fine. I guess I was just tired. I stopped last night and tried to sleep, but I couldn't." She looked at Hank and smiled weakly. "Are you glad to see me anyway?"

Hank picked her up.

It felt wonderful. She wrapped her arms around his neck, smelling the cologne she had given him for Christmas. Had it lasted so long?

He carried her to the bar and carefully helped her sit on one of the stools. "Clea, you come steady your mother, while I give the doctor a call."

"Hank, no. I'll be fine."

He looked at her uncertainly. "You sure?"

"I'm just exhausted. I'm okay. Really."

"You want some coffee?"

Her nerves were ringing, dancing. "God, no. Some orange juice maybe. Let me lie down for awhile on the cot in back. I'll be fine."

They sat with her. Hank held her hand.

Jennifer smiled at him, at Clea. "It's good to see both of you."

"You're not mad at me?" Clea asked. "I wanted to surprise you."

Jennifer shook her head. "It's been too long since we've seen each other."

"I'm going to stay awhile. Hank gave me a job. I'm going to be a waitress here until I go back to school in the fall. But I'll find a place. I don't want to be a bother to you."

"Don't be silly. You'll stay with me. There's loads of room at the house." Jennifer felt safe and protected, away from Jackson Holloway's reach. The fears of the night seemed distant and unreal. But the snake was real.

Clea smiled. "We'll see. I better go back to work."

"She's a good girl," Hank said. "Told her she could only work days. I don't want a bunch of drunk cowboys chasing after her all night."

"She's a woman now, or didn't you notice?"

"Oh, I noticed. She's almost as pretty as you."

"You're sweet."

"You want to tell me what happened?"

"Later, Hank. Let me rest first." She closed her eyes. At least, fainting gave her an excuse for postponing explanations. It would be a brief respite from the hateful truth.

Hank stayed with her until she drifted off to sleep. Even then, he lingered, reluctant to leave her alone, as though fearing she might disappear. But finally, he gently removed his hand and left her to sleep, hoping that her dreams would be pleasant.

But for Jennifer, there were only nightmares.

Robert Shaw nearly laughed in Holloway's face. Shaw was proud of Jennifer Warren. She had escaped, leaving Muscles sitting in front of her condominium complex thinking she was inside. And she was gone, disappeared into the night. God damn, he was proud of her. But instead of laughing, Shaw said, "I spend three months finding her and Muscles loses her in one night."

"Fuck you," James said. He started out of his chair.

"Tell him to keep his seat," Shaw said.

"James . . ."

"I don't need shit from this asshole."

"James," Holloway said calmly, "he's right. You lost her in one night. I'm not pleased with your performance to date."

James sank back into the chair and sulked.

"I suppose I could try and find her again," Shaw said. I know exactly where she is, but I'll be damned if I tell him about Butt Fuck, Arizona.

"That might be best," Holloway said.

"I don't know where to start now though," Shaw said. "She's running. She could be anywhere. Maybe even out of the country. Mexico. South America. Europe."

"Why not fucking Africa?" James said.

"Maybe even Africa," Shaw said, smiling. "I hear Nairobi's nice this time of year."

"She had a pickup ready and waiting. She didn't leave the country."

"Ah, yes, the pickup. I don't suppose you managed to see the license plate."

"Fuck you."

"I take that as 'No, Mister Shaw, I didn't see the license plate.'"

"I think we can assume that," Holloway said. "What will you do now, Robert?"

"I'll have to give it some thought."

Jennifer ran, pursued by a youthful Jackson Holloway. Jennifer ran faster, climbing into the wilderness with the hangman's noose looped about her slender neck. Holloway loped after her, running easily, never tiring, laughing, holding the end of the rope in his hand. Jennifer could run no more. Her chest ached and she gasped for breath. Kill him. Kill him now. She stopped. Turned. He stood before her, looming over her, laughing. The gun was in her hand. She aimed. Pulled the trigger. Jack laughed as the gun turned into a snake, twisting and writhing about her hand, her wrist, her forearm. Jennifer screamed and shook her hand frantically, trying to throw the snake away from her. She could not dislodge it. She screamed again. She was falling. Falling. Falling. Jennifer waited for the noose to break her neck.

"He's holding out on you, Jackson. He knows where she is."

"Yes, I think so too, James."

Jennifer awakened. She could hear Willie Nelson singing on the bar's jukebox.

Dr. George Washington Cordeman was sitting next to the bed. "How are you feeling, Jennifer?"

"What time is it?"

"Oh, about three or so. Hank called and asked me to take a look at you. Says you fainted."

"I guess so."

He took her wrist in his stubby wrinkled fingers and felt for her pulse. Cordeman was old, in his seventies, and people in the Valley worried about what they would do for a doctor when he finally retired or died.

He took her blood pressure, listened to her heart, thumped her back several times, took her temperature, packed his tools away. "Seem fine to me," he said. "You been getting regular rest, eating good?"

"Mostly. I drove all night to get here. I didn't eat very much."

"Just tuckered out, I expect."

"I told Hank not to worry."

"Hank can be a mother hen sometimes. That your daughter out there?"

Jennifer nodded.

"Knew it soon as I walked in. Looks just like you. If I were a few years younger, might propose to her." Cordeman had buried three wives in the Valley's cemetery.

Jennifer smiled. "From what I hear you might do that."

"Don't believe everything you hear from the folks around here. They're all a bunch of tattletales and gossips. You get some rest tonight. You'll be fine. But if you're still feeling poorly, you come in and I'll go over you some more."

"Thanks."

"Hank's frettin' out there. Reckon I'll tell him he can come in now. Says Jesus made you some chicken soup. Don't know what a Mexican knows about chicken soup, but you eat it."

"Okay."

"You do what I tell you now."

"I will," Jennifer said. "Thanks again and take care."

"You too, Jennifer, you too."

TWENTY

Despite her protestations, Jennifer's mind and body rebelled and she was sick, truly sick. She took to her bed in the big lonely house for three days, sleeping as though drugged, awakening briefly to Hank or Clea or the doctor, sometimes all three, looking down on her anxiously. Barely aware of their presence, she stared at them, uncomprehending, as though they were strangers, only to drift off into a blessed unconsciousness again where she floated weightlessly through time and space, haunted only by her past.

She had been many different women under three different names during her life. Now they had all gathered with her in the Valley, gliding in and out of her bedroom as the whim struck one or another of her many guises. They chattered incessantly, demanding and competing for her attention. Kathleen, Sierra, Jennifer, an unholy trinity, all badgering the woman in the bed who desired nothing more than anonymity and a retreat through the weeks, months, years of her existence to the void that preceded creation.

"What? What did you say, Mother?"

Stupid creature, the child thought petulantly. Why can't she understand? "Alfie," Kathleen said, sliding away into sleep. Alfie's my bear. I want Alfie. I want my teddy bear. But they took Alfie away. She was being punished. Please, I won't do it again. Don't kill Alfie. Please don't kill Alfie. You're not my mother. My real mother is in heaven. I hate you. I hate all of you. You killed Alfie. You killed my mommy and daddy. As soon as I'm old, I'm going to run away. I hate you.

"Total exhaustion . . . Running a fever . . . I'll check in on her again this afternoon."

The grass was cool on her bare feet. She wore garlands in her hair. She was so beautiful. He was so handsome. They loved each other. Forever. But forever was only three months. He became a monster, a transformation before her eyes. He hit her, punching her belly, trying to kill the baby within. Don't hit me any more, please. Someday, someday, I'll go there. I'll disappear and wake up in a beautiful mountain valley where the water is clear and cold and the animals come to visit.

But it was hot, burning hot, not at all like a mountain meadow should be, her meadow. The fingers were cool on the flush of her forehead, but they went away. Please, do it again. It feels so good, so cool. She opened her mouth to speak, but her tongue was thick and her lips refused to form the words. So hot.

She saw herself as in a dream-like mirror, looking up, a struggle to keep her eyes open. No. She was standing, and looking down. Looking down at herself. Younger. I was younger then. Was I still Kathleen? Or Sierra? The reflection in the mirror was beautiful with the same delicate features, light hair, sensuous lips. But she wasn't smiling. Her face was clouded with concern, worry. Her mouth frowned. Why don't you smile, Kathleen? Her eyelids drooped, closed, opened again. The mirror was empty. Where did you go, Kathleen? Or were you Sierra? Who are you? Where are you? She slept.

And awakened in darkness.

Alone.

Afraid.

Mommy. Where are you?

At her side, Alfie stirred, snuggled close, purring. She reached out and felt the sleek, thick fur. I didn't know bears purred, Alfie. What a good silly bear to purr for me.

It rained during the night. She wanted to go outside and walk through the chilling rain. But it was dark and silent and she was afraid to move. She pulled the bear close to her for comfort and heard the contented growls as he purred for her. Only for her.

"If she's not better by tomorrow, I'm taking her to the hospital."

I don't need to go to the hospital. He'll find me there. Jackson will find me there. Shelly will do it. She taught me everything. How to breathe. How to push. It's an adventure, Shelly says. I'll be like the brave frontier woman in the old west. I can breathe. I can push. I can do it. Please don't take me to the hospital. I don't want him to find me. He'll hurt the baby. Our baby.

"She's always hated doctors and hospitals. She'd never go when I was little."

That's right. I'm not sick. I'm not sick. Tell them. Just tired. That's all. I just want to sleep.

"The fever's gone down some."

Sleep. No one can hurt you when you sleep. God won't let them hurt you while you're sleeping.

The room was gray. She could see the rain through the window, falling softly on her tree-covered mountains. Jackson was beside her on the bed, helping her sit up, holding the glass to her mouth.

"I squeezed the oranges myself," Jackson said.

It tasted good, oh so good, cool and refreshing.

Dear, sweet Jackson. How I loved you. More than anything.

"Why did you change?" she asked.

"I didn't change," he replied.

"Promise me you won't change again."

"No," he said. "I won't. I'll never change."

"Then I'll love you forever."

"And I'll love you forever."

Forever and forever and forever.

She swirled, twisting and falling, faster and faster, a dizzying fall through the black tunnel, into the underworld where hideous, drooling, fanged monsters chased little girls and ate them for their suppers. But first they had to catch the little girls. She ran. Faster and faster, she ran through the trees with the clinging branches that reached out to trip and hold little girls back so the monsters could catch them. And eat them. For their suppers. Her mother told her that story. It happened to bad little girls.

But I've been good. I've tried so hard to be good. Bad. Bad little girl. I'm not. I'm not. I'm good. Bad. You're not my mother. I don't have a mother. I've never had a mother. You killed her, just like you killed Alfie. I hate you.

Jennifer awakened late in the afternoon of the third day.

Bear was sitting in the chair beside her bed, not Alfie, her Bear, Hank. He smiled, but worried creases marred his forehead.

"I was dreaming," Jennifer said, thinking that she had to remember something, something very important. "How long did I sleep?"

"Nearly three days," Bear said. "You had a fever."

"You're kidding? Three days?" Oscar poked his face from beneath the covers. Jennifer stroked his smooth fur.

Hank nodded. "You scared the shit out of me. Old Clint, too, I guess. He wouldn't leave you. Had to put food and water in here for him."

"I'm sorry," Jennifer said, petting Oscar. "I dreamed he was my teddy bear. I'm starving."

Hank smiled at her again. "Starving we can fix."

He had a wonderful smile. Jennifer saw warmth and

236

love in the gently caressing smile that flowed over her.

"Breakfast," she said. "I want breakfast. Is that okay?"

"For you, darling, anything."

Jennifer sat up in bed. For a moment, the dizziness returned, but then it passed, and Jennifer swung her legs to the floor, and reached for the robe hanging over Hank's chair.

Hank's face was concerned. "Why don't you stay here? I'll serve breakfast in bed."

"I'm fine," Jennifer said. "Really." And she was. She was weak, hungry, but she felt good for the first time since she had left Los Angeles. And then she remembered.

Jackson Holloway was coming to kill her.

Hank helped her into the robe and put his arm around her shoulders.

"Where's Clea?"

"In the living room," Hank said. "She's a good girl. She loves you."

"I know," Jennifer said. "I love her too. I've always loved her."

Jackson would kill Clea too.

But not if we get him first.

Jennifer looked in the mirror over the dresser. "God, I look awful. How can you love an old hag?"

"No taste in women, I guess."

"I want my purse. Where is it?"

"I'll get it." He took it from the floor beside the bed and handed it to her. "It's heavy."

"Everything I own is in it," Jennifer said, feeling the comfortable weight of the revolver hidden away inside. She leaned on Hank for support as they walked into the living room. Oscar followed behind them.

Clea looked up from the couch. She carefully marked her place in the book she was reading, put it on the coffee table, and stood up. "How are you feeling, Mom?"

237

"Much better."

Clea came to her then and hugged her. She was crying. "God, you had all of us so worried."

"I know, baby, I know."

Jennifer showered, letting the steaming hot water cleanse her of the sickness. She dried and brushed her hair. She brushed her teeth. She put on makeup. She dressed in old jeans and a warm bulky sweater and finally emerged to the smell of ham and eggs, feeling rested and whole again.

Hank and Clea were in the kitchen, dancing to the music from the cassette. It was The Doors. They each held a long wooden spoon in one hand and took turns stirring the scrambled eggs, as they passed by the frying pan. Hank danced awkwardly, shambling. Clea twirled gracefully beneath his arm, poking the spoon into the eggs as she circled, laughing. Jennifer watched. It had been a long time since Jennifer had seen her daughter so relaxed, so happy. And Hank, shuffling his feet, his huge bulk swaying back and forth. Jennifer smiled. She had a family. At last, she had a family.

There were flowers on the table. Jennifer read a home-made card and smiled. The flowers were from Kathy and Dave.

Clea saw her and said, "Hey, Mom, this guy's a keeper."

"I know," Jennifer said, going into the kitchen and embracing both of them. "I know."

"You dance with him," Clea said, twisting away from her mother's embrace. "I've got cooking to do."

"No twirling me around," Jennifer said, laughing, enjoying the moment, knowing it wouldn't last long.

Hank drew her close. She rested her face against his. Hank stopped moving his feet and simply held her. "Welcome home," he said.

238

"That's not dancing," Clea said. "How can I cook if I have to keep my eyes closed?"

"You just don't know how to dance," Jennifer said.

"Oscar," Clea cried. "Get your nose out of there."

"Clint," Hank said. "I keep telling you his name's Clint."

"Cat's going to have an identity crisis," Clea said. "Won't know what his name is."

Kathleen, Sierra, Jennifer. Who am I?

After dinner—Jennifer's breakfast—they sat in front of the fireplace. Jennifer and Hank sat on the couch together, holding hands lightly. Clea sprawled sideways in her chair, reading. Jennifer watched the fire, listened to the snapping of the burning wood. She wanted to watch the fire forever, feeding her past into the flames, but she could not. The time had come. Forgive me, Father, for I have sinned . . .

"I have something to tell you," Jennifer said. "I have something to tell both of you . . ."

She confessed.

Jennifer talked quietly, staring into the fire the whole while, not daring to meet their eyes. Each of them, Hank and Clea, knew portions of her history. Now, Jennifer told them the rest—of her marriage to Jackson Holloway, his sudden and inexplicable transformation, of demanding that she go to Mexico and get an abortion, of flight and the things she had done for survival, the explosion and three murders, flight again, the struggle to complete her degree and law school, the messages he sent to her through the personal columns, the preparations she made for escape, the reasons for coming to Hidden Valley, the rattlesnake. Jennifer told them everything and wondered if they believed her. Did she believe it?

And when she finally finished, there was silence. Still, she dared not look at either of them, daughter or lover. It's true, God damn it, it's true. I'm not proud of some of the things I've done, but it's true.

"That son-of-a-bitch."

"Oh, Mom."

Jennifer stared into the fire. "Can you forgive me?" she whispered.

Hank answered by taking her in his arms. Clea came and sat next to Jennifer, putting her hand on her mother's shoulder. "It's all right, Mom, it's all right."

"Is it?" Jennifer asked. "Can I ever make it up to you, Clea?"

"I used to think I hated you. When I found those pictures, I was ashamed . . ."

"You're a whore. My mother's a fucking whore!" Jennifer fled. Clea followed her from room to room, shouting, "Whore! Whore! Whore!"

"I don't know . . . I thought it was your fault, but maybe it wasn't," Clea said. "None of it was your fault."

"I should have told you, Clea, but I was ashamed too. I wanted to protect you."

"Who is he, Mom? Who is my father?"

"Oh, Clea, I've spent half of my life trying to understand Jack, trying to understand why he did the things he did. To me. To others. He was a wonderful person when I met him. I thought he was a God. I was wrong. He fooled me, like he fooled everyone. I don't think Jack has a moral sense. Whatever he does, he believes is right, simply because he is Jackson Holloway. There is no sense of right or wrong in his psychological make up. When he beat me and kept me locked up, it was perfectly justified in his eyes. He loved Nietzsche and the concept of the super man. He thought Raskalnikov in Dostoyevsky's *Crime and Punishment* was perfectly justified in killing the old woman pawnbroker. Jack used his wealth and overwhelming personality as power to do anything he wanted."

"He was a monster," Clea said. "My father was—

is—a monster. You should have told me. It would have made all the difference. I would have understood our relationship."

"Clea, I wanted to protect you," Jennifer repeated helplessly. "I thought it was better to let you think we were simply divorced and had lost track of each other. I Odidn't want you to know what kind of man your father was. I didn't want you to know what kind of woman you had for a mother."

"Don't you understand?" Clea cried. "I needed to know."

"I should have told you," Jennifer said. "I was wrong. I'm sorry. I'm sorry for everything."

Clea swallowed, cleared her throat. There were tears in her eyes. "I know," she said. "I am too."

"But there is one thing I can never condemn him for," Jennifer said. "He gave me you."

Clea nodded and smiled awkwardly. "I'm going to bed now. I'll see you in the morning."

Oscar, sleeping on the rug before the fire, stretched and turned over, went back to sleep. Jennifer envied him. "Poor Clea," she said. "I've taken whatever fantasies she had of her father away."

"She's strong. She can handle it."

I hope so, Jennifer thought. I hope we're both strong enough. We've got so much to make up for.

She turned to Hank. "I've taken away some of your fantasies too. I would understand if you didn't want to marry me now," she said.

"Nothing you've said makes me want to change my mind. I'd like to kill the bastard though. Do you really think he's coming here?"

"No one knows about this place," Jennifer said. "He can't find me here. I'm safe here with you. We're all safe here. Perhaps it's over now."

"Is it?"

"I don't know," Jennifer said, "but I'm through running. This is the last stop."

241

"We'll see it through together," Hank said. "No more secrets."

"No more secrets," Jennifer agreed. "I am empty of secrets at last."

"We should go to the authorities."

"But there's nothing to tell them. Jack is smart. What proof do I have? Some ads in the personal columns signed with initials. How many people have the same initials? Millions probably. Some dried blood on the carpet. I guess a forensics lab could identify it as blood from a rattlesnake. But there's still no proof that Jack put it there."

"What about the bombing?"

"I know he did it. I'm convinced of that, but again, no proof according to the law. Some whispered conversations I overheard while I was locked up in the bedroom? That's my word against his. In fact, he could make a case for desertion. He's a very respected man in the community with powerful political connections. Claim I ran away and took his daughter. Put all the blame on me. Spousal abuse?" Jennifer laughed bitterly. "The bruises don't show on the outside anymore."

"Only on the inside?"

"Oh, yes," Jennifer said. "They're on the inside, all right. I have half a lifetime of bruises inside."

"And so there's nothing we can do?"

"Wait. See what happens. I don't think he'll come, but if he does, I'll be ready for him. Trap him here. In the Valley, he belongs to me. This is my territory now."

"Our territory," Hank said.

"Yes. This is where I intend to spend the rest of my life. I won't let him take that away from us."

"What about Los Angeles? The condo? Your car?"

"I'll call Leo. Give him my power of attorney. When Leo finishes liquidating everything in L.A., it'll be buried so deep in paper that Jack will never be able

242

to trace it. Jennifer Warren will cease to exist in California."

"I'll talk to the Sheriff," Hank said.

"He won't believe me. He'll think I'm crazy. Maybe I am."

"I'll be vague. Just tell him that you've received some threatening telephone calls. Nothing he can put his finger on. But maybe have a deputy drive by occasionally. Check out any strangers. We have to do something."

"God, what a mess."

"We'll get through it," Hank said once again. "I better get going. Will you be all right?"

"Yes, but . . ."

"But?"

"You still love me? You're not just being gallant for a woman in distress?"

"Oh, I love you all right."

"Then, I think you should move in here."

"What about Clea?"

"Hank," Jennifer said. "You're old-fashioned."

He smiled shyly. "It just doesn't seem right now that Clea's here."

"She thinks you're a keeper. I do too."

"I don't want to leave. Believe me."

Jennifer smiled. "If it would make you feel better, we can get married."

"When?"

"Now. Tonight. Tomorrow. As soon as we can get the license."

"You mean it?"

"Yes," Jennifer said, "I certainly do. We'll pack up Clea and find someone to marry us. She'll be pleased. It won't be what we planned, but . . ."

"I don't care, as long as we're together."

"I don't care either. That's why I'm here. I want to be with you."

They watched the fire. Jennifer rested her head on his shoulder. They were content to be together.

Late that night, Jennifer thought she heard someone crying. She left Hank and the warmth of their bed and went to listen quietly at Clea's bedroom but there were no sounds. She eased the door open. Clea was asleep in a patch of moonlight, embracing her pillow as she might a lover, seeking her own warmth and serenity in the night. Perhaps I dreamed it, Jennifer thought. There have been so many tears, so many harsh words. But we can begin to heal now. We've both taken the first steps. She closed the door quietly and went on to the living room.

The last embers of the fire glowed, a dying beacon to guide her steps. She stood at the window, looking out into the night, watching, waiting for Jackson Holloway.

TWENTY-ONE

Robert Shaw reacted too slowly.

He should have realized something was wrong when he did not feel the resistance of the dead bolt as he turned the key. Darlene always kept the dead bolt locked. They both did. But as Shaw was assimilating the information, his hand automatically inserted the key in the second lock of the knob, pushed the door open, and entered the apartment, calling out, "Darlene."

That was a mistake.

When he realized the dead bolt was not on, Shaw should have dropped the two plastic bags of groceries and fled, back to the car for the handgun, and then returned. Or he could have dialed 9-1-1 from the car telephone, making up some bullshit story about a robbery in progress. Let the cops handle it. Apologize after the fact if Darlene had simply forgotten to lock the door.

But comprehension came too late.

Shaw was already inside, calling out for his wife a second time, when the door swung shut slowly behind him and he felt the cold muzzle of the gun at his neck.

"Drop the bags, fuckhead."

Shaw complied.

"That's good. Now, you know the drill. I want you

against the wall and spread 'em."

"Where's Darlene?"

"Darlene's fine. She'll stay that way so long as you're good. The wall, asshole."

"I'm not carrying," Shaw said. He saw Muscles coming down the hallway, smiling, pointing a .45 at him. It looked like his own gun, the one he kept in his desk. Oh, shit. Shaw turned slowly and placed his hands against the door.

"Cover him."

"I've got him," James said.

Shaw was searched expertly. Muscles might be an amateur, but his partner was a pro. Shaw fell when his legs were kicked out from beneath him. His arm was dragged behind him and the cuff snapped tight. His second arm was dragged back. The handcuffs hurt.

"Okay, you can get up now."

Shaw struggled to his knees. James was grinning broadly. "Good afternoon, asshole," he said.

"Darlene?"

"She's waiting in the den. Shall we join her?"

Darlene was facing the door, tied to the straight-backed chair. Duct tape was plastered around her mouth and hair. Her eyes were wide, filled with fear, pleading. Her mascara had run in dark streaks under her eyes.

That tape's going to be a bitch to get off without hurting her, Shaw thought even with the awareness that the tape would be removed only in death.

"Nice of you to provide the rope," James said. "Found it in your bedroom. Like to get a little kinky with Darlene, do you?"

"What do you want?" Shaw asked. Have to play for time. Do something. Make something happen.

"Mr. Holloway thinks you're holding out. Thinks maybe you have some more information. Something you're not telling us."

"He knows you're here?"

"Oh, yes. He asked me to pay a little visit."

"You fucked up. You lost the woman."

James slapped Darlene lightly across the face. "If I don't like your smart mouth, she's going to get it. Keep that in mind. She deserves better from you. She wouldn't tell us a fucking thing."

"She doesn't know anything."

"But you do."

"No."

James ripped Darlene's blouse open. "Are you sure?"

"I've told Holloway everything."

James took a knife from his pocket and flipped it open. He slid the blade between Darlene's breasts and sawed through her brassiere. "Nice boobs," James said, "if you go in for that sort of thing. I do. Ralphie does. You want us to play with your wife's tits, Robert?"

"Let's get it done, man."

"Your name really Ralphie?" Shaw asked. The second man had cold eyes.

The man shrugged. "He can call me anything he likes, so long as I get paid."

"Sooner you tell me about that bitch, the sooner Darlene gets her clothes back on. She might catch a chill if you fuck around with me too long."

Darlene's eyes begged him.

Oh, Christ, what am I going to do?

"Where is she?"

"I don't know. I'm looking for her."

James drew the knife blade lightly across the swell of her breast. A thin red streak followed in its path. Darlene shook her head frantically.

Oh, Christ, honey, I'm sorry.

"Leave her alone," Shaw said. "It's in the safe."

TWENTY-TWO

They were married three days later by a judge in Flagstaff.

It was the same day that a brief news story was belatedly carried as filler in the Arizona newspapers, buried in the back pages among the ads for health clubs and underwear and appliance sales. The story said little more than a Newport Beach, California, couple had been found shot to death, execution style, in their beach front condominium. Involvement with drugs was suspected.

Jennifer did not see the story.

Even if she had been in Los Angeles, it is doubtful she would have seen the story. It did not receive much play there either. It was only another pair of killings related to drugs. Such happenings were all too commonplace.

The three days had been filled with activities. They bought wedding rings, simple gold bands. "We'll pick out a diamond later," Hank told Jennifer. They obtained their wedding license, made arrangements with the judge, sent Hank's best suit to the cleaners, while Jennifer and Clea went through her wardrobe more than once to decide upon her wedding dress. They laughed and giggled together, more like sisters than mother and daughter. Only occasionally did

Clea's eyes cloud over with melancholy and distress. Only occasionally did Jennifer's eyes fill with worry as she thought of the future and what might happen if Jackson Holloway came for her.

Jennifer stole time to make telephone calls to Leo. He was angry, of course, at her sudden unexplained departure.

"I was worried sick about you, Jennifer," he cried.

"I know, Leo. I'm sorry. I would have called sooner, but I was sick, really sick. I couldn't call."

"Are you all right now?"

"I'm fine," Jennifer said. "But I need your help. Please don't ask me to explain though. I can't tell you anything right now. Someday . . . Someday, I'll tell you the whole story."

Leo sighed. "What can I do to help?" he asked.

After hearing her through, Leo agreed to do as she asked. But he said, "I wish you would let me help get you out of whatever trouble you're in, Jennifer."

"I can handle it, Leo." I have to deal with it alone, Jennifer thought. "But thanks."

"Where are you?"

"I'll call you, Leo. It's better that way. For now."

"You're a difficult woman to love, Jennifer."

"It's complicated."

And that was out of the way, for the moment, at least.

Last summer, Jennifer had watched as a spider had created a series of webs across her condominium balcony. Jennifer felt like that spider, spending her lifetime weaving a delicate and elaborate web, only to abandon it, leaving behind strands of tangled and mutilated silk, moving on to a new location, a different life. For two weeks, the spider had demonstrated great perseverance, creating one web after another, sitting at the center of its tiny universe, a black malevolent creature waiting patiently for its prey. Jennifer returned home each evening to stand on the balcony, watching, waiting with the spider. When the sun was just right, the web glittered and sparkled against the setting sun. Then, one night, the spider was gone. Its latest creation was tattered, a dead fly entangled in its silken hold, but the predator had become prey. There was always something or someone bigger. Someone like Jackson Holloway.

Jennifer swept the cobwebs from the balcony.

By tacit agreement, the subject of Jackson Holloway was not brought up during their evenings together. Jennifer, Clea, Hank, ignored his existence, at least openly. Instead, they spoke of the wedding plans, Clea's return to school in the fall, living arrangements, and all of the mundane activities of life in the Valley. They even argued about the hotel. Clea thought it was a good idea for the Valley. "Besides," she would say, "I can get a job there during school vacations."

Kathy came by after school. She and Clea had become friends and Jennifer was surprised to find herself experiencing pangs of jealousy as Kathy transferred affection to Clea. Let her go. It's good for both of them. Kathy still tagged along after Jennifer when they were alone in the big house, but once Clea arrived, the two young women disappeared into Clea's room to listen to their tapes of one new rock group or another. Jennifer felt left out. It was a part of childhood she had missed. Clea had missed it too.

Crazy Maggie appeared suddenly out of the trees one afternoon, wearing a floppy wide-brimmed hat with feathers that might have been in fashion a century ago. "Some folks around here are miffed that you're not having a big wedding," Crazy Maggie said. "Don't pay 'em no mind. Bunch of busy bodies anyway. Just want an excuse to get drunk when someone else's paying."

Maggie disappeared as abruptly as she had arrived.

Jennifer fought the old habit of reading the personal column, but ignoring the newspapers made her nervous and irritable. She didn't really believe that Holloway would send her a signal. If Jackson Holloway came, he would strike without warning. Despite her trepidation, however, once Jennifer succumbed to the siren temptation of the personal column, she calmed, relieved that there were no messages for Kathleen, the woman who no longer existed.

Holloway read the newspapers too. The accounts of the Shaw murders were extensive in Orange County, but it was treated as a dope deal gone bad with little hope of solution. It quickly disappeared from attention. Other crimes pushed it away. There were always more crimes, more murders. Holloway was pleased. Shaw would have been eliminated sooner or later in any case. James and Ralph would have to go too, of course, but not yet. There was still work for them. Real work, Holloway thought and he smiled at the picture of James and Ralph performing manual labor. It's perfect. It's a perfect plan. And when it's over, I'll take care of them myself.

He placed the call.

"Mr. Kendall's office."

"Is Steve in?"

"Mr. Kendall is in conference. May I have him call you?"

Cold, snooty bitch. "Just tell him Jackson Holloway is calling. I believe he'll take my call."

"One moment, please."

Holloway listened to half a commercial on the radio station piped into the telephone system.

"Jackson, how are you?"

"Fine, Steve. Yourself?"

"Busy, but nothing I can't handle."

"Good."

"What can I do for you, Jackson?"

251

"Where are you on the Hidden Valley project? Any activity?"

"I have a couple of advance men up there now and I'm putting together a crew to follow up in a few weeks. Turns out that some of the new property we acquired last year has a slope greater than thirty-five percent. We're going to have to drill some holes, test the geology. It's one God damned thing after another, but it's required. Fucking government regulations."

"I've got a favor to ask, Steve."

"Anything I can do, Jackson."

"Well, it's a little embarrassing."

"Hey, no problem."

"I've got a nephew who needs a job. Day labor would be fine. He's not going to be fussy at this point."

"Yeah, I can put him on. As long as he doesn't mind working."

"He won't mind at all. Gets him out of my hair too. You know what relatives are like."

"Yeah, I do," Kendall said. "I've got a pack of them myself."

"Can you use two men? My nephew has a friend." Holloway knew that Kendall would not refuse.

"Sure. It's not going to be for a couple of weeks though. End of the month probably."

"No hurry," Holloway said. There's plenty of time. I've waited twenty years. "And thanks."

"Glad to do it."

Perfect. Too fucking perfect.

Jennifer followed the path through the trees into the inviolate wilderness where man was forbidden to desecrate pristine beauty, climbing to her favorite place, her clearing high above the world. A tall pine tree, struck by lightning during one of the vicious thunderstorms that roved over the land, had fallen, its wound still fresh and gaping along its trunk. Jennifer felt a great sadness, imagining the tree standing proud and lonely and frightened in the gathering storm, swaying as the winds approached and the world grew dark beneath the massive clouds, awaiting the sacrificial stroke of nature's sword. She heard its anguished cry, its terrible shriek as the tortured wood ripped and fell. In time, a century or more, it would return to the earth, slowly putrefying. But its remains would endure far beyond Jennifer's own death. Clea's children might yet sit upon the fallen remains. But in its place, another tree would grow, a tiny green leaf sprouting from the seed remaining in the earth, its roots burrowing beneath the clearing, incomprehensibly stretching and reaching out to the memory of its forebear. Jennifer turned her back on the tree, looking out over the valley toward the distant rim where more dark clouds lingered. She wondered which tree would be the next to die.

"I love you, Kathleen."

"I love you, Jack."

She stretched to meet his lips, her arms tight around his neck. She gave herself up to him, completely, and without hesitation.

Their wedding party toasted them with red wine. The meadow was thick with the sickly sweet smell of marijuana.

Kathleen smiled up at him, arms still clasped around his neck. "I love you so much."

Jennifer had entered her clearing in joy. She left it in sorrow, grieving for the lost tree, lamenting the loss of her youth and the wasted years.

That evening, Hank and Dave Wilson stood in the driveway, talking for a long time. Jennifer saw them through the window and wondered what they were talking about. Dave Wilson looked grim and nodded as Hank spoke. But when Dave and Kathy drove away and Hank returned to the house, she did not question him. But she noticed that the next time Dave came up, there was a rifle in the rack of his truck. It had been empty before.

After dinner, the three of them did the dishes together, and then sat quietly before the fire, reading, looking up occasionally to make a comment about something or other, before returning to their books.

But the night before the wedding, Jennifer shooed Hank out of the house, back to his own place. "It's bad luck to spend the night before with the bride," Jennifer said.

He went reluctantly.

"We'll be okay," Jennifer said. It was as close as they came to speaking of Jackson Holloway.

"Silly superstition," Hank protested. He didn't want to admit worry either.

Jennifer kissed him. "We're going to spend every night for the rest of our lives together."

Jennifer and Clea stayed up late.

"Nervous, Mom?"

"A little," Jennifer admitted.

"Don't be. He's a good man. Good for you. You're good for him too."

Jack was a good man too. At first. Then he changed. What if Hank changes? I don't think I could stand it a second time. "And how do you know so much?" Jennifer asked.

"Kids always know more than old people."

"I'm not old."

"You will be if you don't go to bed soon."

"I couldn't get to sleep for a while yet. You go ahead, if you want."

"In a few minutes."

They fell silent. The fire crackled. It was dying down. Don't change, Hank, please don't change.

"Mom?"

"Yes?"

"You know, one of the best things about all this, apart from you and Hank getting married, I mean, is . . . well, you know, we're together again. I like it."

"I do too, Clea. I've wanted this for a long time."

"Me too, I guess." Clea paused. "I said some pretty awful things to you before. I'm sorry."

"It wasn't your fault, Clea. I didn't help the situation much either."

"Well, anyway, I love you." Clea went to Jennifer and kissed her. "Good night."

"I love you, too, Clea. Sleep well. I'll close everything up."

Don't change, Hank. Dear God, please don't let him change.

Jennifer was going to marry a stranger.

No. It won't be the same. It can't be the same. But the other men who had entered her life changed, not like Jack, but after a few weeks, even months, they started treating her differently, their love and affection altering perceptibly before her eyes. Like Bennett. In the beginning, he had treated her with respect. But there was always a point, unnoticed by Jennifer, where something inconsequential began a transformation. And once it started, there was no reversal, only the bitter arguments and increasing pain, until the relationship ended in yet another agonizing quarrel with spiteful words that, once uttered, could never be withdrawn. What is there about me that makes men want to hurt me? What am I lacking?

Acrid smoke swirled from the fireplace, stung her eyes, and drifted away again. She wiped at the sudden tears.

And Clea?

Do I know her anymore? Did I ever know her? God, I'm living with strangers. And the person I know least is myself.

* * *

255

The next morning, Hank was late. Jennifer, dressed and ready, stood at the window, looking anxiously down the road for a sign of his truck. If he doesn't come, I won't care. I'll get in the truck and leave, drive south into Mexico, just keep going until I can drive no more. And then? I don't care.

Behind her, Clea said, "He'll be here, Mom, don't worry so much."

"Maybe something's happened. Should I call?"

"He'll be here."

Jennifer heard the truck before she saw it.

"See."

Hank stomped into the house. "God damned people. Somebody tied a bunch of cans to the truck. Started out before I heard the clatter. I thought the engine had fallen out. Had to cut the knots loose, they were so tight." He stopped. "God, you're beautiful."

"The blushing bride thought you'd changed your mind," Clea said.

"I'd have to be crazy to change my mind."

"Yep," Clea said.

Jennifer only smiled, disregarding doubt. He loves me and I love him.

On their way out of the Valley, they passed the property belonging to Kendall Enterprises. A jeep was parked on the slope of a hill, but there was no evidence of a work crew.

"It's starting," Jennifer said.

"More tests," Hank said. "We're making the bastards do more tests. You said make 'em delay. So we're following your instructions."

"I'll be an old woman before that hotel gets built."

"God, I hope so," Hank said.

Clea didn't know the words, but she spent the drive to Flagstaff humming tunes from the wedding songs of *My Fair Lady*. Jennifer and Hank were quiet. And then they were circling the courthouse looking for a parking space. When they arrived at the judicial chambers, they were nearly thirty minutes early, a time spent pacing by Hank, while Jennifer and Clea sat and watched, smiling.

They were married by a judge in his fifties. He was smoking a cigar and dressed in jeans, a bright red wool shirt, and cowboy boots. But when he donned his judicial robe for the ceremony, he wore authority.

"Now, I don't want to see you back in my courtroom in a couple of years, whining that you want a divorce."

"You won't, Judge."

"Better not. God, I love weddings. But I hate divorces." He looked both Jennifer and Hank directly in the eye. Satisfied, he said, "Okay, let's get you started on the road to matrimonial bliss."

After the groom kissed the bride, Jennifer cried a little. Clea cried a great deal. Hank grinned foolishly and happily. The judge resumed smoking the cigar he had decorously placed on the edge of the desk in his chambers. The law clerk who had provided witness to the ceremony congratulated everyone at least twice and would have started around again had a detective not entered chambers at that moment to ask the judge to execute a search warrant. The young detective was taken with Clea, but the wedding party slipped out while the judge was questioning the need for the warrant. On the courthouse steps, Clea produced a bag of rice and threw handfuls of the grain on the bride and groom to their embarrassment and the applause of legal staff leaving the building for lunch. Everyone agreed that it had been a very nice wedding for a civil ceremony.

The wedding luncheon was celebrated in the restaurant of a Holiday Inn where the wedding party of three acclaimed the event with two bottles of champagne. Hank wanted French champagne in anticipation and honor of their delayed honeymoon in Paris, but settled for a California brand when told by their waitress, after a long consultation with others of the restaurant staff, that their French champagne was not chilled.

"This is Flagstaff," Clea said.

"I should have called ahead," Hank said morosely. "I knew it was Flag."

"We'll have French champagne in Paris," Jennifer said. "In Flag, we'll have California."

"That doesn't sound right," Clea said. "We should be drinking beer." She rummaged through her purse for a moment and put an envelope on the table. "Here, this is for both of you. It's a wedding present, the first of many."

Jennifer opened the envelope. "A key?"

"It's to the honeymoon suite. You guys are staying here tonight. It's all arranged. Room service. Anything you want." She lifted her champagne. "I wish you all the best. I know you're going to be very happy. Now give me the truck keys."

"You can't go home alone," Jennifer said.

"Why not?"

"Well . . ."

Clea held out her hand. "The keys, Hank."

"No," Jennifer said. "Don't do it."

"Look," Clea said. "I know what you're thinking, but nothing can happen to me. I don't even know what he looks like. He doesn't know me. He doesn't even know I exist."

"Hank . . ."

"Just give me the keys. I'm not going to live my life in fear."

Jennifer nodded. She sounds just like me. Perhaps I do know her. She is her mother's daughter. "Give her the keys, Hank."

"All right. I'll be back tomorrow. I'm sorry you're only having a one night honeymoon."

"It's a wonderful present, Clea. Thank you."

"See you tomorrow."

"Wait. What are we going to do for clothes?"

258

Clea smiled. "Who needs clothes?"

"Clea . . ." Jennifer blushed.

"See you tomorrow." Clea raced out of the restaurant.

"Well," Jennifer said.

"Well, indeed. I hope they have cable TV. It's going to be a long afternoon. Maybe we can find a Clint Eastwood movie."

"Hank . . ."

"Or maybe we can find something else to do."

"Maybe we can."

"Well, we're certainly on the road to matrimonial bliss."

They took turns undressing each other, slowly at first, and then urgently, clinging to each other, kissing, caressing.

"Oh, God, I love you so much, Jennifer."

"I love you, Kathleen."

"I love you, Jack."

Jennifer started crying.

"What's wrong?"

"I'm happy, darling. And I love you. Don't ever leave me. Please, don't ever leave me."

Hank kissed her tears away.

He carried her to their wedding bed then.

"Clea, where have you been? I called before."

"At Kathy's. I'm fine. Stop worrying. Go back to bed, Mom."

"Clea!"

"Watch TV then. Or something. I'll be all right."

"I wanted to be sure . . ."

"Gotta go, Mom. I've got a bunch of cowboys in for the night. We're having an orgy. You should too."

"Good night, sweetheart."

"Good night, Mom, I love you."

259

"I was just thinking . . ."

"What, darling?"

"I have a new name now. I've had so many names. Sometimes, I wonder who I really am."

"You're still Jennifer, the woman I love."

"You won't change, will you?"

"No, darling."

Jennifer and Hank spent their first night together as wife and husband sleeping close to each other, the one holding the other alternately, as though both feared waking to an empty bed.

Clea arrived as promised the next morning, turning the truck keys over to Hank with a flourish, asking, "So, how's the road to matrimonial bliss?"

"Fraught with peril," Hank said.

"You didn't have your first fight?"

"Wet socks and damp underwear," Jennifer said. "He's grouchy and it's your fault."

"Boy, he gets upset about the littlest things."

"Men are that way, dear."

"It was a great wedding present," Hank said. "Despite the lack of amenities."

When they turned south off the interstate and paused at the edge of the Mogollon Rim, Jennifer remembered how many times she had made the trip alone, or with only Oscar for companionship. This time she said, "We're going home," to her family.

All of the Valley was spread out beneath them, bathed in a glorious clear sunshine.

But the jeep was still parked on the hotel property.

TWENTY-THREE

The shot rang out clearly.

The echo followed, reverberating off the mountain face, rushing back through the Valley. A flock of birds rushed into the air with a collective screech. When the echo died out finally, the landscape was empty and silent.

"Better."

"Better? I didn't even come close."

"Try it again. Don't aim. It's just like pointing your finger. Do it naturally."

The bullet kicked up dirt, two feet to the left of the can.

"You flinched."

Another shot.

The can jumped into the air and fell on its side.

Clea turned to her mother and grinned. "It worked."

"Good shot," Jennifer said. "That was six. Now reload."

Clea released the cylinder and emptied the spent cartridges in her hand and then dropped them on the ground. "Jesus, they're hot."

"Oops," Jennifer said. "I forgot to tell you to let them cool. We'll pick them up later."

"Thanks a lot, Mom." Clea slipped more cartridges into the cylinder, closing it gently. She thumbed the hammer back and fired. The can jumped again.

"You're getting the hang of it now," Jennifer said.

When the revolver was empty again—with four hits out of the six shots fired—Clea let the shell casings fall to the ground and slipped the ear muffs off her head. "Let's see you do it."

"Set the cans up," Jennifer said, pulling her ear muffs off, letting them rest around her neck.

Jennifer waited until Clea was standing behind her before she reloaded the revolver. She fired quickly, methodically, sending all six cans flying.

"Show off," Clea said.

"Practice," Jennifer said. "I don't want to frighten you, but if you ever have to use this, just keep shooting. Don't stop."

"Do you really think . . ."

"No, but you should know how to use it, just in case."

"I'm his daughter," Clea said. "What kind of man would hurt his daughter?"

"He hurt me . . ."

"I know, but . . ." Her words died, like the echo of the shots. "Christ, I wouldn't even be here if he had his way."

Jennifer hugged her. "Don't think about any of that."

"I try not to, but . . ."

"I know. It's the same with me. I'm happy for the first time in my life really, and still . . . To hell with it. You want to try the rifle now?"

"Sure. This is kind of fun. I just wish . . ."

Jennifer and Clea drove slowly back toward the little town. Both windows in the truck were rolled all the way down. After a last snow storm during the weekend after the wedding, the first signs of spring had come to the Valley. The snow had melted except for the last patches

262

that remained in cold shaded canyons where the sun did not reach. Trees that had been skeletal were turning green with their new leaves. Jennifer had seen robins in the yard. The lingering chill of the nights passed quickly and the afternoons were warm. It took the sun longer to disappear behind the mountains.

"Clea?"

"Yeah, Mom?"

"Don't tell Hank what we were doing. I don't want him to worry."

"I won't."

"Thanks."

"You guys are really happy, aren't you?"

"Happier than I thought I could ever be."

"Yeah, it's kind of disgusting, really. All that lovey dovey stuff all the time."

Jennifer smiled. "Wait until you're in love."

"I've been in love. Lots of times."

"Great, isn't it?"

"It's kind of neat, all right."

"Are you lonely here?"

"Sometimes. I wish there were some guys around though. Somebody I could really like. Somebody besides ranch hands."

"You'll be back in school in no time. The summer will pass quickly."

"I know," Clea said. "I can wait. You did."

"I hope you don't have to wait twenty years."

"Me too."

"Hey, darlings," Hank called. "What have my two favorite girls been up to?" He marked his place in *Martin Chuzzlewit* and came around from behind the bar to hug and kiss each of them in turn, ignoring the few patrons. "You smell like gunpowder."

Clea looked at Jennifer.

"Oh, hell," Jennifer said. "We've been out shooting. I

263

thought it was time Clea learned. It wasn't something we could do very well when she was growing up in L.A."

"Good idea," Hank said. "It'll keep some respect in the boys around here. How'd you do, Clea?"

"Okay, I guess. I could hit the cans after awhile."

"She's really good with the rifle. You'd be proud of her."

"I always am. Want a beer or something?"

"Love a beer," Jennifer said.

"Coke for me."

"Belly up to the bar."

Jennifer glanced at the television automatically as she sat at the bar. *High Plains Drifter* was on. Someone broke on the pool table in the back. The balls clattered.

"God, that's good," Jennifer said after the first swallow of beer. "It's almost hot out there."

"You're beginning to drink like a native," Hank said. "People going to think you were born here."

"I'll be sixty before they stop calling me that new girl who lives up west of town," Jennifer drawled.

"Might always be that new girl, Mom."

"Order came in today for the party," Hank said.

"Are you sure it's enough?"

"Got a lifetime supply of liquor for anyplace but here. Probably be gone by midnight. We better be getting some expensive wedding presents out of this."

"Hank! They're our friends. We have to have some kind of reception for them. And I don't want them thinking they have to bring presents. We don't need anything."

"I'll take them," Clea said. "For my trousseau."

"You're as bad as he is," Jennifer said.

The bar and the diner slowly began to fill and the friendly and relaxed atmosphere of the bar closed around them. Rowdy and raucous only late in the evening and on Friday and Saturday nights, it was a comfortable place to be, less a bar usually than a gathering spot for the townspeople to gossip and the ranch hands who dropped in for a beer or two to get the dust from their mouths, watch the Clint Eastwood movie, and argue over whatever was the pressing topic of the day, sports in season, crooked politicians always, the latest weekend spent in the bright lights of Phoenix, lies about hunting and fishing prowess or who was seeing what woman and what they did together, the proposed hotel, a mean horse that couldn't be broken, strayed cattle, guns, pickup trucks, dreams of owning a Corvette, or any of a multitude of other subjects that needed complete discussion.

Clea had settled into her job at Hank's, quickly breaking a dozen or more hearts as she turned down dates and the frequent offers of "Let me take you away from all this." She smiled and bantered with the young men who vied for her attention, her smile, a few moments of her time devoted only to them. Everyone loved Clea and there was a general consensus that Hank's place was much livelier with her presence.

For Jennifer, it was always an opportunity to get away from the house, to be with Hank. She was surprised to find that she missed her work, not the loneliness of Los Angeles, but the daily routine of going to the office and the mental challenge of working through some complex legal problem. Before, the hours and days spent in the Valley were a cherished luxury. Now, there were hours and days to fill with activities. Jennifer did not regret being in the Valley, but she had quickly learned that she was not destined to be a wife only. She loved cooking for Hank, but he also liked to cook and competed with her for time in the kitchen. His chili was better than that of Jesus, but Hank dared not let it get around. Jesus would be devastated. More often than not, they would eat at the bar anyway. Jesus demanded that they sample one or another of his delicacies.

So Jennifer had time to fill. She was planning a computer purchase, everything that would allow her to communicate with the outside world. Leo had offered to send her work as soon as she had a computer and modem up and running. She accepted gratefully. And there was the study for the Arizona bar examination as well. Jennifer was confident that she would pass, but a bar exam was never anything to take lightly. Too many young attorneys, new graduates from law school, failed to pass on their first try.

But Jennifer was happier than she had ever been.

And the bar provided an extended family.

"Hank, Jennifer, Clea," the Doc said.

"Evening, Doc."

"You feeling okay, Jennifer?"

"Just fine, Doc, thanks."

"I still want you to take it easy. Don't overdo it."

"I won't."

"Hank, let me have just a taste of your good whiskey."

Ben Davis emerged from the pool room carrying his cue stick. "Jennifer, Miss Clea, how y'all today?"

"Just fine, Ben."

"Hank, need some more quarters and a couple more beers. Beating Charley so bad, he's embarrassed to come out and face you."

"Don't be too hard on Charley," Jennifer said.

"Ain't taking no prisoners," Ben cackled. "Don't you think for a minute, he wouldn't do it to me. If he could, of course."

"Ben, you coming back in here or you afraid you're gonna get your butt whipped?"

"Have to excuse his language, ladies. He gets right ornery when he loses."

Thad Murphy was in and out quickly. The two cowboys Hank had fought at the Christmas party sat at the far end of the bar, tipping their hats respectfully to

266

Jennifer. "Evening, Hank," they said.

"Evening, boys. The usual?"

"Yes, sir. Mighty hot out there today."

The room quieted.

Two men entered, stood at the door for a moment and then walked past the bar into the dining room. They greeted Hank with a nod and a "Good evening."

"Good evening," Hank replied.

Their voices were loud in the sudden hush.

"God damned carpetbaggers," someone muttered. It was loud enough for the two men to hear. "Don't know why Hank lets 'em come in here."

Jennifer waited until the noise level had returned almost to normal. "Who are they, Hank?"

"A couple of the fellows working up at the hotel site. They're doing some of the preliminary work for the testing they need."

"They're not real popular."

"They're not at fault. They're just doing their job. I can't blame them for that."

Jennifer looked into the dining room. They were sitting at an isolated table, shunned by the others in the room. Like lepers, Jennifer thought.

Jennifer waited up for Hank to come home after closing the bar for the night. It was a part of the routine they had fallen into, established almost by accident. Hank worked late, slept late, and Jennifer adjusted her schedule to his. Sometimes, she rose first, going into the kitchen to pour a first cup of coffee from the pot left for them by Clea, carrying a second cup back to Hank. On other mornings, it was Hank who brought the coffee back to bed. Whoever was the first to get up did so reluctantly, neither wanting to leave the warmth of the other. They could not get enough of each other. Not yet. After Hank left, Jennifer worked around the house or shopped or talked with Leo on the telephone, filling her time one way or another until Clea came home after the luncheon crowd thinned. They would then spend time together or not according to their mood. After school, Kathy might come by, with or without her grandfather. Then, it was time to join Hank at the bar for a drink, or to make supper if he chose to come home for a break before returning to work. And then it was time to wait for his late arrival. Hank took Sunday and Monday as his weekend. That time belonged to them.

Tonight, Clea had already gone to bed. She, too, had established her own pattern, rising early to work the breakfast and lunch shift at the cafe. Jennifer continued to marvel at the nice young woman her daughter had become. They were making up for time lost, creating a new and genuine friendship. All we needed was time together. And honesty.

Despite the warmer nights, Jennifer had lit a fire and sat before it as she waited for Hank. Once the weather turned completely, there wouldn't be many opportunities for using the fireplace and that was one of the great pleasures for Jennifer. Oscar was stretched out at full length on the rug. She sat and watched the flames, book open in her lap, mesmerized by their allure.

Hank was late tonight. Usually, he was home by eleven or eleven-thirty on a week night. But it was almost midnight. Probably going over tomorrow's menu with Jesus, Jennifer thought. He would be home soon. But she closed her eyes and concentrated on sending him a message. I love you, darling. He responded by driving up the steep driveway. Jennifer jumped up and ran to the door and down the steps. She was waiting for him when he got out of the car.

"That's an enthusiastic greeting," he said as she jumped into his arms.

"I missed you."

"I thought old married people were supposed to get tired of each other."

"Nope. Not this old married woman anyway."

They walked arm in arm up the steps. Clea's light was off. "We've got the fire to ourselves," Jennifer said.

"Got any ideas?"

"Two or three."

"You're going to have to let me rest one of these days. You're wearing me out."

"We'll get Doc to prescribe some hormone pills."

"Think that'll work?"

"You haven't needed them yet. Would you like a nightcap?"

"I think I would."

"Go sit in front of the fire. I'll get it."

"You spoil me."

"I hope so. Your usual?"

"Bourbon tonight. Some of that Jack Daniels."

"When did you switch?"

"That's one of the secrets of being a bartender. You get to know what everyone drinks. But you should switch it around. Don't be predictable."

"I'll keep that in mind."

Jennifer poured a shot of the black label in a snifter for Hank and then as an afterthought poured a second drink for herself. When she returned, Oscar was sitting in Hank's lap.

"Fickle damned cat. He wouldn't come near me all night. Just slept."

"That's cause he likes me better. Ain't that right, Clint?"

Oscar purred contentedly. He hadn't stopped purring since that night at the rest stop. For Jennifer, it seemed long ago.

"Got room for one more?" Jennifer asked, snuggling close to Hank without waiting for a response.

"So long as it's you, darling."

"You're sweet."

"Course I am. Isn't that why you married me?"

"Why did you marry me, Bear?"

"Didn't have too many choices around here. It was

269

either you or Crazy Maggie and she doesn't have a cat that likes me."

"I'm serious."

"Me too."

"Come on."

"All right, I'll be serious. I fell in love with you the first time you walked into my life. I saw you and I knew I wanted to spend the rest of my life with you."

"What took you so long then?"

"I was afraid of you. Hell, I was just a bartender and you came in looking so cool and sophisticated."

"I was wearing jeans and an old sweater."

"Designer jeans and cashmere sweater. I didn't think you even saw me."

"Oh, I noticed you all right."

"And what did you think?"

"I couldn't figure you out. Here's this big old bartender reading a book. Something literary, but I don't remember what."

"Henry James," Hank said. *"Wings of the Dove.* I remember everything about that day. 'The Germans wore grey, you wore blue.'"

"All right, Bogie. But it was red."

"Red, blue, don't screw up a good line."

"Who did you see *Casablanca* with the first time?"

"I've never seen it."

"Come on."

"Mary Louise Jenkins."

"Why didn't you marry her. Aren't you supposed to marry the girl you first see *Casablanca* with? Or is it the other way around?"

"I was waiting for you."

"What happened to Mary Louise Jenkins?"

"She got married. Moved to Tucson. Had about ten kids and got fat."

"Was she pretty then?"

"Beautiful."

"Better than me?"

270

"Much."

"Did she have big breasts, like mine?"

"Bigger."

"Nice long legs, like mine?"

"Longer, nicer."

"How about her hair?"

"Silky."

"Blonde?"

"A real blonde."

"I'm a real blonde."

"Not like Mary Louise."

"You should have married her."

"Yeah, but then I'd be living in Tucson with a fat old wife and about ten kids. No fun at all. Besides . . ."

"Besides what?"

"I love you so much it aches inside sometimes. The moments I'm away from you are torture. And when we're together, it's paradise."

"You're a smooth talking devil. I'll say that for you. But I love you just as much. I always will."

Hank put his hand on her breast.

Jennifer closed her eyes, already feeling her nipple swell. "Even if they're not as nice as Mary Louise's?" Jennifer whispered. She squirmed beneath his gentle caress. She was glad she had discarded her bra while she waited for him.

"Oh, I lied about that. Mary Louise was skinny and flat-chested. Had scraggly red hair. And she hated *Casablanca*. Thought it was dumb. It was the only time I took her out."

"She was a foolish woman, but I'm glad you waited for me."

"I've waited for you all my life." He tugged at her blouse, pulling it from the waistband of her jeans. He caressed the warmth of her breast.

"Restaurateur," Jennifer said dreamily, arching and thrusting her body to meet his touch.

"What?"

"You're not a bartender. Oh, don't stop," she said, taking in a sharp breath. "I prefer . . . to think of you . . . as a restaurateur." She gasped. "Oh, God, I'll give you all my money if you'll just keep doing that forever."

"I've already got your money. What else do you have?"

"Anything. You can have anything you want." She pulled him to the floor, touching him. "I don't think you need any hormone pills."

"Clea . . ."

"She's asleep, darling."

"We need a fireplace in the bedroom."

"I'll have it done tomorrow," she said.

"We'll do it over the summer. It can wait that long."

"Yes, yes, but I can't," she cried. "Ah, do it now. Please."

Afterwards, as they still held each other, Jennifer said, "This is the best part of our routine. Do you think we'll ever get tired of it?"

"I don't see how."

"Me neither," Jennifer said happily.

And later, his arms protected her as she waited for sleep. That, too, was a delicious part of their routine, their lives. The nights were never so lonely and fearful now. Jennifer fell asleep, his breath a soothing warmth on her neck.

Outside, time stopped. In the distant timber, a wolf howled, a mournful lament for the full moon hanging motionless in the sky above the valley, creating a ghostly and spectral night for the restless shades of the dead. Shadows formed, dancing grotesquely in the moonlight, creeping ever so slowly toward the house.

The wolf cried out to the night.

TWENTY-FOUR

From the road far below, the house could not be seen. Driving up the long curving driveway through the trees was like taking a journey into oblivion. Indeed, if it were not for the solitary rural mailbox atop its planted post, there was little indication to the casual traveler that anything but a vast wilderness existed further up the hill beyond the road. Place an unschooled child looking west from the road into the timbered mountains and ask what might lie beyond. The reply would be, "Nothing," for there was no indication of human habitat. Tall trees flanked the driveway. Not planted by man to guard the passage to a stately mansion, they were the first outposts of the untamed forest, a dark and brooding presence for the child, and for those who questioned him. Whoever persisted in entering the forbidding trees, however, despite their fear of what unknown creatures might lurk in tangled thickets, concealed by the gloomy shadows, would be rewarded—and relieved—to find the house in the clearing as a brightly-lighted beacon.

The windows of the house blazed with light, shining into the open, fighting bravely against the dark night with no hint of its own sad history when it stood abandoned by those who had once loved it. Colored lanterns glowed from the overhang of the porch, strung there by Clea and Kathy to welcome visitors from the darkness. Already crowded with guests spilling outside from the house, latecomers had to park down the hill and trudge the last hundred or two hundred yards, carrying their wedding presents, guided by laughter and animated conversations.

Jennifer and Hank stood at the door, greeting their guests in a mini-receiving line of two. Everyone wanted to kiss the bride, shake the groom's hand in hearty congratulations, and offer their token in celebration of their union. A table behind the door overflowed with wedding presents. Once, Jennifer caught her daughter's eye and mouthed, "Your trousseau is growing." Clea laughed and continued circulating through the crowded living room with the trays of hors d'oeuvres that Jennifer, Clea, and Kathy had spent days preparing. Kathy also moved through the rooms with trays, occasionally sneaking up to Jennifer and Hank, offering to replenish a drink, or to give Jennifer a quick hug and say, "I'm so happy for you."

Finally, it seemed that there was no one left in the Valley below. They were all crowded into the isolated house. Jennifer and Hank dissolved their receiving line and went through the crowd once more, receiving a second round of acclamation from their well-wishers, joining first one group and then another.

There was a weight room beneath the small three-story apartment building where James lived. He was the only one who used the weights and usually the only person who sat in the adjoining sauna. Located off the underground parking garage with an entrance near the pool, the weight room afforded privacy. James thought the other residents were fools for not taking advantage of the facilities—they preferred sitting around the pool, drinking beer and wine, baking and blistering their bodies in the hot, unhealthy Southern California sun—

but was always pleased to have the room to himself. He always brought a portable radio, tuned to a station that played nothing but Heavy Metal, turned it as high as he wanted—no one ever complained—fastened the heavy leather belt around his waist and began his routine, starting slowly with curls, progressing to heavier weights and more difficult exercises, grunting loudly, obscenely, as the workout became more difficult.

Once, a voyeur, a newcomer to the swimming pool crowd, heard the grunts and crept silently down the steps and along the walkway to the weight room door, expecting to find a couple in the climactic throes of passionate lovemaking. The voyeur was extremely disappointed to find only James, doing bench presses, his hard body glistening with sweat. The voyeur returned to the pool and said, "I thought someone was getting their ears fucked off."

The voyeur didn't know that James made the same exact sounds when lifting weights as when he was in bed with one or another of his partners. They were cries of passion. For James, though, lifting was better than sex, a sensuous pleasure far more prolonged than groping and coupling awkwardly beneath sheets for a few minutes. Lifting conditioned his body, eliminated poisons, and carried his mind into a metaphysical realm where thoughts came to him with a definite clarity. James had been lifting when he determined how Robert Shaw and his wife would die. It had rankled that Shaw thought him to be homosexual. It still did. The last words Shaw heard were when James whispered into his ear, "I'm going to fuck your wife, but first I'm going to play with her tits and let her suck my cock. Give her a taste of a real man." Then James shot him in the back of the head with the silenced .22 target pistol. That had been a disappointing mistake, James thought now. I should have let him watch. But that was over. He added weights to the bar, another fifty pounds, and turned his thoughts to the woman in

275

Arizona. She, too, would pay for humiliating him, tricking him so easily that night.

The party grew louder.

Snatches of conversation, shouts really, for everyone was talking at the top of their voices to make themselves heard, stood out above the clamor.

"God damn hotel anyway. Got no right."

"Don't know what they're doing up there."

"I hear there's more a'coming. Supposed to be here this week."

"Old Matt sure welcomed 'em with open arms."

"He ain't never made so much money renting them cabins a'his."

"Ain't right."

With the bar closed for the first Saturday night anyone in the Valley could remember, Jesus stood happily behind the bar, dispensing strong drink to anyone offering a glass for refill.

"Jesus Christo, Jesus, Hank'd go broke if you was his full-time bartender."

Offended, Jesus defended himself, "I'm a good bartender, amigo, don't you forget it." He continued pouring more whiskey than water, more rum than Coke, more gin than tonic. The room buzzed under his bartending influence.

"Shit howdy."

"Looks like an early spring."

"Gonna be a good year maybe."

"We sure could use one. Been awhile. Been too long."

"Maybe the hotel ain't such a bad idea. Bring some money in here. Get us out of the recession."

"Recession, my ass. It's a full-on depression. Just like the Great Depression. I remember that, all right. Terrible times."

"Times ain't been so good here lately either."

276

"That's for damned sure."

"And then the horse just scraped him off. Used the top rail like a back scratcher. Stood there then waiting for old Charley to get up off his sorry ass. Looked innocent with them big eyes and like no butter gonna melt in its mouth."

Hank and Jennifer continued to circulate, going from one circle of friends and acquaintances to the next. Each group was eager to share their happiness. Around whatever group they happened to join, the maelstrom of the party swirled.

James lifted.

It was no place to take the Lexus, so they were going in a pickup truck Ralph had stolen from out in the Valley someplace. James didn't like the charade of work, but Holloway insisted. "It will give you time to decide the best way to do it," he said. "Once you have a plan, you will call me and I will make the final decision." That's a lot of unnecessary bullshit, James thought. Get in. Get out. Fast. That's the way to do it. But for the money Holloway was paying . . . It was only for a week, ten days at the most. Then James and Ralph would go to the crew foreman and quit. Wait another day or two and then do it. Snatch her. Toss her in a packing crate and deliver her to Holloway. And then the fun would start.

James thought of Jennifer Warren and expelled a long passionate cry that could have been either pleasure or pain—or both.

"Great party."

"Here's to you. All the best. Drink up."

"We're so glad to have you with us, Jennifer."

"That's right. You're one of us now. You need anything, just holler. We take care of our own."

"You're looking a might peaked, Hank. Married life getting you down?"

"Haw. That ain't his problem. Getting it up, more likely."

Clea and Kathy laid out the buffet and the guests ate and continued drinking and talking, laughing and shouting to be heard.

"Octopus ain't coming no more," Crazy Maggie cackled. "It's here. It's here, for sure. Got them big arms out. Gather us all in now."

"Did you try some of that champagne punch?"

"I'll try it if we run out of drinkin' whiskey."

"Ain't likely. Saw Hank loadin' his truck. Got enough to drink here, even for you."

"Better have two truck loads a liquor, way Jesus's pouring."

"Hell you say."

"Hell I don't."

"You leave my partner, Jesus, alone. Just keep on pouring, Jesus. That's the way."

"Don't be startin' no fights now."

"That was a good one at Christmas time. Old Hank sure laid them fellas out quick."

"Never saw it coming."

"Better not fuck with old Hank."

"Better not fuck with me neither."

"That's for damned sure."

"You better get outside and breathe some of that good night air. You getting drunk and it ain't even ten o'clock."

"I'll be here dancing when you sleeping in that ratty old pickup you got."

"Ain't ratty. Just broke in nice. Like a woman. Gotta know the right thing to do."

"I wouldn't mind doing it with her just once."

"Hank kill you and I'd be helping him."

"Wouldn't need no help."

"Daughter's just as pretty. Prettier even."

"Sure make a nice-looking family."

"Sure do."

"Oughta go up there and tell them boys what's what. Tell 'em what they can do with their hotel."

"Oughta ain't nothing. Let's do it."

"Let's have another drink first."

"Good idea. Mighty fine idea, in fact."

Thad Murphy made the first toast after spending ten minutes trying to get everyone crowded into the house and quieted down.

"Let 'er rip, Thad."

"I will, soon as y'all shut the hell up so a man can think."

"What about the ladies, Thad. Ain't good for the mayor to be prejudiced about the ladies. They got the vote too, you know."

"Ladies, too," Thad shouted back. "I'm an equal opportunity mayor. Now y'all listen up. We've done some celebrating here tonight . . ."

"And we got a lot more to do yet," Hank shouted. The crowd cheered and applauded. Jennifer squeezed his arm. "Let the mayor speak," she said.

"Well, it's true," Hank said.

There were additional cheers.

"Well, we can't get to the celebrating unless I get through this toast."

"Let 'em make his toast."

"He'll burn it."

"Oh, hell," Thad said, raising his glass. "Here's to you, Hank and Jennifer, we wish you all the happiness in the world. May all your days be good."

"Nights, too," someone shouted.

"Told you so."

"Hear, hear."

"To Hank and Jennifer."

Crazy Maggie stepped up, pushing Thad Murphy into the background. She held a cup of champagne punch daintily in her hand. "Ladies and gentlemen,

279

charge your glasses." She waited patiently while those who had gulped at the first toast refilled their glasses. The room quieted for Maggie. No one wanted to be the subject of her disapproving glare. Old superstitions die hard.

"This toast is mostly for Jennifer, Hank too, but mostly Jennifer. There's some people in this room consider you a stranger to the Valley, but you ain't. You just come home after a long time away. You been here before. You may not know it, but I do. I seen you here. You was sad then, but no more. You got a right to be happy now. So that's what I'm telling you. Be happy. Welcome home."

"Welcome home," came the refrain from around the room.

"And," Crazy Maggie said, "this is to Hank. You take care of your woman, you hear."

"Yes, ma'am," Hank said.

Crazy Maggie nodded. "All right, then, here's to Hank and his bride. Joy and happiness."

"Joy and happiness."

Crazy Maggie stared at Jennifer with wild, flashing eyes, hinting of something dark and forbidding, a warning. Of all the people in the room, only Jennifer saw more than apparent madness. The others listened and watched the same old Crazy Maggie prattling on in her addled fashion.

Jesus, who had not been drinking yet, shouted, "Viva Senora Jennifer and Senor Hank."

James showered and paced the apartment restlessly. The workout had left him keyed up. He had an erection and suddenly wanted Sarah. There wouldn't be anyone to fuck in Arizona. A waitress or two maybe. It wasn't worth it. He went into his bedroom and glanced across the driveway to the next building. Her lights were on.

He had watched her surreptitiously for weeks. Each

weekday morning she stood in her bra and panties before an uncurtained window ironing the clothes she would wear to work each day. She had big tits and long legs. At first, James thought she was a dyke, but after watching her dress in the freshly ironed dresses and blouses, she transformed herself into a soft and feminine woman. One morning he printed his telephone number on a large piece of cardboard and stood boldly in his window—before he had always stood back, peeking through a part in the blinds—looking down at her, willing her to notice him.

She did and stared back equally boldly.

James smiled and held the telephone number.

She stared at him for a few moments and then reached across and pulled the curtains closed.

Shit.

A few minutes later his telephone rang.

"How long have you been a peeping tom?" a husky voice asked.

"Long enough to know I want you."

"You've seen me. Undress and go stand in your window. You'll have to get on a chair." She hung up.

James did as she had instructed. He thought he saw the curtain move, but he couldn't be sure.

The telephone rang again.

Still naked, he went to answer it.

"Dinner tonight," the husky voice said. "Seven o'clock."

He had been banging her ever since.

"I deserve a going away fuck," he said and dressed quickly in jeans and a plaid wool shirt, the cowboy clothes purchased as camouflage for the Arizona excursion. He left his building and went next door.

Clea and Kathy wheeled out the tiered wedding cake. Together, Jennifer and Hank cut the cake to much applause. They linked arms and grinning foolishly

281

passed each other small slices of cake. Crumbs fell down their chins to more applause and cheers. And then Jennifer sliced the cake, putting each piece on a paper plate, handed it to Hank who passed it on to a waiting guest.

As soon as she could, Jennifer slipped away and looked for Crazy Maggie. She found her on the back porch. The old woman stared into the night.

"What is it?" Jennifer asked quietly, not daring to look at Maggie, fearing what might be revealed in the penetrating eyes.

"Just looking at the night," Maggie said. "I see things out there."

"What things?" Jennifer asked.

"The dark mostly." Maggie cackled. "Just like other folks. But sometimes . . ."

Jennifer waited.

". . . it's like sittin' in a dark room and the curtains are opened, sudden-like, you know . . . and it ain't dark no more. That's what happens. I'm going along through life, minding my own business, muddling through the dark as best I can . . . and then someone opens the curtain on me . . . ain't fair. Didn't ask for it. But you just got to look out through that window. I ain't crazy." Maggie turned to face Jennifer. "I ain't crazy at all."

"I didn't think you were."

Maggie nodded, accepting Jennifer's statement. She turned away again back to the darkness beyond the pool of light from the house. "I just see things."

Jennifer asked again. "What things?"

"You believe in reincarnation?" Maggie asked.

"I don't know," Jennifer replied. She stared into the darkness, waiting for the curtain to lift. "I guess I've never thought much about it."

"Makes sense. If folks don't come back again . . .

282

why heaven and hell must be gettin' pretty crowded now with all the people that been born and died for hundreds of years . . . hear about all them Chinese and Africans and Indians and Americans. Seems like all we do today is have babies. Grow up and die. Don't you ever wonder where God's gonna put 'em all?"

"Recycled souls."

"That's it, exactly," Maggie cried. "Recycling, just like they say we oughta do with garbage. There's some human garbage that don't deserve recycling, but I guess they gotta come back too."

"And that's what you see when the curtain lifts?"

"Sometimes . . . Saw me once. Most people who believe in this reincarnation . . . say they lived before and they was always a king or queen or somebody fancy. Saw me once and wasn't like that a'tall. I was a witch. Least they said I was." Again, she turned to look at Jennifer. "Does that scare you?"

"No," Jennifer said, despite the chill that crawled down her back.

"Burned me at the stake." Maggie cackled her mad laugh again. "Didn't do 'em any good though. Here I am. Just like new. Well, used to be, anyway."

Jennifer smiled and waited.

"Saw you once too."

"Was I someone fancy?"

"Don't make fun of me, girl."

"I'm sorry," Jennifer said quickly. "I didn't mean anything by it."

"All right, then," Maggie said. "I guess maybe you wasn't."

"I'm interested," Jennifer said. "I want to know."

"Shouldn't have ever said anything."

"Please . . ."

"You wasn't anybody fancy. Unless you consider a whore fancy. Wasn't you, a course. Not the way you are now. But it was you, all right. It was what you was before. When I seen it, I knew it was you out there

283

walking through the grass, wearing a long dress and flowers in your hair. You was happy, but it didn't last long."

"What happened?"

"They took you out and hung you."

Sarah was a biter and a scratcher. It was like fucking a wildcat on a roller coaster each time, James thought, all fangs and claws and swooping up and down through the bed. But she never protested when he got rough in return, daring him to do his worst. And he did, climbing on, pinning her arms to the bed, crushing her breasts beneath his hard body, kissing her brutally, fighting her all the time. It was good practice for Arizona.

Behind Jennifer and Maggie, the house rocked with laughter.

"What do you see now?" Jennifer asked.

"Just the night," Maggie lied. "Ain't nothing out there but the night."

"Does it frighten you?"

"Ain't nothing out there to hurt an old woman," Maggie lied again. There was always something in the night that hurt. "Want you to do me a favor."

"Whatever I can."

"Want you to play me a tune on that violin of yours."

Jennifer and Maggie found two empty chairs in a corner of the living room. Jennifer removed the violin from its case, stroking the carved words on its back as always, tenderly, affectionately, absorbing the sadness of the violin's history. She looked at Maggie as she applied resin to the bow string. The chills that had penetrated her soul while listening to Maggie outside had fled in the cheery light and companionship of the party that careened all around them. Now, Jennifer looked at Maggie and saw an old woman who confused past and present. But she was harmless, a well-meaning old woman who had outlived her lovers, husbands, children.

Jennifer lifted the violin to her chin, closed her eyes, and began to play for Maggie. The lilting, melancholy tune was born in a distant past, in the hill country of Appalachia—West Virginia perhaps or maybe Tennessee. It floated through the room and drifted beyond, into the night, speaking of sadness, lamenting the harshness of life, celebrating the release that came with death's cold touch. Jennifer played, her fingers stroking the strings, using the bow to caress and coax the melody from the instrument. The room quieted as she played and everyone listened with rapt attention.

Jennifer, eyes still closed, also listened and wondered as she played something she had never heard or played before. It came to her across moldering decades, remote in dusty time, a long dead voice whispering the notes and chords in her ear. She no longer controlled her fingers, her arms, her mind. She had been taken over by an alien who guided her movements. On and on she played, transfixed, hearing nothing but the beauty of the music, seeing nothing but a vast darkness with shadows that swayed in unhappy contrast to the music, grieving and mourning, inconsolable at some great loss.

The last notes quivered, hung in the air, died. Jennifer opened her eyes slowly. The spell was broken.

"Thank you," Maggie said.

Jennifer's audience burst into applause.

"That was beautiful."

"Just wonderful."

"Didn't know you could play like that."

"I didn't either," Jennifer said.

"Play another."

285

"Something happy this time."

Jennifer lifted the violin and filled the room with bluegrass, happy, foot-stomping bluegrass.

The party resumed for a time and then it too died.

One by one, the windows in the house went dark. The bright glow that had lit the night slowly retreated before the encroaching shadows of darkness. The lanterns and the porch light went shortly after Jennifer and Hank, arm in arm, stood on the porch waving to the last of their departing guests. The cheery lanterns blinked off and the night shadows waited. After that, the lights in the kitchen were turned off. And then Clea's bedroom united with the quivering shades of darkness creeping closer to the isolated home.

Jennifer stood at the bedroom window, looking into the night, wondering what Maggie had seen out there, what spectral vision had disturbed the old woman's mind. But Jennifer saw nothing but the dim reflection of herself. She turned and went to the bed, reaching back to snap the switch on the bedside lamp, and snuggled close to Hank, taking comfort, as always, from his reassuring presence.

But now the night, like a silent predator, was triumphant, surrounding and invading the house.

TWENTY-FIVE

The Kendall Enterprises crew straggled into town by twos and threes, arriving in pickup trucks with camper shells, Broncos, Blazers, even a van or two. Even though their arrival had been anticipated for weeks, their actual presence still came as a shock. Matt Barnes, who owned the Hidden Valley Motel and the adjacent cabins outside town, had been counting the money he would make from their reservations and letting everyone know of his new-found approval of the proposed hotel, so it was no secret. Hank, Harriet Spencer, Thad Murphy, and others around town figured—rightly so—that Matt had cut a secret deal with the hotel people. Otherwise, how could Matt accept the hotel that would drive him out of business. Once the hotel was in, who would stay in Matt's ratty old place? Few enough stayed there now.

But the presence of twenty or so outsiders dawned slowly on most of the Valley's residents, at least those who had been in attendance at Jennifer and Hank's wedding reception. They slept late into the day, awakening only long enough to take more aspirin and gulp water trying to slake the alcohol-induced thirst. A few hardier souls—Ben Davis and Charley White among them—were waiting for Hank's place to open at 11:30, figuring a beer or four or five and one of Jesus's greasy cheeseburgers and a mess of french fries would work far better than aspirin. But Jesus wasn't there either. Late the night before or early in the morning, Jesus had started drinking tequila with salt and lime. When he got to the worm, he decided his cousin could work in his place. It was the last coherent decision he made.

"Shit," Ben Davis said. "Maybe we're gonna have to open up ourselves." He was sitting on the porch, holding his head.

"Got no key," Charley White groaned.

"Break a pane of glass. Just a little one. Hank won't mind. This is a medical emergency."

Just then, Clea drove up in Hank's pickup. Clea had promised to open for Hank and since she had sipped only a little champagne during the toasts, she felt fine.

"Oh, Clea, darling, you've come to save our lives."

"You think I'm Clara Barton?"

"Who's she?" Ben asked.

"She's that waitress up in Flag," Charley said. "The cranky one at the steak house. Don't never get your order right."

"Oh, her."

"Wrong Clara Barton," Clea said, smiling mischievously. "Can't let you boys in until noon. Can't serve alcoholic beverages until then."

"Don't do that to us, honey. You got to have some pity."

"You can't serve us anyway. You ain't twenty-one."

"Guess you'll have to wait till Hank gets here then. And he was still sleeping when I left."

"Serve ourselves. You ain't gonna tell on us, darling?"

"Well . . . If you don't tell anyone I'm underage."

"It's a secret we'll carry to our dying day."

"Which is gonna be about ten minutes from now if you don't open that door."

The beer, and the cheeseburgers and French fries cooked up by Jesus's cousin, worked so well that Charley and Ben were still sitting at the bar arguing about which Clint Eastwood movie to watch next when the first of the outsiders came in, nodding politely as they passed the bar on their way to the dining room.

"Wonder who they are?" Charley asked.

"Probably some of them hotel people."

"Aw, shit, what they wanta come in here for. Bad enough they're gonna spoil the valley. Do we have to drink with 'em too?"

"What we gonna do? Toss 'em out?"

"Why not? Explain to 'em gentle-like why they should go back where they came from."

"Won't do no good."

"Guess not. Better have a couple more beers."

"Now that'll do some good."

James and Ralph arrived before nightfall. They checked into the motel and were assigned to share one of the cabins.

"You could each have one of the single rooms if you want," Matt Barnes said. "But a cabin's better. Got a hot plate so you can make some coffee in the mornings if you want."

"Any place open to get coffee."

"Not much open around here on Sundays. I can let you have some instant if you like. Pay me back when you boys have a chance to do a little shopping."

"That would be real nice of you," James said.

"Yeah, it would," Ralph echoed.

"I'll do it then."

"Any place to get dinner?" Ralph asked. "Any place that's open?"

"Hank's will be open. Down in the middle of town. You can't miss it."

James and Ralph parked the stolen truck with the changed plates in front of number nine, their cabin. Ralph had done a good job on the truck, even going so far as to ensure that the front license plate was smeared with dead bugs. "Cops look for that sort of thing," Ralph explained. "A clean front license plate starts them wondering. You have to pay attention to details.

You're asking for trouble otherwise."

They opened the door to number nine and a musty smell swept over them. "Jesus fucking Christ," Ralph said.

"Just think about the money," James said, dumping his carryall on a bed.

"Let's get a beer while we're thinking about it."

"When did you start drinking beer?"

"When I got to this God forsaken shithole of a place. Look, Jimmy, the right way to do this is to blend in. Don't stand out from the crowd. Like I said before, pay attention to the little details. We want to be accepted by the other guys on the crew. Act like they do. We do not want to be different, believe me. What we want is to be a part of this crowd."

"They're a bunch of assholes."

"Of course they are. So we're going to be assholes too. Beer drinking assholes. Now, let's go find one."

"I don't like beer. I get bloated."

Ralph shook his head. "I don't believe this. Why don't you just wear a fucking tee shirt that says 'L.A. Killer? Looking for hometown broad to kidnap.' You could do it in day-glo colors. A nice pink maybe. That'll go over big in this dump."

"Don't start on me, Ralphie."

"Was I right in leaving a little coke on the Newport job?"

"Yes, but . . ."

"Do the fucking cops think it was dope-related?"

"Yes, but . . ."

"Details, right?"

"Fuck it. I'll drink beer. Do you think they have Heinekins, at least?"

"You're a real pisser, Jimmy. A real pisser. Why don't you just think about the money? Maybe that way, you'll get to liking beer."

"I sincerely doubt it," James said. "I sincerely fucking doubt it."

*　　　*　　　*

Clea was still working when James and Ralph came in, stopped at the door to look around, and then sat at one of the small tables across from the bar. She took menus with her just in case they wanted to order food, but she thought they looked like drinkers.

"Hi, what can I get for you?" She put the menus on the table.

"A couple of beers," Ralph said.

"Do you have Heinekin?" James asked. Ralph rolled his eyes back.

"Sure. Two Heinekins?"

"Bud for me," Ralph said.

"Be right back."

"Good God, what's she doing in this dump?"

"She could be a model. See those tits?"

"Hard to miss. Love to have her wrap those long legs around me. Just hang on, baby, give you the ride of your young life."

"Might not be so bad here, after all. Think she's got a sister?"

"She could handle both of us."

"I don't like sharing."

"Some friend you are."

Clea returned with their beer. "Would you like to order something to eat?"

"Maybe later," Ralph said. "What's good?"

"Everything."

"Including you?"

"Oh, please," Clea said. "You've been here two minutes and you're hitting on me." But she smiled down at them.

"Surprised to see you here. That's all. You should be in movies."

Clea laughed. "Not very original, guys."

"Seriously," Ralph said, "what are you doing here?"

"Working my way through college."

"Where?"

"University of New Mexico. But I'm thinking of transferring to ASU or UA. Closer to home now."

"You say now. Where are you from originally?"

"California . . . Excuse me. Holler if you need anything."

"Hey, wait a minute. I was just being friendly."

"I'm busy."

"Okay, we're not going anywhere."

"Now, we've been here three minutes and you've pissed her off already."

"Fucking college girl," Ralph said. "They all think they're better than us. Fuck her."

"That was the point."

They were on their third beer when James saw Jennifer Warren enter the bar. He averted his face and almost jumped up to run to the men's room so he could avoid her when he realized she had no idea who he was or why he was there. Then he smiled. This is great, he thought. She was followed into the bar by a man. The guy was big. They went to the bar and slid on to bar stools next to the two old guys wearing cowboy hats.

"Hi, Mom," the waitress said. "Hi, Hank. You old married folks recovered yet?"

"Great party," one of the old doofers said.

"Yep," the other old guy agreed. "Ain't had so much fun since grandma got her tit caught in the wringer."

"What's a wringer?" the waitress asked.

"Before your time, Clea, honey," the old guy replied.

James glanced over at the bar casually, as though he was interested in the second fucking Clint Eastwood film they had just put on. So. Her name was Clea. The young chick was her daughter. Christ, what a pair of lookers. She doesn't look old enough to have a daughter that age. And married to the big guy. James turned away and motioned to Ralph with his eyes.

Ralph took another sip of beer before he looked at the bar. He could see Jennifer Warren's face reflected in a mirror behind the bar. He turned back to James and nodded slightly. "Let's order something to eat. Hang around for awhile."

"Good idea," James said. He lifted his beer bottle

and motioned to Clea.

Before the mother and daughter left an hour later, James and Ralph had learned that Jennifer Warren and the big guy named Hank had been married recently, that he had a small ranch but had moved into his wife's big house, that the people in the Valley hated the idea of the hotel and resented the interlopers who had come into town with the crew, that Jennifer was a relative newcomer to the Valley, that all three were well-liked and respected by the patrons who drifted in and out, as well as a dozen or so details of assorted gossip.

Shortly after the two women left, James and Ralph rose, leaving money on the table.

"Come again," Hank said to them.

"We will," James said.

Outside, they stood for a moment on the wooden porch. The night sky was clear and a million stars glowed. "This is perfect," James said.

"Too good to be true," Ralph agreed. He stepped off the porch into a pile of horseshit. "Shit!"

"That's right," James said, disturbing the quiet night with his laughter. "It's shit. Let's go find a pay phone."

Holloway turned the portable telephone off. He had been watching the late news with Janice when the call had come. He got up and carried the phone into his study as he listened to the report. He agreed with James. It *was* too fucking perfect. You're coming home soon, Kathleen. You should not have remarried. That wasn't right. Not right at all. You still belong to me. I'm sorry to take your new cowboy husband away. But it must be done and done it shall be. So ordered. It'll be good to see you again. We have so much to talk about. Lost time to make up for. And Clea. We have a daughter named Clea who is even more beautiful than you were at her age. Darling Clea. What a nice family reunion we'll have.

293

TWENTY-SIX

Kathleen watched, her lips quivering, as he slowly pulled the belt from the loops of his trousers. She wiped at the tears.

"Crying won't do you any good, young lady."

Her foster brother sat at the kitchen table, grinning at her. He stuck his tongue out.

"I didn't spill it. He did."

"Lying will only make it worse. Now march, young lady. You get to your room and wait for me." He swung the belt ominously.

Her cheeks were flushed and burning. He did it. It's not fair. You always spank me for the things he does.

"Get!"

The rabbit screamed in the night, a prolonged and anguished dying cry, as it was run down by a coyote or struck by the talons of an owl or a night hawk.

Jennifer heard its stricken wail and jerked awake. She heard the little girl she had once been screaming across time. I won't do it again, she pleaded. Don't hit me anymore.

Hank's arm was thrown across her body, holding her down. She was sweating. It was just a dream. God, it was just a dream. The first in a long time, the first since she had been sick. Why now? What brought back the tortured memories of an unhappy, despairing childhood? She had not been Kathleen for such a long time now, not since she had run into the night away from Jackson. She had never been Kathleen. That was not her name. That was the institutional name associated with foster parents and torment. I'm not Kathleen. I was never Kathleen. I'm Jennifer Warren Moore now. Kathleen is dead.

The shriek echoed in her mind. That wasn't a dream. One of God's creatures had just died, the victim of another of God's creatures.

Lately, she had taken to throwing bits of lettuce and carrots to the small cottontails that gathered timidly in the late afternoon and early evening at the edge of the backyard. She wondered if she would recognize which one was missing tomorrow. How many would be missing? No more. It's too cruel. All I'm doing is fattening you up for the predators. Go someplace else. Hide. The world is not safe for you. It's not safe for any of us.

God, what brought this on?

Jennifer closed her eyes and willed sleep to come. Beside her, Hank breathed easily, regularly. He did not hear the screams that echoed through the night. Lucky man. Did Clea hear? Did she recognize the scream for what it was. She took delight in the small rabbits, talked to them, gave them names. Would she notice that one was missing? Jennifer hoped not. Clea would cry and blame herself. God, it's just a rabbit. It's the way of nature and nothing can change it. Not now. Not ever. Jennifer opened her eyes and listened. But the night was silent now. The rabbit was dead. Another would take its place. Who cares about a dead rabbit?

I do.

Jennifer carefully moved Hank's arm. He stirred briefly and was quiet again. She slipped from the bed and, taking her robe, left the bedroom. Oscar followed. The floor creaked as she passed Clea's door. She stood in the darkness at the window and looked out at the

Valley. A few lights burned in the distance, evidence that she was not alone in the world. Oscar leaped to the window sill and looked up, his large yellow eyes examining her intently. "Woke you up too, huh, old buddy?" She scratched his ears. Together, they looked out into the night. "What do you see, Oscar? Cat fantasies? An unlimited supply of birds and mice? Rabbits? You're a predator too. Just doing what your instincts command." She shook her head and continued to stare through the window, waiting for a revelation, an epiphany of understanding. But no curtain lifted for Jennifer. She saw nothing but the shadows that crept through the night.

"What are you doing?"

Jennifer turned. Hank was another shadow in the night. "I couldn't sleep. I'm sorry if I woke you."

He came to stand beside her. "No woman. No cat. I got lonely. What's wrong, hon?"

"Just bad dreams, I guess. The past won't leave me alone."

The past. The God damned past. It won't be forgotten. Its bony fingers reach out like the snags disturbing an endless dark river, grasping and tugging at the mind with an icy grip. The past flows unevenly, swirling and twisting with tiny powerful whirlpools, always threatening to suck the unwary voyager into their dizzying bottomless depths. The God damned past. It colors all the days yet to come, smearing and blurring any clarity, any small understanding of the present or the future. Fucking memories.

They went back to bed. Hank's arms surrounded her, drew her close. "Let me into your dreams," Jennifer whispered. "Let me share your dreams. Please."

But with the sun, the restlessness of the night was gone, if not quite forgotten, and there was another day

296

to fill. Jennifer had no specific plans, but there was always something that needed to be done. There were calls that could be made to Los Angeles—to Leo and to Jerome, computer catalogs to read and pore over, another chapter of Arizona law to assimilate, a bathroom tile to replace, a leaky faucet needing a washer, a walk to take through the trees. There was always something to occupy minutes, hours, days, weeks. Jennifer looked forward to the day. It was only the night that brought half-remembered horrors. The night. The God damned night.

The work was easy, boring. They rose early, before first light, drank coffee, had an early breakfast at Hank's, and were at the site by seven o'clock, where they spent the day standing around waiting for the geologists to determine the next bore hole. James—he was Jim to the others on the crew—and Ralph helped unload the gear or humped it if the slope was too steep for one of the trucks. And then there was more standing around while the drills dug deep into the earth and core samples were removed and labeled. Then it was hump time again. They knocked off before dark and went back to the motel for a shower before going to Hank's for a few beers and dinner. Everyone flirted with Clea. She handled it well, putting one or another of the crew in their place without being mean or nasty about it. James could tell the big cowboy didn't like the guys coming on to her, but he didn't interfere. Clea could take care of herself.

The locals continued to avoid the crew, but there was no trouble. A muttered remark was made occasionally, accompanied by a surly glance at the outsiders, but it went no further than that. The crew kept to themselves for the most part. The men on the crew drank heavily at night, but they faded quickly. The long day spent in the open beneath the hot Arizona sun took care of any

297

excess energy and for the most part they were back in the motel and asleep long before the bar's regulars closed down. James and Ralph stayed until closing time one night, checking out the routine, lingering even in the parking lot, watching from the shadows as Hank locked the place up and went around to the back where he kept his pickup.

The plan had slowly taken shape over several days and nights in James's mind. He presented it to Ralph and they discussed it endlessly each night in the motel, arguing over details and timing, revising it, arguing again, revising, keeping it simple. Finally, it was complete. It would work. James explained their concept over the telephone to Holloway. He approved. James was proud of the plan. It was going to work. All they had to do now was wait for the signal. It would come from the foreman, although he did not know it.

"Jennifer, sweetie, I miss you."

"I miss you, too, Jerome. I'll be back to visit one of these days soon."

"I hope so. How's little Oscar?"

"He's fine, Jerome. He likes the country lifestyle."

"I always thought of him as the kitty from the big city. I guess there's no accounting for taste."

Jennifer laughed. "Has anyone been around?" Jennifer asked, trying to make it sound a casual question. "You know, asking about me?"

"No one, sweetie. It's as though you didn't exist."

Good, Jennifer thought.

"Looks like we'll be finished up here Wednesday night," the foreman said. "Thursday morning at the latest. Back home for the weekend. How's that sound, men?"

The crew stood in a circle around the foreman. There was a chorus of approval. James and Ralph exchanged a glance. Ralph nodded.

"Can't be soon enough for me."

"Ain't nothing keeping me in this shithole."

"What a fucking place."

"You believe these people? Actually live here? One of them asked why I wanted to go back to L.A."

"What'd you say?"

"Told the asshole to take a look around, but to keep his eyes open this time."

They all laughed. Hidden Valley was not their favorite place in the entire world. But it was a job.

"It's not a good market," Leo said. "There have been some offers, but not what the place is worth."

"Maybe we should lower the price again."

"It's rock bottom now, Jennifer. Let's wait it out. It will sell."

"All right, Leo, I'll trust your judgment."

After the lunch break, Ralph stood up and walked down the hill a little ways toward the truck. James followed. Ralph lit a cigarette and stood looking out at the Valley. "Gonna be a great place for the rich fuckers when it gets built," he said.

James shrugged. He moved carefully upwind of Ralph's cigarette smoke. "Who gives a shit? We'll be long gone."

"Oh, I don't know. Might come back as a guest sometime. Bring a dolly. Lie around the pool all day and fuck all night."

"We're going to do it tonight."

"Sure. I know that."

"Timing's right. Just what I expected."

"So? We'll do it tonight. You nervous or something?"

"Just want to get it done."

Jennifer drove down the hill through lengthening shadows. It was a little earlier than she usually left, but she had grown lonely and uneasy in the big house. It was nothing she could identify. A vague nervousness came over her late in the afternoon, and she drifted from room to room looking for something to occupy her attention, but finally decided she was simply tired of rattling around alone in the empty house. She freshened up, applied lipstick and headed to the truck. Hank and Clea would be glad to see her. They always were.

The parking spaces in front of the bar were occupied so Jennifer drove around to the back and parked behind Hank's truck. Having the work crew in town had been good for business. Jennifer had thought there might be trouble between some of the hot-headed locals and the outsiders, but the men were quiet, reserved, and kept to themselves while they spent money freely in the bar. The worst that had happened was a brief argument over the pool table, but the outsider simply backed off before any real animosity could develop, Hank said.

Jennifer pushed the door open and her uneasiness vanished instantly. Hank was in his usual place, reading yet another of the Dickens novels from the set she had given him. He glanced up and smiled. She walked over, leaned across the bar and kissed him.

"Hi, darling."

"What are you reading now?"

"The Old Curiosity Shop."

"Aren't you getting just a little sick of Charley?"

"Not yet."

"I didn't mean that you had to read them all at once."

"I've been spacing them out," Hank protested. "He strikes my fancy at the moment."

"Well, can you tear yourself away long enough to get me a glass of wine."

"The lady's slightest desire is my command."

Clea entered the bar from the dining room, carrying a tray loaded with empty beer bottles. They rattled as she went behind the bar. "Hi, Mom. Are you early or is it quitting time already?"

"I'm early, I guess. I was lonely."

"You need to get back to work."

"All in good time."

"You always used to nag me about school."

"It's different with me."

"Yeah, sure." Clea disappeared into the back.

Hank set the glass of wine on the bar.

"Darling?" Jennifer began.

"Yes?"

"Could you take off Saturday?"

"I don't see why not. What's up?"

"I'd like to drive down to Phoenix and get the computer. I've been putting it off too long."

"Maybe we could have an early dinner somewhere."

"I know a nice romantic little spot."

"Perfect."

Clea returned from the kitchen. "Want me to bring some chili home for dinner, Mom? Save cooking."

"Save Jesus's feelings, you mean."

"Well, yeah, that too."

"Sure. We can have chili. Again."

"I'll have to tell Jesus to come up with a new specialty," Hank said.

"Don't hurt his feelings," Jennifer said.

"I'll be subtle and diplomatic."

"Like the last time?" Clea asked.

"What last time?"

"When you told him to get his sorry ass in a cookbook and figure out how to make a decent stew."

301

"Oh. That last time." Hank looked sheepish. "I'll be easier on him this time."

"He moped around here for a week. Jesus is sensitive."

"Stew's good, isn't it?"

"I suppose."

"It's better than good."

"I suppose."

"I rest my case, then."

"Well, I'm getting ready to rest my case."

"Clea!" The shout came from the pool room.

"Well, soon, anyway." She dashed off with a tray in her hands.

Hank poured a glass of wine for himself and came around the bar and sat next to Jennifer. They talked for awhile, exchanging stories about their respective days. There was nothing exciting, nothing consequential.

"Another action-packed day in Hidden Valley, Arizona. This is Jennifer Warren Moore signing off."

"We could go down and watch 'em change the display in the drug store window."

"Are you kidding? They haven't changed the display since I started coming here."

"It'll be something we can talk about for weeks then. A truly memorable occasion."

When others began entering the small bar, the smoke grew thicker, the music louder, and Hank began opening bottles of beer and paying attention to his customers. He was at the other end of the bar listening to some new complaint Thad Murphy was explaining when Jennifer finished her glass of wine and waved goodbye. "I'll see you tonight," she said.

Hank smiled and nodded.

Outside, the last streaks of red glowed over the mountains. The Valley floor was in darkness. Jennifer drove home in silence, not bothering to insert a new cassette in the tape deck. The headlights of her truck flashed across the dark empty house and she wished she had remembered to leave the lights burning. In total darkness, the old house looked its age, run down and ramshackle, frightening. She turned off the engine and reached across the seat for her purse. She sat for a moment with the purse and its revolver heavy in her lap. Looking out at the house, restored with such loving care over her years in Hidden Valley, she saw a grim hulk, haunted with those who had gone before, imagined movement behind its curtains, and eyes peering out at her, the inhabitants slavering predators from the underworld waiting for her entrance. Suddenly, she was afraid and considered waiting for Clea or returning to the bar. She could tell Hank, I forgot something.

"This is silly."

Jennifer got out of the truck and walked boldly to the porch steps. They creaked as she climbed them. She stopped for a moment and listened. Silence. Where was Oscar? Usually, he greeted her at the door, clamoring for her companionship. She inserted her key with a trembling hand. The door was still locked. She put her hand on the knob, turned it, and pushed the door open, quickly reaching inside to snap the light switch.

Everything was as she left it, warm and inviting. There were no monsters, no rattlesnakes, no Jackson Holloway. Oscar was sitting on the back of the couch waiting for her. She put her purse on the table and switched on more lights. "Jennifer, you're a silly goose sometimes." From down the hill, she heard the sound of Clea driving home. Jennifer shook her head and went to the refrigerator and poured two glasses of wine. "Hi, hon," Jennifer said when Clea came racing up the steps and into the house carrying a large container of chili.

"Soup's on," Clea cried. "Is that for me? Thanks, Mom. What a bitch of a day." She took a sip of the wine Jennifer offered. Some of it splashed on her chin. "Oops. Missed my mouth. Again. I better go back to

303

college. I'm going to get varicose veins if I keep waitressing. I've been on my feet all day. That damn crew from the hotel stayed longer than usual. Some of them are pretty creepy, but some of them are nice too. Polite. Hi, Oscar. What, no music?"

"I just got here," Jennifer said. "I haven't had a chance to put anything on. And, you came through the door talking nonstop."

"Have I been rattling again?"

"Just a little."

"What would you like to hear?"

"You choose. Surprise me."

"Oldies but goodies night. Simon and Garfunkel. How's that?"

"Fine," Jennifer said, already hearing the ballads of her youth, her personal night track. The music was always with her, evoking the images from the past—dancing through the sun-washed spring days in Berkeley, walking through foggy nights in San Francisco's North Beach listening to the mournful cry of the foghorns, standing and looking across the bay, past the grim, abandoned hulk of Alcatraz to Sausalito and the Marin hills. "No," Jennifer said. "I've changed my mind. Put on George Strait or Garth Brooks." Why not add to the memories of Hidden Valley? Start a new night track.

"Aw. Mom, I listen to shit-kicking music all day long," Clea complained, but soon the room was filled with the country twang of George Strait.

Clea finally wound down and sat with Jennifer in the living room. Clea was curled up on the couch, feet tucked beneath her. Jennifer was at the end, her bare feet resting on the coffee table. Garth Brooks sang softly in the background, providing peaceful moments to remember, the music for a night track of the future.

"Hank's sure nice, Mom."

"Yes, he is. He's a very good man."

They were content to sit quietly for awhile, sipping their wine, speaking only occasionally. Dinner followed, bowls of the chili, a small salad, and garlic bread. The dishes were rinsed and put in the dishwasher. Clea stayed up for a while, but soon disappeared into her room, leaving Jennifer alone with her computer catalogs.

Oscar climbed into Jennifer's lap and settled down after washing his paws. The cat was soon asleep. Hank would be home soon now. Jennifer dozed.

Hank locked the bar and stood for a moment looking up at the cold distant stars. He hummed a little tune as he walked around to the back of the building. He didn't see the two figures steal quietly from the shadows.

She awakened with a bad taste in her mouth and a headache. Oscar was still in her lap. Jennifer sat up and lifted Oscar from her lap. Her legs had fallen asleep and tingled with sharp little pains as the numbness wore off. She shook her head and looked at her watch. Midnight. Where was Hank? He should be home by now.

Jennifer shook her head again, trying to clear the grogginess away. She went into the bathroom to splash water on her face and brush her teeth. That helped. She went back into the living room. Five minutes had passed. Where is he? She quickly dialed the number of the bar and listened to the phone ring for a long time. He must have worked late and now he's on his way. He'll be here any minute. Jennifer had a sudden urge to smoke a cigarette as she listened for the sound of his truck climbing up the hill to the house.

The minutes passed slowly, agonizingly. The urge to

305

smoke intensified as Jennifer paced the living room. Another five minutes, she thought. I'll give him another five minutes and then I'm going out to look for him. She strained to hear his truck, but the night was deadly quiet.

To hell with it.

Jennifer shrugged into her jacket and went to the table for her purse. Wake Clea? Tell her? Let her sleep. I'll meet Hank on the road. Don't disturb her.

She locked the door and stood on the steps, looking down the hill through the trees for a glimmer of approaching headlights. Nothing.

Walking to the truck, Jennifer passed through one of those eerie chills in the night, a pocket of air where death had passed, leaving behind the cold evidence of his presence.

In the truck, Jennifer removed the revolver from her purse and placed it on the seat beside her. She drove down the hill, still searching the night for Hank's headlights. For as far as she could see, Jennifer was the only person driving through the night.

She passed no one on the road to town.

The bar was dark.

Where is he? Dear God, where is he?

Jennifer pulled around to the back. His truck was there. The door on the driver's side was open. She switched her lights to bright. Then she saw him lying on the ground. He wasn't moving. Oh, God, no. She choked back the scream building inside.

Please, God, no.

He's dead. Hank's dead.

TWENTY-SEVEN

Still unconscious. Concussion. Broken ribs. A collapsed lung. Broken jaw. Internal bleeding. Multiple bruises, abrasions, lacerations. Eyes swollen shut. Very professional beating. Someone left him for dead. You probably saved his life, although he seems strong. Most probably you saved his life by coming along when you did. Dr. Cordeman did a fine job with limited facilities. He's in critical condition. However . . .

There were two Jennifers.

One listened to the doctor drone on listing Hank's injuries. The other watched the scene from afar, noting the surreal details—the doctor in his white hospital coat, the stethoscope that writhed like a snake in death agonies protruded from the right hand pocket, the pens clipped to a holder in his breast pocket, the blue stain from a leaking ballpoint that turned blood red as she watched. The other Jennifer, the one apart from her body, saw the waiting room outside the intensive care unit, the nurse's station down the hall, the orderlies wheeling meals to other rooms, other wards. They were disembodied shades like herself, floating ethereally about their duties. She was isolated from the hospital activity, trapped in another world. How would she get back? Did she want to get back? Better to die with Hank. They would both find release from pain.

"Will he live?" she asked.

"Yes. He suffered a brutal beating, but I don't believe the situation will be life-threatening once he regains consciousness."

"When will that be, Doctor?"

"It's difficult to say with head injuries. Right now, his brain is protecting him from the great physical trauma he suffered. It could be five minutes from now . . . or two weeks."

"Or never?"

"I think that is only a very remote possibility."

"But possible?"

The doctor nodded. "It is possible."

Jennifer nodded. No! she thought. He can't die. I won't let him.

But if he does?

I'll kill Jackson Holloway.

Jennifer rubbed her eyes.

"You should get some rest yourself," the doctor said.

"I know."

The horror of the night rushed back with the terrible mind-numbing realization that Hank was dead. But he wasn't.

He groaned.

Weakly.

He groaned a second time and was silent. Jennifer raced for Cordeman's house. It adjoined his small medical center. She banged on the door, screaming for him to come. When he answered the door, he had a gun in his hand. My God, Jennifer, what is it? Come quick. Now. I can't get him up. He's dying. Who's dying? Hank. Cordeman made a call, stamping a foot impatiently. Where is he? Behind the bar, Jennifer cried before she ran. Behind Hank's place, Cordeman shouted into the phone. He left the gun on the table and grabbed his bag. Percy's bringing the ambulance. Let's go. But Jennifer was gone. The shriek of a siren penetrated Jennifer's despair as she ran back to Hank with desperation in her heart and despair in her mind. He doesn't need the siren, she thought. There's no one out there.

Oh, God. He's out there.

By the time Cordeman arrived, panting and out of breath, Jennifer was kneeling at Hank's side in the red glow cast by the lights on the ambulance, pleading silently with her lover, her friend, her husband, to live. Cordeman pushed her aside rudely and worked on Hank where he had fallen. Percy and someone Jennifer didn't know unloaded the stretcher from the ambulance.

Jennifer paced the waiting room alone until she remembered to call Clea. And then the two of them paced. What happened? I don't know. God damn it, I don't know. He'll be all right, Mom. Hank's strong. They paced. An hour passed. And another. God damn it, I'm going in there. Clea blocked her path. Don't disturb him. Let the doctor work.

Cordeman came into the waiting room. Jennifer and Clea looked at him anxiously. "I think he'll be all right. But we're transferring him to the hospital in Flag. They can do more for him there."

Jennifer rode in the ambulance, holding Hank's limp hand all the way, pleading with him not to die, to fight. Clea followed in the pickup.

The elevator door hissed open. Clea emerged carrying two containers of coffee. She handed one to Jennifer.

"I just talked with the doctor. He thinks Hank will be

okay. If he regains consciousness . . ."

"He will, Mom. I just know he's going to be all right."

"Clea, I want you to leave. Go back to New Mexico for awhile. Until this is over."

"What are you going to do?"

"Wait."

"For him?"

"Yes."

"And then what?"

"I don't know."

"I'm not going."

"Clea, please."

"I'm staying. That's it."

Jennifer sat beside Hank's bed. She prayed. And she waited. When she could stay awake no longer, she relented to Clea's entreaties to go to the motel and rest for a few hours. "I'll stay with him. I'll call you the minute he wakes up."

"I should be here."

"You can't do him any good if you let yourself get sick. He's going to need you."

Jennifer kicked her shoes off and stretched out on the bed. Its twin was rumpled where Clea had napped for a few hours. She closed her eyes but the image of Hank burned behind her eyelids with dazzling clarity. God damn you, Jack. God damn you to hell. Exhaustion overcame rage and anger finally and Jennifer slept into the afternoon.

When Jennifer returned to the hospital, Dave Wilson and Kathy rose from chairs. Ben Davis was there too. And Charley White. Dan Manchester, a deputy sheriff was there as well. He wore civilian clothes. Clea met Jennifer halfway down the hall. "He's still asleep," Clea said.

Jennifer nodded and went to greet the others. Kathy fell into her arms, hugging her. "Thanks, Kathy. It was good of you to come. It was good of all of you to come."

"Aw hell, Jennifer . . ."

"I know. Thank you."

"I want to get the bastards who did this," Dan said. "Hank's a good man and I would have come anyway. I know you got things on your mind but I'd like to ask you a few questions."

"It's all right."

"Why don't we go sit over here? If y'all will excuse us."

Jennifer sat beside Manchester, thinking he looked haggard. He had probably been up since getting called out last night.

"We found some baseball bats," Manchester said. "Two wood bats. I didn't even know they made them anymore. I thought everything was aluminum these days. Anyway, they was tossed in the brush behind the parking lot. Figure there was two assailants used those bats on Hank."

Jennifer shuddered. God damn you, Jack.

"You know anybody that might hold a grudge against Hank?"

"No one that I know," Jennifer said. "Everyone likes Hank."

"I went up and talked to that hotel crew, figuring they was the only outsiders in town, but I can't see any motivation there. They all seemed to like Hank too. Appreciated his hospitality at the bar. So I think they're clean. Is there anybody else?"

"No one." Jennifer shrugged. "I just don't know . . ." I can't tell you about Jack. I have to deal with him myself.

311

"I remembered Hank got in a fight at the Christmas party. Thought about them two fellas, but they ain't even in town at the moment. So unless they snuck in and then snuck out again . . ."

The Christmas party seemed so long ago. So much had happened since then. Jennifer tried to think. It was only four or five months ago. What will the next Christmas be like? "I don't think they did it. They didn't hold a grudge. Hank told me they came in later and apologized for being drunk."

"Well, if you think of anything . . . You let me know, hear?"

"I will, Dan. And thanks again for coming. I appreciate it."

"Hank'll be all right, Jennifer. He's too ornery to . . ."

"I know."

They returned to the others. Jennifer accepted their best wishes for Hank's quick recovery, echoing Manchester's sentiments.

"Old Hank's tough," Ben said. "He'll be back raising hell with his customers in no time."

"We packed a few things for you and Clea," Kathy said.

"You need anything, just holler, Jennifer."

"Thank you all."

"You let us know the minute he wakes up. Don't matter what time it is."

Jennifer nodded.

"Well, we best be getting back."

"I'll go down and get the stuff, Mom."

"Why don't you just go on back to the motel? I'll just stay with Hank for awhile and then come over. I won't be long."

"Okay, Mom."

When the others left for the drive back to the Valley and Clea returned to the motel, Jennifer sat with Hank. She held his hand and prayed for him. She held his hand and waited. Oh, please, God, please let him be all right.

Holloway was angry, angrier than James had ever heard him. "You stupid bastards were supposed to kill him," Holloway said, barely controlling his rage.

"We thought he was dead . . ."

"You thought. You fucking thought! Don't think anymore. I want him dead before you leave that fucking place. And bring those women to me."

"We have to wait. The plan . . ."

"The plan would have worked. It will still work if you don't screw it up anymore. Just get it done." Holloway slammed the phone down. Stupid fucking assholes. It would be a pleasure getting rid of them.

Holloway forced himself to calm down, to think rationally. Kathleen's husband had to die. There was no other way. What if Kathleen told him about me? Did you tell him about me, Kathleen? Did you?

Jennifer glanced at her watch. She had been sitting with Hank for nearly two hours.

His hand moved, squeezing slightly. Jennifer looked up. His eyes opened slowly.

"Hello, darling," he said slowly, painfully. He tried to smile, but it looked like a grimace.

It was a beautiful smile, the best Jennifer had ever seen. "Hello, Bear," she said. Thank you, God, thank you. She reached over and pressed the call button.

"Do I look as bad as I feel?"

"You look terrific to me."

The nurse on duty entered the ICU. "He's awake," Jennifer said.

The nurse smiled. "I'll call the doctor."

"What happened, darling?"

"I don't know, Bear. I was hoping you could tell me."

"I was getting in the truck and something hit me. Felt like another truck and I don't remember anything past that."

"Somebody beat you up. Dan Manchester thinks there were two of them."

"So, the patient's awake," a doctor said. He was new. Jennifer hadn't seen him before. "How are you feeling? Not good, I'll bet."

"Worse. I hurt all over."

"I'll give you something for the pain. Help you sleep." He turned to Jennifer. "Mrs. Moore?"

"Yes."

"I'm Doctor Carradine. Why don't you wait outside for a few minutes. Let me check your guy over. You can come back and say good night then."

"I'll call Clea," Jennifer said. "Tell her you're awake. I'll be back soon, Bear."

"Bear," Jennifer heard the doctor say as she left. "That's a good name for you."

"How is he?" Clea asked, going to the television set and turning it down.

"He hurts all over, but he's going to be fine. He was groggy when I left. The doctor gave him a pain killer and a sedative."

"God, what a relief. I called everyone and told them he was going to be all right."

"Thanks, Clea. I wouldn't have had the energy to do it. I'm exhausted."

"I went out and got a bottle of scotch. Figured you might want a drink. Do you?"

"Did I miss a birthday somewhere?" Jennifer asked. "How'd you buy it?"

"Oh, Mom, I have a false ID."

"That figures."

"Besides, I look twenty-one. You want a drink or do you want to nag all night?"

"A drink would be very nice. And I didn't mean to nag."

"I was just kidding, Mom. Lighten up."

"Oh God, Clea, I was so afraid. I just kept seeing him there on the ground. Not moving."

"Don't think about that now. Hank's going to be fine." Clea went into the bathroom and returned with two glasses, ripping the cellophane free. She poured scotch into the glasses and handed one to Jennifer.

"That tastes good," Jennifer said. "I'll be able to sleep tonight." She stared at the television screen. The late news was just coming on. The anchor stared intently at the camera and mouthed words at Jennifer.

"You want to watch the news, Mom? I'll turn the sound up."

"Not really."

Clea reached over and turned the TV off. She took a sip of her scotch and shuddered. "People like this stuff?"

Jennifer smiled wearily. "You get used to it."

"Mom?"

"Yes?"

"Do you really think *he* did it? Beat Hank up, I mean?"

"Who else would have a reason to hurt Hank?"

"It could have been a couple of strangers. Guys just passing through. Wanted to rob him."

"They didn't take his wallet."

"Maybe you scared them off when you drove up."

"There was no one there. I didn't see anyone on the road."

They fell silent.

"What are we going to do, Mom?" Clea asked finally.

"I don't know," Jennifer replied.

TWENTY-EIGHT

After the attack on Hank, they continued their usual routine, taking care to ensure that they were treated as just two more members of a work crew. When the Deputy Sheriff came up to the site and questioned each of the men, they expressed concern over the brutal assault. "I didn't know him except to say hello to," James said, "but he seemed like a pretty good guy. Always pleasant. Hope he'll be all right."

"Shit," Ralph said. "He was always nice, not like some of the people around here. Maybe that's why they did it. Teach him a lesson. The people around here seem pretty upset about the hotel going in."

"You said *they,*" the deputy said. "How'd you know there was more than one?"

"Hell, just look at the guy. Who's going to take him one-on-one? I sure as hell wouldn't."

"I suppose you're right," the deputy agreed.

James and Ralph watched him trudge down the hill.

"We're in the clear," James said.

"Yeah, but let's get the fucking woman and get out of here."

"Holloway wants the cowboy dead."

"Fuck Holloway. As soon as we're done here tomorrow, I say we head out of town. Go south. Tell everyone we're going for the bright lights of Phoenix.

Get laid. Double back. Come up on the house from behind like we planned and wait for her."

"What if she doesn't come back?"

"She'll be back. She'll need clothes and stuff, even if she stays in Flagstaff. We'll give it a day or two. And then if she doesn't come . . . well, fuck it. I'm outta here. This is getting too screwed up for me. But she'll come."

"She'd better. And the kid better be with her. Holloway wants them both."

"Two's better than one, but one's better than nothing. Holloway'll just have to live with a little disappointment in his life."

TWENTY-NINE

Each day saw improvement in Hank's condition. He was sore, deeply bruised, his head ached and throbbed, and it was painful to breathe even with the tight bandages that wrapped around his rib cage. He had dizzy spells and short blackouts, but he was quickly transferred from the Intensive Care Unit. Two days later, the Flagstaff doctors consented to another transfer, back to Cordeman's small medical center in Hidden Valley, with the sole condition that Hank remain in that facility until Cordeman released him. They estimated a minimum of ten days and a maximum of two weeks under Cordeman's care. Hank blustered, insisting he felt much better, denying the lingering symptoms, maintaining that he did not need further hospitalization. The Flagstaff doctors refused to give in to his demand for outright release. Jennifer joined the fray, siding with the doctors until Hank relented and agreed to remain under Cordeman's care as long as necessary.

After first taking turns watching over Hank, Jennifer insisted that Clea remain close at hand once he had regained consciousness. Mother and daughter became a familiar sight in the hospital, arriving together, on the elevators, striding through the hospital corridors, going to the cafeteria, sitting together at

318

Hank's bedside or outside his room when one or the other of the doctors examined him. Although they seemed inseparable, sharing time and space, Jennifer brooded and worried alone. She avoided any discussion of what had happened and what was yet to come.

It was not a random assault. In Los Angeles, perhaps, Jennifer might accept it as a chance encounter between good guy and bad guys, but not in Hidden Valley. Such things didn't happen in the valley. Someday, perhaps if the hotel was built and an influx of tourists inundated the valley, the crime rate in Hidden Valley might rise. But not now. Not yet. Jennifer Warren Moore was the only person in the valley with a reason to lock the doors of her home. No one else did. No one else needed to use the locks. They trusted their friends and neighbors. If a problem existed, they confronted it openly, honestly, and during the day. They didn't come like predators in the night, striking from ambush without warning.

Jennifer tried again to convince Clea to leave.

Clea refused.

Hank wanted to discuss the situation with Jennifer. "Later, darling, when you're feeling better. I'm fine. Clea's fine. We stay together. We're safe here."

Hank tried to persist, but pain and weakness forced his reluctant acquiescence.

Jennifer continued in self-imposed isolation, driving herself to the point of madness as she struggled to overcome twenty years of fear and deal with the reality of her situation.

Jackson Holloway had found her.

Jennifer had no doubt of that. There could be no other reason for the attempt on Hank's life. Jack had ordered the murder attack on Hank. And Jennifer was also convinced that Hank had been left for dead. His assailants had bungled their work. That Hank was still alive was testimony to his strength and will to live.

Jennifer considered flight.

319

If she left the valley, there was no longer a reason for Holloway to attack Hank or Clea. He wants me. I endanger them, put them at risk. Without me . . .

How can I leave Hank? How can I desert Clea now? We've just found each other again.

God damn you, Jack. Why don't you leave me alone?

And then the argument started.

Hank refused to be put off any longer. Clea agreed with Hank and would not leave the room.

"I'm a part of this too," Clea said simply.

"You're with friends," Hank said. "They'll help."

"They'll be hurt too," Jennifer said. "Look what happened to you." She violated her own rule and stormed out of the room without Clea, going down to the hospital cafeteria fighting back tears.

Unseeing, Jennifer walked through her own hellish trance with heavy weights dragging at her step, threatening to pull her down into the black chasm where she would be lost. She stood at the coffee urn, letting the hot liquid spill over the rim to burn her fingers. The pain shocked her momentarily and she took a napkin to dry her fingers and the cup. But the oppressive lethargy quickly returned as she paid and carried the coffee to an empty table in the corner of the room. Alone in a black shroud, Jennifer fought the demon from the past while all around her the hospital cafeteria gleamed incongruously.

Her coffee, untouched, cooled.

She stared bleakly at Clea when she sat down across from her.

"You're not my mother," Clea said.

The words penetrated Jennifer's mind slowly, painfully.

"You're not my mother," Clea repeated.

Jennifer raised the coffee cup to her lips. Her hand

320

trembled. The coffee sloshed over the side of the cup. It was cold.

"Who are you?" Clea asked. "You're not the mother who fought and struggled to raise me, protect me from . . . him. You're not the woman I watched go to law school and work and still have time to spend with me. You were a survivor then. Now . . . I don't know you anymore. You've given up."

"I don't want anyone hurt . . ."

"Oh, bullshit, Mother! What are you going to do? Run away again? That doesn't seem to be working very well."

"I don't know . . ."

"You're not alone anymore. You've got Hank. Me. There are lots of others who will help you."

"He's your father . . ."

"He's not my father!" Clea cried. "I don't have a father!"

"I carried you everywhere . . . I never left you . . . You were always so good . . . You hardly ever cried . . . Even when I was posing, you would sleep . . . So good . . . And then . . . Then, you went away . . ."

"I'm here now. We'll fight together. We'll all fight. We'll go to the police."

"They can't help. He's protected himself too well. Who's going to believe me?"

"We believe you."

"I know."

"Let's do something about it then."

Yes, Jennifer thought, it's time to do something about it. I should have confronted him a long time ago.

"Go back to Hank. I'll be along in a minute."

"You're not going to do something stupid. Like run away from us?"

"I won't run," Jennifer said. "Not this time."

Jennifer watched Clea walk across the cafeteria. Men watched her go too, glancing surreptitiously, hoping their own women did not see. She's so beautiful, Jennifer thought. And you never cried, Clea. Not even when they were looking for us. You were so brave. You've deserved so much better. I love you. And I love you, Hank.

They were such hollow words, so inadequate for describing the emotions she felt. Once, she had used those same words to describe her feeling for a young Jackson Holloway, the only man she would ever love. It had been true and lasting then—for a few brief months. But he turned on her like a foaming dog, maddened and snarling viciously as he ripped and tore her love to shreds. And he had never left her. Through all the years, she had felt the warm putrid breath of his hatred. She felt it still. He was close, so close. He would destroy her and those she loved.

A cold anger built slowly, starting deep within her soul, spreading, becoming more and more intense. All of the pain and threats of a lifetime now culminated in a blinding, wrathful fury. She let the fierce rage grow as she saw Hank lying in the parking lot. It was an image that would never leave her mind. Jennifer remembered her despair as she ran to him. Jennifer remembered the fear and pain and helpless confusion in Clea's eyes over so many years. Jackson Holloway had hurt her countless times. Now he had hurt those she loved. I have to protect them. I will not let him hurt Hank or Clea. No more, Jack.

Jennifer left the cafeteria and took the elevator back to Hank's floor. They waited for her silently, watching the door. Jennifer saw the relief on Clea's face. Jennifer smiled wearily, disguising her true emotions, the seething outrage within. "I'm sorry, Hank. I'm just too tired. I'm not thinking clearly."

"I'm sorry too, darling. I didn't mean to snap at you."

"I think I'll go back to the motel and rest for an hour or two. We'll talk when I come back."

Hank nodded. "That's probably a good idea."

"I'll stay here with Hank, Mom." Clea turned to Hank. "Feel up to a game of Scrabble?"

"Feel like getting your butt whipped again?"

"Ha!"

"Okay, I'll see you guys later." Jennifer leaned over and kissed each of them in turn. She felt like she was kissing them for the last time.

"See you in a little while."

Jennifer went to the hospital lobby. Outside, she stood on the hospital steps and stared into the western sky. The afternoon sun was a harsh red above the mountains, a complement to Jennifer's ruthless mood. Later, it would relent and soften, its energy spent. But for now it was a bloody gaping hole in the sky. Jennifer would remember it that way. "Here I am, Jack," she whispered. Her fingers curled around the butt of the revolver concealed in her purse. "Let's get it over with, Jack."

Jennifer went to the parking lot, got into the truck, and drove to the Interstate, joining a row of trucks heading east. They were carrying goods and equipment to eastern markets, a mundane occupation. Jennifer was going to meet her destiny. He was waiting for her. Jennifer was positive of that. This night would see an end to it. Jack was waiting for her.

Jennifer swung into the fast lane and passed one big truck after another. Their tires sang to her. Jack is waiting. Jack is waiting. Jack is waiting. One driver touched his air horn, a mournful salute to the beautiful woman driving a pickup truck with a rifle in the gun rack, speeding out of his life. Jennifer waved to him. The horn sounded again. The needle on her speedometer touched sixty-five and climbed higher. Seventy. Seventy-five. She left the pack of trucks behind, disappearing from her rear view mirrors. Suddenly, she was alone on the road, as she had been so many times before. But this time she wasn't running away. Instead, Jennifer was rushing to an appointment she knew should have been kept long ago. All those wasted years.

"She wants some time alone to think, I guess," Clea said.

"God damn it all to hell anyway. What a mess."

"It'll be okay, Hank. We'll take care of it somehow."

Jennifer felt giddy and lightheaded when she turned off the Interstate and soon began the descent into the valley, rehearsing what she would say to Jack when she saw him finally, wanting to berate and curse him, but finally decided simply to say, "Hello, Jack."

And then?

"Maybe I should give her a call and see if she's all right," Clea said.

Hank's forehead was wet with sweat. The pain killer was wearing off again. He smiled wanly. "No, darling. Let her sleep if she can. We can call in a little while if she's not here. I'll leave it alone when she gets back."

"It wasn't your fault, Hank. She's got to face it with us, realize that she's not alone anymore."

And then?
Reason with him?
Leave me alone, Jack. Why are you doing this? I can't hurt you. I don't know anything. I don't want to know anything. I just want to be left alone to live the rest of my life in peace.

Call the Sheriff? My former husband wants to kill me.

"I'm a respected and powerful man, Sheriff. Why would I want to do something like that?"

Shoot him?

Wait for his reply, "Hello, Kathleen."

Then shoot him.

Wouldn't that surprise him?

"Hello, Jack." And pull the trigger.

Jennifer admitted to herself that she didn't know what happened next. She did know that she felt free of the burden she had carried for twenty years. The heavy weights had been lifted from her heart, her shoulders. One way or another it would end today.

You should have waited a few more weeks, Jack. Then we could do this on our anniversary.

"Hank, she's not answering the phone. She's gone."

He opened his eyes. His broken ribs ached and it hurt to breathe. "Are you sure?"

"I let the phone ring and ring. I got the desk clerk to look for the truck. It's not there."

"She's probably on the way back."

"It's ten minutes away. She should be here by now."

"Maybe she stopped for something."

"Hank," Clea said solemnly. "She's gone."

"Shit." He struggled to sit up and fell back. "Help me up, Clea."

"You can't."

"I have to." He threw the blankets off and looked up at her. "Help me." His eyes pleaded with her.

Clea went to him, put her arms around his shoulders and helped him sit up. "Where would she go, Hank?"

"I don't know," he said. He groaned with the effort of moving. "What did she say when you talked with her?"

"She said she wouldn't run. Not this time."

Hank reached for the phone. "Get my clothes."

"What are you doing?"

"Calling the police. Tell them my truck's been stolen. Maybe we'll get lucky and they'll stop her."

"What if they don't?"

"We'll find her ourselves."

Jennifer drove past the hotel site. The hillside was empty. The crew was gone. She turned off the road before entering the township, and drove the corrugated unpaved back road toward her house. Their house. Hank and Jennifer and Clea lived there too. But he had defiled it. No more. She turned off the road again, this time driving into the trees, bumping along an old logging road, long abandoned and overgrown with weeds and brush. When Jennifer finally stopped, she was little more than a mile from her home.

Jennifer sat and listened to the silence. She had disturbed the wilderness with her intrusion, but slowly the woods came alive again. A bird chirped tentatively. Another joined in. The woods filled with the piercing sound of the cicada. Jennifer removed the revolver and checked the cylinder. It was fully loaded. She twisted around and removed the rifle from its rack and reached into the glove compartment for the rifle shells, slipping one after another into the loading port. She took extra shells for both the revolver and rifle, dropping them in a compartment of her purse. She was ready, but still she sat behind the wheel of the truck with the rifle across her lap.

It was time to go.

She waited.

Wondering.

What am I doing?

Hank insisted that the police put the license number out to California law enforcement as well as Arizona. He didn't think she was going to California, but . . .

326

He dialed Dave Wilson's number.

No answer.

God damn it.

Ben Davis.

No answer.

Charley White next.

God damn it.

He called the bar. "Jesus, is anyone there. Dave, Ben, Charley?"

"No, Boss, ain't seen anybody yet. They'll be in soon, I expect."

"Take these numbers down and call them every five minutes until you get someone or until they come in. Then here's what I want you to do . . ."

He spoke rapidly for two minutes.

Clea came in, looking angry and frustrated.

"Do it, Jesus, I'm counting on you." Hank replaced the phone.

"They won't rent me the God damned car," Clea cried. "It's your credit card. You have to sign."

A nurse entered the room in time to hear Hank say, "Shit!"

"What are you doing?"

"Leaving," Hank said.

The nurse retreated, only to return a few moments later followed by one of the doctors.

"What are you doing?" the doctor asked.

"I just had this conversation," Hank said. "I'm leaving."

"You can't do that."

"Watch me."

"You're a God damned fool."

"Maybe."

"We won't be responsible."

"Help me up, Clea."

Jennifer lengthened the shoulder strap on the purse.

The woods quieted again as she got out of the truck and closed the door. She took a hundred steps into the woods, stopped, looked back. The truck had disappeared from sight. She started walking again, confidently. She had roamed the woods for years and had no fear of getting lost. She had no fear at all. The mind-numbing terror she had felt over the years with each new message in the newspapers had disappeared, like the pickup obscured by trees and underbrush, as soon as she made her decision on the hospital steps. It would be over soon. But she felt regret and had to push thoughts of Hank and Clea from her mind. They'll understand. I hope they'll understand. I have to do this myself.

"Faster."
"I'm doing eighty."
"Faster."
Clea pressed the accelerator to the floor.

It took Jennifer little more than fifteen minutes to get near the house, even after stopping frequently to strain her ears listening for some alien sound. Each time there had been nothing but silence. The only sounds were in the wake of her passage, distant and faint as the forest returned to normal. Now she was close, listening again. She couldn't see the house, but it was there. Slowly, cautiously, Jennifer moved forward again, until she saw a streak of red. Another step. Two. Three.

Dave Wilson's old red pickup was parked in front of the house. Dave or Kathy, perhaps both, were at the house.

Jennifer felt foolish and embarrassed. All this for nothing. She put the rifle over her shoulder and stepped out of the trees.

328

THIRTY

Amidst the quiet, familiar surroundings, Jennifer's embarrassment grew as she walked toward the house. Hank and Clea will think I'm crazy. Maybe I am. Perhaps I've been mad for twenty years. All of the certainty—the conviction that Holloway was waiting for her—had vanished. Now she was filled with doubts, but she had been so positive when she stood on the hospital steps, knowing, just as she had known over the years when to go to the newspapers to find another message from Jack. Jennifer berated herself now, feeling ridiculous. She had made a fool of herself. It was absurd to think that Holloway was sitting in her living room, simply waiting for her to walk back into his life. He wasn't stupid. If he came he would appear suddenly in the night, find her when she was alone and unsuspecting. If he came. It still might be that Hank was just the victim of some random assault. Christ, I'm the dumb one. I've got to call Hank and Clea. They'll be frantic.

Oscar's favorite squirrel—the one that drove him to whimpering distraction—scampered along a branch, chattering down at her, laughing at her. They were all going to laugh at her. That might have been Jack's plan all along, to send her into paroxysms of paranoia, always looking over her shoulder, wondering when he would finally come for her, until she was no longer able to function normally. If that's what you wanted, Jack, you've done a pretty good job of it. God damn you!

"Kathy!" Jennifer called. "Dave? It's me."

There was no answer. They must be in the back, Jennifer thought as she opened the door.

They were waiting in the living room.

It was too late to run, too late to raise the rifle, too late.

They had Kathy.

Jennifer knew them from the bar. They had come in with the crew from the hotel site, ate and drank with the others, paid quietly, never caused any trouble. Bastards.

"Come on in. Shut the door."

He was holding Kathy by the arm and pointing his gun at Jennifer. Kathy winced with pain.

Jennifer did as he ordered.

"Put the rifle on the floor. Very carefully. Don't be nervous. Just do as you're told."

The other one was sitting in a chair. There was a pistol on the table next to the chair. Hank's chair. Oscar was in his lap, looking up at her with his large yellow eyes. He started to come to her, but the man held him back by the scruff of the neck. Oscar whined.

Jennifer put the rifle on the floor and stood up again. She clutched the purse to her stomach.

"You got any other guns?"

Jennifer shook her head.

"Dump the purse on the floor."

"It'll mess everything up," Jennifer said calmly.

"Dump it."

Jennifer let the contents of her purse spill on the floor. The revolver remained hidden in the folds. "Satisfied?" she asked, kneeling to scoop everything back.

"Just needed to be sure."

"Where is he?" she asked as she stood.

330

"Who?"

"Jack."

"You'll see him soon enough. We'll take you to him."

He didn't even come himself. Jennifer felt cheated. The son-of-a-bitch didn't even show up.

"I came to feed Oscar," Kathy said. "I saw them sneaking around in the trees and yelled at them. They were running away and I made them come back. I'm sorry, Jennifer. If I hadn't said anything they would have just gone away."

"It wasn't your fault, Kathy. Believe me, it wasn't your fault."

"Where's your pretty little daughter?" It was the man in the chair who spoke.

"Safe."

"We'll see."

"What are you going to do now?" Jennifer was surprised to find there was no tremor in her voice. She felt no fear. She felt nothing.

"Yeah, what are we going to do?" It was the other man who spoke, the one holding Kathy's arm.

"We wait for dark and then we leave. For right now, let's get everyone comfortable. What's your name?"

"Kathy."

"Well, Kathy, you sit right over there at one end of that couch and keep quiet. Jenny, you sit at the other end. Let's make this as easy as possible."

"What are you going to do with us?"

"I already told you. We wait until it's dark and then we leave."

"You don't need Kathy. He just wants me. Let her go. You can lock her in a closet or the shed."

"We'll see. Just sit down."

Jennifer went to the couch and sat down. "It'll be all right, Kathy."

Oscar whined again and was released. He jumped down and came to Jennifer. She put her purse next to her on the couch and patted her lap. Oscar leaped up.

Christ, this isn't what I expected at all. What did you expect? Walk in and find Jack waiting? Jennifer, you're a fool. What are you going to do now? Wait. Wait for dark. Wait for a chance to do something. God damn it, Hank, I'm sorry. I've messed everything up. If I hadn't come, they'd have Kathy. God knows what they would do with her. Now they've got both of us. At least Hank and Clea are safe.

"Who are you?"

The man who had been holding Oscar shrugged. "It doesn't matter."

"What do I call you? Thug Number One and Thug Number Two?"

"That's funny, Jenny, that's very funny. I'm James. He's Ralph."

"How did you find me?"

James laughed. "We've known where you were for months."

"You're the one who put the rattlesnake in my place? Slashed Hank's tires? Kept calling and hanging up?"

"I did the snake bit. I don't know about the other stuff. Maybe Holloway was doing it. He's crazy sometimes."

"I'll tell him you said that."

"I'm not afraid of him."

Maybe not, Jennifer thought. But I am.

"You got anything to drink?" Ralph asked.

"There's beer in the refrigerator. You want me to get it?" Sure, play the gracious hostess, Jennifer.

"You stay put. You want one, Jimmy?"

"Sure, why not? One beer won't hurt."

Ralph went to the kitchen and returned with two bottles of beer. He handed one to James and took a swallow of his own. "I'd offer you one, but it's going to be a long drive and you won't be getting any rest stops." He laughed and took another swallow of beer. Ralph went to the window and looked out.

Jennifer followed his movements. The house was in

332

shadows already and they were creeping further down the hillside. It was going to be dark soon. Think, Jennifer, think. What are you going to do?

Hank used the telephone at the roadside rest area. He was stiff and sore and it was a struggle to walk. A woman from an RV back-tracked when she saw him limping along the walkway to the pay phone. *Christ, I must look like shit.*

"Ben came in and I told him what you said. He went home to get his guns and he knew where Charley was. He'll try to find Dave too if it don't take too much time."

"Did you tell him what I said about not being seen?"

"He said he'd be careful."

"Okay, we'll be there soon."

"It's getting dark and no one's seen her, Boss."

"We'll find her."

Hank hobbled back to the rental car. "Let's go."

"How much longer we gonna wait?" Ralph asked. He was drinking his third bottle of beer.

Oscar had returned to James's lap. He stroked the black fur. "Not much longer. Why don't you go get the truck?"

"Okay."

"Bring the rope when you come back."

"I know what to do."

Sierra turned and put her wrists behind her back and waited patiently while Arthur wrapped the rope around her wrists in the first turns. He was always so gentle when he tied her for the camera. She had learned to trust him over the weeks. She no longer felt the panic of helplessness as she was deprived of movement. Arthur tied the knot.

"It's not too tight?" he asked.

Sierra wiggled her fingers. "It's fine, but I can't get loose either."

"I just don't want to hurt you."

"You're not."

He turned and took another length of rope from the table.

No!

Jennifer's mind screamed. No!

This is not Arthur. This is not make-believe. You can't let them get the ropes on you. If they do . . .

Do something.

Now.

What?

She looked out the window in desperation, hoping to see rescuers. Someone had to come. Dave would wonder where Kathy was. But she had the truck. How could he get here without his truck? They were alone. The shadows stretched across the Valley now. No one is coming. I've got to do it myself. But how? Jennifer turned back to James. Oscar was still in his lap. Damn cat, she thought irrationally.

She heard the engine laboring up the hill. Again, Jennifer looked out the window. Ralph banged the door and reached into the bed of the truck. He pulled out a coil of rope.

No!

Jennifer put the purse in her lap.

"It's dark enough," Ralph said.

"Do the girl first," James said. Oscar stirred. James held him by the nape of his neck.

"Okay, Kathy, this won't hurt."

Kathy looked at Jennifer with panic-stricken eyes.

Ralph pulled her to her feet and dragged her across the room. Jennifer stood up, clutching the purse to her stomach.

"Stay put," James warned.

"Keep an eye on her," Ralph said. Kathy twisted in his grip.

"She's not going to do anything. Are you, Jenny?"

Jennifer's mouth was dry. She shook her head slowly.

Kathy shook Ralph off and ran to Jennifer, falling into her arms, crying, "I'm so sorry, Jennifer, I'm so sorry."

"God damn it," Ralph said.

Later, Jennifer would wonder what possessed her at that moment. There had been no plan in her mind, no course of action she had pre-determined. There was only fear.

It just happened.

Jennifer put her arm around Kathy instinctively, patting her back. The purse was wedged between them. Jennifer's other hand found the revolver.

"Don't cry, Kathy. Everything's going to be all right." She looked at the two men. They weren't worried. They could handle a disarmed woman and a girl. Jennifer saw it in their eyes. Ralph stood casually, swinging the rope back and forth. His pistol was in his belt. James smirked. "Isn't that a tender scene?" he said. He still had Oscar by the neck, twisting his head back.

Jack had smirked that way whenever he was going to inflict pain.

"Come with me, Kathleen." He wrapped his hand in her hair, twisting and pulling, forcing her to her knees. He twisted her head back.

"You're hurting me," Kathleen pleaded, looking up at him.

"Then cooperate and it won't hurt so much."

No!

"Don't hurt the cat," Jennifer said.

"Fuck the cat." He twisted his fingers in Oscar's fur. The cat cried out with the pain and turned, still in his grasp. His claws raked the man's face. He screamed and put both hands to his eyes.

It was a play in slow motion, the actors in the drama moving slowly, deliberately, in the masque. Jennifer

335

saw the other man turn to the one in the chair. She heard Oscar's deep guttural growl. She saw the blood spurting from between his fingers. Oscar fled with a hideous screech. And then Jennifer, still in painfully slow motion, pushed Kathy to the side. Kathy fell to the floor. The purse fell as Jennifer pulled the revolver free.

Ralph turned to look at James. Distracted. James was kneeling in front of the chair, screaming as blood ran down his face. Ralph turned back, dropping the rope, pulling the gun from his belt. It was coming up, slowly, too slowly.

Jennifer fired.

The smirk disappeared from Jack's face. He looked at her, bewildered, eyes wide with amazement.

Another scream filled the room. Kathy? Ralph? James? Both of them?

Jennifer fired again. And again.

Jack was down, twisting and writhing on the floor, holding his knee with both hands. Not Jack. Ralph.

"No!"

"Oh, God damn!"

"No, please don't shoot!"

Both men were on the floor, twisting in pain. James curled up into a fetal position. "Please, don't shoot," he begged. "My eyes. Please."

Jennifer's ears rang from the sound of the gun shots in the enclosed space. With crystal clarity, she saw that neither man was trying to find a weapon. She went to them, pistol ready, bent and scooped up Ralph's gun from the floor. James's gun was still on the table. She retreated again.

"Kathy?"

No answer.

Jennifer backed up, swinging the sights of her gun from one man to the other. "Kathy. Are you all right?" From the corner of her eye, Jennifer could see Kathy kneeling, biting on one clenched fist. "Kathy. God

336

damn it, talk to me."

"I'm . . . I'm all right . . . Jennifer." Her voice drifted to Jennifer from a great distance. "Are you okay?"

"Yes."

"Oh, God, Jennifer. They were going to kill you."

"Not anymore. Now don't fall apart on me. Go to the telephone and call someone. Get some help."

"Who?"

"Anyone. Call your grandfather. Tell him what happened, but that we're all right."

Kathy didn't have to make the call. A truck was coming up the hill. Another followed.

Jennifer's ears still rang. It was difficult for her to understand what the voices from the front yard were saying.

Kathy opened the door. "It's Granddad and Ben and Charley."

"Well, invite them in," Jennifer said.

She began shaking and laughing hysterically. The cavalry had arrived too late.

They were all talking at once.

"Jesus Christ. What happened?"

"What's going on?"

"Are you all right? Kathy? Jennifer?"

"Jennifer, don't cry. Aw hell, Ben, do something."

"That was good shooting, Jenny."

Jennifer cried harder. "I missed."

"No, you didn't. You got 'em."

"I was trying to kill them."

"Well, you scared the shit out of them."

They had to pry the revolver from her fingers. "Let go, hon. It's all over now."

"It's not," Jennifer cried. "It's not."

"Here comes Hank. And Clea."

"What's he doing out of the hospital?"

"Don't know, but it's a good thing he's here."

*   *   *

Hank took charge despite the pain, holding Jennifer while issuing orders to the others. "Better get Doc Cordeman up here. Have him bandage these guys up."

Clea took Kathy into her room.

"Better call the sheriff's people too," Ben offered.

"Not yet. We'll handle this ourselves."

"Whatever you say, Hank. We're with you."

"What the hell's going on, Hank?"

"Jennifer and I have a little problem . . ."

"This is a murderous little group," Hank said. He was propped up in a big chair by pillows.

"Doc Cordeman ain't real pleased. Thinks you oughta be left alone."

"Haw, he thinks Hank oughta be in the hospital."

"Aw hell, he don't get many real patients. Gotta let him have a little slack."

"He's got enough patients now."

"Aw, them scumbags ain't patients. Should've let 'em bleed."

"Mess up the rug that way."

"You gonna show us your incision, Hank?"

"I don't have any incisions."

"You a patient. Supposed to have an incision. I'll show you mine."

"When'd you have an operation?"

"Had my appendix out once."

"Everybody does that."

"I still got mine."

"That's cause you're stingy and mean. Don't wanta give up nothing that belongs to you."

Jennifer looked around the room. Clea sat next to her. Dave Wilson leaned against the wall, slouching next to Ben Davis, who was lifting his shirt, pointing out a faint scar, below the gun belt he wore.

"Aw, tuck your shirt in," Charley White said. "We ain't interested in some old scar. There's ladies present."

338

"We better get started," Hank said. "Let me tell you what we're going to do."

They brought James and Ralph into the living room. They half-carried, half-dragged Ralph.

"I'm going to bleed to death," Ralph said. The bandage over his knee was blood-stained.

"Not before the morning. Plenty of time for what needs doing."

"We've got rights," James said.

"This is fucking Hidden Valley, Arizona. You got no rights here."

James paled, but said nothing.

"We've had a little court here," Hank said. "And we've found you guilty of disruption."

"Disruption?" James cried. "What the hell's disruption?"

Hank smiled. "Disruption's just about the worst thing we could charge you with. It's a hanging offense. See, let me explain. You come in here and disrupt our lives and we don't like it. So we're going to take you out and hang you. Maybe you noticed them big trees out front when you were prowling around. We're going to take you out and hang you by the neck until you're dead."

"Dead, you sons-of-bitches," Dave Wilson said.

"This is bullshit," James said.

"You may think so now," Hank said. "We'll see how you feel at dawn."

"Why wait, Hank? Let's just do it now," Charley said.

"You've got no sense of tradition, Charley. It's always done at dawn."

"Everybody knows that, Charley."

"Seems like a waste of time to me. Just hang 'em."

"Of course," Hank said, turning back to the two prisoners, "there is a way for you to get out of the

339

disruption charges. Then all you'll face is attempted murder, attempted kidnapping. Little things like that."

"Don't listen to him," Ralph said. "They're just trying to fuck with your mind."

Hank shrugged. "You'll have all night to make up your mind. All you have to do is provide evidence against Holloway."

"Fuck you," James said. "Fuck all of you."

"Let's add talking dirty in front of ladies."

"You can only hang them once, Ben."

"Guess, you're right. Too bad, though."

"You got the ropes, Charley?"

"Right here, Hank."

"Well, why don't you just start making the nooses."

"Where'd you learn to tie a noose?" Ben asked.

"I was a boy scout."

"Must've been one hell of a boy scout troop you was in."

"Aw, I just got bored with square knots."

"You can't be serious," James said.

"Oh, we're serious all right. Take them back to the shed, Ben."

"Still say we oughta do it right now."

"This is cruel," Jennifer said.

"Do you have a better idea?"

"No, but what if they won't talk? What do we do then?"

"I don't know," Hank said. "I guess we'll have to hang them."

Jennifer stood under the shower for a long time. She felt violated and hoped that the hot steaming water would cleanse her. But the conflicting emotions within her would not go away. The water could not reach the terrible sick feeling deep within her soul. She had tried

340

to kill a man, two men, and all the logic of the situation was of little consolation. For a moment, she had become one of them, a remorseless beast trying to kill. She knew that they had come for her and for Clea. Kathy had been caught up in Holloway's web. They would have shown no mercy to any of them. There had been no other recourse for Jennifer. She had to fight back in defense of family and home. Still, she was filled with sorrow.

And it wasn't over yet.

Would it ever end?

Not until Jackson Holloway was in prison. There was no other way.

A confession from James and Ralph obtained under duress was inadmissible. There had to be other links to Holloway. He paid them. There had to be some trace. Let the authorities handle it. They'll find the connections. Yes. That was the only way. I'll testify. There is no statute of limitations on murder. I don't care what happens now.

Jennifer turned the shower off and wrapped her body in a large blue bath towel, hugging herself, fighting back the nausea she felt. She dried herself and dressed slowly. When she went back into the living room, she went to Hank and took his hand.

"We're not like them," Jennifer said. "I'm calling the sheriff's station. They'll know what to do."

When the sheriff's deputies opened the door of the shed, James had broken, his nerve failed. He crawled to them pleading. "Don't hang me, please. I'll tell you anything you want to know. Please don't hang me. I don't want to die."

"What's he talking about?"

Hank shrugged. "Beats me," he said.

James confessed everything, implicating Jackson Holloway, the conspiracy to kidnap Jennifer and Clea, the beating of Hank, leaving him for dead. "Holloway told me to kill the cowboy." Separated from James, Ralph held out momentarily, but when confronted with the details James had provided in his statement, said, "Fuck it, I ain't going down alone." He verified everything.

Calls were made to the Newport Beach Police Department. At one A.M., a return call came. Jackson Holloway had been taken into custody and booked on suspicion of conspiracy to commit murder for hire and conspiracy to commit kidnapping. "We're likely to have a bunch more charges," Arizona told Newport Beach. Holloway had called his attorney and refused to make any statement.

It was dawn before the deputies had finished taking all the statements and the house was empty again.

Jennifer had convinced Hank to go to bed. Doctor Cordeman had added the threat of putting him in the hospital.

Jennifer's statement was lengthy, relating an entire lifetime.

It was the longest night of Jennifer's life.

It ended with her standing alone on the porch, watching the first streaks of light break the sky above distant mountains. It was over.

THIRTY-ONE

Jennifer stood in the tiny clearing high above her house and looked out over the world—her world. It was peaceful and serene in the late afternoon and the encroaching shadows cast by the mountains at her back no longer frightened, no longer held menace. The vindictive night track of her mind had fallen silent, as though a hundred disparate records and tapes had been shattered by the burst of gunfire. The haunting melodies and lyrics came from another time and another place now, evoking only memories rather than fear and terror. The wind rustled through the trees. A rabbit hopped into the clearing and looked at her placidly, unafraid, its nose wrinkling as it sought her scent. Jennifer smiled and turned back to the wide expanse of the valley. The view was familiar and comforting. She lingered with the reassuring panorama. But much remained to be done. Although time had passed and their lives had slowly returned to normal, Jennifer still faced one final confrontation with the past. Perhaps then the past would release her. Reluctantly, Jennifer started down the path into the valley.

Because of Jackson Holloway's stature and state-wide—even national—reputation, the media had descended upon both Newport Beach and Hidden Valley in the aftermath of that traumatic night, following the course of events ravenously like the biblical plague of locusts. After all, Holloway had been—and still was—a rich and powerful businessman, an uncanny investor in the projects of other men, an advisor and fund raiser for governors, senators, congressmen.

Jennifer and Hank refused comment and remained secluded in their home. Television reporters did stand-up commentaries in front of the house for a day or two and then returned to their respective stations disappointed.

Hank healed slowly, but returned to his accustomed place behind the bar of his small establishment for longer and longer periods of time each day. Jennifer studied for the bar exam, feeling a sense of freedom for the first time in many years. Holloway could no longer hurt her or the ones she loved. Clea celebrated her birthday and waited tables at Hank's place, saving for her return to college in the fall. Kathy was emotionally shattered for a time by the events of that afternoon and evening, but with the passage of time, a smile returned to her face, and the nightmares grew more and more infrequent.

Jackson Holloway had been arrested, booked, and arraigned. Bail was set at $1 million. Holloway posted the bond and was immediately released. Jennifer had little doubt that he would be held to answer in Superior Court of the County of Orange on all the alleged counts of conspiracy to commit murder for hire and conspiracy to commit kidnapping—if he ever came to trial. James Hodgson and Ralph Hitt testified against Holloway in an effort to gain lesser sentences for their cooperation. Neither James Hodgson nor Ralph Hitt could post bond and they remained in custody.

It was a legal quagmire. Holloway's attorneys—a virtual army—dragged the process out until it seemed that all principals would reach retirement age before any resolution was achieved. His lawyers were skilled.

They fought extradition to Arizona, overwhelmed the prosecution and the legal system with paper, an endless series of motions and requests for continuances while they conducted their own investigations. Lie and deny. While the lawyers refused comment, the media speculated on the possibility of an insanity defense.

During her statements to the various law enforcement agencies investigating the case, Jennifer Warren Moore nee Kathleen Clark related the entire history of her relationship with Jackson Holloway, including the whispered comments overheard when he held her prisoner in their apartment. Federal authorities, in turn, contacted Jennifer Warren Moore and she received a subpoena to appear before a Federal Grand Jury in Los Angeles. The Grand Jury was investigating Holloway's activities during the spring and summer of 1968, particularly those in connection with the bombing of a building in which three people died.

There had been brief flurries of renewed publicity—when another delay in the judicial proceedings was announced, when Janice Holloway filed for divorce, when the Grand Jury was convened. The media attention ebbed and flowed. There was always something else to attract reporters—a rock star arrested for brawling with fans, a film star entering a drug recovery program, a politician indicted. In time, the public would forget. In time, Jennifer hoped she would forget. But first, there was the Grand Jury.

Walking slowly down the hill, Jennifer wondered if she would see Jackson and what she would say if she did. She had seen him often enough on television, always in the midst of his lawyers. He smiled and waved to the cameras, looking confident and relaxed. Jennifer even taped one newscast, playing it over and over again, studying Jackson, looking for the sickness that engendered such relentless hatred. She found no trace of the man who terrorized her, who sent threatening messages through the newspapers, who sent killers after her. When she finally erased the tape, Jennifer had found no understanding of Jackson Holloway. But their confrontation had to come eventually, whether at the Grand Jury or the preliminary hearing. She knew that, accepted it, and wanted it finished. Until she faced the monster, it would not end.

During the summer months there were visitors to Hidden Valley, not many but there were always a few adventurers from Phoenix and Tucson who wanted to escape the burning desert sun for a long weekend in the pastoral setting of central Arizona. When the strangers entered the bar, the locals closed in around Jennifer, Hank, and Clea protectively. Jennifer did not have to turn around at the sound of the door opening and closing to know that new faces had come in. Someone—Ben or Charley or Dave—would suddenly be next to her, leaning back against the bar casually, remaining there until the new people had passed inspection. Someone else—whoever happened to be handy—would follow Clea into the dining room to take up a post at an adjacent table while she took their orders. No one really expected anything to happen. They were all safe in the protective glare of publicity, but . . .

"Who knows what the fuck a crazy man's liable to do," Charley said, hovering next to Jennifer. "Right, Hank?"

"Right, Charley," Hank agreed, turning the page of whatever guidebook to Paris he happened to be reading at the moment.

"Right, Jennifer?"

"Right, Charley."

"Okay then. Let's have another beer."

"Help yourself," Hank said. "On the house."

"That's right neighborly, Hank. You sure you don't

want a couple of us to go over to L.A. with you?"

"We appreciate that, Charley, but it won't be necessary."

"Well, I'm still going to drive you down to Phoenix and pick you up again. Ain't no use arguing about that."

"You know, darling, I don't think two weeks in Paris is long enough. Too many things to see and do."

"You ain't going to eat any of them snails are you?"

"They're a delicacy, Charley."

"Disgusting is what it is. If they're so good, why don't we just go out and grab a few out back? Have Jesus cook up a mess of 'em."

"It's not the same."

"I rest my case."

"Paris will be wonderful," Jennifer said. "I'm really looking forward to it. But first . . ."

"Don't dwell on it, darling."

"I'm not," Jennifer said, even as her mind refused her commands to think only of Paris.

They drove to Phoenix and took a flight to Los Angeles. At LAX, they rented a car and drove to a downtown hotel, following the old familiar route that Jennifer had taken to work for so long. As Hank swore at Los Angeles traffic, Jennifer looked up at the building where she had worked. She tried to pick out the window of her former office, but it was lost in the maze of windows. She would have to see Leo again, but she had begged off on this trip.

"How did you live like this for so long?" Hank asked.

"Why do you think I was always so eager to get back to the valley?"

"Don't you miss it a little, Mom?"

"Not much," Jennifer said. "Not much at all."

"Are you nervous?"

"A little."

347

"Me too," Clea said. "I wonder . . ."

"I know," Jennifer said, "but it'll be fine."

"I'll be there for both of you," Hank said. "Stop worrying."

Jennifer spent a restless night, drifting in and out of sleep, always reaching over to touch Hank, a consoling presence. The memories flooded the dark room. Jack, always Jack. The first time she had seen him. The thrill that passed through her at that moment. Cooking a thick meat sauce for the spaghetti. Drinking red wine during their candlelight dinners. Walking across campus to meet for coffee. Yes, oh yes, I'll marry you. Lying awake after making love as his fingers traced delicate patterns across her skin. The happiness so quickly replaced by fear. Stop it, Jennifer. It will be over tomorrow. Finally. She went to the window and looked out at Los Angeles. He was out there somewhere, refusing to release his clinging hold on her.

Jennifer Warren Moore emerged from the Grand Jury room to the glare of cameras and microphones thrust in her face. Hank and Clea pushed through the crowd, flanking her protectively.

"What did you tell the Grand Jury?"

"No comment," Hank said. He cleared a path for Jennifer and Clea to follow. They hurried after him.

Time stopped.

Jennifer no longer heard the clamor. She stood alone with Jackson Holloway. They were motionless in a silent void, looking at each other.

"Hello, Kathleen," he said.

"Hello, Jack."

"You're as beautiful as ever, Kathleen."

"I'm not Kathleen anymore."

"I know."

"Why, Jack?"

"Because I love you. I've always loved you."

Jennifer saw the lie pass through his eyes, an instantaneous flicker of hatred, quickly replaced by a smile, the same old smile that had enchanted and beguiled her. But the smile did not reach his eyes.

"We have to go, Jackson." An attorney touched him lightly on the arm.

The spell was broken.

He passed by her, so close she could have reached out and touched him. She didn't.

Jennifer turned and watched as he entered the Grand Jury room alone. He didn't look back.

Hank touched her. She looked up at him and smiled. "Let's go home, darling."

EPILOGUE

Paris was their honeymoon and their escape. They arrived after Labor Day when most of the tourists had gone home and the City of Light had been returned to the Parisians. Jennifer and Hank stayed on the Left Bank at a small hotel on the Rue de Seine. They spent their days walking the wide boulevards and the small narrow cobbled streets. They prowled through the student quarter and sat in cafes on the Boulevard Saint Germain where Jean-Paul Sartre, Simone de Beauvoir, and their disciples might have gathered. They strolled the Boulevard Saint Michel amidst groups of university students debating heatedly. In Montparnasse, there were more sidewalk cafes where Hemingway, Fitzgerald, Joyce, and the other expatriates of the twenties had gone after writing. When they crossed over to the Right Bank, they exhausted themselves in the Louvre. They went to Montmartre and climbed to Sacre Coeur and afterwards delighted in the paintings displayed by one artist after another in the small square. They walked along the Seine each afternoon when the city was pale in the gentle rays of the falling sun. They explored Notre Dame, arguing over movie versions. Jennifer preferred Charles Laughton. Hank argued strenuously for Sophia Loren. "I know what you liked about her," Jennifer said. "Still do," Hank replied.

At night, they loved each other to the squalls of cats and the rumble of trucks going to market, the sounds of Paris that Jennifer would always remember.

Each morning, out of old habit and an uneasiness long ingrained, Jennifer turned to the personal column in the *International Herald Tribune.* She expected to find nothing, of course, other than the normal spate of ads searching for a true love encountered briefly through the window of a rushing train in the Metro, birthday wishes, one lover urging another to come home, someone asking for the whereabouts of a friend. But despite the passage of months, Jennifer still suffered moments of doubt when Jackson Holloway attempted to drag her back, deep into the murky depths of the past.

One morning, during their second week in Paris, Hank purchased the *Herald Tribune* at a newspaper kiosk, folding it under his arm without glancing at it. They walked on to a sidewalk cafe and ordered coffee before Hank opened the newspaper. "My God," he said.

"What is it?" Jennifer asked, suddenly alarmed.

"Holloway's dead."

"What happened?" Jennifer cried.

Hank passed the newspaper across the table. "Bottom right," he said.

Jennifer read the brief wire service report.

"In a bizarre twist to an already bizarre case, Jackson Holloway, a prominent businessman, was shot to death by his estranged wife, apparently in self defense.

"Janice Holloway claimed that her husband had returned to their Newport Beach home, beating her as he attempted to rape her. Holloway said that she kept a pistol because she feared retaliation by her husband and that she managed to reach it during an ensuing struggle.

351

"According to authorities, Holloway was shot three times and pronounced dead at the scene.

"Holloway, the target of a Federal Grand Jury investigation and already facing other allegations that he . . ."

Jennifer put the paper down and looked across at Hank.

"It's over now."

Jennifer nodded. "Let's go back and call Clea. I want to make sure she's okay."

They left the paper on the table. At the corner, Jennifer looked back and saw it fluttering in a sudden breeze. It blew to the ground. Jennifer watched as a waiter picked it up, glanced at it briefly, and then stuffed it in a trash receptacle on the sidewalk.

"Goodbye, Jack," she whispered.